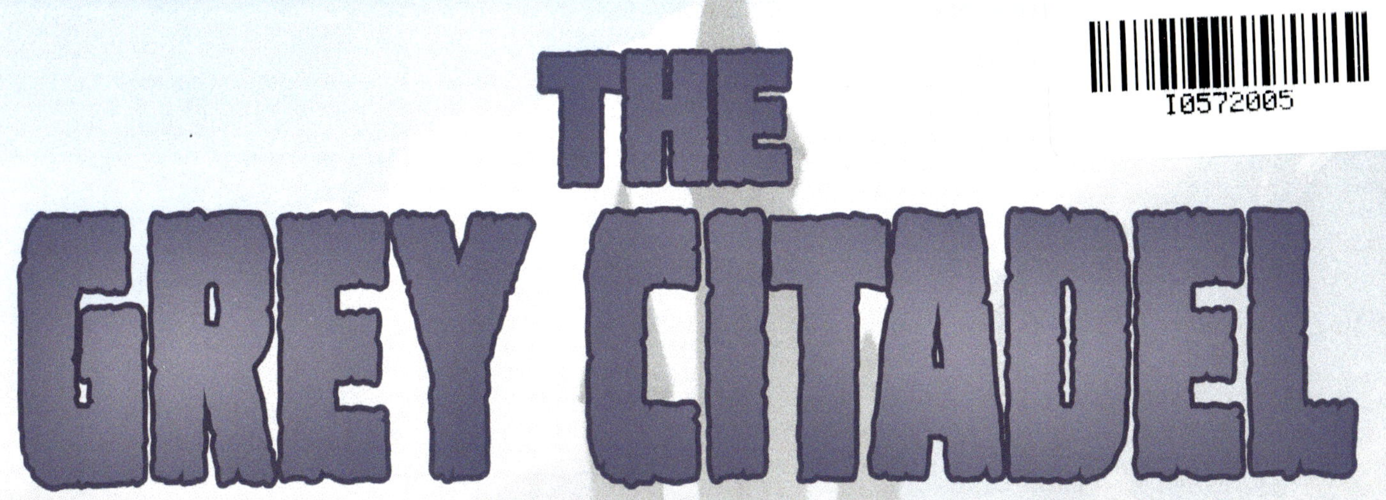

Author: Nathan Douglas Paul
Project Manager: Zach Glazar
Editor: Jeff Harkness, Andrew Bates, and Mike Johnstone
Swords & Wizardry Conversion: Jeff Harkness
Art Direction: Casey Christofferson
Layout and Graphic Design: Charles A. Wright
Cover Design: Charle A. Wright
Cover Art: Michael Syrigos
Interior Art: Michael Syrigos, Brian LeBlanc, and Tyler Walpole
Cartography: Robert Altbauer

FROG GOD GAMES

ISBN: 978-1-62283-858-5

FROG GOD GAMES IS:

Bill Webb, Matthew J. Finch, Zach Glazar, Charles A. Wright, Edwin Nagy, Mike Badolato, John Barnhouse

Table of Contents

INTRODUCTION

The Grey Citadel is an adventure designed for a party of four or more characters of at least 5th level. It combines wilderness adventuring, urban detective work, and underground exploration.

The Grey Citadel of Dun Eamon is a vibrant and busy city, full of adventure and opportunity, but its prosperity is threatened by the actions of a series of factions working together and separately to destabilize the community. Demons roam the streets, criminals rule the night, and an important local power figure is missing … with no apparent connection. The heroes become involved in a chain of events that leads them through every social element of the city, into the hearts of its inhabitants, and far below its streets in search of answers.

ADVENTURE BACKGROUND

Before the first patriarch of the Angus clan founded his trading post on the River Eamon, the greatest threat to his descendants was already brewing in distant lands. An ambitious conjurer named Mamuthek conspired to build a device that he could use to dominate the kingdom in which he dwelled. His completed project — which created an aperture in the planar barrier through which outsiders could be called — was powerful, but not without flaws. The most dangerous of these flaws was that it lacked the ability to grant control over the creature to the summoner. Mamuthek found this out when the creature he had called ended his coup and his life. *Mamuthek's Aperture* has since drifted across the known world, bringing death everywhere it is used, and none have managed to unlock its secrets. Very recently, one wizard came close, but she did not learn enough to prevent the carnage that goes hand-in-hand with *Mamuthek's Aperture*.

Elinda Bannon is a magic-user who specializes in artifacts and magical devices. She dwells in the Grey Citadel and was the most recent owner of Mamuthek's creation. She had great success in her research, with one exception: She believed the device was used for communicating across the planes, not for summoning. She acquired the artifact and activated it. The unforeseen result of her experimentation was that the device recognized and retrieved the previous being called, a powerful succubus demon named Lilith. Imprisoned in the Abyss for transgressions against a demon prince, Lilith did not hesitate when the shimmering portal opened in her cell. Two hundred years had passed since *Mamuthek's Aperture* last offered her passage into mortal realms, and she was glad to return. She defeated the wizard, took the device, and fled into the water-carved caverns beneath the city.

When she arrived, she found that a gang of thieves was already ensconced in her chosen lair. Their master, a wily rogue named Devlin, had led them there after their guild was expelled from a neighboring city. Lilith quickly seduced Devlin, giving her effective control of a skilled group of evil agents with a competent understanding of the city. They immediately began securing the components she needed to activate the artifact and reinforce her position with an army of outsiders. She also allied herself with Gethrax, a fallen paladin who found her a new patron. Many elements of the city, both aboveground and below, that had once lived in relative harmony are now being drawn together in a deceptive and violent plot that will affect each and every life in the Dun Eamon. The heroes' arrival coincides with the disappearance of Elinda Bannon and the emergence on and below the streets of the minions (both summoned and seduced) of the new owner of *Mamuthek's Aperture*.

HOW TO USE THIS MODULE

This adventure involves a city-based investigation and a difficult dungeon that are intricately intertwined, with actions aboveground being reflected in the events below. That is not to say that simply kicking in doors and spilling a great deal of blood won't complete the adventure; there is plenty of mayhem for those who crave it (and maybe more than some would choose!). Hopefully, though, the players will realize that clever, attentive roleplaying in the city will give them several advantages when they descend into the underground, allowing them to reap great rewards without undue risk.

You may either bring the party directly to the Grey Citadel and begin the adventure proper, or, if you wish, you may begin by having the party travel to the city itself. If you choose the latter, feel free to either use encounters appropriate to your campaign world or include one or more of the encounters or areas detailed in **Appendix D: Wilderness Encounters** found at the back of this book.

READ-ALOUD TEXT

Text blocks are provided for some locations and encounters, but not all. Usually, these text blocks involve important roleplaying encounters with NPCs or dungeon locations that might be difficult to visualize. Other times, they are included to reinforce the character and feeling of the adventure. Use as much or as little as you wish. When read-aloud text is absent, the description has been written with paraphrasing in mind.

ENCOUNTER TYPES: KEYED, TIMED, AND RANDOM

Encounters are handled in three different ways in this adventure:

Random Encounters can be selected or randomized from the **City Random Encounters Table** (see **Chapter One**) whenever you think it appropriate.

Timed Encounters happen at specific times in the storyline, although they can be modified, rescheduled, or canceled without disrupting the plot.

Keyed Encounters take place at a specific location (such as a room in a dungeon) whenever the characters choose to go there (locations important to the plot are fully developed; others are structured, but left for you to detail in the future).

NOTATION

All of the descriptions in this adventure are titled with a letter and number combination that indicates where or when the encounter is to be used. Keyed Encounters include a letter referring to the map key, and a number referring to the area or room within that location (for example, D-1 is **Location D**, the Market Tavern, and **Area 1**, The Coat Hall). Dungeon levels are similarly titled with the number of the dungeon level and the number of the area (for example, **Area 2-9** is the ninth room on the second level). Timed encounters are titled with a number for the day, a number for the encounter, and a short phrase (for example, **Timed Encounter 1.2** is the second event on the first day).

BACKGROUND

The real facts behind the mystery are best understood by reading the entire adventure carefully and possibly by re-reading the **Mystery Elements** section (see **Chapter Two**). Here are a few facts to keep in mind as you do so:

• The succubus Lilith is building an army of outsiders and plotting to take control of Dun Eamon.

• The wizard Elinda Bannon took it upon herself to undo the damage she did with her experiments and pursued the fleeing demon. She was defeated and is now being held captive in Lilith's lair.

• Devlin and the Ebon Union thieves' guild are hard at work providing materials for the artifact's operation, but they may take time out to make an attempt on the party.

• A fallen paladin named Gethrax has loosely allied himself with Lilith and the Ebon Union.

• An NPC adventuring party called the Band of the Crimson Mantle is competing with the heroes, leading to some potentially interesting side effects.

Good detective work in the city will be rewarded with information about the dungeon, including the identities of its occupants, their weaknesses, and the weapons to use against them.

THE RULE OF THREE

The adventure elements are arranged in groups of three to make tracking the heroes' progress easier. The mystery is composed of three elements: wizard, thieves, and demons. Each element offers three ways that the heroes can approach the mystery: they can collect three clues left by the wizard; they can analyze three major burglaries of the thieves; or they can investigate three citizens seduced by the succubus. Each of these approaches reveals secrets that serve the heroes well when they venture underground. Not all (or even any) of the leads must be pursued, but each one increases the heroes' chances of success. These clues are described fully in the **Mystery Elements** section (see **Chapter Two**) and referenced in the appropriate Keyed Encounter.

Elinda's Clues: These are located in the Tower Library (**Area L-8**) and lead to the Secret Workshop (**Area L-9**), the Temple Courtyard (**Area I-9**), and Stump's Hovel (**Area S**). These clues reveal a potent weapon against the demon and the artifact's functions.

Lilith's Thralls: The men who have been *charmed* by Lilith include Ulf Ironfist, the master smith (**Area Q-4**); Herrick Mendon, a merchant (**Area H-4**); and Danver, the miller (**Area R**). Each of these men guards an entrance to the caverns.

The Crime Scenes: Burglaries have been committed at several locations: The Root-Cutter's Shop (**Area T**), the Seer's Parlor (**Area N**), and the Finesmith's Shop (**Area H-9**). The stolen items suggest the nature and origins of the dungeon creatures.

Also in groups of three are the Timed Encounters. These are events scheduled to take place during the first three days the heroes are in the city, with three events to occur on each day. Some of them involve combat, others focus on roleplaying, and some could go either way. They do not represent a rigid timeline, nor do the heroes need to participate in all of the encounters; feel free to change, reschedule, or cancel them to suit your style of play. Letting the plot lead the players through them in order without "railroading" them, however, should be possible. Refer to the table below for the various Timed Encounters:

Day One: 1.1 — An NPC adventuring party celebrates a victory over the demons; 1.2 — Arb Angus enlists the heroes' help; 1.3 — The party encounters demons in the streets (night).

Day Two: 2.1 — A local shares his suspicions (morning); 2.2 — The NPC adventurers challenge the party; 2.3 — Demons actively hunt the heroes (night).

Day Three: 3.1 — Thieves storm the inn and attack the party (early morning); 3.2 — The rival adventurers enter the sewers; 3.3 — The heroes interrupt a burglary (evening).

TIMELINE

In the course of the investigation, the players will likely ask many "when" questions. Nothing in the adventure hinges directly on timing, but a brief timeline of past and future events is provided below for the sake of consistency. Day 1 marks the party's arrival in the city; negative numbers indicate the amount of time before the party's arrival (for instance, "–2 days" is two days before the heroes arrive, and so forth).

Completing the adventure may require several trips into the underground tunnels over several days. Parties may find it difficult to complete the dungeon portion without visiting the surface at least once. The days that the party spends completing its investigation and adventuring underground have no specific events in the city; assume that Lilith's demons continue to terrorize the population as the Mist Watch struggles to maintain order. Emphasize the deteriorating conditions each time the party returns to the city.

Time	Event
–1 month	Elinda leaves to retrieve *Mamuthek's Aperture*.
–2 weeks	Elinda returns to Dun Eamon with the artifact.
–13 days	Elinda buys silver from Crenshaw the Finesmith.
–12 days	Elinda activates the artifact, summons Lilith, and is defeated.
–11 days	Lilith arrives in her new home on Level 4.
–10 days	Elinda places her clues and pursues Lilith.
–8 days	Lilith steals charms from Amarathea the Seer.
–7 days	Dretches appear in the streets (thanks to the Abyssal iron ore).
–6 days	Lilith seduces Devlin; thieves steal silver from Crenshaw.
–5 days	Lilith seduces Ulf Ironfist.
–4 days	Lilith seduces Herrick Mendon; the Band arrives.
–3 days	Lilith seduces Danver; thieves steal items from Caledon.
–2 days	Large groups of dretches panic the citizens; Elinda is captured.
–1 day	Tunnels are now full of Lilith's summoned creatures.
Day 1	The party arrives in the city; Timed Encounter 1.1, 1.2, and 1.3.
Day 2	Investigation begins; Timed Encounters 2.1, 2.2, and 2.3.
Day 3	Timed Encounters 3.1, 3.2, and 3.3.
Day 4+	Investigation and demon attacks continue, if necessary.*

REPLACEMENT CHARACTERS

Many adventures include pre-generated characters, either for player use or to give an idea of what types of heroes best suit the adventure. In this module, potential characters have been written into the story as NPCs. They are not intended to be the starting party and would need to be converted into characters if you wish your players to use them. They can provide additional characters for a party whose numbers are dropping or perhaps extra support for a small or underpowered party — but they are not high-powered heroes. Rasputin, Fitch, Brother Melph, Stump, or even Yelm have skills and abilities that can benefit the party over the course of the adventure. Some of them, notably Rasputin, Stump, and Yelm, also have small roles to play as NPCs, so handing them over too early might require some adjustment. Once the party wraps up the city investigation and is ready to proceed underground, most of these NPCs will have served their purpose and likely have a motivation to join the party as well. See **Appendix A: NPCs** for stats and descriptions.

ADAPTING THE ADVENTURE

The Grey Citadel is written for a party of four characters of 5th level. The mysteries in the city should present adequate roleplaying and problem-solving challenges for a group of any level. City encounters consist mostly of groups of creatures and so are adaptable by varying the number of creatures encountered (dretches, guild thieves, mongrels of Yith, and so forth). The dungeon encounters will need more adjustment, possibly including adjustment of trap damage and replacement of powerful creatures.

Lower-level parties will need to take their time and rest frequently, but a large 3rd- or 4th-level party can gain enough experience during the city portion to survive an upper dungeon level, which earns them enough experience to survive the next level, and so on. A 5th-level party is presumed to have done a thorough investigation in the city and thus gained an advantage against the underground foes (such as taking acid to deal with the troll). More powerful parties (6th-level characters or parties numbering six or more) will find that they can survive the encounters without needing those advantages and go longer without rest. Parties of 7th-level and higher will need most of the encounters upgraded (extra trolls and so forth) to provide a significant challenge.

SETTING

The setting should be easy to insert into any fantasy campaign; all you need is a city and an underground cavern complex. The city could easily be relocated to any location — desert, arctic, or anything in between. The special conditions are present for effect, but are not necessary. Similarly, the river, the trade road, the frontier location, and the economic politics are not necessary to the plot, although many of the hooks for future development relate to them.

The surrounding wilderness areas are not of great importance to the city and the adventures to be had there, allowing easy integration of the adventure into your specific campaign world. If, however, you desire more information on the surrounding wilderness and perhaps a few more adventure hooks and NPCs, that material is presented in the **Appendix D: Wilderness Encounters** detailed in the back of this module. If desired, you may use some of those encounters as the characters travel to the Grey Citadel before running the primary adventure.

Chapter One: The City of Dun Eamon – An Overview

This adventure takes place in the city of Dun Eamon, the center of government for Eamonvale. Located high in the mist-shrouded mountain crags of the Stoneheart Mountains, it is a city like no other. Locally known as the Grey Citadel, Dun Eamon is an important trading city and a key crossing point on the turbulent river. Thanks to its economy, Dun Eamon is highly successful, but its remote location also ensures that it will never be terribly sophisticated.

The River Eamon has only one viable crossing in the Stoneheart Mountains — a broad ford at the base of a plunging waterfall. Just below the ford, the river tumbles several hundred feet over a second waterfall before continuing down the rocky gorge. Midway across the ford, a huge slab of bedrock divides the river into two channels. On this island, many generations ago, Eamon Angus staked a claim and founded a tiny trading post. Now, centuries later, expansion of the duchies and kingdoms on either side of the Stoneheart Mountains and the development of trade between them have caused the tiny trading center and waystation to grow into a heavily fortified citadel, with the charter and lordship still in the hands of the Angus family.

Three brothers rule the city. Arb Angus is the eldest; he inherited the land and title from his father. Bron is the middle brother and the captain of the Mist Watch. Cael is the youngest brother and master of the Temple of Fortitude. More than 5,000 citizens dwell within the city walls and pay homage to the brothers.

The Grey Citadel is renowned as the location of the finest forges in the land. Nearly any tool, weapon, or other metal item can be crafted here, and the quality of their alloys and the strength of their castings are unsurpassed. The quality and availability of tools and the location on the trade road have resulted in Dun Eamon becoming a city of artisans and craftsmen. The attention of foreign guilds wishing to expand their influence and tap the region's unique market has also been attracted, but the Angus family has always enforced strict regulations that limit guild activity and encourage free trade. Today's rulers are no exception, and their policies have not made them popular among the powerful merchant houses.

In addition to its mercantile presence, the Grey Citadel is a well-known frontier fortress. In times of war, its walls are the outer line of defense for the lowland below the Stoneheart Mountains. Many hunters and trappers pass through the gates every season to sell their pelts and to resupply for another trip into the wild mountains. It is a hiring point for caravan laborers and guards for the dangerous journey over the mountains to the distant kingdoms beyond. Traveling minstrels, adventurers, and highwaymen all call the city home from time to time.

City Random Encounters Table

These encounters should be used to provide action, inspire roleplaying, and develop the unique character of Dun Eamon. They can also be used to develop the plot with the delivery of an important rumor at the right moment.

1d8	Encounter
1	**Mist Watch City Patrol (9 soldiers, 1 sergeant):** With the developing events in the city, patrols are larger, more frequent, and increasingly reactive. They have standing orders to question anyone out after dark or who appears to be engaged in questionable behavior. Reactions depend on the party's activities, reputation, and level of cooperation.
2	**Cutpurse:** Equally at home working a crowded market or dark side street, these thieves of the Ebon Union always try to flee a confrontation, attempting to lose pursuers before going underground through one of the drains in the market. They fight only as a last resort.
3	**Dretches (1d2):** When encountered in numbers this small, these creatures are usually wandering erratically instead of serving their demonic mistress. They create a panic whenever they appear in public view. They are most often found scavenging scraps in an alley refuse pile.
4	**Confrontational Drunk:** An inebriated caravan guard stumbles into the party and belligerently challenges a random character. If diplomacy fails, the heroes should make an effort to end the fight without loss of life to avoid repercussions.
5	**Perfumed Harlot:** These women roam the city in revealing gowns and heavy makeup, attempting to attract wealthy (or at least employed) men to various dances and festivals at the inns or to rendezvous at the bathhouse. They know 1d3 rumors from the **City Rumors Table** in **Chapter Two** if questioned.

1d8	Encounter
6	**Raving Prophet:** These wild-eyed fanatics pester anyone who shows an interest in their rants, which will always pertain to a deity/faction/cult of which the party has never heard, unless it benefits an outside story connection. They know a single rumor from the **City Rumors Table** in **Chapter Two** if asked, but always twist it to favor their cause.
7	**Ragged Beggar:** There are very few independent beggars in the citadel; 90% have been bullied into loyalty to the guild, but 30% of those report secretly to Rasputin as well. Any beggar knows 1d4 rumors from the **City Rumors Table** in **Chapter Two** (reroll those that pertain to the thieves' guild unless the beggar is one of the truly independent 10%).
8	**The Elite:** One of the three Angus brothers (see **Appendix A: NPCs**) is out on business in the city (chosen or determined randomly). **Arb** may be responding to a simple legal or economic matter; **Bron** might be investigating a crime or reviewing Watch stations; **Cael** will most likely be ministering to his congregation's needs. All are on business unrelated to the demon crisis and, depending on the heroes' level of involvement, may approach the characters for an update. Day or night, **2 trusted soldiers** accompany them from the Mist Watch or the acolytes of the temple, as appropriate.

Confrontational Drunk, Male or Female Human: HD 1d6hp; **AC** 9[10]; **Atk** dagger (1d4); **Move** 12; **Save** 18; **AL** Any; **CL/XP** B/10; **Special:** drunk (−1 to hit and saves). (*Monstrosities* 254)
Equipment: dagger, pouch with 1d10 cp, 1 sp.

Cutpurse, Male or Female Human (Thf2): HP 2d4; **AC** 7[12]; **Atk** dagger (1d4); **Move** 12; **Save** 14; **AL** C; **CL/XP** 2/30; **Special:** +2 save bonus vs. traps and magical devices, backstab (x2), thieving skills. (see **Appendix A: NPCs**)
Thieving Skills: Climb 86%, Tasks/Traps 20%, Hear 3 in 6, Hide 15%, Silent 25%, Locks 15%.
Equipment: leather armor, 2 daggers, pouch of caltrops (1d4 damage, halves movement in 10ft-diameter area), pouch with 2d10 gp and 2d10 sp.

Dretch Demons (1d2): HD 4; **AC** 2[17]; **Atk** 2 claws (1d4), bite (1d6); **Move** 9; **Save** 13; **AL** C; **CL/XP** 6/400; **Special:** spell-like abilities. (*Monstrosities* 92)
Spell-like abilities: 1/day—*darkness 15ft radius*, stinking cloud (20ft radius, save or nauseated for 1d4+1 rounds), summon 1d4 giant rats.

Mist Watch Soldier, Male or Female Human Warrior: HD 1; **AC** 5[14]; **Atk** longsword (1d8), spear (1d6) or longbow x2 (1d6); **Move** 12; **Save** 17; **AL** L or N; **CL/XP** 1/15; **Special:** none. (*Monstrosities* 257 or **Appendix A: NPCs**)
Equipment: ring mail, steel shield, longsword, spear, longbow, quiver of 20 arrows.

Mist Watch Sergeant, Male or Female Human Warrior: HD 3; **AC** 4[15]; **Atk** longsword (1d8), spear (1d6) or longbow x2 (1d6); **Move** 12; **Save** 14; **AL** L or N; **CL/XP** 3/60;
Special: none. (*Monstrosities* 256 or **Appendix A: NPCs**)
Equipment: chainmail, steel shield, longsword, spear, longbow, quiver of 20 arrows, potion of healing, signal horn, rank chain.

Perfumed Harlot, Female Human: HD 1d6hp; **AC** 9[10]; **Atk** none; **Move** 12; **Save** 18; **AL** Any; **CL/XP** B/10; **Special:** drunk (−1 to hit and saves). (*Monstrosities* 254)
Equipment: gown, vial of scented oils (1 sp), pouch with 2d8 sp.

Ragged Beggar, Male or Female Human: HD 1d6hp; **AC** 9[10]; **Atk** none; **Move** 12; **Save** 18; **AL** Any; **CL/XP** B/10; **Special:** drunk (−1 to hit and saves). (*Monstrosities* 254)
Equipment: wooden bowl with 2d6 cp.

Raving Prophet, Male or Female Human Acolyte (Clr1): HP 1d6; **AC** 9[10]; **Atk** club (1d4); **Move** 12; **Save** 15; **AL** Any; **CL/XP** 1/15; **Special:** +2 save vs. paralysis and poison, banish undead.
Equipment: robes, club.

The people of Dun Eamon are hardy and self-sufficient; hardships are taken in stride, and respect is reserved for those who have earned it. Two dominant social groups exist in the city, and they are usually at odds with each other. The woodsmen who occupy the forested slopes around the citadel regard the merchant class as arrogant foreigners from pampered lowland cities; the merchants regard the woodsmen as savages whose uncouth lifestyle they tolerate only in the interests of profit. Rangers and druids are welcomed into the community, as are fighters to a slightly lesser degree. Paladins are not unwelcome, but the citizens are intolerant of judgment by outsiders. Dun Eamon attracts plenty of thieves, mostly bandits and highwaymen rather than burglars. Magic-users and monks are uncommon, mostly due to the lack of social refinement. Clerics are not treated any differently than anywhere else. Adventuring parties are generally regarded as a natural part of the traffic through the gates.

In appearance, the Grey Citadel of Dun Eamon is imposing yet dreary. Its stone buildings are quarried from the same grey basalt as the bedrock on which they sit, as are the city walls and the keep. The rest of the buildings are half-timbered two- and three-story structures, with roofs of thatch or shingle. The cobblestone streets and alleys are always shiny and damp, and everything in the city hosts at least a thin sheen of green moss; many buildings even have thick clumps of ferns growing on the roof. Amid the green-fostered slopes and drifting grey rain clouds, the grey-green edifices of the city blend right in.

CITY RANDOM ENCOUNTERS AFTER NIGHTFALL TABLE

After nightfall, use the following table:

1d8	Encounter
1–2	Mist Watch Night Patrol (9 soldiers, 1 sergeant)
3–4	1d2 Ebon Union cutpurses
5–6	1d4 dretches
7	1d4 confrontational drunks
8	Ragged beggar

Confrontational Drunk, Male or Female Human: HD 1d6hp; **AC** 9[10]; **Atk** dagger (1d4); **Move** 12; **Save** 18; **AL** Any; **CL/XP** B/10; **Special:** drunk (−1 to hit and saves).

(*Monstrosities* 254)
Equipment: dagger, pouch with 1d10 cp, 1 sp.

Dretch Demons (1d4): HD 4; AC 2[17]; **Atk** 2 claws (1d4), bite (1d6); **Move** 9; **Save** 13; **AL** C; **CL/XP** 6/400; **Special:** spell-like abilities. (*Monstrosities* 92)
Spell-like abilities: 1/day—*darkness 15ft radius*, *stinking cloud* (20ft radius, save or nauseated for 1d4+1 rounds), *summon* 1d4 giant rats.

Mist Watch Soldier, Male or Female Human Warrior: HD 1; AC 5[14]; **Atk** longsword (1d8), spear (1d6) or longbow x2 (1d6); **Move** 12; **Save** 17; **AL** L or N; **CL/XP** 1/15; **Special:** none. (*Monstrosities* 257 or **Appendix A: NPCs**)
Equipment: ring mail, steel shield, longsword, spear, longbow, quiver of 20 arrows.

Mist Watch Sergeant, Male or Female Human Warrior: HD 3; AC 4[15]; **Atk** longsword (1d8), spear (1d6) or longbow x2 (1d6); **Move** 12; **Save** 14; **AL** L or N; **CL/XP** 3/60; **Special:** none. (*Monstrosities* 256 or **Appendix A: NPCs**)
Equipment: chainmail, steel shield, longsword, spear, longbow, quiver of 20 arrows, potion of healing, signal horn, rank chain.

Ragged Beggar, Male or Female Human: HD 1d6hp; AC 9[10]; **Atk** none; **Move** 12; **Save** 18; **AL** Any; **CL/XP** B/10; **Special:** drunk (–1 to hit and saves). (*Monstrosities* 254)
Equipment: wooden bowl with 2d6 cp.

The trade road bisects Dun Eamon through the lower city, and a massive gatehouse guards each entrance where the road rises up from the ford. A rampart wall surrounds the entire island, with watchtowers evenly distributed along it. Where the second falls spill over the edge, the island rises steeply to a flat-topped promontory. On this slab of rock sits the upper city, consisting of the craftsman's district, the vast market, and the largest taverns. Rising from the very tip of the island and towering over the dizzying waterfall is the Angus castle and keep, the central point of defense for the entire region.

CONDITIONS IN THE CITY

The Grey Citadel has some special characteristics that make roleplaying within its walls dangerous and unforgettable. Two special rules apply whenever the heroes are outdoors in the city.

Visibility: The city's position on a ford between two waterfalls and the combination of rain and fog that drift down the slopes constantly shroud the city in thick mists and drizzle. The result of this constant precipitation is badly restricted visibility (with an appropriate penalty to attack as you decide, typically a –1 or –2, or even a –4 in extreme fog).

Footing: Eamonvale's moist climate ensures heavy growth of mosses and lichens in the city, and nearly every surface has a thin green coat of slick vegetation. As a result, footing is treacherous, especially for visitors who are unused to the conditions (those who have been in the city for less than one month). Walking under normal circumstances does not present a problem, but once another activity (such as combat, running, etc.) distracts a character, they face a chance of slipping on the slimy surface. The character must make a saving throw. If this save fails, the character slips and takes 1d4 points of damage and suffers a –1 penalty to hit and saves for 1d4 rounds. Incoming attacks against the character during this time gain a +1 to-hit bonus. Use your judgment on when and how to apply the footing conditions.

THE UNDERGROUND CAVERNS

Beneath the city, thousands of years of erosion have carved a complex network of tunnels and chambers. In addition to the natural caverns, a burial crypt and a halfling stronghold add variety to the dungeon levels.

The descriptions of the underground caverns beneath Dun Eamon are divided into four levels, although several passageways connect them and the party need not visit every level to be successful. The encounters in these levels are based on a party of four characters of 5th level as the minimum requirements for survival: such a party will find the dungeon challenging and should expect to need regular rest, well-refined tactics, and a broad range of abilities to succeed. Hirelings or NPC allies from the city are other options that can reduce the overall wear and tear on the party.

Parties entering through the drains in the market will have a good chance of exploring the levels chronologically. The first three levels are connected by side tunnels that allow them to be explored in any order. The final (and most challenging) level can be reached only after completing at least one of the upper levels.

The Band of the Crimson Mantle has likely been in the dungeon longer than the party, and the heroes have several opportunities to interact with them. Dresden has been killed and his body remains on Level 2. The bulk of the Band waits to share an encounter with the party on Level 3, and the survivors of that encounter may be involved in the final confrontation on Level 4.

Lilith's use of *Mamuthek's Aperture* with the items she stole from various citizens has resulted in several creatures summoned directly from the Abyss.

CHAPTER TWO: TIMED ENCOUNTERS, RUMORS, AND MYSTERY ELEMENTS

This adventure is driven by three components: **Timed Encounters** are events that happen to the heroes, essentially bringing the story to them. **Rumors** are the results of their investigation and can be gained at every turn, from anyone in the city. **Mystery Elements** are the "hot" leads that bring the heroes closer to the answers they seek.

TIMED ENCOUNTERS

These encounters are milestone events in the timeline that serve to draw the heroes into the plot — for they are victims as much as anyone in the city. Not all of the encounters are combat encounters; some of them are strictly roleplaying oriented and should help enforce the notion that city life goes on around the characters.

TIMED ENCOUNTER 1.1: ARRIVAL AMID REVELRY

Use this encounter soon after the heroes enter the Grey Citadel, perhaps after they have stabled their mounts and are looking for lodgings. The Band of the Crimson Mantle has defeated and crucified a dretch, and it is parading the demon through the streets as a trophy. A crowd of relieved citizens follows the adventurers, who are on their way to the keep to claim their bounty.

> As you move down the cobbled streets, a commotion catches your attention a few blocks away. From where you stand, a group of hardy-looking adventures dressed in red are apparently bearing a corpse up the street on a crucifix. A crowd of people surrounds them, laughing and cheering. They seem to be going up the hill toward the city center and the castle on the bluff.

Be prepared to elaborate further on the grisly, bloated, and obviously non-human nature of the corpse or to describe the Band of the Crimson Mantle (see **Appendix A: NPCs**). If the heroes join the procession, they witness Lord Angus presenting a sack of coin to Pratchett, the Band's leader. Pratchett panders to the crowd, playing the hero, while the others stand back; Isidra looks disgusted with the bravado, Dresden looks typically on edge, and Yelm just looks uncomfortable, like he would rather be someplace else. The corpse is hung on the wall next to the gatehouse.

The heroes can gather quite a bit of information from the citizens. General "What's going on?" questions produce responses that tell of the demon infestation and are full of praise for the Band of the Crimson Mantle, derogatory toward Elinda Bannon, and apprehensive about the city's future. Refer to the **City Rumors Table** later in this chapter for specific rumors and responses.

TIMED ENCOUNTER 1.2: THE LORD'S OFFER

This encounter begins after the heroes have been in the city for a short time, perhaps moving about the market or leaving their lodgings to explore. It can also be inserted directly following **Timed Encounter 1.1**. If the party does not seek out the local authorities on their own, a young herald approaches with a summons to the gate of the keep from **Lord Arb Angus** of Eamonvale.

When the heroes attend or approach on their own, Arb voices his concerns over the events in the city and offers a proposal to the party. Allow the heroes' reputation to precede them if they have one in the region. Arb stands at the gatehouse of the castle, flanked by a Mist Watch unit. He is gregariously greeting citizens and visitors, but breaks away to attend to the heroes.

> "Well met, travelers. Allow me to extend a welcome on behalf of the citizens of Dun Eamon. I am Arb Angus, Lord of Eamonvale, and I have a proposition for you.
>
> "Your arrival is ill-timed, yet fortuitous, for while you have come during trying times, I believe you may be able to assist us. Dun Eamon has been troubled by a plague unlike we have known before, a plague of evil creatures who walk like men but kill and plunder without remorse — demons, I am quite certain, from a world beyond our own. While I have known them to exist, I never dreamed that they would appear in the streets of the Grey Citadel.
>
> "The Mist Watch is able to safeguard the citizens and their property for the most part, but the origins of the problem are a mystery. I have offered a bounty on slain demons, and a few adventurers, such as the group you may have seen earlier, have been able to collect. Yet I fear that killing a few demons will not bring an end to our troubles. While my people need victories like this afternoon, I need someone who can finish the job.
>
> "A separate circumstance has arisen as well. A wizard who lives here in the citadel has disappeared. The timing may or may not be coincidental; she vanished just prior to the first appearance of the creatures. Knowledge of this may aid you in your investigation; I pray that your success may return her to us unharmed.
>
> "I am prepared to offer a reward to anyone who can successfully identify and eradicate the source of the infestation. Of course, the original bounty still stands: 50 gold ducats for every demon slain. Find and eliminate the source of the threat, and another 2,000 ducats will be yours, as well as my gratitude.
>
> "What say you?"

If the party asks, Arb is willing to advance 50 gp to the party to begin the investigation. He answers any questions truthfully, according to his knowledge. He knows that Elinda Bannon was last seen three nights before the demon's appearance, and he knows about the three burglaries, but does not speculate as to their significance. He also has heard most of the rumors from the **City Rumors Table** (see later in this chapter), but does not reveal them unless questioned directly — they are just rumors, after all.

Arb Angus, Male Human, Lord of Eamonvale (Rgr9):
HP 71; AC 2[17]; **Atk** *+2 bastard sword* (1d8+2) or longbow x2 (1d6); **Move** 12; **Save** 4 (+2, ring); **AL** L; **CL/XP** 9/1100; **Special:** +9 damage vs. giants and goblin-types, alertness, spells (1), tracking. (see **Appendix A: NPCs**)
Spells: 1st—*detect evil.*
Equipment: *bracers of defense AC 4[15], +2 bastard sword,* short sword, longbow, 20 arrows, *ring of protection +2,* gold band of lordship, amulet of the Angus crest, emerald signet ring (500 gp).

Timed Encounter 1.3:
The Demon Attack

This encounter brings the heroes face-to-face with the demons that are terrorizing the city. Introduce it when the heroes are settled at the inn on the evening of their arrival. You may need to modify the text for characters that are not in the common room (sleeping, tending horses, returning from business, and so on).

The cheerful, noisy atmosphere of the common room is abruptly shattered by a scream of unmistakable horror coming from beyond the side door of the inn. The sudden hush in the room is broken only by the sound of weapons being readied, but nobody seems eager to leave the safety of the inn to investigate. They know all too well what most likely waits outside. The scream comes from a boy, **Mert**, who is returning home late with his merchant father **Kelvin**. A roaming group of **6 dretches** has cornered them behind the inn, and unless the heroes intervene, Mert and Kelvin are overpowered in a few rounds. Read the following when the party exists the inn:

The two citizens are cornered at the bottom of the ramp between the upper and lower city, right below the woodlot. They are surrounded by four of the dretches, which are closing in; two more wait in the mist. If the heroes position themselves between the dretches and their intended prey, the father grabs his son and rushes for the inn's side door. Unless the party has a favorable reputation at the inn (having bought several rounds, and so on), the patrons do not join in the fight, but they stand guard at the open door to admit retreating characters. The exception is **Rasputin**, who intervenes (with thrown daggers) if one or more of the heroes loses consciousness. After 10 rounds, a Watch Patrol arrives on the run. This patrol is made up of **9 guards** and **1 sergeant**. This patrol also has a 25% chance of a **constable** and a 10% chance of a **mist mage** being present.

Tactics: The dretches' strength is in their numbers, so they use simple mob tactics to maximize their advantage, attempting to surround individuals. They fight until four of them are slain, then attempt to retreat into the darkness, using their stench to cover their escape. Once broken, they do not attempt to stay together but flee randomly into different parts of the city to continue their mischief. Tracking them does not lead the heroes to any place of importance.

Development: The dretches carry no treasure, but a reward of another kind awaits the heroes if they succeed. Word travels quickly in the Grey Citadel, and by morning the heroes find that their notoriety has opened many doors. Citizens are more inclined to cooperate with

Timed Encounter 1-3: The Demons Attack

Elevation Detail

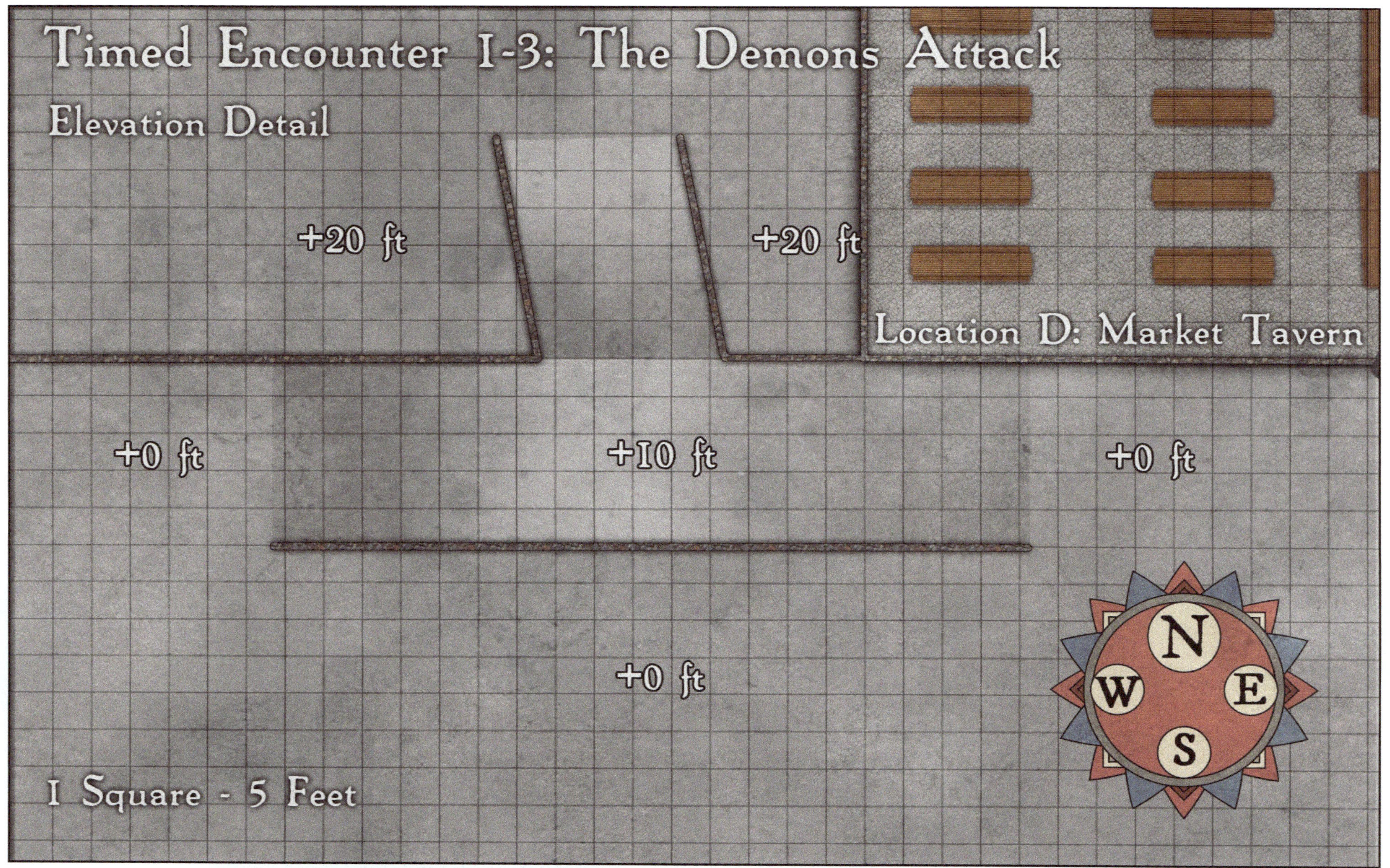

the investigation, the ruling family is impressed, and every innkeeper and merchant in the city is competing for their business.

The Band of the Crimson Mantle is not happy at being outdone, however, which sets the stage for **Timed Encounter 2.2: Unfriendly Competition**. Thanks to the eyes and ears of the thieves' guild, Lilith needs very little time to order the assassination attempt described in **Timed Encounter 3.1: The Guild Strikes**.

Whether Rasputin participates or not, he invites the party to join him for a late breakfast, described in **Timed Encounter 2.1: Rasputin Speaks Out**. If Kelvin and Mert survive, they give each hero a waterproof cape or hooded cloak.

Kelvin, Male Human: HP 5; AC 9[10]; Atk staff (1d6); Move 12; Save 18; AL L; CL/XP B/10; Special: none. (*Monstrosities* 254)

Mert, Male Human: HP 4; AC 9[10]; Atk strike (1hp); Move 12; Save 18; AL L; CL/XP B/10; Special: none. (*Monstrosities* 254)

Dretch Demons (6): HD 4; HP 22, 20x2, 19, 18, 17; AC 2[17]; Atk 2 claws (1d4), bite (1d6); Move 9; Save 13; AL C; CL/XP 6/400; Special: spell-like abilities. (*Monstrosities* 92) Spell-like abilities: 1/day—*darkness 15ft radius*, stinking cloud (20ft radius, save or nauseated for 1d4+1 rounds), summon 1d4 giant rats.

Mist Watch Constable, Male or Female Human Warrior (Ftr3): HD 3; AC 4[15]; Atk *+1 longsword* (1d8+1) or longbow x2 (1d6); Move 12; Save 12; AL C; CL/XP 3/60; Special: multiple attacks (3) vs. creatures with 1 or fewer HD. (see **Appendix A: NPCs**) Equipment: chainmail, large steel shield, *+1 longsword*, longbow and quiver of 20 arrows, signal horn, rank chain.

Mist Mage, Male or Female Human Wizard (MU4): HD 4d4; AC 9[10] or 2[17] (missile) and 4[15] (melee) from *shield* spell; Atk dagger (1d4) or *wand of magic missiles* (1d4); Move 12; Save 12; AL L or N; CL/XP 4/240; Special: +2 saves vs. spells, wands and staffs, spells (3/2). (see **Appendix A: NPCs**) Spells: 1st—*charm person, light, shield*; 2nd—*detect evil, phantasmal force*. Equipment: robes, dagger, *wand of magic missiles* (2d4 charges), *potion of healing*, spellbook.

Mist Watch Soldier, Male or Female Human Warrior: HD 1; AC 5[14]; Atk longsword (1d8), spear (1d6) or longbow x2 (1d6); Move 12; Save 17; AL L or N; CL/XP 1/15; Special: none. (*Monstrosities* 257 or **Appendix A: NPCs**) Equipment: ring mail, steel shield, longsword, spear, longbow, quiver of 20 arrows.

Mist Watch Sergeant, Male or Female Human Warrior: HD 3; AC 4[15]; Atk longsword (1d8), spear (1d6) or longbow x2 (1d6); Move 12; Save 14; AL L or N; CL/XP 3/60; Special: none. (*Monstrosities* 256 or **Appendix A: NPCs**) Equipment: chainmail, steel shield, longsword, spear, longbow, quiver of 20 arrows, potion of healing, signal horn, rank chain.

Rasputin, Half-Elf Male Thief Performer (Thf6): HP 20; AC 5[14]; Atk *+1 dagger that returns to the hand* (1d4+1) or short sword (1d6) or throwing dagger (1d4); Move 12; Save 10; AL N; CL/XP 6/400; Special: +2 save bonus vs. traps and magical devices, backstab (x3), darkvision (60ft), read languages, thieving skills. (see **Appendix A: NPCs**) Thieving Skills: Climb 90%, Tasks/Traps 40%, Hear 4 in 6, Hide 35%, Silent 45%, Locks 35%. Equipment: *bracers of defense AC 6[13]*, gaudy clothing and jewelry, *+1 dagger that returns to the hand* (in boot), short sword, 4 throwing daggers, *ring of protection +1*, balalaika, props (dice, cards, juggling balls, and so forth), pouch containing 54 gp, 22 sp, 18 cp, and hacksilver ingot worth 90 gp, pet monkey (Vlado).

TIMED ENCOUNTER 2.1: RASPUTIN SPEAKS OUT

The heroes may find their way to the local performer in their search for information, following other people's recommendations or their own instincts. Unless the party approaches Rasputin, use this encounter on the morning of the second day in the city.

As the heroes descend the stairs in the morning, a small monkey wearing a red vest and fez approaches them. The monkey seems quite insistent that they accompany him to a table at the rear of the common area, where **Rasputin** waits for them. He has an important piece of information for their investigation and wishes to enter into an agreement with them. Whenever the heroes approach Rasputin, introduce him and read the following in your best eastern European accent:

"I know a great deal about what goes on in this city. I know, for example, that Arb Angus wants your help in eliminating the demons and finding the missing wizard. I know from watching you last evening that you are capable, but I also know a few things that may help you in your quest. I suggest we exchange information in hopes that we can work together to mutual benefit.

"Many of my sources have ceased to provide me with information; others are nowhere to be found. The thieves of the city are no longer independent; they have formed some sort of organization and, frankly, they are making my life very difficult. I will find out what I can to assist your investigation, and you will tell me if you discover who is marshalling the thieves. Like many people in the city, I am a merchant, not of goods, but of words. Most people hear my words as pretty songs, but you may hear far more, if you know how to listen. Come and watch one of my nightly performances here, put a few coins in Vlado's cup, and you shall hear what I know.

"Now be careful, and let me give you some advice: listen to everyone, but trust no one."

You may need to modify the text slightly to accommodate the heroes' reactions or other major deviations from the plot. They may wish to question Rasputin further, but he is very reserved with his information; he insists that they come see his next performance before he gives them anything more. Remember, Rasputin may be used to feed important rumors to stumped parties, he can support them in a fight, and he could even replace a deceased character. He is a valuable tool, so consider how best to play him.

For example, his next performance can yield information about the three burglaries. If the party watches (and tips) any of his performances that day, he sings of the "cutter of roots," the "seer of stones," and the "winder of golden wire." These are the three citizens whose shops were burgled to provide for the operation of the summoning device, though Rasputin does not know this. Chatting with nearby patrons reveals the theme of his song and the location of the shops; otherwise,

the party may just need to figure it out through trial and error (i.e., "If I wanted a root cut, who would I see?"). Use the same format to deliver any other information the party might be missing, over several performances if necessary.

Rasputin, Half-Elf Male Thief Performer (Thf6): HP 20; AC 5[14]; **Atk** *+1 dagger that returns to the hand* (1d4+1) or short sword (1d6) or throwing dagger (1d4); **Move** 12; **Save** 10; **AL** N; **CL/XP** 6/400; **Special:** +2 save bonus vs. traps and magical devices, backstab (x3), darkvision (60ft), read languages, thieving skills. (see **Appendix A: NPCs**)
Thieving Skills: Climb 90%, Tasks/Traps 40%, Hear 4 in 6, Hide 35%, Silent 45%, Locks 35%.
Equipment: *bracers of defense AC 6[13]*, gaudy clothing and jewelry, *+1 dagger that returns to the hand* (in boot), short sword, 4 throwing daggers, *ring of protection +1*, balalaika, props (dice, cards, juggling balls, and so forth), pouch containing 54 gp, 22 sp, 18 cp, and hacksilver ingot worth 90 gp, pet monkey (Vlado).

Vlado, Monkey (Pet): HD 1d4 hp; **HP** 3; **AC** 7[12]; **Atk** 2 claws (1d3); **Move** 15; **Save** 18; **AL** N; **CL/XP** A/5; **Special:** none.
Equipment: vest, fez, hurdy-gurdy, tin cup.

TIMED ENCOUNTER 2.2:
UNFRIENDLY COMPETITION

Use this encounter on the second afternoon or any time after the heroes distinguish themselves in the city (after successfully completing **Timed Encounter 1.3**, for example). **The Band of the Crimson Mantle** confronts the heroes and warns them to stand down. Consider adding some **hired bandits** if the party greatly outnumbers the Band. This encounter is appropriate whenever the party is in a relatively peaceful setting or at least during a quiet moment. Potential opportunities are at the Market Tavern, in the market, or in the Crafthall. If it develops into a combat encounter, be prepared to improvise the location. A bystander summons the Mist Watch, which arrives seven rounds after the Band enters. Read or paraphrase the following:

> You are interrupted by crash of an opening door, and all eyes turn to stare at the newcomers. The party of adventurers you saw in the city parading the crucified demon is walking toward you, wearing their distinctive red garb. The dark half-elf is in front and looks to be in charge. The pale, gaunt woman, the wild-eyed halfling, and the tattooed warrior are right behind him, all looking fierce and determined.
>
> "You think there's enough room in this town for all of us?" the dark half-elf says. "I think not! This demon plague is our business, you lot need to stand down. We'll wrap this mystery up before you get yourselves killed — you'd better leave the glory work to the real heroes!"

The heroes have a great deal of control over where this encounter goes. If they respond nonviolently, play out the exchange of venomous remarks as far as the heroes wish. If this is the case, Pratchett eventually spits at someone's feet, makes one last colorful remark, and retreats with his group in tow. The band did not come here looking for a fight, but they are ready for one. If the party rises to the occasion, returns their taunts, or otherwise escalates the threat of violence, the situation may deteriorate into a brawl.

The Band of the Crimson Mantle

The entire band — **Pratchett**, **Isidra**, **Dresden**, and **Yelm** — is present for this encounter.

Pratchett, Male Half-Elf Thief (Thf5): HP 14; AC 6[13];
Atk short sword (1d6) or *+2 light crossbow* (1d4+1) or leather sap (1d4 nonlethal); **Move** 12; **Save** 11; **AL** C; **CL/XP** 5/240;
Special: +2 save bonus vs. traps and magical devices, backstab (x2), darkvision (60ft), detect secret doors (4-in-6 chance), read languages, thieving skills. (see **Appendix A: NPCs**)
Thieving Skills: Climb 89%, Tasks/Traps 35%, Hear 4 in 6, Hide 30%, Silent 40%, Locks 30%.
Equipment: *+1 leather armor*, short sword, leather sap, *+2 light crossbow*, 20 bolts (8 pre-poisoned); large vial of purple worm poison (8 applications; save or additional 1d6 damage); 50ft silk rope, grappling iron, thieves' tools, flint and steel, hooded lantern, 2 flasks of oil, 2 days' trail rations, waterskin, pouch (contains 65 gp, 18 sp, and 4 garnets [worth 120 gp, two worth 100 gp each, and 90 gp), map to his secret cache of supplies and treasure.

Isidra, Female Human Priest of the God of Death (Clr5): HP 23; AC 3[16]; Atk heavy mace (1d6); **Move** 12; **Save** 10 (+1, ring); **AL** C; **CL/XP** 5/240; **Special:** +2 save vs. paralysis and poison, banish undead, spells (2/2). (see **Appendix A: NPCs**)
Spells: 1st—*cause light wounds* (x2); 2nd—*hold person*, *silence 15ft radius*.
Equipment: *+1 ring mail* (see special note below), small steel shield with unholy symbol of the God of Death, heavy mace, *ring of protection +1*, *potion of healing* (x3), scroll (*detect magic* and *speak with dead*), mummified hand of a small child, 2 days' trail rations, waterskin, 2 torches, pouch (containing 32 gp and 18 sp), silver necklace with 3 tiny black pearls worth 500 gp total.

Dresden the Mad, Male Halfling Mage (MU5): HP 14; AC 6[13] or 2[17] (missile) and 4[15] (melee) from *shield* spell; Atk dagger (1d4) or sling (1d4); **Move** 12; **Save** 11; **AL** C; **CL/XP** 5/240; **Special:** +1 to-hit missile weapons bonus, +2 saves vs. spells, +4 save vs. magic, wands and staffs, spells (4/2/1). (see **Appendix A: NPCs**)
Spells: 1st—*charm person*, *magic missile*, *shield*, *sleep*; 2nd—*invisibility*, *web*; 3rd—*fireball*.
Equipment: *bracers of defense AC 6[13]*, dirty red robes, dagger, sling with 30 stones, *ring of fire resistance*, *potion of flying*, *potion of gaseous form*, 2 scrolls (*haste* and *knock*), assorted rocks (his "friends"), 2 days' trail rations, clay flask, pet toad named Pebble.

Yelm, Male Human Barbarian (Ftr5): HP 31; AC 5[14]; Atk *+1 bastard sword* (1d8+3) or throwing axe (1d6+2) or strike (1d4+2); **Move** 12; **Save** 10; **AL** N; **CL/XP** 5/240; **Special:** +2 to hit and damage strength bonus, multiple attacks (5) vs. creatures with 1 or fewer HD. (see **Appendix A: NPCs**)
Equipment: chainmail, stained kilt, *+1 bastard sword*, 4 throwing axes, 2 flasks of oil, wineskin, flask of whiskey, 5 days' trail rations, 6 torches, 50ft hemp rope, silver beck torc worth 20 gp, silver-trimmed drinking horn worth 12 gp, hacksilver armband worth 8 gp, pouch containing 25 gp and 16 sp.

Bandits (if needed): HD 1; AC 7[12]; **Atk** weapon (1d8);
Move 12; Save 17; AL C; CL/XP 1/15; Special: none. (*Monstrosities* 254)

Tactics: The Band does not use lethal force unless their lives are in danger, as they have no desire to wind up in jail. Pratchett produces a leather sap, and Yelm wades in enthusiastically with his fists. Isidra and Dresden use their spells as needed. If the fight goes badly against them, or when the watch is summoned, the Band tries to escape the fight (spiced by lots of threats and oaths).

Development: At a minimum, the heroes may need to explain what happened to the watch when it arrives. They may also be responsible for damages, depending on where the incident takes place. At worst, they may be responsible for someone's death. Keep these issues in mind as you develop the encounter. On the positive side, the band has shown its true colors. As a result, a sympathetic bystander might approach the heroes with some basic information about their skills and hierarchy; paraphrase a few select items from their background in **Appendix A: NPCs**.

Timed Encounter 2.3: Howlers in the Night

Use this encounter any time on the day following the dretch attack, probably the second day in the city. The later in the day it occurs, the less time heroes have to recover before **Timed Encounter 3.1: The Guild Strikes**. It can occur anywhere in the city.

> As you move down the street, a long, mournful howl rises through the misty air, chilling your spine. Immediately following it are the cries of panicking citizens, and they sound as if they are coming right toward you.

In addition to fighting the **3 mongrels of yith**, the heroes may try to deal with the tide of panicked citizens. With the fleeing citizens are **4 watchmen** whose unit has been decimated. The party may be able to reinforce its numbers with the soldiers or a mob armed with improvised weapons. Reward good roleplaying — especially good "stand together" speeches — with a small knot of temporary followers. This development can complicate the combat but it also helps the heroes preserve their spells and hit points and makes for a cinematic fight scene.

The **10 citizens** have no weapons, though they fight with anything they are given.

Mongrels of Yith (3): HD 4; HP 28, 25, 23; AC 4[15]; **Atk** bite (1d6+1); **Move** 15; **Save** 13; **AL** C; **CL/XP** 4/120; **Special:** terrifying howl (save or flee in fear for 1d6 rounds). (see **Appendix B: New Monsters**)

Watchmen, Male or Female Humans (4): HD 1; AC 7[12]; Atk longsword (1d8); **Move** 12; **Save** 17; **AL** N; **CL/XP** 1/15; **Special:** none. (*Monstrosities* 257)

Commoners, Male or Female Humans (10): HD 1d6hp; HP 6, 5, 4x3, 3x2, 2, 1x2; AC 9[10]; Atk weapon (1d4); **Move** 12; **Save** 18; **AL** N; **CL/XP** B/10; **Special:** none. (*Monstrosities* 254)

Tactics

Give the party at least five rounds between the citizens and the mongrels to rally, plan a defense, or take up positions. The howlers were sent into the city to hunt the heroes, and they attack citizens only for fun or if they try to stand their ground. The mongrels of Yith are instinctive pack hunters, and when they encounter the party, they attempt to encircle it. They attack by charging in and then racing away. Each mongrel continues this action as long as the party remains in a defensive posture. As soon as a mongrel is charged or followed, it turns and focuses on that opponent. The heroes must decide when they shift from defense to offense.

The commoners have no combat skills and need the party's leadership to survive. They fight defensively the characters inspire and encourage them.

DEVELOPMENT

Even after these mongrels are defeated, there is a 60% chance per hour that one or more mongrels in or around the city use their terrifying howl. Chances are that the heroes will not be affected unless they pursue the creature (which is up to you to administrate). The effects on the population are profound, however; people tend to stay inside or hurry from place to place, sleepless and haunted. Reinforce this "city under siege" atmosphere to the heroes when they next venture into the city.

TIMED ENCOUNTER 3.1: THE GUILD STRIKES

Use this encounter early in the morning following the encounter with the mongrels of Yith. Lilith has ordered Devlin to eliminate the party, and he sends two guild agents, **Kubris** and **Thurf**, to lead a gang to do the job. The guild intends to strike while the party is weakened from the previous night's battle, and unless the heroes were highly successful at rallying citizens to fight with them, they may not be fully recovered. During the fighting, Fitch the barman is wounded and struck unconscious, and Molly the bartender is killed to prevent her from identifying the assassins (she had been informing for the Ebon Union; see **Area D-2** for more on Fitch and Molly).

In this battle, remember that most of the party was likely sound asleep. You could allow the characters to react normally, or you might have each player roll 1d4 to see how long it takes them to shake off their drowsiness. Also, they might need to don their armor or fight without it. Until the heroes provide a light source, the encounter takes place in darkness. This encounter is probably very different from the party's usual methods, with unarmored fighters and spell-less spellcasters swinging fists in the dark.

Non-thief characters have a 1-in-6 chance to hear the following; thieves use their Hear Sounds score. Read the following to those who succeed:

Tactics: If the heroes only took one room, the attack takes place as described in the table below. If they occupy two rooms, divide the attackers evenly (ignore any further rooms, as the attackers prefer to focus their strength). If eight thieves are killed (or four, if either Kubris or Thurf is among them, or if both of them are killed), the survivors attempt to withdraw. If the ram fails to break down the door, the heroes barricade themselves in, or the heroes meet the thieves in the gallery, the rounds may need to be adjusted, but the plan is the same. The thieves have carefully timed their attack on the party and act in a specific order:

Round	Actions
Round 0	The thieves enter the inn and surprise the barman dozing by the fire; establish characters' levels of drowsiness.
Round 1	The thieves ascend the stairs and prepare their rams; the heroes take their 1st actions (rising, arming themselves, and so on).
Round 2	The thieves smash in the door(s) with their rams (1-in-6 chance it fails on each try); **2 bandits** enter the room; heroes take second action.
Round 3	**4 bandits** enter the room; heroes take third action.
Round 4	**4 knives** enter the room and move to flank the heroes; **2 nets** burst through the shutters and swing in on ropes; heroes take fourth action.
Round 5	The Thugs and Knives pair off and attack characters; the Nets will seek out spellcasters from behind the party and try to entangle them; heroes take fifth action.
Round 6	**Kubris** and **Thurf** arrive from downstairs to join in the fight (Kubris murders Molly at this time); Kubris tries to disarm the most threatening characters, and Thurf tries to crush the largest ones; heroes take sixth action.
Round 10	A **watch patrol** (9 soldiers, 1 sergeant) arrives downstairs.

Kubris, Male Human (Thf4): HP 13; AC 7[12]; Atk rapier
(1d6); **Move** 12; **Save** 12; **AL** C; **CL/XP** 4/120; **Special:** +2
save bonus vs. traps and magical devices, backstab (x2), read
languages, thieving skills.
Thieving Skills: Climb 88%, Tasks/Traps 30%, Hear 4 in 6,
Hide 25%, Silent 35%, Locks 25%.
Equipment: leather armor, silvered rapier, pouch (13 gp
and 19 sp), pouch of powdered silver (8 gp).
Note: Kubris is a mean and spiteful man, detested by
everyone except Thurf, who idolizes him, and Devlin, who
needs a man willing to do the unspeaking with only financial
conditions to be met. He has greasy black hair and stained
armor, but despite his slovenly appearance, he is a quick
and capable swordsman. He aspired to be a great mercenary
captain, but his greed and maliciousness have led him down
the dark path too many times to turn back.

Thurf, Male Human (Ftr4): HP 24; AC 7[12]; Atk flail (1d8);
Move 12; **Save** 11; **AL** C; **CL/XP** 4/120; **Special:** multiple
attacks (4) vs. creatures with 1 or fewer HD.
Equipment: leather armor, flail.
Note: Thurf is as large and powerful as he is slow and
thick-witted, with broad shoulders and fierce black eyes. His
career as a mason was cut short by a lethal outburst of rage.
Kubris tool him on as a friend and as a bit of reinforcing
muscle, and the pair was notorious as thugs, enforcers, and
extortionists in the city by the time Devlin's gang arrived.

Bandits, Male or Female Human (6): HD 1; HP 6, 5x3,
4, 3; AC 6[13]; Atk short sword (1d6) or club (1d6), dagger
(1d4); **Move** 12; **Save** 17; **AL** C; **CL/XP** 1/15; **Special:** none.
(*Monstrosities* 254)
Equipment: leather armor, short sword or club, dagger,
small wooden shield, pouch with 1d4 gp and 2d6 sp.

Knives, Male or Female Human (Thf1) (4): HP 4, 3x2,
2; AC 7[12]; Atk dagger (1d4); **Move** 12; **Save** 15; **AL** C;
CL/XP 1/15; **Special:** +2 save bonus vs. traps and magical
devices, backstab (x2), thieving skills. (see **Appendix A:
NPCs**)
Thieving Skills: Climb 85%, Tasks/Traps 15%, Hear 3 in 6,
Hide 10%, Silent 20%, Locks 10%.
Equipment: leather armor, 2 daggers, pouch of caltrops
(1d4 damage, halves movement in 10ft-diameter area), pouch
with 1d4 gp and 2d6 sp, 10 % chance of a small pouch of
powdered silver skimmed from a previous heist (worth 1d4
gp).

Nets, Male or Female Human (Thf2) (2): HP 6, 5; AC
7[12]; Atk net (save or entangled) or dagger (1d4); **Move**
12; **Save** 14; **AL** C; **CL/XP** 2/30; **Special:** +2 save bonus vs.
traps and magical devices, backstab (x2), thieving skills. (see
Appendix A: NPCs)
Thieving Skills: Climb 86%, Tasks/Traps 20%, Hear 3 in 6,
Hide 15%, Silent 25%, Locks 15%.
Equipment: leather armor, net, dagger, pouch of caltrops
(1d4 damage, halves movement in 10ft-diameter area), 50ft
silk rope, grappling hook, pouch with 1d8 gp and 2d10 sp,
10% chance of a small pouch of powdered silver skimmed
from a previous heist (worth 2d4 gp).

**Mist Watch Soldiers, Male or Female Human Warriors
(9):** HD 1; HP 8, 7x2, 6x3, 5, 4x2; AC 5[14]; Atk longsword
(1d8), spear (1d6) or longbow x2 (1d6); **Move** 12; **Save** 17;
AL L or N; **CL/XP** 1/15; **Special:** none. (*Monstrosities* 257

or **Appendix A: NPCs**)
Equipment: ring mail, steel shield, longsword, spear,
longbow, quiver of 20 arrows.

Mist Watch Sergeant, Male or Female Human Warrior:
HD 3; HP 18; AC 4[15]; Atk longsword (1d8), spear (1d6)
or longbow x2 (1d6); **Move** 12; **Save** 14; **AL** L or N; **CL/XP**
3/60; **Special:** none. (*Monstrosities* 256 or **Appendix A:
NPCs**)
Equipment: chainmail, steel shield, longsword, spear,
longbow, quiver of 20 arrows, potion of healing, signal horn,
rank chain.

DEVELOPMENT

At this point, the party may be badly weakened or even dwindling
in number, depending on the battles with demons and assassination
attempts. The death of Molly, the serving girl, is a good pretense
on which to integrate new party members. Depending on what the
party lacks (magic, muscle, and so on), Rasputin and Fitch now have
enough personal stake in the matter to want to join in the quest. At
this point in the adventure, either NPC could become a permanent
character without derailing the plot.

TIMED ENCOUNTER 3.2:
THE RIVALS DEPART

Wherever the party is on the afternoon of the third day, allow
them to hear of the Band of the Crimson Mantle and their mission
belowground. A friendly NPC (Fitch or Rasputin) or an excited child
on the run tells them that the "heroes" are going underground in
search of the source of the demons. If the party chooses to attend,
use the following:

> As you reach the market, you can see that the words of
> the citizens were true … half the city has turned out to
> see the adventurers off. A drain has been opened in the
> middle of the market, and a huge knot of people crowd
> around it. An escort of Mist Watch soldiers looks on as the
> four adventurers in their red capes light torches and sling
> on their packs.
>
> The half-elf cries out to the gathered crowd: "Friends,
> citizens, take heart, for the Band of the Crimson Mantle
> goes now to seek the source of your troubles. Do not fear
> for our safety; instead, prepare the feast for our return, for
> we will be victorious! Farewell!"
>
> A huge cheer goes up from the crowd; the members of
> the Band raise their torches in salute and descend through
> the drain.

If the heroes scan the crowd, they may find the Angus brothers on
hand. They find the brothers watching the display with interest. Their
sentiments toward the Band are unchanged: They believe the adventurers
are good for the morale of the city, but doubt that they will meet with
success. Stump is with them, but he is certain the Band will fail based on
his assessment of them and his knowledge of dungeoneering.

The heroes may find themselves being looked at questioningly by
those who know of their investigation. If the party had no idea that the
underground caverns were involved, this event hands that information
to them. More likely, they have found one or more of the secret
entrances to the tunnels — something the Band did not find — and
using the hidden entrances can save them time and energy. They may
choose to abandon whatever leads they were following and pursue the

Band, or they may continue with their detective work and discover advantages to aid them in their quest. The party may even disagree on the proper course of action — possibly leading them to an interesting discussion over a few pints!

TIMED ENCOUNTER 3.3: CAUGHT IN THE ACT

This incident provides an opportunity to learn more about the activities of the Ebon Union and their connections to the demons. The party also gets another chance to learn about one of the secret entrances to the tunnels. Use this encounter any time late on the third day while the party is in or near the market. The characters notice cloaked figures descending a drainpipe from the roof of a house at the end of Grocer's Lane.

A team of thieves from the Ebon Union has robbed the home of a wealthy merchant in the city; the party notices them as they leave the scene. Out of laziness and to avoid getting soaked, the burglars choose to disobey orders and return via the secret entrance in the basement of the now-empty Ironworks (**Area Q**). The gang consists of **2 bolts**, **2 cutpurses**, and **4 knives**, and **Gulik**, a wizard who usually accompanies housebreaker heists.

Gulik, Male Human Ebon Union Mage (MU5): HP 15; **AC** 8[11] or 2[17] (missile) and 4[15] (melee) from *shield* spell; **Atk** dagger (1d4); **Move** 12; **Save** 10 (+1, ring); **AL** C; **CL/ XP** 5/240; **Special:** +2 saves vs. spells, wands and staffs, spells (4/2/1).
Spells: 1st—*charm person, magic missile* (x2), *shield*; 2nd— *invisibility, phantasmal force*; 3rd—*lightning bolt*.
Equipment: robes, dagger, *ring of protection +1, potion of gaseous form*, scroll (*confusion*), scroll (*haste*), spellbook, water flask, pet cat Jak.

Jak, Pet Cat: HD 1d4 hp; **HP** 3; **AC** 8[11]; **Atk** 2 claws (1hp); **Move** 12; **Save** 18; **AL** N; **CL/XP** B/10; **Special:** none. **Equipment:** jeweled collar (65 gp).

Bolts, Male or Female Human (Thf2) (2): HP 2d4; **HP** 6, 5; **AC** 7[12]; **Atk** dagger (1d4) or light crossbow (1d4+1); **Move** 12; **Save** 14; **AL** C; **CL/XP** 2/30; **Special:** +2 save bonus vs. traps and magical devices, backstab (x2), thieving skills. (see **Appendix A: NPCs**)
Thieving Skills: Climb 86%, Tasks/Traps 20%, Hear 3 in 6, Hide 15%, Silent 25%, Locks 15%.
Equipment: leather armor, 2 daggers, light crossbow, 20 bolts, pouch of caltrops (1d4 damage, halves movement in 10ft-diameter area), pouch with 1d8 gp and 2d10 sp.

Cutpurses (2), Male or Female Human (Thf2): HP 2d4; **HP** 7, 4; **AC** 7[12]; **Atk** dagger (1d4); **Move** 12; **Save** 14; **AL** C; **CL/XP** 2/30; **Special:** +2 save bonus vs. traps and magical devices, backstab (x2), thieving skills. (see **Appendix A: NPCs**)
Thieving Skills: Climb 86%, Tasks/Traps 20%, Hear 3 in 6, Hide 15%, Silent 25%, Locks 15%.
Equipment: leather armor, 2 daggers, pouch of caltrops (1d4 damage, halves movement in 10ft-diameter area), pouch with 2d10 gp and 2d10 sp.

Knives, Male or Female Human (Thf1) (4): HP 4x2, 3, 2; **AC** 7[12]; **Atk** dagger (1d4); **Move** 12; **Save** 15; **AL** C; **CL/XP** 1/15; **Special:** +2 save bonus vs. traps and magical devices, backstab (x2), thieving skills. (see **Appendix A: NPCs**)
Thieving Skills: Climb 85%, Tasks/Traps 15%, Hear 3 in 6, Hide 10%, Silent 20%, Locks 10%.
Equipment: leather armor, 2 daggers, pouch of caltrops (1d4 damage, halves movement in 10ft-diameter area), pouch with 1d4 gp and 2d6 sp, 10 % chance of a small pouch of powdered silver skimmed from a previous heist (worth 1d4 gp).

Tactics: The activities and reactions of the Ebon Union thieves and the actual location for this encounter depend on the heroes. The encounter begins when the party spots the thieves leaving the scene of the burglary. The heroes may decide to confront the thieves on the spot, or they might try to follow them back to their destination. The thieves' initial reaction is the same regardless of location.

When they are accosted, either by force, by ambush, or by shouts, the thieves assume they have been spotted either by the watch or by some private security faction. Their reaction is an attempt to escape with the booty. The knives turn and make a stand to allow the cutpurses to make a run for the nearest access point with the loot. The bolts move past the knives and take up firing positions to cover the retreat. Gulik follows the bolts and uses spells to discourage pursuit. If this encounter happens in the market or at the scene of the crime (at the end of Grocer's Lane), citizens scatter and cry for the watch, and the thieves head for the drains in the market (**Areas F** and **G**).

If the thieves are allowed to enter the Ironworks unmolested, they take up positions in the shadows of the shop to ensure they have not attracted any attention. If they are out of the market and near the Ironworks when confronted, they attempt to draw their pursuers inside and dispatch them.

The thieves make a stand in the Ironworks. From just inside the foundry (**Area Q-4**), Gulik casts spells at the party while the thieves move in to fight. Remember the special factors for fighting in and around hot forges (**Area Q-2** and **Q-4**).

Gulik and the others are determined not to reveal the secret entrance and do not enter the storeroom (**Area Q-7**). If they are discovered, they fight to the death or attempt to flee into the city to hide. If the heroes dispatch them, they must draw conclusions about the significance of the Ironworks on their own.

RUMORS IN THE CITY

In this mystery, the success of the heroes — and even the difficulty of achieving it — is directly related to the depth of their investigation. The heroes should be prepared to ask lots of questions, follow up on answers, and constantly weigh the worth of the information they receive. You must likewise be prepared to adapt to unforeseen questions, make up answers, and humor the players as they pursue fruitless dead-ends. The rumors describe rumors; more specific facts can be found in the **Mystery Elements** section.

These rumors are categorized by subject for when the heroes are pursuing a particular topic. Be prepared to recycle and paraphrase rumors as needed, because they represent the majority viewpoints of the community. Do not underestimate the significance of the rumor information, and be careful not to distribute too much at one time — limit one rumor per NPC unless otherwise indicated.

Unless the heroes are asking about one of the specific topics, randomize the subject.

1d6	Rumor Subject
1	The Demons
2	The Underground
3	The Brothers
4	The Wizard
5	The Thieves
6	Other Rumors

RUMORS ABOUT THE DEMONS

1d12	Rumor
1–4	"The foreign merchants have always plotted to overthrow the brothers' rule. I fear that this is their insidious doing." (*False*. The Angus family has never been popular with foreign guilds, but they have no hand in the demonic infestation.)
5–7	"There's a fine reward from Lord Angus for the body of a demon. You look like the kind of bunch to collect it." (*True*. Angus is offering 50 gp for the body of what he defines as a demon, currently a dretch.)
8	"I saw a dark, powerful figure skulking around town the other night … it seems to me it was over by the mill. With all the talk of demons abroad, I'd rather stay in at night, if you know what I mean." (*Mostly True*. This man actually saw Gethrax leaving the mill on some nightly errand.)
9	"Someone says that one of the market drains was open this morning, with horrid claw marks all around. Whatever it is that plagues us, it dwells beneath the streets." (*Mostly true*. The claw marks are an embellishment, but an emerging dretch did leave the grate open.)
10	"An old legend tells of a demon prince who was imprisoned at the bottom of the pool below the falls. I fear he has broken free and dwells deep beneath the city." (*False*. The legend is a wives' tale, although a powerful demon does dwell below the city.)
11	"I saw one of the beasts in the market one night, with my own eyes. Horrible and hunched it was, with a blubbery face and dripping lips. If I never see such a thing again, it will be too soon." (*True*. This man saw a dretch.)
12	"I reckon it's got something to do with that damned witch in the tower [i.e., Bannon]. Always with the flashing lights and smoke; she's in league with them demons, and now she's gone off to join 'em." (*Partly True*. Bannon is responsible for the demons, but she has gone to eliminate them, not to join them.)

RUMORS ABOUT THE UNDERGROUND

1d12	Rumor
1–4	"I don't believe all the talk of demons underground. They say there's an underground river beneath the city, runs right down the middle. Nothing could live in those sewers." (*Partly True*. The underground river is there, but so are many nasty creatures.)
5–7	"There's a cesspit under the mill, where all the sawdust and grain hulls are thrown. They say it's spawned its own lifeforce." (*True*. The caves below the mill are infested with sentient plants and fungi.)
8–9	"This city came under siege many years ago, and the heroes that saved it were buried in lavish tombs near the gates of the keep. Those burial chambers are still under there …" (*True*. The catacombs are beneath the market.)
10–11	"Every so often, somebody disappears without a trace, no bodies, no remnants. They say a tribe of evil, flesh-eating halflings live below the city." (*False*. The halflings are long gone, but their halls are now occupied by the Ebon Union. The body snatcher is more likely Gethrax.)
12	"It's rumored that an ancient, forgotten race had a great city right under our feet, abandoned now, but still rich with treasures and fearsome traps." (*True*. The Ebon Union occupies the gatehouse of an old halfling city.)

RUMORS ABOUT THE BROTHERS

1d12	Rumor
1–6	"Them boys are the best thing that's ever happened to the city, an' I been here for three generations of Angus law. Tough an' fair, they are, bless 'em." (*True*. This is the general sentiment toward the brothers.)
7–9	"There's talk that Lord Arb and Captain Bron are feuding over Elinda Bannon. Now of all times, when we need them the most." (*False*. Arb and Bron both figure in the affections of Bannon, but neither lets anything come before their responsibilities.)
10–11	"We've had some tough winters, an' bad crops, but nuthin' like this has ever happened. I can't say I'm sure Lord Angus'll see us through it." (*True*. Some citizens are losing faith in their leaders in this time of troubles.)
12	"The Angus bloodline is corrupt! Old Colm Angus was in league with dark gods, and now we all must pay the price!" (*False*. This man feels the Angus clan wronged his family in a previous generation.)

R

1d12	Rumor
1–6	"That crazy woman! Just look at what she's brought down upon us this time! Left just in time to save her own hide, too." (*Partly True.* Elinda Bannon is responsible for the demon problem, but she has left to solve it. This is becoming the majority view toward Bannon.)
7–8	"I don't care what the others say, she's always been a sweet girl. She lost her father so young and was raised the best that old halfling knew how, so it's no surprise she's a bit … eccentric." (*True.* This may lead the heroes to Stump, who can provide more insight about Elinda Bannon.)
9–10	"She used to work with Ulf Nine-Fingers, over at the Ironworks. They say he ain't been quite right since she left." (*True.* Elinda and Ulf collaborated on magic items, but now Lilith has seduced him.)
11	"I hear she has a secret laboratory where she performs all sorts of strange experiments. Some folks say it's guarded by a dragon!" (*Mostly True.* Except for the dragon.)
12	"A couple of weeks ago, she came home from a long journey with something in a big strongbox. Things just ain't been right 'round here since then." (*True.* Elinda traveled far to acquire *Mamuthek's Aperture,* which began causing problems almost as soon as it arrived.)

Rumors about the Thieves or Robberies

1d12	Rumor
1–4	"It's the damned trade guilds. They've always envied our market, and I believe this is their effort to upset our economy." (*False.* The foreign merchants exploit the circumstances, but they are not the cause.)
5–6	"They got old Herrick Mendon shook up real bad. I've heard he ain't been himself since all this started." (*Mostly False.* Mendon the Merchant has not been himself since Lilith seduced him.)
7–8	"Ha! Some thieves — they robbed the old halfling hag of her magic rock collection! Bet they were disappointed when they didn't turn out to be diamonds or something!" (*True.* The thieves did steal the seer's "magic rocks," which are not diamonds but mineral samples from other planes.)
9–10	"They hit Crenshaw's shop over at the Crafthall … if the Crafthall ain't safe, then nothin' is." (*True.* Crenshaw was not the only victim, however.)
11	"I heard they ran a buncha thieves outta Reme [or any large city in your campaign world.] Betcha them scoundrels set up shop here." (*True.*)
12	"The merchants say there's a gang of highwaymen robbing travelers on the road outside the city — perhaps they are moving into the city." (*Mostly True.* The Ebon Union has an allied wilderness counterpart.)

1d12	Rumor
1–5	"Buncha kids wuz throwin' rocks at some sorta big lizard down on the rocks yesterday. Ain't never seen nuthin' like it. Mighty strange stuff afoot these days, mighty strange." (*True.* The children attacked a lizardfolk infant who had made its way out of the forest. Returning it unharmed to the tribe can win favor with the leaders; see **Appendix D: Wilderness Encounters** and **Area U** in **Chapter Three** for details.)
6–8	"The girls who work at the baths are real disappointed. I guess Herrick Mendon quit bringin' his business in; he used to be good for a nightly massage." (*True.* Mendon has not engaged the services of the ladies since his first visit from Lilith.)
9–11	"They say a bunch of drunks broke into the herbalist's shop lookin' for wormwood juice. Oughta crack down on 'em if ye ask me! (*Partly True.* Caledon's shop was robbed, but it was thieves, not drunks.)
12	"Danver finally got hisself a woman! Somebody seen her comin' outta the millworks the other evening." (*True.* It was Lilith leaving the building on business in the city.)

MYSTERY ELEMENTS

In this adventure, a great deal of information (and advantage) can be gained by thoroughly investigating a series of recent events. The guidelines for revealing information to the players are presented below using the "rule of three" as described in **Chapter One**. All pertinent NPCs are fully described and profiled in the appropriate Keyed Encounter locations, which are referenced below.

These clues, especially those regarding the thefts and the seduced citizens, can be introduced in several ways. The best way is to have the heroes draw their own conclusions from rumors and interviews (as in, "Hmmm. It sounds like a lot of people are 'acting strangely,' doesn't it?" or "Burglaries, huh? So who was robbed?"). If they gather too few rumors or ignore obvious leads, Rasputin, Arb Angus, and other NPCs can help fill in the gaps (i.e., "There has been a rash of burglaries lately. You should look into it.").

Force-feeding your players all the clues should not be necessary; just drop the first one in their laps (such as the wizard reference in **Timed Encounter 1.2: The Lord's Offer** or the thieves' guild reference in **Timed Encounter 2.1: Rasputin Speaks Out**) and see how far they can follow it.

THE CRIME SCENES

Three unusual crimes have occurred in the city since the disappearance of Elinda Bannon and the beginning of the demon attacks. All have certain elements in common: the thieves were efficient, seemed to know what they were looking for, and took uncommon items of questionable value. If the heroes investigate the three crime scenes carefully and interview the victims, they should be able to establish connections with some of the other components of the mystery, such as Bannon's activities and the corrupted citizens. The party may find out about these crimes from listening to rumors or receiving tips from Lord Angus, Rasputin, or other citizens.

Visiting the Seer

In a cramped shop in the lower city, the heroes can find **Amarathea the Seer** (see **Area N** for details), one of the burglary victims. Lilith herself entered the shop soon after her arrival, looking for planar material to fuel her summoning device. When Amarathea is asked about the robberies, she responds as follows in her "little old lady" voice:

> "I don't know why anyone would want to rob a harmless old woman. There are those who mistrust my gift, but I've never done anyone any harm. They stole simple things, but things that were important to me. Money I can do without or get more of. But they left that and took some of my charms, my precious charms."

If asked to describe her "charms," Amarathea says they were all "trinkets from the far corners of this world … and other worlds as well" — meaning other planes. Some of the items were planar in origin:

- A chunk of iron ore from the Abyss
- A moonstone from a fortress on the Astral Plane
- A vial of soil from the fields of Elysium
- A piece of obsidian from the Elemental Plane of Fire

The other items were all mundane common minerals from exotic locations (volcanoes, great canyons, other unique landforms) of the Material Plane. She wore them all on a cord around her neck, the chunks of stone, pendants, and little glass vials all rattling together. She believed that having them would help gain the favor of natives of those regions if she encountered them while "seeing."

The collection included what Lilith hoped to find: the Abyssal core, which she uses to establish the source plane for the creatures summoned with *Mamuthek's Aperture*. The other items are still in Lilith's possession and could also be used with the device. If the heroes deduce the nature of the artifact, knowledge of the Elysian soil can give them a powerful weapon.

While the heroes are visiting, Amarathea insists on performing a "seeing" for them (see **Area N** for details).

Visiting the Root-Cutter

Caledon (see **Area T** for details) is a druid who runs a small herbalist shop in the city. The thieves came here a few nights ago and made off with several organic components to use with *Mamuthek's Aperture* (see **Appendix C: New Magical Items**). Caledon is not terribly perturbed at the incident, although the components were quite rare. If he is questioned, read or paraphrase the following:

> "I always fancied myself the least likely to be burgled. People know that I take most of my work in trade and keep very little of value. It was the oddest burglary I could imagine; the items stolen were all body parts from exotic creatures that I experiment with in some of my preparations. I cannot imagine them being of any use to anyone else.
>
> "The one oddity that strikes me, though, is that Herrick Mendon was in here just the day before the robbery. He was asking me about flowers, of all things — and he is not by any accounts a romantic man. Before he left, he asked about my use of organic material in my concoctions, and I showed him a few of the things that were later stolen. Still, I don't imagine that he has anything to do with it. He seemed a bit out of sorts, and I sent him home with some herbal tea to ease his mind."

Caledon wondered about the crime coinciding with Elinda's disappearance, but does not suspect her; he says she had never expressed any interest in anything with which she could not tinker. He actually believes that the burglars were drunks looking for his distilled essence of wormwood (absinthe).

A few more clues are revealed through this conversation. The involvement of organic components points to another feature of *Mamuthek's Aperture*; it uses them to identify the type of creature to be summoned. It also highlights the involvement of Herrick Mendon and the possibility of romance; investigating him can yield another crop of clues. Like the other burglaries, this one suggests that the thieves were efficient, skilled, and looking for something in particular.

If the characters ask Caledon to list the items that were stolen, they will have gained the most valuable information of all. The items were used to power the summoning device, and Caledon's list reads like a roster of the most powerful underground inhabitants. Most of them were things that Caledon had agreed to take in trade from desperate adventurers, and he was experimenting with their properties in his preparations. The heroes might also discover that he actually has items in his shop that can be very effective against them. The items that were stolen include:

- A mummified hand from a troll
- Antennae from a rust monster
- The tooth of a cave leech
- The horn of a minotaur
- The venomous stinger of a monstrous scorpion

Visiting the Finesmith

Crenshaw the Finesmith (see **Area H-9** for details) is a master craftsman of detailed metalwork. He is also one of the victims of the thieves' guild. He had a large bag of powdered silver stolen from his floor vault in the Crafthall several nights ago. When he is asked to describe the incident, read or paraphrase the following:

> "Whoever they were, it seems they knew what they were doing. The watch saw nothing, and there is always a patrol somewhere in the market. They left not a mark on the gate on the shop, nor did they damage the vault when they opened it. That vault has a lock of my own creation on it — the most secure lock I have known.
>
> "They took all the coin — about 80 gold ducats and a bag of powdered silver that I use for casting custom items. Taking the silver seemed odd. It is not easily transacted, and several items were more valuable and no harder to liquidate: gold and silver wire, gold leaf, and a small quantity of mithral. All were untouched.
>
> "I'm certain it has something to do with that witch, Bannon. She was in here just a week earlier buying powdered silver herself, and now she's gone off and left all this trouble in her place."

If the heroes request to see the vault, Crenshaw asks them to step outside while he opens it (**Area H-9**). It contains items jointly owned by him and Lord Angus, both raw materials and nearly-finished products.

This conversation might suggest to the heroes that the thieves were well-organized, skilled, and under orders to steal certain items. Also, this is an important occurrence of powdered silver. The powdered silver is a material component used in several spells, especially wards. In this instance, it is needed to establish the *protection from evil* circle that is created when *Mamuthek's Aperture* is activated. The knowledge that Bannon purchased silver here may help the party understand the device's properties.

Lilith's Thralls

Lilith has seduced three men of the Grey Citadel for the purpose of protecting and supporting her activities and those of the Ebon Union, which is also under her control. Clever heroes will observe that the three men have several common characteristics: they have no family; they are not known as being especially romantic; and they all have workplaces with deep basements — and entrances to the underground caverns. The party may find out about these men from listening to rumors or receiving tips from Lord Angus, Rasputin, or other citizens.

The Smith

Ulf "Nine-Fingers" Ironfist (see **Area Q-4** for details) is the master smith of the Ironworks. Lilith (in dwarven form) seduced him just after she took residence in the caverns. She needed his basement as an access point for her forays into the city to gather components for the operation of *Mamuthek's Aperture*, and later to allow the thieves of the Ebon Union to do the same. Ulf believes she is a clan chief's daughter whose family has sworn to remain underground, where they feel dwarves belong. He thinks she plans to run away and join him on the surface, but for now he contents himself with periodic visits in the caves below the forge.

Speaking with employees at the forge (**Area Q**) might reveal certain clues that pertain to the mystery:

• Ulf has not taken up the hammer in several days (he is weakening, thanks to the repeat visits from the succubus).

• He does not spend as much time on the forge floor as he used to (he is often underground or in his quarters dreaming of his love).

• He has made a few foolish mistakes in the little work he does do, such as mixing ores improperly or using the wrong furnace (also a result of his lost levels).

• He busies himself with odd projects (such as reinforcing the door to the basement).

The Merchant

Herrick Mendon (see **Area H-4** for details) is the merchant who manages the Crafthall and storehouse for Lord Angus. Lilith chose him as a victim because he knew the sources she would need for her material supplies and because, like Ulf Ironfist, his basement had an opening into the caverns. Mendon believes Lilith is an agent from a foreign guild sent to gather information about Dun Eamon's markets and products, and she has promised him a lucrative position in the guild when they usurp control of the local economy. He has given up any information she has asked about, much of which is useless to her, but serves to conceal the important questions, such as where powdered silver can be found. They meet regularly in the basement storehouse.

Speaking with the tenant craftsmen upstairs (**Area H**) can shed some light on Mendon's odd behavior of late:

• He has been oddly forgiving in his collection of late rents (he profits more from Lilith's meeting than he does from skimming rent payments).

• He no longer harasses craftsmen about paying to draw the materials they need from the storehouse; he's more insistent that they get what they want and get out (he is nervous that the site of his rendezvous might be discovered).

• He actually made a loan of a few silver coins to a man who asked in jest (he needed to clear his office to make it to a meeting with Lilith).

The Miller

Danver the Miller (see **Area R** for details) is the engineer who supervises the waterworks and runs the gristmill. He is a lecherous man whose weakness was easily identified and exploited by Lilith: women. She rarely appears to him in the same guise twice, and he is pleased with his apparent success with romance. Lilith needed access to his mill for an additional entrance to her caverns, and she also had him try to grind silver coins to supply her with powdered silver.

The stout laborers who move all the grain to and from the mill (**Area R**) have noticed changes in Danver's personality of late and are willing to discuss them if asked:

• He does not heckle every farmer's daughter that enters the mill with a bushel of wheat. In fact, he now chides them for "letting him get away" (since meeting various forms of Lilith, his newfound charm has made him confident).

• He is hardly seen around the taverns and inns he used to frequent (most of his evenings are spent preparing for and entertaining Lilith).

• He recently spent a large sum of money on the newest and gaudiest clothing and jewelry in Raiment Row.

ELINDA'S TRAIL OF CLUES

Despite her hurried departure, Elinda Bannon left a careful trail of clues to her great mistake and her current activities. The clues are deliberately cryptic; Elinda is quite vain and wished to leave what information she could in case she failed, but in such a way that it would not betray her error if she were successful. The clues are also geared toward those close to her — namely, Stump and the Angus brothers — so the heroes must work hard to gain the information for themselves.

Before she left her ruined library, Elinda left a single sheet of parchment with a note on it. Lying across the drawers of her toppled desk, the page radiates mild magic and reads:

> *Play chess*
> *Wind Papa's clock*
> *Clean birdcage*

Although the note reads like a "to-do" list, these things are actually instructions on how to assemble three parts of a puzzle. Anyone who knows her well recognizes the connections: she loves to play chess (she plays with Cael once each week); she learned her first spells from her foster father (who never remembers to wind the clock she gave him); the birdcage is in the workshop (Stump and the brothers only know that the directions to the workshop are "in the desk").

In each of these locations (**Areas S**, **I-9**, and **L-9**, respectively; see **Chapter Three**), Elinda has hidden a small scrap of unmarked fabric. Each scrap radiates an aura of magic and is actually one of three fragments of an amulet that Elinda recovered and magically hid. When the scraps of fabric are dropped, they transform into the three broken shards of the amulet and radiate residual magic. The amulet was the device that held the succubus imprisoned on her home plane, a device that ceased to function and shattered into three parts when Lilith was called through *Mamuthek's Aperture*. Although its magic is gone, the amulet is engraved with the demon's name — Lilith, a name that is abhorrent to her (see **Dungeon Area 4-12** for more on Lilith).

With each scrap of fabric is a small piece of parchment containing a short bit of poetry; Elinda intentionally disguised her advice so she could salvage her reputation. The three poems, if interpreted correctly, reveal what little she understands about the device and its properties. Consider copying the poems onto separate sheets of paper as player handouts.

IN THE WORKSHOP

One scrap of fabric and a poem are hidden in Elinda's secret workshop (**Area L-9**). Stump and the Angus brothers only know that the directions to it are "in the desk." Under the lining of the birdcage where her pet owl roosts is an envelope. In it is the scrap (actually the left third of the amulet that bears the letters "LI") and the following poem:

> *Intent to reach across the void*
> *Great thoughts to proffer and collect*
> *Instead unpacked an Aperture*
> *That every cloud could not protect.*

With this poem, Elinda hopes the finder realizes that what she thought was a device for communication across the planes actually summoned a demon to her. She also alludes to the failure of silver wards — the lining of "every cloud." She capitalizes the word aperture in reference to *Mamuthek's Aperture*.

AT THE TEMPLE

In the courtyard at the Temple of Fortitude (**Area I-9**) is a section of alternating black and white tiles used for large-scale games of chess. A small shed nearby holds the game pieces and an envelope with Elinda's clue. The envelope holds the right third of the amulet (with the letters "TH") in fabric form. A piece of parchment bears a short poem:

> *From stony beach to mountain peak*
> *To mighty marbled hall*
> *These building blocks of worlds,*
> *They choose*
> *From whence it comes to conquer all.*

In this poem, Elinda describes the role of minerals in deciding the source plane for the creatures summoned by *Mamuthek's Aperture*.

AT STUMP'S HOVEL

In the midst of Stump's cluttered shack (**Area S**) stands a finely crafted grandfather clock, a gift from Elinda to her foster father. In the case where the winding key is stored is another envelope. It contains the middle third of the amulet (with the letters "LI") in fabric form, and another piece of poetry:

> *With the remnant of a thing that*
> *Once was living, choose the form*
> *Of the beckoned creature stepping*
> *From a worldly shimmering door.*

Here, Elinda describes the other component for the operation of *Mamuthek's Aperture*: an organic item to determine the creature summoned.

When the three pieces of the amulet are collected and the name "Lilith" is read near the sheet of paper from the desk, the three clues fade and new page is revealed:

> I know not what I have done, only that it is most frightening and unintentional. I fear that you read this now only because I have failed to set things right myself. In my attempt to communicate with beings from beyond out world, I have loosed a great evil upon our community. Wherever I must go now, I am sure that darkness waits for me. I can only hope for absolution in my success or forgiveness in my failure. I do not understand what manner of creature this is, only that the amulet you hold may be the only key to its destruction. Should I not return, you — whoever you are — must act to right my wrongs.
> — *Elinda Bannon*

Collectively, this information gives the heroes several important advantages. They can guess the identity of their ultimate foe (an evil being from another plane) and have gained a weapon to use against it (her true name). They can speculate about the involvement of *Mamuthek's Aperture* and how it works, and they can connect it to the burglaries. Also, they have some information that can help them begin to clear Elinda's name.

Chapter Three: The Grey Citadel Encounter Areas

Dun Eamon is a bustling, vibrant frontier city, too large and complex to detail completely. Thus, the areas that will most likely draw the heroes' attention during their investigation are described below. Most of the NPCs are simply good sources for rumors and other information, and others have links to potential further adventures. Areas in the city with a specific connection to the mystery include a reference to the **Mystery Elements** section in **Chapter Two**.

Area A: The Gatehouse

The party has no reason to linger here, but the unique nature of Dun Eamon's defenses deserves description. The River Eamon flows swiftly here, spreading out across the broad basalt spillway. Across the shallow ford, the mighty gatehouse of the Grey Citadel leers out of the drifting mists like an open maw. A steep ramp from the ford approaches it, and a dozen armored men with pikes and shields flank its base. A portcullis stands half-raised at the front of the gatehouse; beyond that, heavy ironbound doors stand open as well. The top of it bristles with ballistae and the steel caps of sentries.

A **constable** always accompanies the **Mist Watch unit** (which consists of **9 soldiers** and **1 sergeant**) that guards the gate. He questions every prospective visitor as to place of origin, duration of stay, and purpose of visit. He oversees the collecting of entrance taxes (1 sp per beast and 1 sp per cart or carriage to pay for upkeep of the streets). There is no charge for visitors on foot, but anyone with goods to transact must visit the Caravan Camp (**Area C**) and meet with Lord Angus' chief steward Semerion, who registers and taxes their goods. He warns the party that the use of magic, the open worship of dark gods, and the practice of slavery are all forbidden within the city walls, but requires no surrender or binding of weapons or other items.

The area just inside the gate always attracts more than its share of beggars, hired swords, and harlots, all waiting for caravans to enter or leave the city. Consider using the **City Random Encounters Table** in **Chapter One** as the party enters.

Mist Watch Constable, Male or Female Human Warrior (Ftr3): HD 3; AC 4[15]; Atk +1 longsword (1d8+1) or longbow x2 (1d6); Move 12; Save 12; AL C; CL/XP 3/60; Special: multiple attacks (3) vs. creatures with 1 or fewer HD. (see **Appendix A: NPCs**)
Equipment: chainmail, large steel shield, +1 longsword, longbow and quiver of 20 arrows, signal horn, rank chain.

Mist Watch Soldier, Male or Female Human Warriors (9): HD 1; AC 5[14]; Atk longsword (1d8), spear (1d6) or longbow x2 (1d6); Move 12; Save 17; AL L or N; CL/XP 1/15; Special: none. (**Monstrosities** 257 or **Appendix A: NPCs**)
Equipment: ring mail, steel shield, longsword, spear, longbow, quiver of 20 arrows.

Mist Watch Sergeant, Male or Female Human Warrior: HD 3; AC 4[15]; Atk longsword (1d8), spear (1d6) or longbow x2 (1d6); Move 12; Save 14; AL L or N; CL/XP 3/60; Special: none. (**Monstrosities** 256 or **Appendix A: NPCs**)
Equipment: chainmail, steel shield, longsword, spear, longbow, quiver of 20 arrows, potion of healing, signal horn, rank chain.

Area B: The Public Stables

Located adjacent to the caravan camp (**Area C**), this long wooden building houses the public stables and is identified by an iron sign that trails rust down the stone walls. The smell of dry hay, oiled leather, and horses is dominant inside the stables. The air is warm from the body heat of the animals, especially compared to the cold drizzle outside. Down the row, a powerful stallion kicks and snorts. Stabling options are as follows: 5 sp for 1 day; 3 gp for 1 week; 5 gp for 2 weeks. Extra rations of oats and vegetables are available for 1 sp per day; grooming for another 1 sp per day.

Tad does most of the grooming and feeding at the stables; his uncle **Edgar** does the mending and bookkeeping. In addition, both are paid informants — nobody knows more about who comes and goes. Each evening, Edgar meets with a member of the Ebon Union at the Hole, who then reports to Devlin, who reports to Lilith. Tad reports to both Rasputin and Bron Angus, although each knows about the other. By the time the heroes have found lodging, nearly everyone of consequence in town knows of their arrival.

The stables have one other secret, and the heroes might be the first to find it out. One of the horses — a tall, powerful stallion — is not a horse at all. It is a *polymorphed* man named **Weck**, originally a warrior from a far-off land who ran afoul of a powerful sorcerer while infiltrating his domain. He has been sold several times (his owners usually find him difficult to handle) and is currently owned by a wealthy merchant in the city. Edgar and Tad are unaware of this oddity.

A druid or ranger notices something distinctly odd and even unhorse-like about the stallion. Anyone else simply sees frantic snorting and pawing. Only the horse's vocal mechanism prevents Weck from communicating; however, he understands Common perfectly well and is more than ready to play charades. A *speak with animals* spell is also sufficient.

Once communication is established, Weck pleads with the party to restore him, offering them anything, including servitude, if they will do so. A *dispel magic* spell (vs. a 13th-level caster) returns him to his true form, including his non-magical armor, weapons, and supplies. If the *dispel magic* fails (and it may, given the party's level), he begs to be purchased or stolen so the heroes might try again.

Edgar is a surly and bitter old man who runs the stables for Lord Angus only to settle his bar tabs and gambling debts.

Edgar, Male Human Stable Groom: HP 5; AC 9[10]; Atk club (1d4); Move 12; Save 18; AL Any; CL/XP B/10; Special: none. (**Monstrosities** 254)

Tad is Edgar's cheerful nephew and has a room in the hayloft.
Tad, Male Human Stableboy: HP 3; AC 9[10]; Atk whip (1d6); Move 12; Save 18; AL Any; CL/XP B/10; Special: none. (**Monstrosities** 254)

Weck, Riding Horse (Polymorphed Human): HD 2; HP 13; AC 7[12]; Atk bite (1d2); Move 18; Save 16; AL N; CL/XP 2/30; Special: none. (**Monstrosities** 252)
Note: *Dispel magic* (vs. a 13th-level caster) is required to restore Weck to human form. He cannot speak as a horse, but understands Common.

If restored, Weck is extremely loyal to his saviors. He is unwilling to ride a horse except in the most extreme circumstances. In human form, he has the following profile:

A - Gatehouse
B - Public Stables
C - Caravan Camp
D - Market Tavern
E - Market
F - Rainment Row
G - Grocer's Lane
H - Crafthall
I - Temple of Fortitude
J - Garrison
K - Angus Keep
L - Bannon's Tower
M - Shrine of the Sun
N - Seer's Parlor
O - The Hole
P - The Bathhouse
Q - Ironworks
R - The Millworks
S - Stump's Hovel
T - The Rootcutter
U - Waterfront

The Grey Citadel
At Dun Eamon

Weck, Male Human Warrior (Ftr3): HD 3; HP 19; AC 4[15]; Atk longsword (1d8); **Move** 12; **Save** 12; **AL** L; **CL/XP** 3/60; **Special:** multiple attacks (3) vs. creatures with 1 or fewer HD. **Equipment:** chainmail, small shield, adventurer's clothing, longsword, dagger, bedroll, pouch with 23 gp and 12 sp.

Area C: The Caravan Camp

In the lower city, a wide area has been left clear of buildings for the maneuvering, loading, and unloading of the large merchant caravans that are always passing through the Grey Citadel. The stables (**Area B**) sit on one edge of the camp, handling care and feeding of the merchants' horse teams. Beyond the stables, a wide stone ramp leads to the upper city and the market (**Area E**). Around the perimeter of the clearing, dozens of wagons are parked close together, many with tents slung between them.

The caravan camp is always a busy place. During the day, **caravan laborers** busily shift goods from the wagons to carts and handbarrows for delivery around the city, and replace them with the products the merchants purchase from the local craftsmen. Some of the laborers are usually **acolytes** from the Temple of Fortitude (**Area I**). Any visitor with goods for trade is expected to visit **Semerion**, the chief steward of the Angus clan (who is always accompanied by a unit of the **Mist Watch** [9 soldiers, 1 sergeant]). He assesses the suitability of the materials and assigns a tax based on their value: 10% for foreign merchants, 3% for residents of Eamonvale.

At night, bonfires are lit and spits of meat and kettles of stew are hung at the edges. Kegs are procured and opened; fiddles, flutes, and drums are unpacked; and the singing, dancing, and gambling continue into the wee hours. The fierce rivalry between merchants of different trade guilds and dynasties often extends to their employees; fights are common here, as are contests of strength and skill such as wrestling, knife throwing, and lifting sacks of produce.

Most of the contraband transactions in the city take place here rather than in the market. Greedy merchants often barter goods that are illicit under Angus laws, such as poisons, exotic spell components, narcotics, and slaves. Under cover of night, they buy stolen goods for a fraction of their value for resale in other cities. If the heroes wish to buy or sell any such goods, they most likely deal with **Kinnan the Dark**.

A small, open shrine sits at the base of the slope leading to the market. A small stone building with a small fireplace and a dozen cramped bunks, it is dedicated to the God of Roads and is maintained by the wandering clerics of that faith. There is a good chance that **Brother Melph** is here offering healing and counseling services to travelers.

Rasputin mingles freely here during the day, considering the value of information as it trickles in from the road and following leads regarding his lost niece.

Finally, the caravan camp is a gathering place for mercenaries seeking employment as **caravan guards**, messengers, and even simple thugs. They usually lounge around outside the stable building, boasting, drinking, and heckling the laborers until their coin runs out and they are forced to find menial work themselves. Hireling NPC warriors can be found here and possibly a low-level fighter or two.

Brother Melph, Male Human Priest (Clr5): HP 21; AC 7[12]; Atk *+1 staff* (1d6+1); **Move** 12; **Save** 11; **AL** L; **CL/XP** 5/240; **Special:** +2 save versus paralysis and poison, banish undead, spells (2/2). (see **Appendix A: NPCs**) **Spells:** 1st—*cure light wounds* (x2); 2nd—*bless, hold person*. **Equipment:** cleric's vestments, leather armor, heavy cloak, *+1 staff* (a gift from the nymph Bernya, in return for his service along the roads of her wilderness), bedroll, holy symbol, 3 days' trail rations. **Note:** Brother Melph is a cheerful priest of the God of Roads who offers his clerical skills and traveling stories at the caravan camp. Brother Melph is one of several NPCs who

can serve as a pre-generated or replacement characters or as a temporary addition to or permanent part of the party.

Caravan Laborers, Male or Female Humans: HD 1d6hp; AC 9[10]; Atk dagger (1d4); **Move** 12; **Save** 18; **AL** Any; **CL/XP** B/10; **Special:** none. (*Monstrosities* 254) **Equipment:** cloak, dagger, shoulder yoke or wheelbarrow, pouch with 2d6 sp. **Note:** The caravan laborers in the camp are usually hard at work during the day and hard at play during the night.

Caravan Guards: HD 1; AC 7[12]; Atk longsword (1d8), dagger (1d4) or light crossbow (1d4+1); **Move** 12; **Save** 17; **AL** Any; **CL/XP** 1/15; **Special:** none. (*Monstrosities* 257) **Equipment:** leather armor, cloak, longsword, dagger, light crossbow, 20 bolts, pouch with 3d6 sp. **Note:** The caravan guards are typically sluggish, half-drunk, and lazy while their caravans are in town.

Kinnan the Dark, Male Elf Warrior (Ftr4): HP 24; AC 7[12]; Atk rapier (1d6); **Move** 12; **Save** 11; **AL** C; **CL/XP** 4/120; **Special:** darkvision (60ft), detect secret doors (4-in-6), multiple attacks (4) vs. creatures with 1 or fewer HD. **Equipment:** Leather armor, rapier, platinum ring (35 gp), pouch with 24 gp.

Description: Kinnan is called "the dark" because of his jet-black hair and dark eyes. He is every bit the charlatan, able to go from smiling and friendly to serious and threatening in the blink of an eye. Kinnan is independent, but he has ties with the Ebon Union through Rorin, the smuggler and fence found at the Hole.

Mist Watch Sergeant, Male or Female Human Warrior: HD 3; AC 4[15]; Atk longsword (1d8), spear (1d6) or longbow x2 (1d6); **Move** 12; **Save** 14; **AL** L or N; **CL/XP** 3/60; **Special:** none. (*Monstrosities* 256 or **Appendix A: NPCs**) **Equipment:** chainmail, steel shield, longsword, spear, longbow, quiver of 20 arrows, potion of healing, signal horn, rank chain.

Mist Watch Soldier, Male or Female Human Warriors (9): HD 1; AC 5[14]; Atk longsword (1d8), spear (1d6) or longbow x2 (1d6); **Move** 12; **Save** 17; **AL** L or N; **CL/XP** 1/15; **Special:** none. (*Monstrosities* 257 or **Appendix A: NPCs**) **Equipment:** ring mail, steel shield, longsword, spear, longbow, quiver of 20 arrows.

Rasputin, Half-Elf Male Thief Performer (Thf6): HP 20; AC 5[14]; Atk *+1 dagger that returns to the hand* (1d4+1) or short sword (1d6) or throwing dagger (1d4); **Move** 12; **Save** 10; **AL** N; **CL/XP** 6/400; **Special:** +2 save bonus vs. traps and magical devices, backstab (x3), darkvision (60ft), read languages, thieving skills. (see **Appendix A: NPCs**) **Thieving Skills:** Climb 90%, Tasks/Traps 40%, Hear 4 in 6, Hide 35%, Silent 45%, Locks 35%. **Equipment:** *bracers of defense AC 6[13]*, gaudy clothing and jewelry, *+1 dagger that returns to the hand* (in boot), short sword, 4 throwing daggers, *ring of protection +1*, balalaika, props (dice, cards, juggling balls, and so forth), pouch containing 54 gp, 22 sp, 18 cp, and hacksilver ingot worth 90 gp, pet monkey (Vlado).

Vlado, Monkey (Pet): HD 1d4 hp; HP 3; AC 7[12]; Atk 2 claws (1d3); **Move** 15; **Save** 18; **AL** N; **CL/XP** A/5; **Special:** none.

Equipment: vest, fez, hurdy-gurdy, tin cup.

Note: Rasputin may question the party about their travels in hopes of finding new information about his niece, at your discretion.

Semerion, Male Human Chief Steward: HP 23; AC 7[12]; **Atk** dagger (1d4); **Move** 12; **Save** 12; **AL** L; **CL/XP** 5/240; **Special:** none. (*Monstrosities* 256)
Equipment: leather armor, cloak, dagger, journal, quill, 2d4 sp.
Note: Semerion manages the flow of goods through Dun Eamon's markets.

Temple Acolytes, Male or Female Human Acolyte (Clr2): HP 2d6; AC 9[10]; **Atk** mace (1d6); **Move** 12; **Save** 14; **AL** L or N; **CL/XP** 2/30; **Special:** +2 save vs. paralysis and poison, banish undead, spells (1).
Spells: 1st—*cure light wounds.*
Equipment: robes, leather arm bands with holy symbols.
Note: The acolytes are faithful servants of the God of Strength.

AREA D: THE MARKET TAVERN

This is one of the oldest stone buildings in the citadel, seated firmly on the bedrock slab that hosted the original trading post. It now stands on the edge of the market square, open all day and all night. The service here is not luxurious, but it is always friendly and reasonably priced. The food is hot and wholesome, the beer cold and plentiful, and the beds warm and dry. The menu attests to the concentration of dwarves in the community with its extensive selection of strong spirits and rich meads, as well as to the halflings with several fine cheeses. Hostel style lodging is available for cheap, with private rooms also available.

Exterior doors and ground floor windows are sturdy and secure. All interior doors here are locked, except for unoccupied rooms and the dormitories.

AREA D-1: COAT HALL

A short corridor leads from the front doors into the common room. Its walls are covered thickly with coats, cloaks, and rain capes hung on wooden pegs. Rows of boots and overshoes line the floor, and two large barrels hold cudgels and staves. Searching the garments in the hall yields 2d10 cp and 1d4 sp.

AREA D-2: THE COMMON ROOM

The largest room in the inn has an open-beam ceiling that reveals the second story rooms. It is nearly filled with trestle tables, and on each side a staircase leads to the upper level. Heavy iron chandeliers that are anchored to heavy oak beams that support the upper floor light the room. A long bar occupies one end; behind it are doors to the kitchen and cellar. Opposite the entry, an enormous fireplace heats the room, and in the far corner, an exit leads to a small woodlot. Other than the wee hours of the morning, dozens of customers and a continuous rumble of conversation are always in this room.

In addition to a large staff of commoners, most of the following personalities (**Agatha**, **Fitch**, **Horace**, **Molly**, and **Rasputin**) are present here or elsewhere in the tavern.

Agatha, Female Human: HP 7; AC 9[10]; **Atk** ladle (1d2); **Move** 12; **Save** 16; **AL** L; **CL/XP** 2/30; **Special:** none. (*Monstrosities* 254)
Equipment: dress, ladle.
Note: Agatha is the owner and tavern hostess. She is a large, motherly woman who rules with a warm smile and an iron fist and carries a ladle in her apron strings to discourage rowdiness.

Fitch the Barman, Male Dwarf (Ftr5): HP 32; AC 4[15]; **Atk** +1 battle axe (1d8+1) or leather sap (1d4 nonlethal); **Move** 12; **Save** 9 (+1, ring); **AL** L; **CL/XP** 5/240; **Special:** +4 save vs. magic, darkvision (60ft), multiple attacks (5) vs. creatures with 1 or fewer HD.
Equipment: *+1 battle axe*, dwarven chainmail, *ring of protection +1*, *potion of heroism*, leather sap, 85 gp.
Note: Fitch is the Market Tavern's grim dwarven barkeeper and keeper of the peace. Fitch is one of several NPCs who can serve as a pre-generated or replacement character or as a temporary addition to or permanent member of the party.

Horace, Male Human: HD 5; AC 9[10]; **Atk** strike (1d3); **Move** 12; **Save** 18; **AL** N; **CL/XP** B/10; **Special:** none. (*Monstrosities* 254)
Note: Horace is a dimwitted lad who busses tables, washes dishes, and changes linens. He works tirelessly and is well-liked by the staff and patrons; no one tolerates any teasing. Though he was never terribly clever to begin with, he is under the curse of a magical grimoire that he snuck a peek at while cleaning the room of an adventuring wizard.

Molly, Female Human Serving Girl: HP 3; AC 9[10]; **Atk** dagger (1d4); **Move** 12; **Save** 18; **AL** N; **CL/XP** B/10; **Special:** none. (*Monstrosities* 254)
Equipment: dress, dagger.
Note: Molly is a teenage girl who helps Agatha serve meals and drinks, but fancies herself an adventurer. To the chagrin of her employers, she spends every free minute listening to stories from the travelers and telling her own embellished tales of conquering the cellars with her knife "Ratsticker." (**Note:** Molly has been bribed into informing for the Ebon Union; nobody else is aware of this, and her allegiances lead to her death during **Timed Encounter 3.1: The Guild Strikes** as described in **Chapter Two**. The charming, naïve girl should be seen as a victim of tragic times, so give the party ample time and roleplaying opportunities to become fond of her.)

Rasputin, Half-Elf Male Thief Performer (Thf6): HP 20; AC 5[14]; **Atk** +1 dagger that returns to the hand (1d4+1) or short sword (1d6) or throwing dagger (1d4); **Move** 12; **Save** 10; **AL** N; **CL/XP** 6/400; **Special:** +2 save bonus vs. traps and magical devices, backstab (x3), darkvision (60ft), read languages, thieving skills. (see **Appendix A: NPCs**)
Thieving Skills: Climb 90%, Tasks/Traps 40%, Hear 4 in 6, Hide 35%, Silent 45%, Locks 35%.
Equipment: *bracers of defense AC 6[13]*, gaudy clothing and jewelry, *+1 dagger that returns to the hand* (in boot), short sword, 4 throwing daggers, *ring of protection +1*, balalaika, props (dice, cards, juggling balls, and so forth), pouch containing 54 gp, 22 sp, 18 cp, and hacksilver ingot worth 90 gp, pet monkey (Vlado).

Vlado, Monkey (Pet): HD 1d4 hp; HP 3; AC 7[12]; **Atk** 2 claws (1d3); **Move** 15; **Save** 18; **AL** N; **CL/XP** A/5; **Special:** none.
Equipment: vest, fez, hurdy-gurdy, tin cup.
Note: Rasputin performs here regularly.

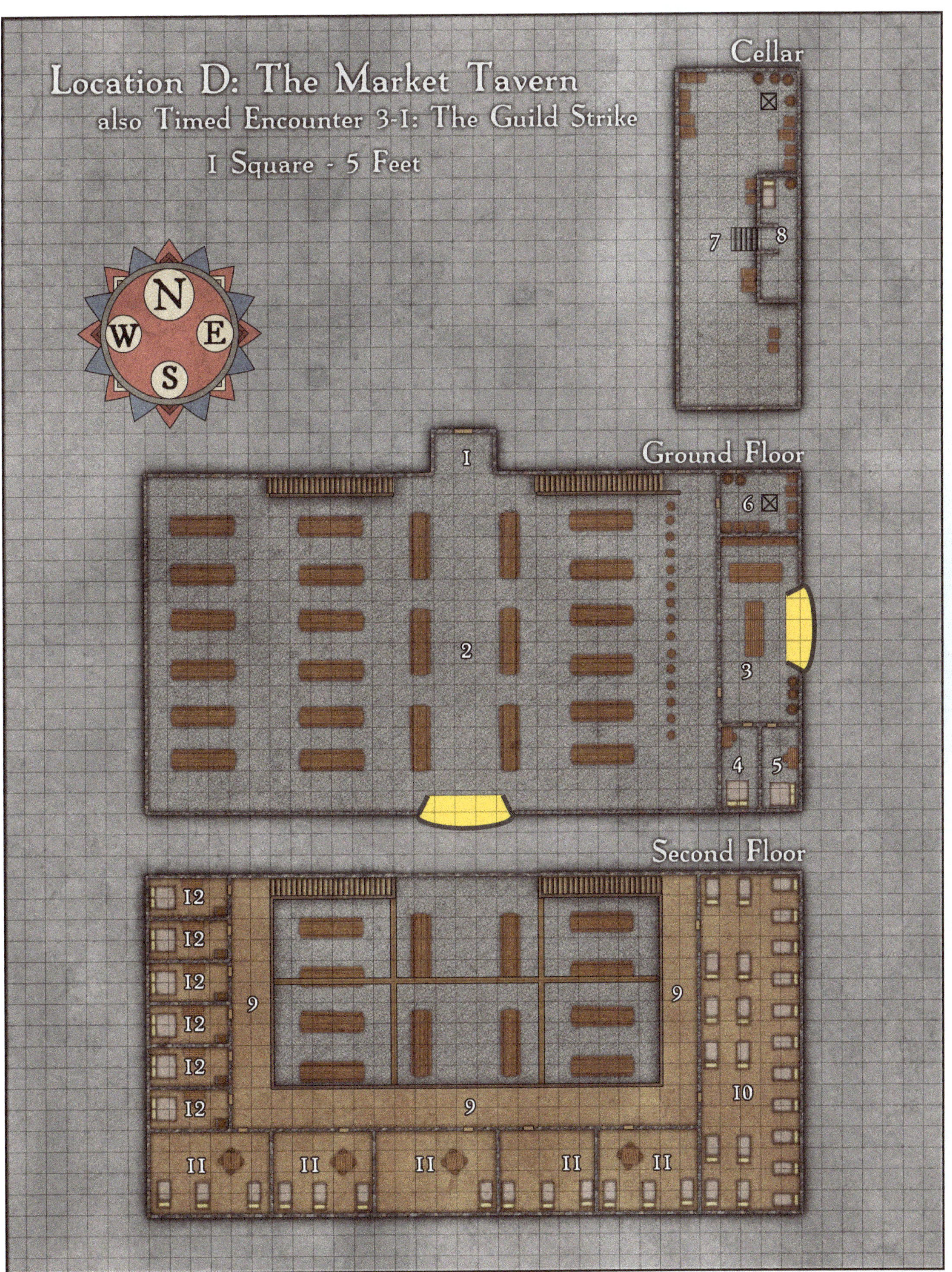

Location D: The Market Tavern
also Timed Encounter 3-1: The Guild Strike
1 Square - 5 Feet
N
W
E
S
Cellar
7
8
Ground Floor
1
2
3
4
5
6
Second Floor
12
12
12
12
12
12
9
9
9
10
11
11
11
11
11

Area D-3: Kitchen

Through the door to the right of the bar is the kitchen, which is dominated by two huge tables, a pantry, and another fireplace. An iron cane holds numerous kettles and cauldrons over the hearth. The pantry is stocked with dry goods of all sorts, and on the top shelf, a box labeled "peppercorns" holds four *potions of healing*. Two doors lead from this room into the small apartments for the staff.

Area D-4: Fitch's Room

This room holds a small bed, a desk and chair, a chamber pot, and a washbasin. Fitch generally lives in squalor, a byproduct of running the tidy bar. His room is strewn with dirty mugs, clothing, and crumpled scraps of paper; he is in the process of writing his memoirs. In a locked chest are the more valuable trappings of his days as a dungeon delver.

The chest contains a partial map of a notorious dungeon (which you may use to introduce future adventures, if you choose), a suit of dwarven plate mail, a *+1 battle axe*, a *ring of protection +1*, a *potion of heroism*, an outline of his book, and a pouch with 85 gp.

Area D-5: Agatha's Room

This room has a canopy bed and a large desk, on which Agatha keeps the books for the tavern. The furnishings here are provincial but very tasteful; the proprietress wishes she could display her nice things in the common room, but she knows they would never last the night.

Area D-6: Taproom

The door to the left of the bar leads into a dim room where great casks sit on wooden racks. Also stored here are numerous smaller casks of spirits and bottles of wine. A trapdoor leads to the cellar, and a block and tackle is connected to the beam above to hoist the casks up from the cellar.

Area D-7: Cellar

The large cellar stores an extra cord of wood, large barrels of ale and cider, and crates of apples, potatoes, turnips, and carrots. A wooden loft holds sleeping quarters for Molly and Horace. A large rolling door opens onto the street behind, which is the setting for **Timed Encounter 1.3: The Demons Attack** (see **Chapter Two**).

Area D-8: The Loft

This wooden platform is raised off the damp floor and split into two small chambers that are kept warm by the kitchen hearth overhead. Molly's room is tidy and simple, with a pallet bed heaped with furs and a wooden box for her meager possessions, which include a ragdoll from her childhood and her mother's wedding veil. Horace's room is cluttered with junk that he scavenges from all over the city. He has numerous broken tools, chunks of scrap iron, and rejected projects from the Crafthall. He also has a rusted longsword and a helm from a suit of full plate.

Area D-9: The Galley

A sturdy railing protects intoxicated guests as they navigate one of two staircases to the gallery. A broad wooden walkway runs around three sides of the common room, lined with the doors to the guest quarters. The thick hemp ropes that support the chandeliers are anchored here.

Area D-10: The Dormitory

This large bunkroom is located on the upper floor. It is full of bunks stacked three high, and it echoes with the sound of snoring, night or day.

Area D-11: Small Bunkrooms

There are three of these rooms, which are more comfortably appointed than the dormitory. One is usually kept for individuals who want a bit more space but do not mind sharing. Agatha makes an effort to rent the others to groups, usually adventurers, mercenary companies, or the entourages of visiting merchants or dignitaries. Each one has six bunks, a table and chairs, a chamber pot, and a dressing screen.

Area D-12: Private Rooms

These rooms are nicely if not lavishly decorated. Agatha prides herself on the décor and always hesitates before renting one to a filthy adventurer fresh off the road (she always makes a point of how nice the baths are!).

Area E: The Market

The central area of the market is a sea of carts, wagons, tents, and even semi-permanent wooden structures. The occupants are numerous and diverse, local and foreign, and sell every item imaginable. Most of them are aggressive salesmen and skilled negotiators; they generally offer prices 30% higher than normal costs but are willing to negotiate down. Some of the merchants are listed below:

Tarsh the Cordwainer

Tarsh makes cord and rope with the help of his two sons. He brings his wares to market twice w week and returns with raw materials. His regular travels bring him lots of news; he knows one rumor from the **City Rumors Table** (see **Chapter Two**).

Tarsh the Cordwainer, Male Human Ropemaker: HP 5; AC 9[10]; **Atk** dagger (1d6); **Move** 12; **Save** 18; **AL** L; **CL/XP** B/10; **Special:** none. (***Monstrosities*** 254)
Equipment: dagger, 50ft coil of rope.

Gurt Anford

Gurt Anford is a merchant of 10-foot poles; he carries a bundle of them on his back as he walks around the market. He is actually an expert craftsman and makes several poles that disassemble for packing. He can list endless uses for a 10-foot pole; his favorite is "for reaching things you can't reach with a 9-foot pole." He sells a 10-foot pole for 2 sp; a collapsing pole sells for 1 gp.

Gurt Anford, Male Human Woodworker: HP 3; AC 7[12]; **Atk** staff (1d6); **Move** 12; **Save** 18; **AL** L; **CL/XP** B/10; **Special:** none. (***Monstrosities*** 254)
Equipment: leather armor, staff, bundle of 10-foot poles.

Filip the Hatter

Filip succumbed to the noxious fumes from the liquid mercury he uses to shape felt hats of all sorts. He is no longer sane and often insists that he "has a hat that cries out" for a particular character's head and sits him or her down while he shapes it to fit. He sells hats or caps for 3 sp; the price triples for custom work.

Filip the Hatter, Male Half-Elf Hatmaker: HP 4; AC 9[10]; **Atk** weapon (1d6); **Move** 12; **Save** 18; **AL** N; **CL/XP** B/10; **Special:** darkvision (60ft), detect secret doors (4-in-6 chance). (***Monstrosities*** 254)

Orin Potter

Orin Potter is a skilled maker of clay pots, mugs, and other containers. He is very shaggy, nearly invisible behind his tangled beard, and spends all day at his pedal-driven pottery wheel muttering about how he should be given a shop in the Crafthall and how much he hates Herrick Mendon.

Orin Potter, Male Halfling Potter: HP 14; AC 9[10]; **Atk** war hammer (1d4); **Move** 9; **Save** 13; **AL** N; **CL/XP** 4/120; **Special:** +1 to-hit missile bonus, +4 save vs. magic. (***Monstrosities*** 254)
Equipment: war hammer, 2d4 sp.

Oberlin

Oberlin is a juggler, acrobat, contortionist, and orator of colorful limericks who performs in the busy market. The heroes probably notice his flying props before they see him. He travels for most of the year and hears many stories; you may allow him to (a) know of the heroes and laud them with a fantastic tale, for which he will privately try to collect a fee; (b) give them a lead on a future adventure; (c) drop a rumor or two regarding this adventure.

Oberlin, Male Human Street Performer: HP 12; AC 9[10]; **Atk** staff (1d6); **Move** 12; **Save** 14; **AL** N; **CL/XP** 3/60; **Special:** none. (***Monstrosities*** 254)
Equipment: staff, juggling clubs.

Dora and her Daughters

Dora and her three very attractive daughters (**Frieda**, **Maike**, and **Shara**) make and sell candles in front of their canopied cart. A peasant widow, Dora hopes to marry her girls well to merchants, nobles, or perhaps even successful adventurers. The girls are content to help their old mother dip candles and avoid the advances of the city's men.

Dora, Female Human Candlemaker: HP 4; AC 9[10]; **Atk** none; **Move** 12; **Save** 18; **AL** L; **CL/XP** B/10; **Special:** none. (***Monstrosities*** 254)

Frieda, Maike, and Shara, Female Humans, Daughters of Dora: HP 3x3; AC 9[10]; **Atk** none; **Move** 12; **Save** 18; **AL** L; **CL/XP** B/10; **Special:** none. (***Monstrosities*** 254)

Area F: Raiment Row

This area, framed by a variety of carts, tents, wagons, and canopies, is one of several semi-permanent boulevards in the market. The trappers from the forest display their furs at one end; the weavers and dyers offer bulk cloth at the other; and the tailors, cobblers, and tanners line the avenue in between.

Nearly any garment can be found here, but the fact that Dun Eamon is a frontier city in a temperate rain forest ensures the popularity of sensible clothing. Furs, woolens, and waterproof goods can be bargained down to 10%–25% more. There is a drain in the street here that leads to **Dungeon Area 1-1**.

The party may run into some acquaintances here. **Kelvin** and **Mert** (from **Timed Encounter 1.3: The Demons Attack** in **Chapter Two**) and **Logan the Furrier** (from **Appendix D: Wilderness Encounters**) both market their wares here and may have interesting rumors to pass along. Other interesting occupants of Raiment Row (who can also supply information from the **City Rumors Table** found in **Chapter Two**) include:

Sabinna the Rug-Weaver

Sabinna is a toothless old halfling woman who weaves rugs and tapestries by hand. She is currently weaving a coat of arms for a local merchant and gladly takes commissions.

Sabinna the Rug-Weaver, Female Halfling Rugmaker: HP 3; AC 9[10]; **Atk** none; **Move** 9; **Save** 18; **AL** L; **CL/XP** B/10; **Special:** +1 to-hit missile bonus, +4 save vs. magic. (*Monstrosities* 254)

Alphonse

Alphonse specializes in a rare elven method of tanning hides that produces the supplest leather, which he stitches into customized, skin-tight garments.

Alphonse, Male Elf Tanner: HP 6; AC 7[12]; **Atk** dagger (1d4); **Move** 12; **Save** 18; **AL** L; **CL/XP** B/10; **Special:** darkvision (60ft), detect secret doors (4-in-6 chance). (*Monstrosities* 254)
Equipment: leather armor, dagger.

Mercy

Mercy is a young orphan girl in a patchwork cloak who begs for fabric scraps on Raiment Row. With them, she makes colorful clothing for the poor and quilts to sell for food money.

Mercy, Female Human, Orphan: HP 2; AC 9[10]; **Atk** none; **Move** 12; **Save** 18; **AL** L; **CL/XP** B/10; **Special:** none. (*Monstrosities* 254)

Egan Taldo

Egan is a wily textile merchant — the man to see if one has rare fabrics to buy or sell. He is secretly in league with a foreign merchant guild and is highly suspicious of everyone.

Egan Taldo, Male Human Textile Merchant: HD 13; AC 9[10]; **Atk** dagger (1d4); **Move** 12; **Save** 14; **AL** N; **CL/XP** 3/60; **Special:** none. (*Monstrosities* 254)
Equipment: dagger.

Area G: Grocer's Lane

This strip of carts and wagons borders the side of the market opposite Raiment Row. Its merchants are more temporary; many of them are crofters who come to sell their produce once a fortnight. Meats, fish, grains, breads, fruits, and vegetables can all be purchased here, as well as dried rations, imported spices, and beverages of many kinds. A drain in the street here leads **to Dungeon Area 1-3**. Many colorful characters do business daily in Grocer's Lane:

Matilda

Matilda is a large, red-faced woman in a bloodstained apron. She prepares and sells meat, fowl, and fish, as well as sausages and pickled organ meats. Her cart is right over the drain to facilitate cleanup; she knows the rumor about the claw marks and open grate.

Matilda, Female Human, Butcher: HP 6; AC 9[10]; **Atk** knife (1d4); **Move** 12; **Save** 18; **AL** L; **CL/XP** B/10; **Special:** none. (*Monstrosities* 254)
Equipment: apron, knife.

Cedrix

Cedrix is a gaunt man who sells durable and easily preserved foods, including dried fruit, fish, and beef jerky; dry salamis; hard cheese; and unleavened bread. Most adventurers visit him before leaving town; he knows a rumor about the underground from them.

Cedrix, Male Human Trader: HP 4; AC 9[10]; **Atk** staff (1d6); **Move** 12; **Save** 18; **AL** L; **CL/XP** B/10; **Special:** none. (*Monstrosities* 254)
Equipment: staff.

Aloysius

Aloysius is a well-traveled elf who markets exotic bottled wines and spirits from distant lands. He also has small casks of brandy, cider, and ale that he purchases from local farmers. He attracts attention by blowing fire with mouthfuls of high-proof alcohol.

Alphonse, Male Elf Brewer and Trader: HP 9; AC 7[12]; **Atk** short sword (1d6); **Move** 12; **Save** 16; **AL** L; **CL/XP** 2/30; **Special:** darkvision (60ft), detect secret doors (4-in-6 chance). (*Monstrosities* 254)
Equipment: leather armor, short sword.

Ephraim

Ephraim always has his pony cart laden with bundles of spices, both domestic and exotic. Some of his spices have medicinal properties, including one that has the effect of a *potion of healing* (5 gp, only one dose can be used per day).

Ephraim, Male Halfling Trader: HP 4; AC 9[10]; **Atk** club; **Move** 9; **Save** 18; **AL** L; **CL/XP** B/10; **Special:** +1 to-hit missile bonus, +4 save vs. magic. (*Monstrosities* 254)
Equipment: club, pouch with 2d4 sp.

Nik Ghoerkin

Nik Ghoerkin makes delightful pickles from the wild cucurbits that grow in the forest. His pickles are inexpensive (6 cp per jar), but could fetch a high price in foreign lands where such things are unknown. He also sells pickled eggs, garlic, pork knuckles, and onions.

Nik Ghoerkin, Male Human Merchant: HP 5; AC 9[10]; **Atk** dagger (1d4); **Move** 12; **Save** 18; **AL** L; **CL/XP** B/10; **Special:** none. (*Monstrosities* 254)
Equipment: cloak, dagger, pouch containing 2d6 cp.

Area H: The Crafthall

An earlier Lord Angus built this long, wooden building to create both working and mercantile space for the city's craftsmen. It consists of a series of workshops facing each other across a wide corridor for the maneuvering of materials and products. Only the most capable and established artisans have shops here, and an appointment as an apprentice is the only way for a craftsman to gain entrance. Many of the products manufactured here are for export or are commissioned pieces for specific clients, and many of them are of masterwork quality.

The building is a noisy roar of men's voices, clattering looms, and pounding tools. It is warm and dry here, and the smells of leather, wool, and freshly cut wood are thick in the air. The occupants are mostly men, all sturdy-looking laboring folk with leather aprons and rough, calloused hands. At night, the exterior doors to the Crafthall are securely locked. All interior doors and shop gates are locked as well.

The party may come here while investigating Mendon the Merchant or the burglary at the Finesmith's Shop. The craftsmen are generally

willing to talk, as long as their work is not interrupted; see **Mystery Elements** in **Chapter Two** for their comments on Herrick Mendon and the tale of Crenshaw the Finesmith.

AREA H-1: THE COOPERAGE

In this shaving-strewn shop, casks and barrels of all sizes are manufactured, as well as wooden boxes and chests. A master and several apprentices work here, and they are capable of building secret compartments, false bottoms, and so on.

AREA H-2: CARPENTRY AND WOODWORK

All manner of wooden goods are fashioned here, from furniture to fine walking staves. The master here can make scroll tubes of oiled hardwood that are strong, light, and waterproof (2 gp).

AREA H-3: BOWYER & FLETCHER

Two brothers who excel in manufacturing bows and arrows (but not crossbows) staff this shop. Bows and arrows, are available, as are specialty arrows (hollow message compartments, 1 gp; whistling signal heads, 5 sp; glass vials, 2 gp; flammable, 5 sp; all have a –1 to-hit penalty). They know nearly everything pertaining to the wilderness area outside the city. They also make Arb Angus' personal hunting bow and arrows, and regard him very highly (paraphrase rumors to that effect).

Gerg and **Fej** spent their youth in the surrounding forest and are expert huntsmen; anyone sharing at least one hour with them or buying them a drink gains a +1 saving throw bonus to one saving throw made in the wilderness in the Eamonvale region.

Gerg and Fej, Male Human Boyers/Fletchers (Rgr3): HP 30, 24; AC 7[12]; **Atk** hand axe (1d6) or longbow x2 (1d6);

Move 12; **Save** 12; **AL** L; **CL/XP** 3/60; **Special:** +3 damage vs. giants and goblin-types, alertness, tracking.
Equipment: leather armor, hand axe, longbow, quiver of 20 arrows, bedroll, waterskin, 3 days' worth of rations.

AREA H-4: MENDON'S OFFICE

In this small but finely-appointed room, **Herrick Mendon** manages the entire Crafthall. He is employed by Arb Angus to purchase much of the raw material in bulk and resell it to the craftsmen. With the financial backing of the lord's coffers, he can afford large quantities and makes a profit for Angus while selling it to shops at the normal rate. All the materials, both raw and finished, are catalogued by him and locked in the vast storeroom beneath the workshops. A **locked trapdoor** reveals a narrow staircase to the storeroom (**Area H-12**).

Herrick Mendon, Male Human Crafthall Manager:
HP 30 (currently 4); **AC** 7[12]; **Atk** dagger (1d4); **Move** 9; **Save** 9 (+2, ring); **AL** L; **CL/XP** 6/400; **Special:** none. (*Monstrosities* 254)
Equipment: luxurious clothing, dagger, *ring of protection +2*, scales, magnifying lens, pouch with 65 gp and 30 sp, keys to Crafthall doors.

Description: Mendon is unscrupulous, miserly, and materialistic, but an excellent choice for the job he does. His appetite matches his purse, his girth is perhaps the greatest in the city, and he is almost always eating some delicate confection or exotic grilled treat. Mendon is currently weak and appears sick as a result of Lilith's embrace. Lilith's frequent visits have not given him the chance to recover.

AREA H-5: LEATHER GOODS

This shop is geared toward the manufacture and sale of leather products including satchels and bags, clothing and armor (leather, studded, or hide). Elaborate book covers, scroll tubes, map cases, quivers, and scabbards are all available as well. They also manufacture the highly heat-resistant work clothing for the forges.

AREA H-6: BINDER & PARCHMENT MAKER

A wizened old halfling and his assistants run this foul smelling shop, where great vats of pulp simmer over red-hot braziers. The halfling offers parchment, paper, and books (including spellbooks) of many sizes, some with latches or locks on the cover.

AREA H-7: TINSMITH

Tin, bronze, copper, and other metals are shaped into implements and utensils in this hot, smoky shop. Cutlery, pots and pans, containers, and decorative coverings are all made here.

AREA H-8: WEAVER

Several massive looms clatter back and forth in this large area, manned by a dozen workers. Three supervisors oversee the blending of colors and patterns. Only large quantities of trade-quality fabric can be purchased here.

AREA H-9: THE FINESMITH

Crenshaw the Finesmith avoids taking jewelry commissions, focusing instead on decorative items, weapon hilts, frames, book covers, fasteners, and any other item requiring intricate metalwork. He collaborates regularly with other craftsmen, adding their skill to his to produce the magnificent wares displayed in this small shop. His apprentices make jewelry settings for the halflings in **Area H-10**.

Crenshaw was also the victim of one of the burglaries, which may be the reason that draws the party to the Crafthall. All of this powdered silver was stolen from the **locked, trapped vault** built into the floor. The lock consists of three keys that must be turned in a particular order to avoid arming the trap. The vault contains 80 gp, 12 silver ingots worth 20 gp each, silver wire worth 20 gp, gold leaf worth 80 gp, gold wire worth 100 gp, 6 gold ingots worth 60 gp each, a platinum ingot worth 200 gp, an envelope of mithral chips worth 200 gp, and 6 works in progress (sword hilts, latches, book binding, and so forth) worth 2d6 x 10 gp in materials.

Anyone opening vault without using the three keys in proper order triggers a *lightning bolt* trap that does 6d6 points of damage to anyone within 20 feet of the vault (save for half damage).

Crenshaw the Finesmith, Male Human Craftsman: HP 32; **AC** 7[12]; **Atk** dagger (1d4); **Move** 9; **Save** 9 (+2, ring); **AL** L; **CL/XP** 6/400; **Special:** none. (*Monstrosities* 254) **Equipment:** monocle, craftsman's tools, 3 keys to the floor vault.

Description: Crenshaw is a slender man with a bad stutter and a permanent squint from wearing his monocle. See **Mystery Elements** in **Chapter Two** for his comments on the robbery.

AREA H-10: THE GEMCUTTER'S SHOP

Entirely staffed by halflings, the gemcutter's shop is a hushed and secretive place amid the clatter and bustle of the Crafthall. In addition to selling their own precious stones, the halflings consider buying stones as well, cut or uncut, provided they are worth at least 500 gp in their finished state.

AREA H-11: THE LIFT

A huge lift at the far end of the Crafthall is used to move heavy loads of materials into and out of the storeroom. A sturdy gated railing to prevent accidents surrounds a 10-foot-by-10-foot lift. That section of floor is reinforced with heavy beams and connected at each corner to block and tackle with thick hemp ropes. The ropes can be tied off to iron cleats for loading and unloading, but the lift is always stored in the lowered position. A combined strength of 30 is required to raise the lift; up to 4 characters can contribute their strength scores. One character must make a saving throw to secure the lift. Should the lift fall on anyone, it deals 8d6 points of damage unless saving throw is made to jump out of the way. At night, Mendon closes a sturdy set of double doors over the opening and padlocks them.

AREA H-12: THE STOREROOM

This massive warehouse takes up the entire lower level of the Crafthall. All raw materials and finished goods are stored here: limber, bales of wool, refined metals, furniture, bolts of fabric, barrels, and boxes are all around. Half of this level is belowground, and a wide ramp leads up to double doors opening onto the market. A staircase leads up to a trapdoor to Mendon's office (**Area H-4**), which is locked from the other side. The large doors above the lift are also locked from above at night (see **Area H-11**).

Mendon keeps watch over an entrance to the underground caverns hidden in this storeroom. The passageway is concealed under the flagstones directly beneath the lift. As the lift is always stored in the lowered position and as the flagstones are not a good place to be while the lift is in use, the secret passageway is fairly safe. To discover the entrance, the party needs to open the large double doors above and raise the lift. With the lift raised, characters have a 2-in-6 chance to locate the loose paving stones in the floor (elves and dwarves have a 4-in-6 chance). When the stones are lifted, a rush of moist, stale air is released — an indicator of the flooded crypt below. The opening leads to **Dungeon Area 1-4**.

AREA I: THE TEMPLE OF FORTITUDE

The temple sits in a large open section in the lower city. A majority of the population of the Grey Citadel worships the God of Strength, as do most of the hardy farmers, hunters, and trappers who live and work beyond the city walls. Strength, endurance, and perseverance are requisite qualities for survival in the harsh landscape of the frontier, and the congregation and clergy of the Temple of Fortitude embody such qualities and more. Part of the recent success of the temple is due to the leadership of Cael Angus, the young master and spiritual leader (see **Appendix A: NPCs**). He has developed a way to support the temple with a minimum of required tithes. While not engaged in training, meditation, or maintenance, **acolytes** from the temple hire themselves out as stevedores in the caravan camp. The merchants are glad to have a workforce that is strong, diligent, and not too eager to head for the taverns, and the acolytes give most of their earnings to the temple's coffers.

While the investigation of the mystery may lead the party here, the temple does not play a major role in this adventure. Enough information is provided here to support the plot, but mapping the area and developing further personalities for its inhabitants are left up to you. In addition to the acolytes, a few **clerics** are always on hand to deal with emergencies of faith or injury.

Temple Acolytes, Male or Female Human Acolyte (Clr2): **HP** 2d6; **AC** 9[10]; **Atk** mace (1d6); **Move** 12; **Save** 14; **AL** L or N; **CL/XP** 2/30; **Special:** +2 save vs. paralysis and poison, banish undead, spells (1). **Spells:** 1st—*cure light wounds*. **Equipment:** robes, leather arm bands with holy symbols.

Note: The acolytes are faithful servants of the God of Strength.

Clerics of Strength, Male or Female Human Priests of the God of Strength (Clr5): HP 5d6; AC 5[14]; **Atk** heavy mace (1d6); **Move** 12; **Save** 11; **AL** L; **CL/XP** 5/240; **Special:** +2 save vs. paralysis and poison, banish undead, spells (2/2).
Spells: 1st—*cure light wounds, detect evil*; 2nd—*bless, hold person*.
Equipment: chainmail, heavy mace, *potion of healing* (x2), holy symbol.

Area I-1: The Entry Vault

This chamber is built from huge blocks of grey stone, but floored with imported marble. On the sides of the short corridor are six massive statues of the God of Strength, facing inward. Two of the six are actually **stone golems** enchanted to protect the temple; they periodically rearrange themselves and the other, inert statues. They are activated by a command word known only to Cael or one of his ranking clerics, one of which is always in attendance. They also animate automatically if any of the holy relics are removed without Cael's authority, if a weapon is drawn in anger anywhere in the temple, or if any magic other than that granted by the patron god is used there.

Stone Golems (2): HD 12; HP 60; AC 5[14]; **Atk** fist (3d8); **Move** 6; **Save** 3; **CL/XP** 16/3200; **Special:** +2 or better magic weapon to hit, immune to most magic (slowed by fire, damaged by rock to mud). (***Monstrosities*** 222)

Area I-2: The Chamber of Worship

This vast room is bare of any decoration except for a massive symbol of the God of Strength opposite the entry. There are no pews or benches, only a bare stone floor on which to conduct the rituals and tests of strength and physical prowess that constitute the acts of faith for the devout. Wrestling matches, strength training, combat training, and sparring bouts are all held here; no activity is sacrilege unless it shows weakness under the gaze of the patron deity.

Columns run the length of the chamber, supporting the vaulted ceiling. Between the columns are doors leading to **Areas 3** through **9**. Above the doors, huge windows let the grey light filter in. A few acolytes are always here, either training or performing maintenance tasks and who can welcome the heroes and summon Master Cael at their request.

Area I-3: The Chapel

This small room is decorated with a few finely-crafted tapestries of various trials of strength. A dozen stone benches are arranged before a simple altar. This chapel is reserved for silent meditation or important rituals.

Area I-4: The Dormitory

In this long, narrow room are the beds and personal effects of the temple's acolytes. Each bunk has a rough woolen blanket and straw mattress, and the footlockers hold only the most basic personal items.

Area I-5: The Priests' Quarters

These simple rooms allow the clerics of the God of Strength space and privacy for their chosen studies and meditations. Each one holds a bed, wardrobe, washbasin, and chamber pot. Most have a small bookcase with the cleric's personal writings and a few treasured books detailing the many instances of manifestation of avatars of their deity. One bookcase is kept vacant for visiting clerics of the same (or even a sympathetic) faith.

Area I-6: Cael's Quarters

The master's chamber is as stark as the rest of the temple. He has a wardrobe with his ceremonial clothing and a large table covered with correspondence, research, and notes. A large chest holds his most precious holy icons and texts. He sleeps on the same type of straw mattress as the acolytes.

Area I-7: The Refectory

In this long chamber, the priests and acolytes prepare and eat their meals. Long tables and benches run down both sides of the room. A huge fireplace dominates one end of the room, including a roasting spit, bread ovens, and a smoking cabinet. The occupants of the temple cook and clean for themselves, making food on long tables and washing in an enormous cauldron on the hearth. A trapdoor in the floor leads to the cellar, where dry goods are stored.

Area I-8: Storeroom

In this tiny, neat room the priests store all manner of training devices for use in the Chamber of Worship. Wooden weapons, padded armor, weights, climbing ropes, and all sorts of strength building aids can be found here.

Area I-9: The Courtyard

This enclosure provides another venue of meditation. It also hosts the temple's vegetable and herb gardens. Several stone benches situated under fruit trees allow space for reflection. A black and white tile patio serves as a board for games of chess; the oversized game pieces are in a small shed (which also holds one of Elinda's clues, as described in the **Mystery Elements** section of **Chapter Two**).

Area J: The Garrison

The garrison is a large, two-story wooden building on a stone foundation. It is big enough to house, feed, and train the members of the Mist Watch. Bron and the high-ranking officers have quarters here, and the building also holds an armory and a jail.

The garrison is not intimately involved in this adventure. It is a likely location for a meeting with **Bron Angus** (see **Appendix A: NPCs**) or a sure destination for heroes who make trouble in the city. It consists of several large dormitories, an armory, a training ground, a cell block, and a mess hall and quarters for the officers and commanders. See **Appendix A: NPCs** for soldiers, sergeants, constables, and others who might be found in the garrison.

Area K: The Keep

The castle and keep of the Angus clan are not integral to the plot of this adventure. This description offers a venue to meet with Lord Angus; any further exploration is beyond the scope of this module and left up to you.

Area K-1: The Gatehouse

The gate usually stands open during the day, guarded by a **Mist Watch** patrol of **9 soldiers** and a **sergeant**. A steward is always here as well, handling castle business and taking requests for audiences with Arb Angus. As often as not, however, Angus is here himself, meeting with his citizens in an informal manner, though important issues are discussed within the castle walls.

The gatehouse is easily defended with an array of arrow slits, murder holes, two sets of ironclad doors, and a portcullis, which is closed at night. Use the description of the city gatehouse (**Area A**) for more details.

Mist Watch Sergeant, Male or Female Human Warrior: HD 3; **AC** 4[15]; **Atk** longsword (1d8), spear (1d6) or longbow x2 (1d6); **Move** 12; **Save** 14; **AL** L or N; **CL/XP** 3/60; **Special:** none. (*Monstrosities* 256 or **Appendix A: NPCs**)
Equipment: chainmail, steel shield, longsword, spear, longbow, quiver of 20 arrows, potion of healing, signal horn, rank chain.

Mist Watch Soldier, Male or Female Human Warriors (9): HD 1; **AC** 5[14]; **Atk** longsword (1d8), spear (1d6) or longbow x2 (1d6); **Move** 12; **Save** 17; **AL** L or N; **CL/XP** 1/15; **Special:** none. (*Monstrosities* 257 or **Appendix A: NPCs**)
Equipment: ring mail, steel shield, longsword, spear, longbow, quiver of 20 arrows.

AREA L: THE WIZARD'S TOWER

Elinda's Bannon's tower is situated on the parapet wall just below where it joins the castle wall. Her family has lived there for several generations — for as long as they have been loyal servants of the ruling family. Elinda is the first generation in two centuries not to serve the Angus clan directly as a steward, bailiff, or in some other official role. Instead, she provides counsel to the brothers on the various elements of arcane magic and its relationship to government.

The tower itself has been heavily modified to suit Elinda's needs as a wizard. She keeps only a small apartment on the second floor; the rest is dedicated to her research. The entire tower is extensively warded against intrusion, as the heroes will likely find out if and when their investigation leads them here.

A wealth of treasure here might reward heroes that survive the defenses, but they will have to answer for it if Elinda is rescued (see **Chapter Eight: Resolution**).

A flight of stairs leads up to the parapet wall from the edge of the city neighborhoods. Citizens are not permitted on the wall, so the **Mist Watch** patrols present the first line of defense for Elinda's tower. Heroes intending to enter must possess a writ of admittance from Lord Angus or be willing to approach using stealth under cover of darkness or distraction. Angus is not unwilling to authorize the heroes to enter if their investigation is proceeding well, but he warns them that he can do nothing about the wards.

Mist Watch Lookout, Male or Female Human Warriors (2): HD 1; **HP** 7, 5; **AC** 5[14]; **Atk** longsword (1d8), spear (1d6) or longbow x2 (1d6); **Move** 12; **Save** 17; **AL** L or N; **CL/XP** 1/15; **Special:** none. (*Monstrosities* 257)
Equipment: ring mail, steel shield, longsword, spear, longbow, quiver of 20 arrows, signal horn, spyglass

AREA L-1: THE HALLWAY OF DOORS

A locked iron door seals the entrance to the tower. Opening the door by any means other than the single magical key (in Lilith's possession) arms all the traps on the approach to Elinda's apartments.

The lowest level of her tower has been reworked into a long, winding corridor divided into sections by normal wooden doors. This corridor is sprinkled with single-use **traps** that range from mildly embarrassing to potentially deadly. In some cases, the doors themselves are trapped; in others, the spaces between them are trapped. Each time a trap is triggered, a *magic mouth* (in the form of perfect, red female lips) appears to speak command words to activate the trap.

Door 1. Stepping through this doorway triggers a *teleport* trap. The victim of this trap must succeed at a saving throw or immediately be teleported into the middle of the market (**Area E**). In addition, the victim is colored purple from head to toe. The Mist Watch is familiar with such occurrences.

Door 2. This door is unlocked, but when it is opened, the **trapped** floor in front of it (where the party presumably stands while opening the door) is affected by *transmute rock to mud*. The *magic mouth* immediately casts *transmute mud to rock*, trapping intruders who fail a saving throw to quickly pull themselves free.

<<Location L: The Wizard's Tower Map>>

Door 3. An iron key hangs on a chain next to this unlocked door. Reading the cloth tag ("unwelcome") on the key for this door triggers the *suggestion* trap. The spell suggests that characters who fail a saving throw "go report your disgraceful activities here to the commander of the garrison."

Door 4. This door appears to have multiple **traps**: one on the knob, one on the hinges, and one on the frame. These traps are not dangerous, but they are intended to help Elinda identify intruders. Each time one of the trapped parts of the door is touched (such as by an attempt to "disarm" the trap), a *wizard eye* captures an image of the room. The images appear in Elinda's workshop (**Area L-9**), so the party may be surprised to see evidence of their entry when they get there.

Door 5. Turning the knob on this door triggers a **flame trap**. The door is not locked, but it does open from the hinged side (that is, backward). The trap creates a semicircle of flame that does 3d6 points of damage (save for half) to anyone within 10 feet of the door.

Door 6. This door is unlocked and not trapped, but the floor beyond it hides a **pit trap**. Anyone who falls into the 20-foot-deep pit takes no damage as they splash down into 10 feet of water. One round after the pit opens, a heavy beam on two chains swings down from the ceiling and strikes anyone still behind (on the entry side) of the pit. The beam deals 1d6 points of damage to anyone it strikes, and they must make a saving throw or be tossed into the pit. On the next round, a *magic mouth* summons 1d4+1 diminished water elementals. The elementals remain for eight rounds before disappearing.

Diminished Water Elementals (1d4+1): HD 2; **AC** 2[17]; **Atk** strike (1d6); **Move** 6 (swim 18); **Save** 16; **AL** N; **CL/XP** 2/30; **Special:** none.

AREA L-2: THE STAIRWELL

A spiral staircase leads upward from the end of the winding corridor. Additional traps could be placed on its steps, if desired.

AREA L-3: CORRIDOR

The hallway bisects the tower from the spiral staircase to a narrow window on the opposite side. On either side of the corridor are two doors. The staircase continues up to **Area L-8**.

AREA L-4: THE SITTING ROOM

This is a simple, neat room in which Elinda entertains prospective clients and longtime friends. It holds comfortable horsehair chairs, potted plants, and a small bookcase filled with a few books on non-magical subjects. Elinda uses magic to rearrange this room for dinner parties when the mood strikes her.

On the wall amid several oil paintings of family members is a wooden plaque; it bears no inscription, only two brass hooks. This is where Elinda's foster father's *+1 short sword* hung until she took it as she left (the other part of the matched pair is in **Area S: Stump's Hovel**). The lacquer is faded around the outline of a sheathed sword.

AREA L-5: THE KITCHEN

Elinda's kitchen is small but functional. A fireplace in a corner has an opening in the chimney to her bedchamber. A tall table and stools provide an area for food preparation and dining. A wooden pantry holds her food supplies, mostly dry goods bought in bulk for her long journeys. On the table are a full waterskin, some small crusty loaves, and a cheese wrapped in wax that Elinda prepared for her mission but then left behind to save weight. Also scattered around are several open

sacks and boxes of food, salted herring, nuts, and dried fruit —
more evidence of her frantic packing.

AREA L-6: THE BEDCHAMBER

Elinda's bedchamber is back-to-back with the kitchen, sharing
its chimney. She has an elegant canopy bed, a large wardrobe, a
large chest, a dressing screen, and a washbasin.

The wardrobe is filled with her everyday working garments
(leather breeches and linen shirts), her traveling clothes, and a
few fine gowns. A dressmaker's mannequin stands inside wearing
nothing but a non-magical leather cap with an iron band around it.

The **locked chest** contains Elinda's family heirlooms. In it are
the symbols of office of previous agents of the Angus family.
Opening the chest reveals various badges of office (an amulet, a
circlet, a scepter, and so on) collectively worth 700 gp in materials
alone and much more to an antiquarian with an interest in the
region; a pouch with 500 gp; a large emerald (800 gp); a rod of
solid platinum (200 gp); and a small pouch of mithral shavings
(30 gp).

AREA L-7: PRIVY

A small chamber beyond the parlor holds a simple privy. A few
books sit on a small stand; one of them is false and holds a *potion
of fire resistance*.

AREA L-8: THE LIBRARY

This room holds Elinda's extensive library, now in disarray
from her battle with Lilith. The large, circular chamber is a
picture of destruction. The finely carved bookshelves that once
encircled it have been smashed into kindling, and book and papers
are strewn in shin-deep piles from wall to wall. Visible amid the
wreckage are an ornate writing desk, a rolling ladder, a divan, and
a sideboard, all upended and badly damaged. Many clues to the
mystery can be found here, as well as the secret needed to find
and unlock the door to Elinda's workshop. Sorting through the
literature on the floor is a week's worth of work, and non-magical
texts exist on every possible subject, in no particular order.
Randomly generate the subject on any volume picked up off the
floor as appropriate to your campaign world. Other contents of the
room, however, are more useful.

The sideboard has been overturned, but most of its contents,
in crystal decanters, are intact (total value 300 gp). Elinda kept
a valuable stock of spirits on hand for when her halfling mentor
(Stump) could be talked into a visit. She also kept a few potions
here for easy access; she took most of these when she left, but
in her rush, she took the cognac and left a single *potion of extra
healing*.

The divan, once comfortably stuffed and upholstered in red
velvet, now has a large "X" slashed into the middle cushion.
Beneath the stuffing is a wooden panel with a recess that is best
described as "a large 'T'-shaped indentation with a curved top and
a dozen small holes on either side." This is where Elinda kept her
crossbow and magical bolts, and she took them in a hurry when
she left to pursue Lilith.

The greatest wealth of information can be found on the desk,
which lies on its back in the middle of the room. A single sheet
of paper, which radiates magic, lies across the drawers (a hint
that it was left after the desk was tipped). This is an important
clue; see the **Mystery Elements** section in **Chapter Two** for a
full description.

The desk also conceals the secret of Elinda's hidden workshop
and is extensively **trapped** against intruders. The paneled front
of the roll-top is stuck. Two knobs on the front tear free if forced
and detonate two *web* spells, automatically hitting the character
or characters who forced the desk. A hidden catch opens the desk
without breaking the bags.

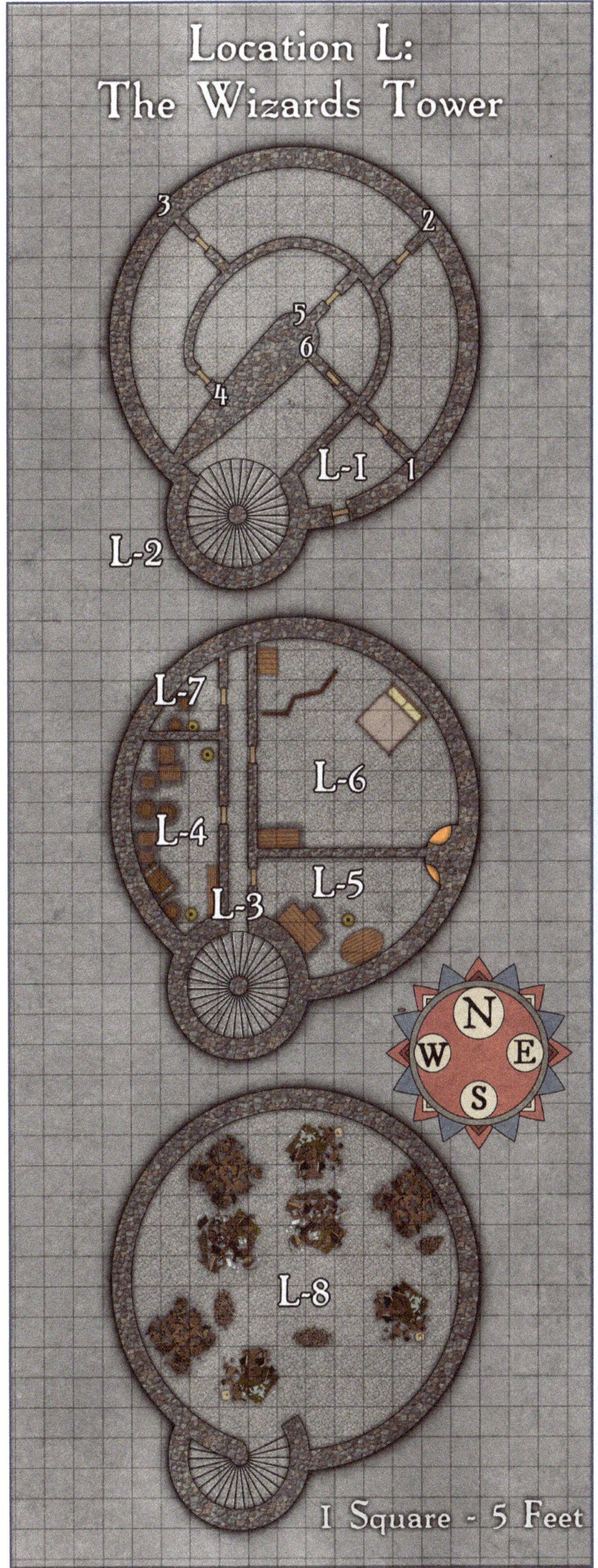

Once the top of the desk is opened, the assortment of quills, parchments, and spilled ink is a mess, but the blotting paper is the only thing that appears to have stayed in place. It is lightly stuck to the desktop with adhesive and comes free easily. On the underside are a few words in elegant script that read, "When nimble fingers come to pry, I beg them to stay, to answer why." On the panel below the blotter is a lock, which is broken, but the key hangs from a satin ribbon on a small nail inside the desk. If the key or any other sharp object is inserted into the keyhole, it bursts a bladder of liquid that paralyzes anyone who fails a saving throw for 2d4 rounds. Using the key in this way does nothing to release the *wizard lock* that actually secures the panel.

When the panel is finally removed by magic or force, a carved message on the underside reads "Welcome" and triggers *explosive runes*, which might be especially dangerous to anyone paralyzed or immobilized.

This arrangement may seem excessively frustrating (or deadly), but it is with good reason. Beneath the false top is one of a pair of tiny *gates* formed from exhausted magical rings, one of Elinda's most prized magical items. It is built into a wooden recess just the right size, and through it the stone floor of her workshop is visible. Her workshop is actually a tiny cottage located miles away in the middle of an impassable bog (see **Area L-9**). The other ring is built into the underside of a table in the workshop. When Elinda steps through the top of her desk, she drops to the floor in the workshop. She crafted a *belt of reduction* (see **Appendix C: New Magical Items**) that allows her to use the miniature *gate*. She took this belt with her, so the heroes will need to find their own means of fitting through (**Note:** This encounter could strand some or all of the heroes on either side).

Area L-9: The Workshop

Elinda's laboratory and workshop are hidden nearly 80 miles away from Dun Eamon. She keeps a small cottage in the middle of the Trackless Mire, a notorious peat bog that is inhospitable to all. No crofters or trappers cross its marshes, no predators hunt its moors; in fact, with the exception of its rich bird and insect life, nothing is there at all — truly a perfect place for a secret retreat. The floor is stone, the walls paneled in wood, and the roof is of thatch. Two closed windows and a well-made door keep out natural light; outside, a gentle wind rattles the shutters. Like the library, books and papers are strewn about, as well as bent and twisted metal, shattered glass, splashes of colored liquids, and a battered birdcage. The walls, floor, and ceiling are scored with sooty black lines in an irregular, feathery pattern.

If the heroes open the door or windows, they see that they are no longer in the city, nor is it even visible. Instead, they see only a bleak moor covered with wind-blown heather and the occasional outcropping of rock. Travel across the moor is dangerous due to hidden caves, deep bogs, and sinkholes. It is 50 miles in any direction to the nearest settlement and 80 miles to Dun Eamon. No navigational landmarks are visible in the drifting mist.

Elinda's workshop was the place where she did most of her tinkering, both experimenting with ancient magical items and devising items of her own creation. She kept here the portion of her massive library that pertained to her current projects. On the wall are three wooden frames holding recorded images that probably show the party struggling with the door traps in **Area L-1**. These are invariably poor images and depict the party picking and scratching where they should not be. The frames can be destroyed, but nothing short of that removes the images.

Two long benches stand along opposite walls, each covered with tools, dirty dishes, bits of broken mechanical components, and grease-stained notes. A table in the middle of the room (the one with the magical ring *gate* in the bottom) is covered with books, scrolls, loose papers, and wooden crates (of more papers). The birdcage is empty, but holds one of Elinda's clues described in the **Mystery Elements** section of **Chapter Two**. The clutter and destruction combine to make finding anything of value here difficult, but several magic items can be found by searching: *lenses of charming*, a *wand of magic missiles* (6 charges), five scrolls (*explosive runes*, *fly*, *knock*, *teleport*, *water breathing*), and three potions (*fire resistance*, *heroism*, *levitate*).

Note: As Elinda is a student of all things magical, her workshop could conceivably hold any item. If a particular item would greatly benefit the heroes (providing an ability they lack), it can be easily inserted here in place of one of the items listed above. Elinda is not concerned if her wand, potions, and scrolls are used to facilitate her rescue, but her ring *gates* and other valuable items should be returned.

Area M: The Shrine of the Sun

In the corner of the market is a forgotten shrine to the Sun God. A traveling cleric decided that the people of the Grey Citadel needed more sunshine in their lives and built the shrine with the permission of the Angus family. Despite the cleric's resolve, the damp climate finally wore him down, and he abandoned his efforts and departed for sunnier realms.

The shrine holds a secret compartment that opens only if in direct sunlight (or equivalent magical effect) and in contact with a holy symbol of the Sun God. Inside are four scrolls (each with *cure serious wounds*). Only the Angus brothers (and the original cleric) know about these items.

Area N: The Seer's Parlor

This tiny, shabby storefront is marked only by a large purple eye painted over door. Inside, **Amarathea the Seer** offers divinations, charms, and readings, including tarot, palmistry, and other forms. The shop is set in the lower city, near the Caravan Camp (**Area C**). Amarathea was one of the victims of the robberies, and this may be what leads the party here (see the **Mystery Elements** section in **Chapter Two** for more information).

Inside the shop, charms and tokens of every sort hang from the ceiling, prompting customers to duck low upon entry. A beaded curtain screens the back half of the shop, though flickering candles can be seen beyond it. In that area, threadbare cushions surround a small round table. Amarathea is seated on the far side of the table, which is covered by trays of small pebbles, carved runes, tarot cards, and bones. A flat, polished crystal lens sits on a bed of velvet in the center of the table: Amarathea's (non-magical) scrying stone.

Whether the heroes come here investigating the mystery or on their own business, Amarathea insists on a "seeing." She tries to extract payment (3 gp), but does the reading for free if refused; she does this periodically when "an aura is unusually strong." The reading can take whatever form the player wishes: palmistry, tarot, or anything else; Amarathea can use her supernatural divination ability with any of them. Some or all of the following can be applied to one character's reading or to several party members, or you can devise your own cryptic divinations:

"*You have a journey before you. Impulsive departure will send you down the road unprepared, but restraint will ensure you take with you what you need.*" (She sees their imminent progress into the caverns. She can see that the information that awaits them in investigating the city will help them below.)

"*Darkness reaches out to do you harm; only by remaining alert and on guard will you prevail.*" (She can see the intended assassination[s] by the Ebon Union, although not with any specific detail).

"*Your actions are mirrored by others; one who seems a foe may yet become a friend.*" (She can see that the efforts of the Band of the Crimson Mantle are parallel to those of the party. She also knows that one of them — Yelm the Barbarian — is not committed to the path of evil.)

Amarathea the Seer, Female Halfling (MU6): HP 14; **AC** 9[10] or 2[17] (missile) and 4[15] (melee) from *shield* spell; **Atk** staff (1d6); **Move** 9; **Save** 10; **AL** L; **CL/XP** 6/400; **Special:** +1 to-hit bonus with missile weapons, +2 saves vs. spells, wands and staffs, +4 savs vs. magic, divination (1/ day, receives a powerful image regarding the immediate

future of an individual or group; she is not necessarily able to interpret what she sees), spells (4/2/2).
Spells: 1st—*detect magic, magic missile, read magic, shield;* 2nd—*detect evil, ESP;* 3rd—*clairvoyance* (x2).
Equipment: scrying lens, numerous odd charms.

Description: Amarathea is a shrunken old woman with her greying hair in a tight bun. Her gift has manifested itself in every generation in her home village due to a shattered *crystal ball* lying in the bottom of their well. Like each seer before her, Amarathea was cast out of the village before her visions could bring harm, and she eventually found her way to Dun Eamon.

AREA O. THE HOLE

When this tavern opened several decades ago, the new owner valued it more than anything "in the whole world." In fact, the iron-lettered sign outside still reads "The Whole World Tavern." The first "W" hangs at an angle from a single nail, and these days, the place is better known as "the Hole."

This disreputable drinking establishment is located in the lower city. It provides cheap beer, watered wine, and day-old bread, plus a kettle of something like soup is usually on the fire. Vodrik, the grandson of the original owner and current proprietor, makes it his business to ignore everything that goes on in his bar. Thus, the Hole is the location of choice for illegal transactions, dark conspiracies, and secret meetings — probably the only reason it is still open. Exterior doors and ground floor windows are sturdy and secure and locked after-hours. All interior doors here are locked.

AREA O-1. THE BARROOM

This main room is always dark and smoky. Its low ceiling is thickly woven with cobwebs, and every floorboard and barstool creaks with age. A short bar and two large kegs stand on one wall, and a small fire smolders in a hearth at the back. The tables are round, allowing more privacy for the small groups of men that huddle there. Weapons are never collected at the door, and most customers leave their cloaks on, ready to run out at a moment's notice. The following are regular encounters at the Hole:

Vodrik is the owner-operator of the Hole. He keeps a battle axe under the counter and a *potion of giant strength* among the bottles, more for self-preservation than for keeping order in his bar.

Vodrik, Male Human Tavern Owner: HP 12; **AC** 7[12]; **Atk** battle axe (1d8); **Move** 12; **Save** 14; **AL** N; **CL/XP** 3/60; **Special:** none. (***Monstrosities*** 254)
Equipment: leather armor, battle axe.

Rorin is a fence and procurement agent for the Ebon Union; he finds buyers for their stolen goods and secures for them what is not worth the risk of stealing, such as food. He also maintains contact with Kinnan the Dark (see **Area C**).

Rorin, Male or Female Human Ebon Union Shifter (Thf2): HP 2d4; **AC** 7[12]; **Atk** dagger (1d4); **Move** 12; **Save** 14; **AL** C; **CL/XP** 2/30; **Special:** +2 save bonus vs. traps and magical devices, backstab (x2), thieving skills. (see **Appendix A: NPCs**)
Thieving Skills: Climb 86%, Tasks/Traps 20%, Hear 3 in 6, Hide 15%, Silent 25%, Locks 15%.
Equipment: leather armor, net, 2 daggers, pouch of caltrops (1d4 damage, halves movement in 10ft-diameter area), scales, pouch with 2d10 gp and 2d10 sp, 10% chance of a small pouch of powdered silver skimmed from a previous heist (worth 2d4 gp).

Yav is the local drunk and has been known to consume alcohol even while asleep in his usual chair near the fire. Every drink bought for him results in a rumor from the **City Rumors Table** (see **Chapter Two**) until he is too drunk to be coherent (after 1d6 more drinks than he has already consumed).

Yav, Male Human Drunkard: HP 3; **AC** 9[10]; **Atk** dagger (1d4); **Move** 12; **Save** 18; **AL** N; **CL/XP** B/10; **Special:** none. (***Monstrosities*** 254)
Equipment: dagger.

Stump comes here to drink when his house gets tiresome. Unlike most of the clients, he listens carefully to everything said in his presence, regardless of how drunk he is.

Stump, Male Halfling Thief (Thf6): HP 17; **AC** 6[13]; **Atk** *+1* short sword (1d6+1), dagger (1d4), or light crossbow (1d4+1); **Move** 12; **Save** 10; **AL** N; **CL/XP** 6/400; **Special:** +1 to-hit missile weapon bonus, +2 save bonus vs. traps and magical devices, +4 save vs. magic, backstab (x3), read languages, thieving skills. (see **Appendix A: NPCs**)
Thieving Skills: Climb 70%, Tasks/Traps 30%, Hear 4 in 6, Hide 45%, Silent 55%, Locks 25%.
Equipment: *+1 leather armor, +1 short sword,* light crossbow, 20 bolts, maps of several dungeon complexes, extra prosthetics, thieves' tools, *potion of invisibility, potion of frozen concoction.*

Drunken Caravan Workers are always present (2d4 of them).
Drunken Caravan Laborers, Male or Female Humans: HD 1d6hp; **AC** 9[10]; **Atk** dagger (1d4); **Move** 12; **Save** 18; **AL** Any; **CL/XP** B/10; **Special:** drunken (–1 to-hit and saves). (***Monstrosities*** 254)
Equipment: cloak, dagger, shoulder yoke or wheelbarrow, pouch with 2d6 sp.

Edgar (Area B) comes in from the public stables each evening to sell information to Rorin.
Edgar, Male Human Stable Groom: HP 5; **AC** 9[10]; **Atk** club (1d4); **Move** 12; **Save** 18; **AL** Any; **CL/XP** B/10; **Special:** none. (***Monstrosities*** 254)
Equipment: club.

AREA O-2. THE TAPROOM

This small storeroom behind the bar is where Vodrik keeps (and waters down) the wine and ale. A small pantry of dry goods holds ingredients bought from the week-old bins in Grocer's Lane: sprouting potatoes, worm-eaten turnips, and stunted carrots better fit for horses than humans. A back door opens onto the alley behind the bar, and a narrow staircase leads up to the loft.

AREA O-3. THE LOFT

Vodrik lives alone in this cramped room above the bar. A pallet bed, a pile of musty clothes, and a few dirty dishes are obvious. Hidden in the bedding are a purse with 185 gp and a *ring of poison resistance* given to him by his father (though neither of them were aware of its properties).

Area O-4. The Alley

Sometimes transactions take place behind the Hole in this refuse-choked alley. It is littered with smashed casks and rotting garbage and has a **rat swarm** (see **Dungeon Area 1-2**) running about at any given time.

Rat Swarm: HD 5; AC 7[12]; Atk swarm (1d6); **Move** 12; **Save** 12; **AL** N; **CL/XP** 5/240; **Special:** 10% of contracting disease.

Area P. The Bathhouse

The bathhouse is another of the Grey Citadel's unique institutions. Situated on the slope below the market, it takes advantage of a geothermal natural hot spring bubbling up from the volcanically active bedrock below the city. It is a gathering place for negotiating merchants, weary adventurers, and wayward lovers. Public and private baths are available, as well as several services.

Note: This location includes a potentially lethal encounter with a guild assassin; character death is a strong possibility, so you may wish to modify this encounter accordingly.

Bathhouse Services

Baths: 5 sp per visit to the public bath, 2 gp per hour in a private room.

Refreshments: Food and drink available for 5 sp, private rooms only.

Laundry: 5 cp per client, undergarments only.

Massage: 1 sp per masseuse per hour, private rooms only.

Area P-1: The Entry

The main entrance to the baths is on the fringe of the market. Across a broad stone porch is a set of double doors, where one of the staff collects the fees and informs clients that no weapons larger than a dagger are permitted. Just inside are doors to the men's and women's dressing chambers and the main office and supply room. A corridor leads toward the back of the building and the private rooms.

Area P-2: The Office

The baths are run by a motherly old crone named **Dendra**, who seems to turn a blind eye to what goes on in the tubs but observes much more than is believed. She knows very little about Tabitha (see **Area P-6**). Her office is a simple affair, mostly dedicated to linens, with a small desk for bookkeeping. A staircase leads down to the laundry.

Dendra, Female Human Bathhouse Proprietress: HP 4; AC 9[10]; Atk none; **Move** 12; **Save** 18; **AL** N; **CL/XP** B/10; **Special:** none. (*Monstrosities* 254)

Area P-3: The Basement

In this steamy, stone-floored chamber, the hot water from the rubs above is used to do laundry for clients while they bathe. Any of the girls who are not serving refreshments or providing massages upstairs are at work at the huge tubs. The girls have a distinct hierarchy: the newest ones do the hardest work, while the most established ones barely lift a finger. The talk here is mostly about the lack of business from Herrick Mendon (see the **City Rumors Table** in **Chapter Two**). **Bathhouse Girls** staff the baths above and the laundry below.

Bathhouse Girls, Female Human Bathhouse Employee (varies): HP 1d6; AC 9[10]; Atk none; **Move** 12; **Save** 18; **AL** N; **CL/XP** B/10; **Special:** none. (*Monstrosities* 254)

Area P-4: The Dressing Chambers

Here, clients change into the linen togas provided, putting their own garments into bags of netting to take into the public bath. An attendant is on hand to help clients undress and offer laundry services. The attendant in the men's chamber, a boy named **Ry**, is a thief as well, and pilfers small coins from the client's pockets. If caught, he begs to be let off and may know an interesting rumor or two. Ry is a skinny little street urchin with an uncertain future. A single door leads into the bath.

Ry, Male Human Chamber Boy (Thf1): HP 2; AC 9[10]; Atk dagger (1d4); **Move** 12; **Save** 15; **AL** C; **CL/XP** 1/15; **Special:** +2 save bonus vs. traps and magical devices, backstab (x2), thieving skills.
Thieving Skills: Climb 85%, Tasks/Traps 15%, Hear 3 in 6, Hide 10%, Silent 20%, Locks 10%.
Equipment: dagger, 1d4 sp.

Area P-5: The Public Bath

A large, shallow pool occupies most of this torch-lit room. A ledge around the perimeter allows for seating, and the center of the pool is four feet deep. Steps descend from the edge nearest the door, and steaming water burbles from an iron pipe in one wall. At any given time, there are 3d8 occupants, 75% of whom are men. They converse in low voices or rest quietly, paying little attention to newcomers. If a conversation is initiated, bathers will know a random item from the **City Rumors Table** (see **Chapter Two**).

Area P-6: Private Baths

If a client expresses interest in a private room, an attendant is summoned from the laundry to escort him or her. The private rooms are small, with a round tub in the center of the floor, and are nicely furnished. An iron chandelier lights the room, a screen is provided for disrobing, and wooden planks are laid across the tub as a massage table. The attendants mention refreshments and massage services before leaving.

One of the masseuses is **Tabitha**, an assassin and member of the Ebon Union. If a single member of the party books a private bath any time after **Timed Encounter 1.3: The Demons Attack** (see **Chapter Two**), she sells or volunteers her "services" to take action against the lone character. She is fanatically loyal to the guild and eager to prove herself to Devlin.

Tabitha, Female Human Ebon Union Assassin (Asn7): HP 37; AC 9[10]; Atk dagger (1d4 + paralyzing poison); **Move** 12; **Save** 9; **AL** C; **CL/XP** 7/600; **Special:** backstab (x3), disguise, poison use, thieving skills.
Thieving Skills: Climb 89%, Tasks/Traps 35%, Hear 4 in 6, Hide 30%, Silent 40%, Locks 30%.
Equipment: silk robe with rope belt (10ft), dagger, 10 needles, poison (1 vial, 2 applications left, save or paralyzed for 3d4+2 rounds), scented oils worth 4 gp, pouch with 15 sp.

Description: Tabitha began working with the Ebon Union before they were expelled from their previous home; in fact, she was the one who traveled to the Grey Citadel and assessed the potential for the Ebon Union to set up an operation. She has told everyone that she is "looking for a new home for her several brothers" while "they handle selling the family farm." She serves Devlin by eliminating his rivals, as well as by distracting merchants and caravan guards. Rather than strike by force or lie in wait, she prefers to use her charms to get right under her victim's nose before dealing her deathblow. She is slim, dark-haired, and attractive.

Tactics: Tabitha waits, if possible, until the character is disrobed and enjoying the massage. After massaging (and studying) the character for three rounds, she attempts to paralyze the character with a dose of poison delivered via a slim needle. If this attack succeeds, and the character fails his or her saving throw, Tabitha has 3d4+2 rounds of paralysis to complete the act. During this time, she rolls the character off the boards and into the bath. Her robe is belted with a silk rope, which she removes and uses to bind the character's hands and feet. She holds the character under the surface until he or she drowns in 1d4+1 rounds. Pending outside intervention, this character may be doomed, and Tabitha smiles quite evilly through the bubbles until they stop struggling. When they do, Tabitha removes the rope, collects her things, and slips out.

If the paralysis save succeeds, Tabitha has a backup plan. She carries a small blade coated with the same poison. She attempts to wound the character to give the poison another chance to act on them. If the character is wounded and fails a new saving throw, the character becomes paralyzed as above and Tabitha drowns him in the tub. If the character makes the saving throw, Tabitha attempts to fight her way to the door and escape.

Needless to say, this encounter can complicate matters. If the character survives, he may (a) have a captive or (b) have to explain to the authorities why he killed his masseuse. If he did not survive the first attempt, it appears he drowned in the bath, in which case Dendra contacts the Mist Watch and tries to minimize bad publicity. If he dies with an injury from the second attempt, the murder becomes very public. If a character is foolish enough to relinquish his weapons, remove his armor, *and* lie face down with his back to a total stranger, he may just deserve this fate!

AREA Q: THE IRONWORKS

This large stone building sits midway across the lower city, and its several chimneys constantly spouting smoke and fire make it easy to recognize. The renown of these ironworks is something with which the heroes should be familiar, for they are widely known as the finest in the realm. Harnessing the power of moving water to drive their bellows and regulate the cooling mechanisms, the Ironworks of Dun Eamon have a more consistent temperature than most, and the quality metal goods they produce are widely sought. As with the Crafthall, the Angus family owns the building, and they grant the rights to work there to the most talented craftsmen. Ulf Ironfist is the best smith there and runs the Ironworks for Lord Angus, who helps secure large quantities of quality ore at reasonable prices. The ringing of hammer and anvil and the shouts of workers can be heard from outside. Exterior doors and ground floor windows are sturdy and secure. All interior doors here are locked.

The Ironworks is a potentially exciting and lethal location for a fight. The heroes should have an opportunity to track a gang of housebreakers here on their way to the lair of the Ebon Union (see **Timed Encounter 3.3** in **Chapter Two**). If the heroes accost them or are noticed, they fight rather than betray the secret of their location any further.

At some point, the heroes may investigate the Ironworks in connection with the mysterious events. The apprentices here revere Ulf's knowledge, but have no love for the wrath that arises when an important project is flawed or compromised. If the heroes can question an employee away from the master, they can relate information about Ulf's strange behavior (see the **Mystery Elements** section in **Chapter Two**).

AREA Q-1: ENTRANCE

A small, stone-walled yard in front of the building provides a quiet place for workers to meet with a client. At any time, **1d3 dwarven workers** are here, usually smoking their pipes and discussing forge practices. They each know one rumor from the **City Rumors Table** (see **Chapter Two**). In addition, they also know of Ulf's strange

behavior, but discuss it only if questioned directly.

Ironworks Workers, Male or Female Dwarves (1d3): HD 1d6hp; AC 9[10]; **Atk** war hammer (1d4); **Move** 9; **Save** 18; **AL** L or N; **CL/XP** B/10; **Special:** +4 save vs. magic, darkvision (60ft). (*Monstrosities* 254)
Equipment: leather apron, thick gloves, war hammer, pipe.

AREA Q-2: MAIN FLOOR

A dozen men at anvils in this large, smoky room manufacture everything from horseshoes to axe heads. Grinding wheels, hand tools, and buckets of water and oil are arranged down both sides of the room, and the glowing mouths of the great forges gape on the back wall. A double door between the forges leads to the foundry. A single door at one end leads to the shop.

This area (as well as **Area Q-4**) is especially dangerous in combat. Coming in contact with the glowing coals in any of the forges deals 2d6 points of damage per round. A number of items are left in the forges at any given time, and they are red-hot. If force to fight, the workers often grab the hot irons to swing at intruders. Anyone not wearing protective gloves takes 1d4 points of damage each round while holding the irons. The irons do 1d8 points of damage, and the target must make a saving throw to avoid his clothing catching on fire.

Ironworks Workers, Male or Female Dwarves (4d4): HD 1d6hp; AC 9[10]; **Atk** war hammer (1d4); **Move** 9; **Save** 18; **AL** L or N; **CL/XP** B/10; **Special:** +4 save vs. magic, darkvision (60ft). (*Monstrosities* 254)
Equipment: leather apron, thick gloves, war hammer, pipe.

AREA Q-3: THE SHOP

In this adjacent, windowless room, all the wares produced in the Ironworks are for sale: tools, weapons, metal armor, and hardware. All normal items are available at the costs listed in the *Swords & Wizardry Complete Rulebook*. A dwarf named **Dregdim** runs the shop, and the door is locked whenever he is away or in the foundry. The room also has a hidden floor vault that is always locked (−40% Open Locks check to open).

Hidden Vault: The vault contains 1,000 gp worth of precious metals that would be useful only to a metallurgist and 200 gp in coins. All other items (such as mithral, finished items and magic items, and so forth) are locked in the Angus vault in the keep and catalogued for sale.

Dregdim, Male Dwarf, Ironworks Shop Smith: HP 26; AC 9[10]; **Atk** war hammer (1d4); **Move** 9; **Save** 13; **AL** N; **CL/XP** 4/120; **Special:** +4 save vs. magic, darkvision (60ft). (*Monstrosities* 254)
Equipment: leather apron, thick gloves, war hammer.

AREA Q-4: THE FOUNDRY

This hot chamber is thick with fumes from smelted ores. All the mixing of metals is done here, as well as the casting of iron and steel. Several smaller forges stand back-to-back with the large ones in the other room. **Ulf Ironfist** and the other masters do their work here, where a larger range of furnace temperatures is available. Two huge anvils stand unused at one end of the room; at the other end, doors lead to the storeroom and Ulf's quarters. The forges here can be very dangerous during a fight (see **Area Q-2**).

When encountered at the ironworks, Ulf is usually in this room, supervising one project or another. He is the master smith of the ironworks, a lifetime craftsman, and a brilliant metallurgist. He oversees the efforts of a dozen forge laborers and also advises the other smiths and apprentices. He rarely undertakes projects himself, as only the most challenging (and lucrative) creations entice him.

Location Q: The Ironworks
also Timed Encounter 3-3: Caught in the Act

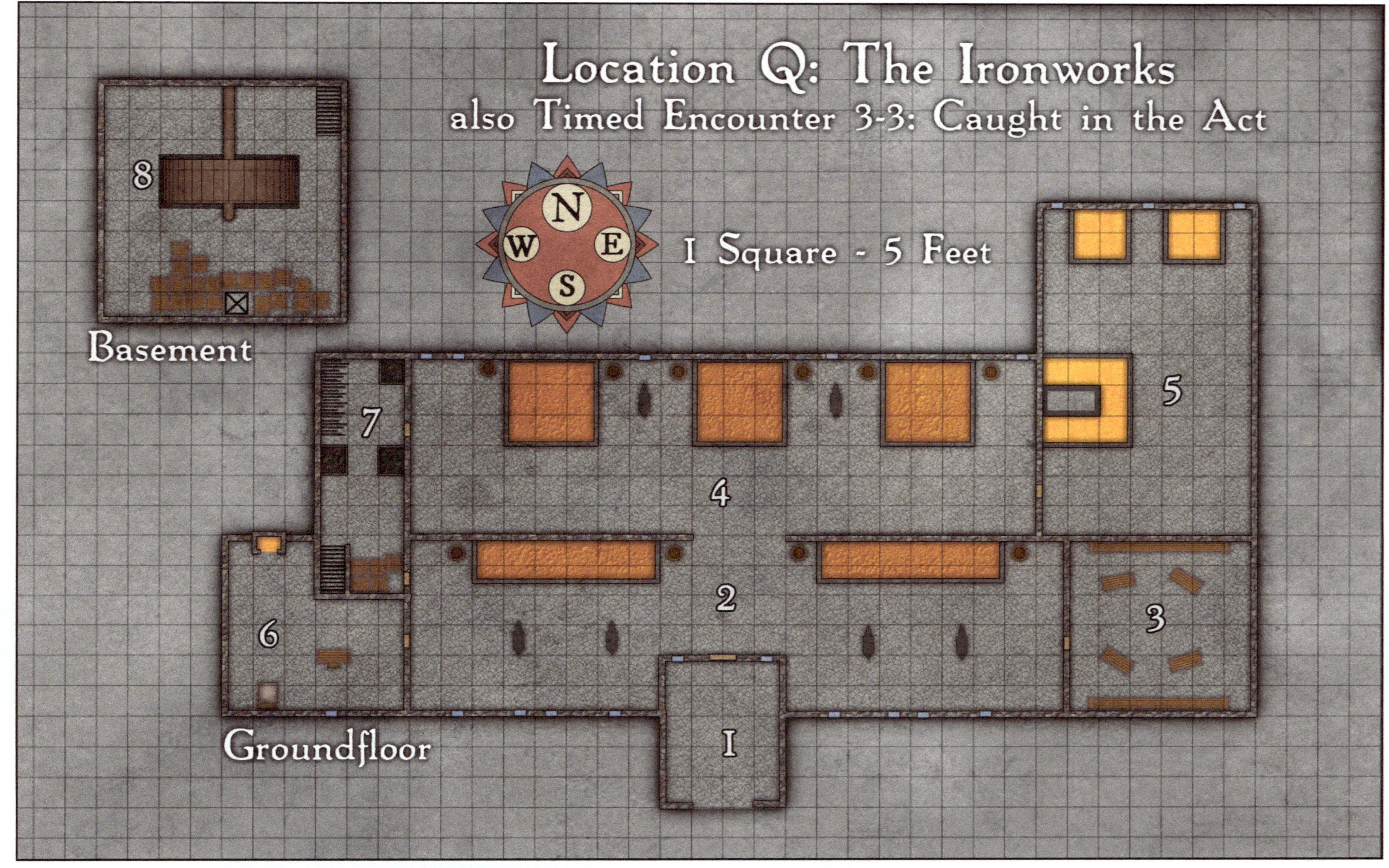

Ulf "Nine-Fingers" Ironfist, Male Dwarf (Ftr7): HP 45 (currently 6); **AC** 9[10]; **Atk** *+2 war hammer* (1d4+2); **Move** 12; **Save** 8; **AL** L; **CL/XP** 7/600; **Special:** +4 save vs. magic, darkvision (60ft), multiple attacks (7) vs. creatures with 1 or fewer HD.
Equipment: +2 war hammer, artisan's tools, key to door in **Area Q-7**.
Note: Ulf is weak and sickly looking after repeated visits by Lilith and her deadly embrace.

Description: Ulf is a strong, squat figure with a singed beard and a face that has been frequently scarred by flying slag. He is also missing the ring finger on his right hand, the result of an old foundry accident, and he hates being called "Ulf Nine-Fingers." Working with metal is his bread and butter; he has no time for anything else, including family or friends. He is the quintessential dwarf — gruff, deliberate, and resolute.

Area Q-5: The Glassworks

This small shop sits adjacent to the foundry room. It was built during the reign of Arb's father to maximize on the forge's waterwheel. His agents traveled far abroad to find the master craftsmen to design and operate the business, and the glass and crystal they produce is beyond compare. The dwarven smiths were not thrilled about keeping company with the foreign masters who work at their back door, but they give grudging respect to their ability.

Two masters and three apprentices work at the glassworks, which has one large furnace powered in the same manner as the forges, plus two smaller cooling furnaces. Shelves in the shop hold all manner of glassware and decorative items, plus stacks of valuable window-glass.

Glassworks Masters, Male Humans (2): HP 10, 8; **AC** 9[10]; **Atk** dagger (1d4); **Move** 12; **Save** 16; **AL** L; **CL/XP** 2/30; **Special:** none. (*Monstrosities* 254)
Equipment: dagger, glass-working tools.

Glassworks Apprentices, Male or Female Humans (3): HD 4x2, 3; **AC** 9[10]; **Atk** club (1d4); **Move** 9; **Save** 18; **AL** L; **CL/XP** B/10; **Special:** none. (*Monstrosities* 254)
Equipment: club.

Area Q-6: Ulf's Apartment

Ulf Ironfist keeps a neat, organized living space. A sturdy dwarf-sized bed and wardrobe occupy one wall; on the opposite wall is a small fireplace with an iron spit and kettle crane in it. In the middle of the room is a large wooden table with a stool. Books stacked on the table and on a small shelf at the far wall provide extensive resources on metallurgy, foundry practices, and iron working.

Area Q-7: Storeroom

This room houses large crates and hoppers filled with raw ores and also piles of unshaped iron rods. A door in the back leads downstairs to **Dungeon Area 1-6**. It is locked, and only Ulf Ironfist, Devlin, and Lilith have keys. The door is well-made and brand new; Ulf constructed it himself under Lilith's *suggestion*.

Area Q-8: The Basement

Hewn from dark stone, the forge's basement is oppressively hot, and the combined thunder of moving water and the wooden groan of the bellows is deafening. The upper half of a waterwheel rises from the middle of the floor, churning and spraying icy water. On the wall opposite the rough stone stairs are stacks of wooden crates.

The crates conceal the opening to the underground network of tunnels. Ulf arranged them after Lilith first *charmed* him. One of the largest crates is bolted to the stone floor and has a hinged top that conceals a secret door. The bottom of this crate is missing, and a wooden ladder descends through the old drain to **Dungeon Area 3-1**. Now that the drain no longer serves its purpose, several inches of water have pooled around the crates, which should indicate something is amiss.

Also, Ulf left himself a reminder of which tunnel to enter for his rendezvous with Lilith (he is notoriously forgetful). Written on the wall above the crate in dwarven script is the following note:

> *From house of iron toward the molten core,*
> *To embrace the Dwarf-maid I adore,*
> *Take the path at outstretched Dwarven arm,*
> *That brings back memories of Dwarven harm.*

The reference is to Ulf's missing ring finger on his right hand. When held at arm's length, the stump of his finger indicates the second tunnel from the right, the only one that leads into the cavern complex.

Area R: The Mill and Waterworks

This building sits in the lower city and taps an underground channel of the River Eamon. Its huge waterwheel drives several axles that provide power for the gristmill and the lumber saws. **Danver the Miller** is the engineer who supervises the operation and maintains the waterworks.

Lilith seduced Danver soon after Herrick Mendon. She wanted access to the city from more than one location, and the foundations of the waterworks are adjacent to Level 2 of the underground caverns. Yet these entrances are less frequently used because of the variety of molds and fungi that feed on the sawdust and grain washed from the mill. Only Lilith, Devlin, Gethrax, and a few thieves are willing to brave the hazards to use this entrance. The **City Rumors Table** (see **Chapter Two**) includes a sighting of Gethrax around the mill.

Danver is usually found moving between the sawmill and gristmill. The employees have noticed his odd behavior and are willing to talk about it (see the **Mystery Elements** section in **Chapter Two**).

Danver the Miller, Male Human: HP 37 (currently 6); AC 9[10]; **Atk** dagger (1d4); **Move** 12; **Save** 11; **AL** N; **CL/XP** 6/400; **Special:** none. (*Monstrosities* 254)
Equipment: tasteless wardrobe, dagger, engineering tools (abacus, calipers, and so forth), overly strong cologne (6 vials).
Note: Danver is weak and sickly looking after repeated visits by Lilith and her deadly embrace.

Description: Danver fancies himself an attractive bachelor, though those days have long gone by. His education in engineering took place in a large city, where bright students could spend the evening hours with the women of their choice. He finds Dun Eamon to be too rough and unsophisticated and the women too "uptight." Any of the local women characterize him as a "dirty old man." He is skinny and gaunt, his clothing is cheap but gaudy, and he usually smells overpoweringly of scented oils.

Area R-1: Sawmill

This half of the building houses the massive saws that process the timber from the forested slopes above the falls. The trees are floated over the falls in huge bundles — an awesome sight — and hauled up through the city from the landing. Most of the lumber produced is for construction in the city and in the outlying villages. Six men work here, moving cut and uncut timber and supervising the saws. A large, obvious trapdoor in the floor leads down to the waterworks below.

Area R-2: Gristmill

The other half of the mill holds one large and two small millstones that grind most of the grain produced in the valley. Danver collects a measure of grain from each bushel he grinds; this grain supplies the city's reserves in the castle or is ground and sold to bakeries and households in Grocer's Lane (**Area G**). Four men monitor the grindstone and move heavy bags of grain to and from waiting carts.

An important clue awaits the heroes at the smallest millwheel. The grindstones had been separated and cleaned of all grain residues, then used at Lilith's *suggestion* to grind silver coins with which to ward *Mamuthek's Aperture*. The experiment damaged the wheel, and it has not been used to grind flour since then. Anyone searching the area finds traces of silver powder on the floor around the stone. A combined strength of 25 is needed to separate the stones to reveal a silvery gouge around the circumference and a few coin fragments.

Area R-3: The Waterworks

This chamber is built into the bedrock of the island city. The floor is rough, unworked stone. A channel allows water to rush through the base of the building where the massive wheel is suspended.

An entrance to the underground caverns can be found here, though it is seldom used. At the point where the axle passes through the stone foundation into the mill, a deep crack in the rock allows water to drain away. All the wastewater from the mill building eventually drains through this crack, which leads to **Dungeon Area 2-1**. All the sawdust and grain hulls are washed down through the crack as well; the rotten stench of stagnant water and fermentation wafts up through the crack on a warm breeze. To enter here, heroes must roll below their dexterity on 4d6; failure results in 1d6 points of damage from the moving cogs and axles.

Area S: Stump's Hovel

The old halfling adventurer **Stump** lives by himself near the caravan camp (**Area C**). His home is a rundown shack, mostly because his missing hand hinders him in making repairs. He lives on the profits of his last adventure and mostly contents himself with alcohol instead of companionship. Inside, a small fireplace warms the single room, which also contains a bed, wardrobe, table, stool, locked chest, and a grandfather clock (which holds one of Elinda's clues as described in the **Mystery Elements** section of **Chapter Two**). Over the fireplace is a wooden plaque with two brass hooks: Stump's *+1 short sword* hangs here. He fought with a matched pair in his adventuring days, but he gave the other one to Elinda after he lost his hand (an identical plaque hands in her sitting room in **Area L-4**). The rest of his adventuring equipment is in the chest.

The heroes most likely come here for information about Elinda (although they might also approach Stump regarding the tunnels). He is troubled by her disappearance and by the deterioration of her reputation. He is very defensive of her and will not tolerate any insinuation of wrongdoing. If and when the heroes question him, he has little to offer. He can confirm her obsession with all things magical and mechanical; he knows that she left recently to pursue another artifact in far-off lands and that she returned with it just a few days before her disappearance. In his opinion, she has never had any interest in summoning or had anything to do with it.

Stump, Male Halfling Thief (Thf6): HP 17; AC 6[13];
  Atk *+1 short sword* (1d6+1), dagger (1d4), or light crossbow
  (1d4+1); **Move** 12; **Save** 10; **AL** N; **CL/XP** 6/400;
  Special: +1 to-hit missile weapon bonus, +2 save bonus vs.
  traps and magical devices, +4 save vs. magic, backstab (x3),
  read languages, thieving skills. (see **Appendix A: NPCs**)
  Thieving Skills: Climb 70%, Tasks/Traps 30%, Hear 4 in 6,
  Hide 45%, Silent 55%, Locks 25%.
  Equipment: *+1 leather armor*, *+1 short sword*, light
  crossbow, 20 bolts, maps of several dungeon complexes, extra
  prosthetics, thieves' tools, *potion of invisibility*, *potion of
  frozen concoction*.
  Note: Stump (which is a nickname) lost his left hand while
  defusing a trap and has since had it replaced with an
  eight-inch-long steel spike. This spike deals damage as a
  dagger. The sharp spike is interchangeable with a hook and
  blunt-tipped spike as well. The loss of his hand has hurt his
  thieving skills, however.

Stump is a bitter, drunken old halfling and is completely unpleasant to
deal with. He is also one of several NPCs who can serve as a pre-generated
or replacement character or as a temporary addition to or permanent part
of the party. See **Appendix A: NPCs** for his complete profile.

A large locked chest contains Stump's equipment. It contains a light
crossbow, 20 bolts, *+1 leather armor*, maps of several dungeon complexes,
thieves' tools, *potion of invisibility*, *potion of frozen concoction*.

AREA T: THE ROOT-CUTTER'S SHOP

Caledon the Root-Cutter operates a small herbalist shop in
the lower city. The druid makes and sells potions, poultices, and
alchemical distillations and keeps a huge garden of exotic plants
and herbs. He is usually willing to trade goods or services for his
preparations, including exotic plant and animal substances.

Inside, baskets of ferns hang from overhead beams and the humid
air is rich with smells of earth and organic matter. The floor is soft
and mossy, the walls are covered in lichen, and potted plants clutter
every available surface. A large brazier sits in the middle of the shop,
with several small cauldrons suspended at different heights above it.
His companion, an ancient wolf named **Gareth**, usually sleeps curled
around the base of the brazier. Caledon is most often seated at a counter
opposite the door, trimming buds, docking roots, or scraping bark for
his preparations. He appears unaware of visitors until they speak, but
he is merely allowing them to absorb the tranquility of his shop for
as long as they like. He sells his products, but he is not concerned
about money. Usually, he is willing to trade for any rare substances,
especially those botanical in nature.

He keeps a stock of healing preparations on hand and ready for
sale: a bowl of holly berries (x12, 1 gp each, each berry heals 1d6
points of damage, but consuming more than one per day causes nausea
and vomiting), *potions of healing* (x4, 50 gp each), and *potions of
extra healing* (x2, 300 gp each). He also has some scrolls for sale:
speak with animals (x2, 150 gp each), *speak with plants* (300 gp), and
neutralize poison (x2, 400 gp).

Note: Caledon is one of the people visited by Ebon Union thieves
seeking components for *Mamuthek's Aperture*. The robbery and
Caledon's reaction are described in the **Mystery Elements** section of
Chapter Two.

Caledon, Male Human (Drd8): HP 34; AC 9[10]; **Atk**
  walking stick (1d4); **Move** 12; **Save** 8; **AL** L; **CL/XP** 8/800;
  Special: +2 save vs. fire, immune to fey charms, shape
  change (3/day), spells (4/3/2/1).
  Spells: 1st—*detect magic*, *faerie fire*, *locate animals*, *purify
  water*; 2nd—*cure light wounds*, *heat metal*, *warp wood*; 3rd—
  cure disease, *plant growth*; 4th—*hallucinatory forest*.
  Equipment: *+2 leather armor*, walking stick (treat as club),
  apron with towel and shears, alchemical lab.

Description: Caledon's curly brown hair and beard are worn in
long braids and are just beginning to show flecks of grey; he wears
a woolen vest and trousers with a leather apron. He began his career
as a member of a rural druidic order, but they soon grew wary of his
"tampering with the natural order," despite his good intentions. When
he was banished from the circle, he chose to leave his cherished woods
behind and come to the city where his skills could benefit a greater
number of people. He travels often in search of new plants and grows
many of them in his shop. He also maintains contact with a nymph
named Bernya who dwells in the wilderness outside the city (see the
Appendix D: Wilderness Encounters) and provides Caledon with
some rare components.

Gareth, Wolf: HD 2+2; HP 14; AC 7[12]; **Atk** bite (1d4+1);
  Move 18; **Save** 16; **AL** N; **CL/XP** 2/30; **Special:** none.
  (*Monstrosities* 513)

AREA U: THE WATERFRONT

The citadel has a small gate at the edge nearest the pool at the base
of the waterfall. This gate is not so heavily guarded as the main gates,
but it would be very difficult to access unnoticed. A few citizens make
their living fishing in the deep pool, and the large bales of lumber that
are floated over the falls from upstream are retrieved here and hauled
to the sawmill.

Beneath one of the moss-covered docks is a **lizardfolk youth** (see
Appendix D: Wilderness Encounters and the **City Rumors Table**
in **Chapter Two** for additional material). Druids and rangers have a
4-in-6 chance to notice tracks in the mud; 1-in-6 for all others. If a
character notices the prints, it leads the party to the space under the
dock. The young creature is injured, half-starved, and frightened of
its uncertain fate and the possibility of punishment on its return to its
village. Returning it to its village can be beneficial to the party, but the
citizens of Dun Eamon would kill the child if given the opportunity.

Lizardfolk Youth: HD 1+1; HP 5 (currently 2); AC 5[14];
  Atk 2 claws (1d3), bite (1d4); **Move** 6 (swim 12); **Save**
  17; **AL** N; **CL/XP** 1/15; **Special:** breathe underwater.
  (*Monstrosities* 302)

Chapter Four: Level 1 – Tales From the Crypt

This is the uppermost level of the subterranean caverns below Dun Eamon, although direct routes to lower levels exist and the party will not necessarily come here first. Half of the level is made up of refuse-filled sewer tunnels; the other half is a flooded crypt. Rats, carrion creepers, and an otyugh populate the sewers. The crypt is home to a small band of grimlocks displaced from their home below and a cave leech summoned by Lilith. There is also a wight and two dangerous traps capable of producing dozens of undead.

The tombs date from a great battle fought in the valley long ago and nearly forgotten. The people of the valley buried their heroes at the base of the castle, an area that was later covered over to make room for the market. The remains interred here include heroes of several races, a great holy warrior, and an ancestor of the Angus clan.

Area 1-1: Entry Chamber – Raiment Row Drain

This stinking pit is awash in dark water and choked with rotting piles of garbage and discarded fabric. Dim light filters down from the drain 20 feet above, and in the watery reflections, a passage can be seen leading into darkness. One wall is made of mortared stone, and a section seems to have collapsed, revealing an entrance to the crypt. Gethrax's *box o' darkness traps* (see **Area 1-9**) are positioned so that entering the crypt without triggering them is impossible. The piles of fabric cast off from Raiment Row above help conceal this chamber's occupant: an **otyugh**. This muck-dweller hides beneath piles of rotten

Level 1: Tales From The Crypt

Entrances: The drain in Raiment Row empties into **Area 1-1**. The drain in Grocer's Lane empties into **Area 1-3**. A tunnel from **Area H-12** in the Crafthall leads to **Area 1-4**.

Exits: Area 1-7 opens into the waterfall well in **Area 2-24**. A tunnel in **Area 1-6** leads to **Area 3-9**. The unstable floor in **Area 1-16** may collapse, dumping characters into **Area 2-6**.

Wandering Monsters: Very few wandering monsters are on this level; most keep to their lairs or defend their food source. Check for wandering monster encounters every hour or after any loud event, although only the carrion creepers or cave leech investigate noise with food in mind.

1d20	Encounter
1	**1d2 grimlocks** (scavenging for food, subtract from **Area 1-10**)
2	**1d3 rat swarms** (subtract from **Area 1-2**)
3	**1d6+1 giant rats** (subtract from **Area 1-4**)
4	**1d4+1 carrion creepers** from their lair on this level
5	Ebon Union **thug**
6–20	No Encounter

Carrion Creepers (1d4+1): HD 2+4; AC 7[12]; **Atk** bite (1 hp) and 6 tentacles (paralysis); **Move** 12; **Save** 14; **AL** N; **CL/XP** 4/120; **Special:** paralysis (save or paralysis for 2d6 turns). (*Swords & Wizardry Complete Rulebook*)

Ebon Union Thug, Male or Female Human: HD 1; AC 6[13]; **Atk** short sword (1d6) or club (1d6), dagger (1d4); **Move** 12; **Save** 17; **AL** C; **CL/XP** 1/15; **Special:** none. (*Monstrosities* 254)
Equipment: leather armor, short sword or club, dagger, small wooden shield, pouch with 1d4 gp and 2d6 sp.

Giant Rats (1d6+1): HD 1d4hp; AC 7[12]; **Atk** bite (1d3); **Move** 12; **Save** 18; **AL** N; **CL/XP** A/5; **Special:** 5% are diseased. (*Monstrosities* 384)

Grimlocks (1d2): HD 3; AC 4[15]; **Atk** 2 slams (1d4) or stone axe (1d6); **Move** 12; **Save** 14; **AL** C; **CL/XP** 4/120; **Special:** immunities (gaze attacks, illusions, and visual effects). (*Tome of Horrors 4* 116)
Equipment: tattered hides, stone axe.

Rat Swarm: HD 5; AC 7[12]; **Atk** swarm (1d6); **Move** 12; **Save** 12; **AL** N; **CL/XP** 5/240; **Special:** 10% of contracting disease.

Detections: The whole level radiates faint evil from the *box o' darkness traps* (see **Appendix C: New Magical Items**) in the corridors of **Area 1-9**.

Continuous Effects: The natural caverns and tunnels are shin-deep in stinking black water; the crypt corridors are only inches deep. Any character running through the water has a 3-in-6 chance of striking a hidden obstacle and must make a saving throw to avoid tripping and falling face first and take 1d4 points of damage. Any character that falls prone for any reason on this level has a 10% chance (per immersion) of contracting sewer plague (save avoids, 1d6 damage per day, *cure disease* to end ongoing damage). A thorough search beneath the water reveals 1d4 gp of coins (mostly silver and copper) per minute of sifting through the muck, which also requires a save to avoid disease. Unless the heroes have a light source with them, the entire level is in near total darkness.

Standard Features: In the sewage caverns, the walls are of rough stone and the floor is a combination of loose cobblestones, sand, and garbage. The overhead clearance is 10 feet in the tunnels and 15 feet in the rooms. In the crypt, the walls are of mortared stone and the floors are flagstone. All doors are of stone and open inward. The ceilings are 10 feet high and barrel-vaulted.

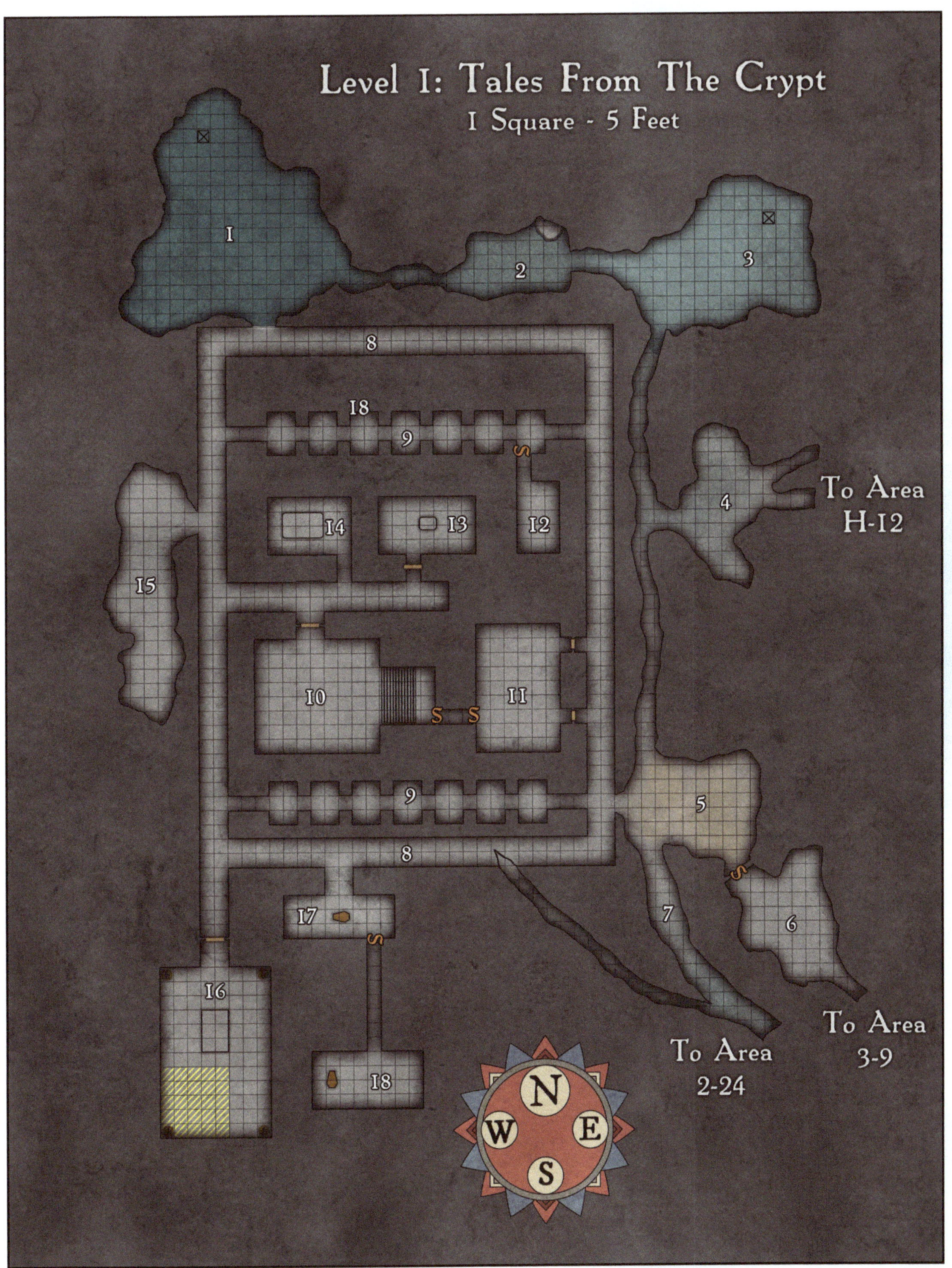

Level 1: Tales From The Crypt
1 Square - 5 Feet
1
2
3
4
5
6
7
8
8
9
9
10
11
12
13
14
15
16
17
18
18
To Area H-12
To Area 2-24
To Area 3-9
N
E
S
W

cloth and has a *cloak of protection +1* draped over it that fell into the sewers. If the cloak isn't washed before it is worn, the wearer is subject to sewer plague.

Otyugh: HD 7; **HP** 49; **AC** 2[17]; **Atk** 2 tentacles (1d8), bite (1d4+1); **Move** 6; **Save** 8 (+1, cloak); **AL** N; **CL/XP** 8/800; **Special:** disease (90% chance of contracting fatal disease, death in 3d6 days unless cured). (*Monstrosities* 367)
Note: The otyugh has a cloak of protection +1 draped and hooked across it that fell down from the sewers above. The cloak can be pulled off the beast to end its benefits, but doing so grants the otyugh a +2 to-hit bonus against the creature attempting to do so.

Tactics: This otyugh attacks any creature entering its lair, although it waits to attack until the heroes move to investigate one of the openings.

AREA 1-2: THE RAT CAVE

The water is only ankle-deep in this oblong chamber, and the bits of trash floating about show signs of being chewed. With the water shallow and the food plentiful, **6 swarms of rats** have taken up residence in this room. Their lair is deep in the shadows on a rock ledge 10 feet off the ground. The climber is most likely attacked upon arrival. A *potion of frozen concoction* is hidden near the back in a pile of droppings; an adventurer had been trying to use it to escape the otyugh and dropped it when he was surprised by a face full of rats.

Rat Swarms (6): HD 5; **HP** 36, 33, 32; **AC** 7[12]; **Atk** swarm (1d6); **Move** 12; **Save** 12; **AL** N; **CL/XP** 5/240; **Special:** 10% of contracting disease.

Tactics: The rats leap onto any characters who peek over the edge. Staying on the wall when this happens requires a saving throw.

AREA 1-3: ENTRY CHAMBER — GROCER'S LANE DRAIN

Situated right below Grocer's Lane, this chamber collects all the rotten produce from the market above. The squirming of maggots is audible, and the stench brings bile to the throat of any character passing through. If anyone falls prone in this area, the saving throw against contracting sewer plague is made with a −2 penalty. Lurking near the exit tunnel are **8 carrion creepers**, four on either side. Submerged in the corner of the area opposite the entrance are two bodies (an Ebon Union cutpurse who failed to make it back home safely one night, and a beggar who refused to inform for the Ebon Union). On the cutpurse are two daggers, an entrails-stained set of leather armor, a pouch of caltrops, a pouch with 6 gp and 20 sp, and a silvered short sword. A secret compartment is in the short sword's hilt. The hilt contains a slip of paper which reads "green first," a clue relating to a trap in **Area 3-22**. On the beggar is a signet ring worth 150 gp, or 450 gp if returned to the beggar's family in a far-off land of your choosing.

Carrion Creepers (8): HD 2+4; **HP** 18, 16, 14x2, 13, 10x2, 9; **AC** 7[12]; **Atk** bite (1 hp) and 6 tentacles (paralysis); **Move** 12; **Save** 14; **AL** N; **CL/XP** 4/120; **Special:** paralysis (save or paralysis for 2d6 turns). (*Swords & Wizardry Complete Rulebook*)

Tactics: The carrion creepers lurk on either side of the entry (the light from the drain sometimes lures prey into their lair). They lash out from hiding, attempting to surprise the first two heroes. They instinctively fight until slain.

AREA 1-4: ENTRY CHAMBER — THE CRAFTHALL TUNNEL

This small room has a raised floor that is mostly free of water. Bones are scattered all over, and at the base of one wall is a pile of broken pottery and glass. At the back of the room are two deep cracks in the wall. This room is the arrival point of a long tunnel from the basement of the Crafthall (**Area H-12**). It is infested with **8 giant rats** that the thieves have learned to distract with sugary sweets such as jam and honey. Upon arrival, they smash a jar or two against the far wall and slip past the rats while they eat. The rats' lair in one of the cracks contains their non-combatant young (**2d6 rats**). Within in this crack is also a chewed satchel containing a chewed roll of blank parchment, a pouch with 28 gp, and an unopened jar of strawberry jam that acts as a *potion of healing*. The other crack leads to the passage to the Crafthall.

Giant Rats (8): HD 1d4hp; **HP** 4x2, 3x3, 2x3; **AC** 7[12]; **Atk** bite (1d3); **Move** 12; **Save** 18; **AL** N; **CL/XP** A/5; **Special:** 5% are diseased. (*Monstrosities* 384)

Tactics: The giant rats attack as soon as they are aware of beings approaching their lair, unless they are distracted with sweets. When 75% of them are killed, the remaining rats retreat into their lair to defend their offspring.

AREA 1-5: STIRGES AND SECRETS

Most of this room has a relatively dry sandy floor. Obvious tracks lead across it from a deep fissure on one wall into the murky water of the natural corridor. A few burned scraps of rag lie scattered around the room. One of the walls is of mortared stone, which has collapsed to reveal a chamber beyond. The quiet buzzing of **6 stirges** reverberates in the crevices of the ceiling above. Immediately lighting the oily rags keeps them at bay; otherwise, they attack the party just after they arrive. Wedged in a crack in the ceiling, 12 rat corpses can be found in what appears be the stirges' larder. One of the rats is noticeably heavier than the others as it has a string of pearls worth 900 gp in its belly.

In the crack on the wall is a pivoting stone door with a pair of iron rings at the base. This door hides the entrance to a cavern used by the Ebon Union as a stop on their way to their lair on Level 3. The door requires a combined strength of 22 to open, or only 16 if a staff is inserted into the rings for leverage.

The collapsed stone wall leads to **Area 1-8**. Stepping through it possibly triggers a trap in **Area 1-9**.

Stirges (6): HD 1+1; **HP** 6, 5, 4x3, 3; **AC** 7[12]; **Atk** proboscis (1d3 + blood drain); **Move** 3 (fly 18); **Save** 17; **AL** N; **CL/XP** 2/30; **Special:** +2 to hit bonus, blood drain (automatic 1d4 after hit). (*Monstrosities* 461)

Tactics: The stirges attack as soon as they have reason to believe prey is below; note that they may react to the skeletons that result from the trap in **Area 1-9** depending on the party's location when the trap is triggered. The only thing that deters them is smoke; if the oily rags are lit or some other smoke is introduced, the stirges retreat into the cracks.

AREA 1-6: THE READY ROOM

Compared to the foul mess that is unavoidable elsewhere, this small cavern is nearly livable. A pile of rags looks like it could be a bed, and a few crates arranged in a corner have several candle stubs and dirty cups on them. A faint spot of light touches one wall. At the back, a low tunnel descends into darkness. There is a 10% chance per hour that an Ebon Union individual or group arrives; randomly determine which direction they are heading and use the profile from the Ebon Union section of **Appendix A: NPCs**. Check for this possibility as soon as the heroes arrive.

This is the staging area for the Ebon Union's forays into the city. They usually rest here after the climb up from their lair or stockpile supplies here to be carried down. A hairline crack in the ceiling allows whatever sunlight or moonlight exists above to filter down, where a mirror reflects it into the room so the thieves can establish the hour of the day. The tunnel in the back leads down to **Area 3-9**.

A sack with five rations and three bottles of wine (8 gp each) wrapped in cloth sits on a table. Also on the makeshift table is a deck of playing cards that has been magically treated to resist moisture and dirt (possibly valued as high as 1,000 gp, but only worth so much to a handful of people, easily mistaken for more powerful magical cards). The mirror jammed in the ceiling is made of silver and tortoise shell. This mirror is worth 35 gp.

AREA 1-7: OUTFLOW TUNNEL

This tunnel slopes down toward the sound of rushing water. Some distance down it picks up the drainage from **Area 1-8**. It eventually leads to the huge waterfall well described in **Area 2-24**.

AREA 1-8: PERIMETER CORRIDOR

The first time the heroes enter this area from either **Area 1-1** or **Area 1-5**, they almost certainly trigger a trap left in **Area 1-9** by Gethrax (refer to this area for complete details).

This corridor is 10 feet wide and runs all the way around the tomb complex. The walls are breached at three places, leading to **Areas 1-1**, **1-5**, and **1-15**. In one corridor, a wide crack at floor level drains away water toward **Area 1-7**. Only a halfling or dwarf character could fit through this tunnel and would be subject to disease, but halfway down is a corroded tin box containing a garnet necklace worth 360 gp.

AREA 1-9: CRYPT CORRIDORS

Burial niches in both walls dominate this long narrow corridor. They are lined up head to toe from one end to the other and are stacked three high. In most of them are ancient corpses, no longer clad in flesh, but still wearing armor and sometimes clutching weapons. These are the long-dead heroes of the near-forgotten war that threatened the valley. They were loyal defenders of the island city when it came under siege and so were buried here near the keep's gate to guard it for eternity. Thieves have already scavenged most of this area, so only a few bits of treasure remain. In one burial niche is a stone statue in place of a corpse; the stone wall behind it conceals a secret door to **Area 1-12**. The door is locked. In the other burial niche and scattered around on the floor are two rusty daggers, a small steel shield, and 25 gp worth of coins in silver.

Read the following as the party approaches within 50 feet of either *box o' darkness trap* (see **Appendix C: New Magical Items**):

> As you move into the corridor, a strange sound reaches your ears. It sounds like the cries of happy children playing and the cheerful notes of a wind-up music box.

If the party can see the box at the end of five rounds, add the following:

> The top of the box pops open on hidden hinges, and a one-inch figure rotates slowly inside. The cheerful music slowly winds to a stop, the pitch falling off in a tuneless moan. A thick, oily mist begins to seep from the box, spreading out around you, and the figure rotates to face you as the music dies out. It is a reaper in black, bearing a scythe. All around you, the dead begin to stir …

These portable magical traps were designed by evil priests to hamper the efforts of Lawful creatures. Gethrax placed them to further secure the caverns against the righteous, and he felt (rightly) that the crypt below the market was the most accessible area. Parties are likely surprised by the first one and may even be holding it when the top pops open and the evil mists seep out. If the heroes keep their wits about them, they may react quickly enough to minimize the effect of the second one — by moving it, blessing the area, or perhaps some other creative solution.

The traps are armed when wound up, and from then on are triggered by the approach of any Lawful humanoid within 50 feet. When triggered, they begin to play a pleasant tune as would a child's music box, and the sound of laughing children can be heard. After five rounds, the music slows, and thick black fog seeps out of the box, expanding to cover a 50-foot radius. This sickly fog animates **10 skeletons** from the dead scattered about the area. Undead within this area receive +1 hit point and a +1 bonus to attacks, damage, and saving throws. Checks to turn the undead suffer a –3 penalty for 10 hours in this area. On the bottom of the box is an engraved sigil (see also **Area 3-17** and **Appendix D: Wilderness Encounters**) that may lead the party to the powerful creator of the *boxes o' darkness* in a later quest.

Skeletons (10): HD 1; **HP** 9, 8, 7x3, 6x2, 5, 4x2; **AC** 8[11]; **Atk** strike (1d6); **Move** 12; **Save** 16 (+1, *box o' darkness*); **AL** N; **CL/XP** 1/15; **Special:** immune to sleep and charm spells. (*Monstrosities* 428)
Note: The skeletons gain +1 to hit, damage, and saves in the area around the *box o' darkness trap*. They can be turned with a –3 penalty.

Area 1-10: Chapel

This room appears to have been a place of worship at some point, complete with curtained altar. Unless the heroes have taken steps to infiltrate the room, **6 grimlocks** leap up to attack as the door opens. If the heroes enter through the secret corridor from **Area 1-11**, they emerge behind a tapestry and have a good chance to surprise the creatures. Their leader **Bashrib** and another **grimlock** are hidden beneath the altar and almost certainly surprise the heroes regardless of which way they come in.

The chapel was included in the tomb to represent the dominant belief system in the valley at the time; feel free to use any non-evil deity, forgotten or otherwise. The chapel was taken over by Bashrib's grimlock band when they were displaced by the arrival of the Ebon Union. Most of their treasure is in a large locked chest in the corner, but a few items are in **Area 1-11**. The chest can be broken open or unlocked with thieves' tools. Additionally, Bashrib carries the key to this chest around his neck.

Within the chest there are 180 gp, 260 sp, three pieces of uncut amber (worth 80 gp, 95 gp, and 110 gp), a silver-plated dagger with a turquoise and jet handle (worth 380 gp), and an ivory statue of a horse (worth 65 gp). Within the room there is a mildewed tapestry (used as bedding) with gold thread in it worth 250 gp. A secret door can be found behind the altar tapestries. The door opens easily, leads through a passageway to **Area 1-11**, and has a disgusting treasure of its own: 3 silver bowls (12 gp each, or 24 gp if sold to a temple of the appropriate deity) that the grimlocks use as chamber pots.

If any of the gridlocks survive the encounter, they might be convinced to share some of what they know about the dungeon. They might be charmed, intimidated, or even tortured; let the roleplaying abilities of the players determine what their characters learn. If Bashrib survives, he attempts to barter for his survival with information, perhaps even agreeing to guide the party through the parts of the dungeon he knows. All of the grimlocks are familiar with Level 3; their lair used to be in the troll cave (**Area 3-29**).

Bashrib, Grimlock Leader: HD 4; **HP** 28; **AC** 4[15]; **Atk** 2 slams (1d4) or by war hammer (1d4); **Move** 12; **Save** 13; **AL** C; **CL/XP** 5/240; **Special:** immunities (gaze attacks, illusions, and visual effects). (*Tome of Horrors 4* 116)
Equipment: tattered hides, war hammer, key to treasure chest, jade necklace (85 gp).

Grimlocks (7): HD 3; **HP** 22, 20x2, 19, 16, 14, 13; **AC** 4[15]; **Atk** 2 slams (1d4) or stone axe (1d6); **Move** 12; **Save** 14; **AL** C; **CL/XP** 4/120; **Special:** immunities (gaze attacks, illusions, and visual effects). (*Tome of Horrors 4* 116)
Equipment: tattered hides, stone axe.

Tactics: Regardless of how the fight begins, Bashrib and his mate wait two rounds behind the altar before leaping out and attacking the heroes closest to them, preferably ones with their backs turned to the altar. Bashrib is very irate at having his snuggling time interrupted.

Area 1-11: Memorial

This rectangular room is devoid of furnishings save for a bed of furs made up in a corner. The walls are exquisitely carved in bas-relief and depict an epic battle between an allied force of humans, dwarves, and halflings and a great evil horde of orcs and orc-kin. These carvings are a tribute to the epic battle for the valley in which so many great heroes lost their lives. The carvings themselves are worth several thousand gold pieces each, but the logistics of removing them are complicated, as each panel weighs thousands of pounds and was actually carved in this room. Of course, the citizens will not take kindly to their relics being removed, even if they have forgotten that they exist. A secret door leads to **Area 1-10**. The door can be broken open or unlocked with thieves' tools. A few items of the grimlocks' treasure are hidden in the stinking furs. This includes a silver pitcher (matches the chalices in the tunnel, worth 80 gp or 160 gp if sold to a temple of the appropriated deity), and a pouch with 11 moonstones. Of these moonstones, four are worth 40 gp, another four are worth 50 gp, two are worth 60 gp, and one is worth 70 gp.

Area 1-12: Hidden Burial Vault

The craftsmen who built the tombs created this hidden vault. In addition to the great heroes who fell in battle, scores of commoners died, and the stonemasons were allowed to place a stone statue in the vault to represent their dead. Regardless, they created this small antechamber behind a secret door to honor the dead of the lower classes. Hundreds of skulls line the walls in great piles, and a number of items of treasure (clearly those of common folk) were left with the dead in keeping with various belief systems. These items include 12 clay jugs of stale beer (1 sp for the jugs), seven bottles of fine wine (8 gp each), three bottles of not-so-fine wine (worthless), two sets of high quality artisan's tools (55 gp each), silver holy symbol of a good-aligned deity (25 gp), and a small oak cask of several hundred-year old unblended "cask-strength" whiskey (80 gp, or 2,000 gp if sold to a collector or master distiller).

The vault is reached by squeezing through a trapped passage behind a secret door in the stone carving of a craftsman in **Area 1-9**. The door can be broken open or unlocked with thieves' tools. Upon opening the door, a **falling block trap** drops and strikes any character in front of the door unless they make a saving throw to dive out of the way. Anyone who fails the saving throw is crushed by the block and takes 3d6 points of damage (but can make another saving throw for half damage).

Area 1-13: Dwarven Burial Vault

The door to this area is locked and trapped. The door can be broken open or unlocked with thieves' tools. A **field of spikes** drops from the ceiling as a character enters the room. This trap catches anyone within five feet of either side of the door. Characters in the area must make a saving throw to dive out of the way. On a failed saving throw, the character takes 4d6 points of damage (but can make another saving throw for half damage).

This room is decorated with beautiful carvings and graceful stone arches. The burial niches that line these walls are slightly shorter than the ones in the other corridors, and a large stone casket dominates the center of the room.

This tomb is dedicated to the many dwarves that fell in the great battle, and their leaders and heroes are buried here. Ten dwarven warriors in rotted robes hold dwarven battle axes across their chests. The central casket is the tomb of the dwarf lord Gedgrath; his name and title are carved on the lid in dwarven script. Removing the lid requires a combined 26 strength. Gedgrath is lying in state here. His items and the weapons of the other dwarves make up the treasure. This includes 10 dwarven battle axes (300 gp), finely-engraved dwarven plate armor (1,800 gp), a jewel-encrusted battle axe (820 gp), and a mithral crown studded with fire opals (5,500 gp). If the party brings all of these items to the dwarven market at once, questions might be raised as to how they acquired these items.

Area 1-14: Halfling Burial Vault

The door to this vault has been smashed to rubble. Inside are a large marble slab and a few burial niches, but the bones of the dead are scattered on the ground. The air is noticeably colder in this chamber, which has already been looted. It is a tribute to the halfling heroes of the great battle; the marble slab has their story and the history of the battle inscribed on it, which may be of interest to characters interested in historical events. It could also reference the villains' stronghold that was sealed but never cleansed; this detail is left to your discretion for further development. A patch of **brown mold** and a pitiful treasure of 1 sp per party member wait in the corner.

Brown Mold: HD n/a; **AC** n/a; **Atk** none; **Move** 0; **Save** n/a; AL N; **CL/XP** 4/120; **Special:** drains heat (5ft radius, 2d8 damage per round, no save), healed by fire (doubles size), vulnerable to cold (200%). (*Monstrosities* 335)

Area 1-15: The Cave Leech's Lair

This rough-walled stone chamber is lit by an unseen source. A **cave leech** dwells in a smaller cave to one side of the main room. Lilith summoned it after she had the Ebon Union rob the herbalist's shop; if the heroes have not already made the connection, they may realize that a cave leech's tooth was one of the stolen items, but only if they can identify the creature. It attacks with its many tentacles as soon as the party enters its lair. The leech unknowingly has a collection of treasure left over from a past meal. Floating in a magical bubble about 15 feet above the ground in the smaller chamber are a red *potion of fire resistance*, a blue *potion of flying*, and a green *potion of gaseous form*. If the treasure bubble is not restrained, it floats upward at a rate of one foot per round. The bubble can be popped with any sharp weapon.

The cave leech waits in the smaller section of the cave until the party enters, possibly drawn by the light of the potion. It attempts to strike characters with its tentacles to drain their blood.

Cave Leech: HD 5; AC 9[10]; Atk 8 tentacles (1d4) or bite (1d6); Move 3; Save 12; AL N; CL/XP 6/400; Special: blood drain (each strike drains 1d4 blood). (**The Tome of Horrors Complete** 88)

AREA 1-16: ANGUS TOMB

The doors to this chamber are locked. The doors can be broken open or unlocked with thieves' tools.

Double doors give way into a vault at the end of the corridor. A large casket sits in the center of the rectangular room, unadorned except for some carved script on the lid. Rotting tapestries hang from brass rods on all four walls, and brass braziers stand empty in all four corners. The brazier in the southwest corner seems to be leaning at an off angle. This room is the final resting place of the Lord Angus who marshaled the army and masterminded the defense of the citadel during the war. He was laid to rest in a place of honor, and for many weeks, mourners passed around his tomb. Their path in the floor is worn. The inscription on the lid reads:

> *Colm Angus*
> *Lord of Eamonvale*
> *Slain on the Ramparts*
> *For the Sake of his People*
> *Let None Disturb his Rest*

A great hunter, he was buried with a treasure of his personal hunting weapons, although the *sword of Angus* was passed on through his heirs to Arb. The tomb can be opened with a combined 25 strength. The tomb contains four brass braziers (worth 20 gp each), a silvered longbow, and 16 *+1 arrows*.

The brazier in the southwest corner leans because the floor it sits on is ready to collapse. Dwarves have a 3-in-6 chance to detect this danger; 1-in-6 for all others. Any weight greater than 150 pounds on a 10-foot-by-10-foot square around the brazier triggers a collapse. The floor in a 25-foot-by-25-foot area in the corner buckles momentarily before collapsing. Characters on the falling floor take 6d6 points of damage from the collapse and the falling stone blocks that follow them down. All characters who fall can make a saving throw for half damage. If the saving throw is failed, the character is also trapped under the debris and must be rescued. The collapse spills some or all of the party into **Area 2-6**, which has its own nasty surprises.

AREA 1-17: THE PALADIN'S CENOTAPH

No doors restrict access to this small room. It holds only a large marble tomb raised off the floor on a slab of granite. An inscription on the pedestal reads:

> *Let none forget Roark the Righteous,*
> *Paladin of the North and Defender of Eamonvale,*
> *Lost on the Last Day as he Ended the*
> *Dark Reign of the Dead Lord*
> *Bless Him*
> *That He May Never Succumb*
> *To the Curse of Unlife*

The citizens of Eamonvale were unwilling to see Roark buried here because of the manner of his death. The cenotaph was placed to commemorate his death, but the heir to the Angus lordship buried his

body in a secret chamber anyway. The "tomb" is actually a block of solid marble carved to represent a burial vault. It does not open.

Roark was a paladin from the distant north who heeded the call of the imperiled valley and rode to aid the defense. A cadre of powerful necromancers and undead beings led the invaders, and a wight fatally wounded Roark even as he struck it down. He bade the citizens prepare a consecrated grave for him as he struggled with the curse. They laid him down before the injuries claimed him, and even as he passed, his spirit struggled against the spawn within. His soul remains trapped within the husk of his body, barely holding the wight impulse at bay, and as the evil influences on this level have increased, his grip on undeath has been slipping.

Nothing here indicates that Roark is anywhere in this room, but secret door is disguised as stone, but formed of iron on the inside. The door can be broken or unlocked with thieves' tools. Behind it lies Roark's tomb, hidden from would-be grave robbers in hopes that what he might become would never see the light of day.

AREA 1-18: THE PALADIN'S TOMB

This room is small and simple — no tapestries, no carvings, no furnishings. A marker in the stone floor indicates that it is the final resting place of Roark the Righteous. The lid to Roark's tomb is massively heavy, requiring a combined 30 strength to open it. If the lid is pried off the floor vault, it shifts the fragile balance of good and evil, tipping the scales against Roark's spirit and freeing the undead creature he should have become ages ago. Information from the memorial statue in **Area 1-17** and in the read-aloud text below should hint at the necessary means to defeat the **wight**.

> Inside the recess beneath the lid is the body of Roark the Righteous. His skeletal remains are clad in age-tarnished mail, a large shield rests across his torso, and his penitently folded hands hold a large sword, point down across the shield. A whispery voice suddenly whirls around you like an icy wind. "You have unleashed me … my fight is lost … again!" The voice cries out "Noooooo!" as the skeletal corpse leaps up and flings itself at you!

Roark the Righteous wears chainmail armor and carries a *+1 freezing longsword*. The powerful spirit of Roark's living self is nearly able to keep the wight from animating his corpse. Destroying the wight destroys Roark as well, but an extensive quest may allow Roark's spirit to be salvaged and laid to rest. This development is up to you.

The wight abandons the shield and attacks until it is killed, turned, or overcome by Roark's spirit. Based on the clues on the statue and in the text block, the heroes may be able to help Roark overcome the wight and return his own corpse to the tomb. The pedestal says, "Bless Him," and a *bless* spell allows Roark to regain control of his remains for 1d6+1 rounds and fling them back into the burial recess. The heroes must still return the lid to its original position, and the wight remains subdued only temporarily; the party may still need to find a permanent solution.

Roark the Righteous, Wight: HD 8; HP 54; AC 5[14]; Atk claw (1d6 + level drain) or +1 freezing longsword (1d8+1 + 1d6 cold); Move 9; Save 8; AL C; CL/XP 9/1100; Special: +1 or better magic or silver weapons to hit, level drain (1 level with hit), vulnerability (bless spell stuns it for 1d6+1 rounds). (**Monstrosities** 510)

Chapter Five: Level 2 — Fungus Among Us

This is the second level below the surface, although it can be reached directly via the tunnel below the mill. The caverns here were carved by the force of moving water and still tend to be more wet than dry. The steady flow of organic waste from the mill has spawned a great deal of botanical and fungal growth on this level — some of it quite intelligent. Among the vegetable denizens of the swampy caverns are a shambling mound and some assassin vines, and non-botanical life abounds in the form of monstrous cave crayfish and comical (but deadly) giant dire frogs. Lilith's summoned rust monsters are here as well. The most dangerous occupant is Gethrax, one of Lilith's allies, who makes his lair here to be close to the surface.

The hazards here generally keep the thieves from passing through, but Lilith and Devlin use this level to access the surface from time to time. Several adventurers seeking bounties on the demons penetrated this far into the dungeon before meeting their ends. As the plants have

Level 2: Fungus Among Us

Entrances: This level has only one surface access point: a slimy tunnel winding down from the basement of the mill. The unstable floor in **Area 1-16** may collapse, dumping the characters in **Area 2-6**. A passage from **Area 1-7** arrives in the waterfall room, **Area 2-24**.

Exits: The waterfall room in **Area 2-24** has an underground river that flows out to Level 4. A secret passage in **Area 2-17** leads to **Area 3-9**. If the heroes were to bring down the ceiling in **Area 2-6**, they could climb up to **Area 1-16**.

Wandering Monsters: Many of the creatures on this level are plants and tend to wait rather than actively look for their prey. A few of the creatures, however, do move about — check for a wandering monster encounter every hour or after any loud event.

1d20	Encounter
1–2	1d3 bat swarms (subtract from **Area 2-2**)
3–4	1d2 rat swarms (subtract from **Area 2-23**)
5	1d6+1 giant rats (subtract from **Area 2-5**)
6	Gethrax (see **Area 2-17**)
7	Sogrin the ogre (see **Area 2-16**)
8	Rust monster (subtract from **Area 2-10**)
9–20	No Encounter

Bat Swarm: HD 4; AC 7[12]; **Atk** swarm (1d4); **Move** 12; **Save** 13; **AL** N; **CL/XP** 4/120; **Special:** 10% of contracting disease.

Gethrax, Male Human, Fallen Paladin in service to the Ebon Union (Ftr6/Clr5): HP 61; AC 2[17]; **Atk** *+1 longsword* (1d8+7); **Move** 12; **Save** Ftr 9/Clr 11; **AL** C; **CL/XP** 11/1700; **Special:** +2 to hit and damage strength bonus, +2 save vs. paralysis or poison, banish undead, multiple attacks (6) vs. creatures with 1 or fewer HD, spells (2/2).
Spells: 1st—*cause light wounds* (x2); 2nd—*hold person, silence 15ft radius*.
Equipment: *+2 chainmail*, shield, *gauntlets of ogre power*, *+1 longsword, box o' darkness trap* (unwound; see **Appendix C: New Magical Items**), *ring of animate dead* (see **Appendix C: New Magical Items**), cursed *ring of invisibility* (ring and hand must be bathed in still-warm blood once a week or it ceases to function for current wearer).

Giant Rats (1d6+1): HD 1d4hp; AC 7[12]; **Atk** bite (1d3); **Move** 12; **Save** 18; **AL** N; **CL/XP** A/5; **Special:** 5% are diseased. (*Monstrosities* 384)

Rat Swarm: HD 5; AC 7[12]; **Atk** swarm (1d6); **Move** 12; **Save** 12; **AL** N; **CL/XP** 5/240; **Special:** 10% of contracting disease.

Rust Monster: HD 5; AC 2[17]; **Atk** 2 antennae (cause rust); **Move** 12; **Save** 12; **AL** N; **CL/XP** 5/240; **Special:** cause rust (touch destroys armor/weapons; magic weapons get 10% chance per +1 bonus to resist destruction). (*Monstrosities* 406)

Sogrin, Ogre: HD 6; HP 40; AC 5[14]; **Atk** club (1d10+1); **Move** 9; **Save** 11; **AL** C; **CL/XP** 6/400; **Special:** none. (*Monstrosities* 356)
Equipment: club, sack containing *potion of extra healing* and *potion of treasure finding*, pouch containing 60 gp, 50 sp, and a dead rat.

Detections: The level has a strong life force, but neither good nor evil seems to dominate it … rather, hunger is the driving force of these creatures. The lair of Gethrax radiates potent evil.

Continuous Effects: This level is a major drainage for the city, and the constant flow of runoff and nutrients ensures that the caves and corridors are always full of water and slime. Any character running or fighting in the muck must make a saving throw or fall prone; the character takes no damage thanks to the thick moss growing everywhere. Enough luminescent fungi are scattered throughout this level that the overall lighting is the equivalent of dim light.

Standard Features: The walls here are of rough, unworked stone, and the floor and ceiling are uneven and studded with stalactites and stalagmites. Tunnels are generally rounded with water trickling down the middle; rooms have pools of standing water with thick carpets of bright green algae. Secret doors on this level are actually curtains of moss and fungus. Overhead clearance is 10 feet in the tunnels and 15 feet in the caverns, measured from the water level (some caverns have pools that go much deeper).

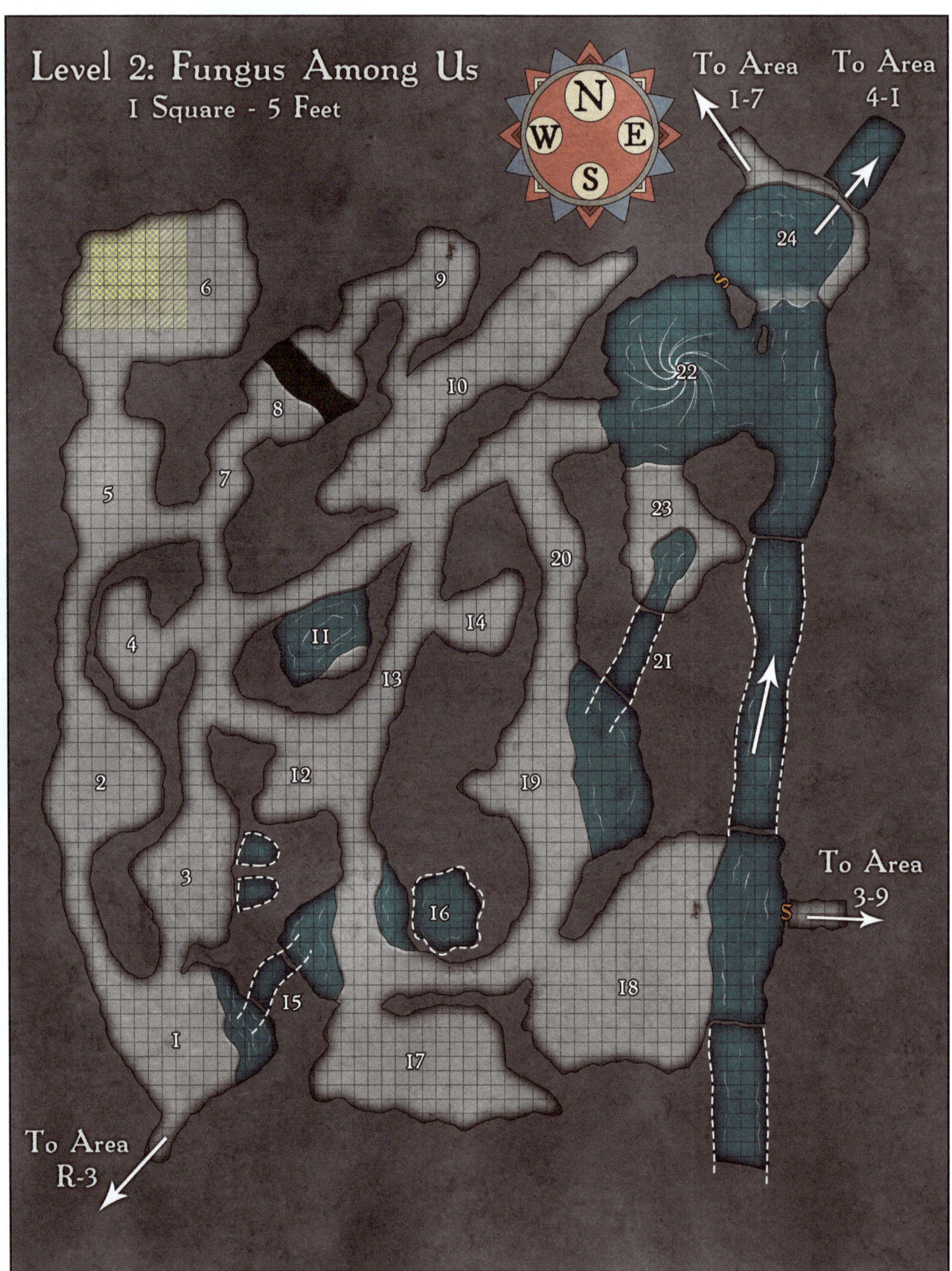

Level 2: Fungus Among Us
1 Square - 5 Feet
N
W E
S
To Area 1-7
To Area 4-1
To Area 3-9
To Area R-3
1
2
3
4
5
6
7
8
9
10
11
12
13
14
15
16
17
18
19
20
21
22
23
24

little use for the bodies beyond nourishment, the possessions of the fallen make up most of the treasure here.

Area 2-1: Entry Chamber — The Millworks Basement

This wedge-shaped cavern has tunnels leading to other areas on Level 2 and one leading to **Area R-3** in the mill. A pool of stagnant, stinking water in the corner conceals a water-filled tunnel (see **Area 2-15**) that leads to **Area 2-16**.

Area 2-2: Going Batty

This cave holds a relatively harmless surprise for the party: **4 bats swarms**. As soon as they are disturbed by loud noise, attacks, or major changes in their environment, the bats take flight, wheel crazily around the party for a 1d4+1 rounds (during which time each swarm tries to nip the characters with their many sharp fangs) and then fly off into some other part of the cave. They inflict superficial injuries, spread lots of guano, and alert Gethrax (**Area 2-17**) to the intruders.

Bat Swarms (4): HD 4; HP 30, 27, 23, 19; AC 7[12]; **Atk** swarm (1d4); **Move** 12; **Save** 13; **AL** N; **CL/XP** 4/120; **Special:** 10% of contracting disease.

Area 2-3: Albino Cave Crayfish

Glowing blue fungi on the ceiling light this long, narrow cavern. The floor is flat for the first time and is covered with a spongy layer of mossy growth. A trickle of water can be heard at the far end. The flat surface in this area is not actually the cavern floor, but a floating bed of moss on the surface of a pool of stagnant water. Living in the pool are **4 monstrous crayfish**.

Characters who aren't testing the floor have a 1-in-6 chance to notice what it is made of. A safe passage across the moss can then be discerned by tapping the moss a pole. Failing this, the heaviest members of the party likely fall through the surface of the moss bed to be trapped underneath. Any creature weighing 200 pounds or more must make a saving throw if they attempt to cross the cave. On a failed save, the mossy blanket closes over the hero's head as they fall in darkness.

A character trapped under the floating moss has a 1-in-6 chance to find their way back to the original hole through which they fell. An alternative is to make a new hole; in this case, 20 points of damage done to any five-foot section creates a new opening. Characters under the moss can also tear a hole by making an Open Doors check. Other heroes may attempt to assist, but they are subject to the 200-pound weight limit. Dispersing body weight by slithering on one's belly or using long or flat objects (ladders, large weapons, and so forth) increases the limit to 300 pounds; doing both increases it to 400 pounds.

Several previous adventurers died here, and a rich treasure awaits anyone exploring the pool. Underneath the blanket of moss, characters can find a breastplate, a longsword, 4 *+1 arrows*, a jar of ointment (four applications) that heals 2d6 points of damage per application, and a pouch with 49 gp.

Monstrous Crayfish (4): HD 4; HP 29, 25, 24, 19; AC 4[15]; Atk 2 claws (1d6); **Move** 9 (swim 15); **Save** 13; **AL** N; **CL/XP** 4/120; **Special:** surprise (2-in-6 chance). (**The Tome of Horrors Complete** 113)

Tactics: When the first character enters the pool, the crayfish leave their holes and approach slowly. They fight until reduced to 25% of their original hit points before retreating into their deep holes.

Area 2-4: And Then There Were Two

The pale, blubbery creature crouched here is a **dretch** and should look familiar from the party's adventures in the city above. It is scratching strange circles in the sand … that is, it is luring in the party to use its *stinking cloud* ability. Hiding nearby is another **dretch** the characters have a 1-in-6 chance to spot.

Dretch Demons (2): HD 4; HP 30, 27; AC 2[17]; **Atk** 2 claws (1d4), bite (1d6); **Move** 9; **Save** 13; **AL** C; **CL/XP** 6/400; **Special:** spell-like abilities. (**Monstrosities** 92) **Spell-like abilities:** 1/day—*darkness 15ft radius*, stinking cloud (20ft radius, save or nauseated for 1d4+1 rounds), summon 1d4 giant rats.

Area 2-5: Giant Rats

This area seems to have been set up as a camp of some sort. The remains of a small fire and a few chewed bones are tucked up against the back wall, and some tatters of woolen cloth may have once been a bedroll. This cave is home to **8 hungry giant rats** that are dangerous on their own and even more so if they strike while the party is suffering the effects of the collapse in **Area 2-6**. Their nest is in a small hollow behind the shredded bedroll; they keep their treasure here, still on the back of a dungeoneer who failed to return to the surface. The dungeoneer is wearing a backpack containing a set of clothes, three torches, a short sword, a scroll tube with 3 scrolls (*mirror image*, *telekinesis*, and *wizard eye*), and a coin purse containing 32 pp.

Giant Rats (8): HD 1d4hp; HP 4x2, 3x4, 2x2; AC 7[12]; **Atk** bite (1d3); **Move** 12; **Save** 18; **AL** N; **CL/XP** A/5; **Special:** 5% are diseased. (**Monstrosities** 384)

Tactics: The giant rats are defensive of their lair, although no young are present at this time. They fight aggressively until six of them are killed, at which point they flee into the caverns to seek another home.

Area 2-6: Bring the House Down

This chamber is different from any other on this level in that a portion of its roof is constructed of mortared stone. This section supports **Area 1-16** above, although not very well. Any loud noise, concussion of applied force (striking, leaning, pushing, and so on) against the columns or ceiling brings it down on top of the heroes.

Dwarves have a 3-in-6 chance to detect this danger; 1-in-6 for all others. Characters take 6d6 points of damage from the collapse and the falling stone blocks. All characters can make a saving throw with a −3 penalty for half damage. If the saving throw is failed, the character is also trapped under the debris and must be rescued.

If the **giant rats** in **Area 2-5** have not already been dealt with in some manner, they investigate the collapse. This encounter may hamper the rescue of pinned characters.

Area 2-7: Just a Fun Guy

Hidden among the multitudes of mushrooms and fungi that cling to the walls of the corridor is a **violet fungus**. It is well fed and inactive and does not attack the party unless alerted by the **shriekers** in **Area 2-8** or attacked.

Tactics: This fungus does not attack the party on sight. If it is attacked or if it hears the shriekers in **Area 2-8**, it moves as fast as it can to attack. Its primitive, fungal instincts kick in, and it fights until destroyed.

Violet Fungus: HD 3; **HP** 19; **AC** 7[12]; **Atk** 4 tendrils (rot); **Move** 1; **Save** 14; **AL** N; **CL/XP** 4/120; **Special:** tendrils cause rot (save or flesh rots for 1d4 damage per hour; *cure disease* ends damage). (*Monstrosities* 183)

AREA 2-8: THE 'SHROOM ROOM

This narrow cave is split by a fissure so deep that the bottom is beyond the reach of the party's lights. Tunnel openings are on both sides of the fissure. The entire room is densely populated with slimy fungi; a particularly tall purple variety dominates the north side. Some of the tall purple mushrooms are **shriekers** and **2 violet fungi** are hidden at the edges of the chasm. The chasm is 10 feet wide. Characters who attempt to jump the chasm must roll below their dexterity on 3d6; if they fail, they can make a saving throw to grab the opposite ledge before they fall (and likely are killed unless they have some magical item to save themselves). The landing on either side is slick and requires a saving throw to avoid falling prone and taking 1d4 points of damage.

For the purposes of this adventure, the fissure is bottomless, and any character or item falling into it is lost. Alternatively, you may use it to integrate other dungeon areas or place a river at the bottom that drains into **Area 2-24**.

Lying under a mound of fungal growth is the body of an independent thief who fatefully tried his hand at dungeon delving; his belongings make up the treasure for this area. The mound contains a chain shirt, a dagger, a velvet envelope containing three silver and emerald hairpins worth 1,200 gp, a gold bracelet worth 60 gp, and a pouch containing 18 gp and 20 sp.

Shriekers: HD 3; **HP** 21; **AC** 7[12]; **Atk** none; **Move** 1; **Save** 14; **AL** N; **CL/XP** 3/60; **Special:** shriek (1 point of damage per round to all within 30ft). (*Monstrosities* 423)

Violet Fungi (2): HD 3; **HP** 20, 16; **AC** 7[12]; **Atk** 4 tendrils (rot); **Move** 1; **Save** 14; **AL** N; **CL/XP** 4/120; **Special:** tendrils cause rot (save or flesh rots for 1d4 damage per hour; *cure disease* ends damage). (*Monstrosities* 183)

Tactics: The shriekers react to any light or movement within 10 feet or anywhere on their side of the fissure. If some party members are more inclined or equipped than others to jump the fissure, this probably means that the party is split up for this encounter. The distribution of heroes between the two sides is especially important if the violet fungus from **Area 2-7** has not been killed; it arrives after three rounds of shrieking. All of these fungi fight (and shriek) instinctively until killed.

AREA 2-9: THE LITTLE MADMAN

This small cave has two tunnels at one end. A crumpled body lies in the corner farthest from the tunnel entrances. The robes are tattered and dirty, but even from a distance they seem to be the colors of the Band of the Crimson Mantle. This is the body of Dresden the Mad (unless you choose to alter these events). When the Band engaged the rust monsters from **Area 2-10**, Dresden was separated from the group. The other members had far more to fear from the creatures, and they fled with their metal items, leaving the little halfling to his fate. Rust stains are around his body, and he has been scavenged of all metal items, but his remaining equipment makes up the treasure for this area. Note that any loud noises may attract the rust monsters from

next door. On his body is a sling, a pouch of rocks, a *potion of flying*, a *potion of gaseous form*, and two scrolls (*haste* and *knock*).

AREA 2-10: RUST MONSTERS

Bits of wood and leather stained with rust litter the floor in this long, narrow room. Two domed, earth-colored creatures with the appearance of large beetles burst from a burrow at the far end and rush toward the heroes as they enter. These **2 rust monsters** are more of Lilith's summoned creatures that she turned loose in the caverns to guard against intruders. Their treasure is entirely non-metal and is mostly buried in their burrow. Within the burrow is 50 feet of silk rope, a jeweled leather belt with no buckle worth 160 gp, and four improvised clubs.

Tactics: The rust monsters rush directly toward the largest source of metal in the party, although they do not attack the same target if several similar volumes of metal are present. They do not pursue fleeing adventurers if a meal of rusted metal is available. If both are reduced to 25% of their original hit points or if one is killed, they flee.

Rust Monsters (2): HD 5; **HP** 36, 32; **AC** 2[17]; **Atk** 2 antennae (cause rust); **Move** 12; **Save** 12; **AL** N; **CL/XP** 5/240; **Special:** cause rust (touch destroys armor/weapons; magic weapons get 10% chance per +1 bonus to resist destruction). (*Monstrosities* 406)

AREA 2-11: THE ORACLE FROGS

On the right side of this tunnel is a large, dark pool of water. Sitting on a stone ledge at the back are three very large, placid-looking frogs. Their eyes swivel to watch the heroes as they walk past. A few coins are visible in the murky pool below the ledge. These **3 giant dire frogs** possess rudimentary intelligence and a gift for extra-sensory visions. They answer one question per character per day, to a maximum of three per day. Before a question is answered, an item worth at least 1 gp must be tossed into the pool below the frogs.

These three giant dire frogs have a unique shared ability to perform minor acts of clairvoyance and fortune-telling. They answer a maximum of three questions per day, but only one question per character per day. All three frogs must be alive and together to answer questions. Treat the questions as premonitions with a 70% chance of accuracy. The answers are limited by the frogs' vocal capabilities and always consist of three syllables, one from each frog. For example, asking about a mysterious cave in which lurks a dangerous, plant-based creature might result in an answer such as *"vines ... bring ... death."* Simple questions such as "Who are you?" still count toward the daily limit and produce simple answers such as *"We ... are ... frogs."* There is a 50% chance that the syllables/words are in the wrong order and require deciphering by the asker.

The pool is full of the frogs' treasure, but it is trapped with a curse that follows anyone who steals from it. If a creature takes an item from the frogs' pool, they must make a saving throw or be cursed. You are free to come up with colorful curses such as "can eat only insects" or "can speak only in single syllables." At the bottom of the pool is a *potion of frozen concoction*, a drinking horn worth 65 gp, and a collection of 78 gp and 130 sp.

If attacked, the giant dire frogs fight until killed. They are unwilling to leave the dungeon voluntarily and resist any attempts to capture them. There is a 20% chance that the frogs are hungry and attack on sight.

Giant Dire Frog (3): HD 4; **HP** 30x3; **AC** 2[17]; **Atk** bite (2d6), tongue (entangle); **Move** 12 (swim 15) or 50ft leap; **Save** 13; **AL** N; **CL/XP** 5/240; **Special:** entangle (if tongue hits, automatic bite damage; Open Doors check to escape),

fortune-telling (answer 3 questions per day), leap (50ft). (*The Tome of Horrors Complete* 629)

Tactics: The giant dire frogs fight only if attacked. Any other activity is met with total apathy. If an opportunity to escape a fight is possible, they take it; otherwise, they fight to the best of their abilities until dead.

AREA 2-12: AWWWWW, RATS!

A huge pile of rotten plant matter and flotsam washed up in a sandy corner of this room. A **rat swarm** hollowed out a nest in the pile of garbage, which also conceals their treasure. Within the pile of garbage, a coin purse containing 4 pp, 11 gp, and 54 sp can be found. In addition, a mummified human hand bearing the tattoo of a dragon (actually the icon of a distant cult) can be found.

Rat Swarm: HD 5; **HP** 29; **AC** 7[12]; **Atk** swarm (1d6); **Move** 12; **Save** 12; **AL** N; **CL/XP** 5/240; **Special:** 10% of contracting disease.

Tactics: These rats are more likely to flee than fight, although they attack any creature between them and the mouth of their cave for one or two rounds on their way out.

AREA 2-13: ASSASSIN VINES

This corridor has an unusually low ceiling. Up ahead, backlit by a purple glow, is a pile of something on the ground — bodies. More specifically, the remains of bodies: bones, armor, weapons, and baggage lie strewn across the corridor, surrounded by hundreds of tiny mushrooms of every color. The **2 assassin vines** that dwell on the ceiling of this corridor do not strike until the remains of their past victims attract the party. Their treasure is spread over the length of the corridor, along with the remains of the deceased owners. This includes a suit of half plate with skeletal remains still inside, a 50-foot length of hemp rope that breaks if a load greater than 100 pounds is place on it, and a pair of *boots of leaping* (one still has a foot inside). The glow from down the tunnel originates in **Area 2-14**.

Assassin Vines (2): HD 7; **HP** 48, 42; **AC** 5[14]; **Atk** vine (1d6+1); **Move** 1; **Save** 9; **AL** N; **CL/XP** 8/800; **Special:** animate plants (30ft range, immobilize any creature that fails a saving throw). (*Monstrosities* 23)

Tactics: As soon as one or more creatures enter the corridor below them, the vines attack, lashing out with their tough vines.

AREA 2-14: A COZY HOLLOW

This small alcove is just big enough for the party to enter. Light is provided by clumps of phosphorescent fungus, and the floor is relatively dry, providing a good place for a break.

An etched sigil on the wall of this cave is the stylized initials "E.B." Elinda Bannon spent a few hours here when she passed through several days ago.

AREA 2-15: UNDERWATER TUNNEL

This underwater tunnel connects **Areas 2-1** and **2-16**. Passing through it safely requires a character to have a swim speed or to roll equal to or below their dexterity on 3d6 three consecutive times. The character takes 1d6 points of damage for each failed check and possibly drowns (cumulative 10% chance per failed check). Thus, a character with 14 dexterity who rolls 10, 15, and 16 takes 2d6 points of damage during the underwater swim. Assuming they don't drown (20% chance in this example), they make it through the tunnel.

Halfway through the tunnel is the treasure of an unsuccessful swimmer, though the skeleton has long-since washed away. The treasure is a solid gold bust of a merchant patriarch from a nearby kingdom wrapped in canvas. It is worth 900 gp although it is possibly worth more to the merchant house.

AREA 2-16: AN OGRE'S TEARS

A motionless pool of dark water stands on either side of the tunnel, with a narrow gravel path leading between. A water-filled tunnel (see **Area 2-15**) connects one of the pools with **Area 2-1**. A slab of rock at the back of the other does not quite touch the surface of the water, leaving a small pocket of air and darkness beyond. Deep, heavy sobbing can be heard from within this watery cave. This is the hiding place of **Sogrin the ogre**, who was wounded by Gethrax. He ventured into the caverns from downriver looking for a new lair, but Gethrax was not very accepting of his new neighbor. Sogrin goes on the defensive as soon as the party approaches, but fights only if pressed. A gunnysack is tied to his belt.

Sogrin, Ogre: HD 6; HP 40; AC 5[14]; **Atk** club (1d10+1); **Move** 9; **Save** 11; **AL** C; **CL/XP** 6/400; **Special:** none. (*Monstrosities* 356)
> **Equipment:** club, sack containing *potion of extra healing* and *potion of treasure finding*, pouch containing 60 gp, 50 sp, and a dead rat.

Tactics: Sogrin is wounded from his last fight and does not feel like another one just yet. He tries to frighten the party with loud, smelly bellowing and false lunges with his club. If given the opportunity, he flees past the party and hides elsewhere. He is not above making peace with the heroes and even considers joining them to fight Gethrax, if they make such an offer. How long he stays and his overall disposition as an NPC is up to you.

AREA 2-17: THE DEAD MAN'S PARTY

This low-ceilinged cavern stinks of fresh death and the salty-sweet odor of blood. In one corner is the source of the stench: a pile of eviscerated corpses under a cloud of black flies. This is the lair of **Gethrax**. He visits the city regularly, causing havoc here and there and returning with news for his patron, Lilith. He has also trapped Level 1 with his *box o' darkness traps* (see **Appendix C: New Magical Items**), a device crafted by a sinister order. He waits, invisible and bathed in blood, in the far corner behind the bodies. He may know that the party is coming due to the bats in **Area 2-2** being disturbed or from various other events or loud noises.

This area is desecrated, and undead created here receive +1 hit point per hit die and a +1 bonus to attack, damage, and saving throw rolls. Undead within this area have advantage on saving throws against being turned. The bodies (beggars, drunks, harlots, and other "unmissed" types) are the results of Gethrax's deranged anatomical exploration and his blood rituals. Each corpse has a chunk of black stone in its eye socket — they are prepared to be *animated*, and a DC 15 Intelligence (Arcana) check reveals this.

Gethrax, Male Human, Fallen Paladin in service to the Ebon Union (Ftr6/Clr5): HP 61; AC 2[17]; **Atk** *+1 longsword* (1d8+7); **Move** 12; **Save** Ftr 9/Clr 11; **AL** C; **CL/XP** 11/1700; **Special:** +2 to hit and damage strength bonus, +2 save vs. paralysis or poison, banish undead, multiple attacks (6) vs. creatures with 1 or fewer HD, spells (2/2).
> **Spells:** 1st—*cause light wounds* (x2); 2nd—*hold person*, *silence 15ft radius*.
> **Equipment:** *+2 chainmail*, shield, *gauntlets of ogre power*, *+1 longsword*, *box o' darkness trap* (unwound; see **Appendix C: New Magical Items**), *ring of animate dead* (see **Appendix C: New Magical Items**), cursed *ring of invisibility* (ring and hand must be bathed in still-warm blood once a week or it ceases to function for current wearer).

Description: Gethrax was a mercenary fighter who signed on with an evil warband that was hired to hamper the efforts of a holy crusade against a cult of evil priests. Thanks to Gethrax's leadership, the band of paladins and clerics was destroyed before they reached the cult's fortress deep in the Stoneheart Mountains. His success with the mercenaries and his obvious lust for carnage won him a position in the

cult, and he began learning their dark arts for himself. His wanderings have spread evil far and wide in the name of his order, and his pact with Lilith has made him even more dangerous. He serves as her eyes and ears in the city and in the Ebon Union, and he has no compunction about killing for her or anyone else. Eventually, he hopes that her takeover of Dun Eamon will be advantageous for his secret sect.

Tactics: Gethrax prefers to use his *ring of invisibility* to surprise his victims. He waits invisibly at the rear of his chamber, behind the pile of corpses. When the party is at least partially distracted by the corpses, he uses his *ring of animate dead* on the pile to create **2d6 zombies** from the freshest corpses. If all the undead are destroyed (or are about to be), Gethrax turns visible and attacks, a terrible apparition in gore-caked armor. He chooses escape over death if possible, but if given no opportunity for escape, he spends his final round winding up his last *box o' darkness* trap. This *box* animates **2 skeletons** in the area (see **Appendix C: New Magical Items**). While the skeletons attack, Gethrax turns invisible and tries to escape.

Zombies (2d6): HD 2; AC 8[11]; **Atk** strike (1d8); **Move** 6; **Save** 16; **AL** N; **CL/XP** 2/30; **Special:** immune to sleep and charm. (*Monstrosities* 529)

Skeletons (2): HD 1; AC 8[11]; **Atk** strike (1d6); **Move** 12; **Save** 17; **AL** N; **CL/XP** 1/15; **Special:** immune to sleep and charm spells. (*Monstrosities* 428)

AREA 2-18: THE RIVER ROOM

A powerful underground river flows along the back wall of this cavern, and a body lies near it. Across the swift flowing river is a secret door that leads to Level 3, where the Ebon Union has their lair. A small ledge on the far side of the river holds a tunnel entrance that the thieves use to come and go from their lair. It is concealed by drooping strands of algae but is not otherwise secured. The door opens easily. One must cross the river to gain access; the river is 10 feet wide at this point and flows toward **Area 2-22**. The river can be crossed with a successful saving throw.

The thief (whose body holds this room's treasure) was headed for the door when Gethrax surprised him in an unusually malicious mood. The presence of his corpse may help the heroes locate the secret door. On the thief's body is a leather pack containing a jeweled ebony inkpot and pen (40 gp), gold hourglass (100 gp), empty map case with inlaid mother-of-pearl (35 gp), a set of thieves' tools, 50 feet of silk rope, a grappling hook, two daggers, a set leather armor, and a coin pouch containing 6 gp and 10 sp.

AREA 2-19: DARKMANTLES

The corridor widens here, and a deep pool of murky water is on one side, and a small alcove is on the other. A shovel and a crowbar lie half-buried in the middle of the soggy floor. The tools are the leavings of an ill-fated pair of fortune-seekers whose bodies in the pool make up the treasure. Nearby is a shield, a morningstar, a hooded lantern, and a coin purse containing 18 gp and 20 sp. A group of **4 darkmantles** on the ceiling waits for the heroes to investigate the pool, the chamber, or the odd debris, although they are stationed directly above the tools. From the pool, an underwater passage (see **Area 2-21**) leads to **Area 2-23**.

Darkmantles (4): HD 1+2; HP 10, 7, 6, 4; AC 4[15]; **Atk** grab (1d4); **Move** 3 (fly 3); **Save** 17; **AL** N; **CL/XP** 2/30; **Special:** *darkness 15ft radius* (at will), grab (save or 1d4 damage and suffocation), suffocation (automatic 1d4 damage each round after grab). (*Monstrosities* 85)

Tactics: The darkmantles hang hidden over the center of the chamber, indistinguishable from the cave ceiling. If a character enters the center of the area at any time, the darkmantles release their grip on the ceiling and attack. If the initial attacks miss, they use their *darkness 15ft radius* to cover their flight back to the ceiling for another attempt. All of these creatures fight until slain. A character whose vision is obscured by darkmantles or darkness must make a saving throw each round to avoid falling prone (15% chance of falling into pool) and suffering 1d4 points of damage.

AREA 2-20: SLIMED

This low tunnel has many stalactites hanging from the ceiling. In addition to the water dripping down, **green slime** waits here to drop onto unsuspecting parties, usually attacking the second or third person to pass under it. That character immediately notices a burning sensation on exposed flesh as the wet, slimy mass falls from above. A previous victim lies nearly completely buried in the tunnel with a few bits of treasure. The body has a hand axe, a *potion of invisibility*, and a coin pouch containing 8 gp and 20 sp.

Green Slime: Green slime isn't technically a monster, just an extremely dangerous hazard in underground tombs and other such places. Any metal or organic substance it touches begins to turn to green slime (saving throw avoids). It can be killed with fire or extreme cold, and the transformation process can be arrested by the use of a *cure disease* spell. (**Monstrosities** 228)

AREA 2-21: UNDERWATER TUNNEL

This tunnel is full of black water and connects **Area 2-19** to **Area 2-23**. Passing through it safely requires a character to have a swim speed or to roll equal to or below their dexterity on 3d6 three consecutive times. The character takes 1d6 points of damage for each failed check and possibly drowns (cumulative 10% chance per failed check). Thus, a character with 14 dexterity who rolls 10, 15, and 16 takes 2d6 points of damage during the underwater swim. Assuming they don't drown (20% chance in this example), they make it through the tunnel. Characters arriving in **Area 2-23** break the surface in the middle of a very large pile of rats.

AREA 2-22: THE BIG POOL

A great pool of murky water dominates this large cavern. Debris and driftwood are piled up around the edges, where the sheer walls come right down to the water. On the far wall, a swift current runs across the pool to an exit tunnel and pours over what could only be a giant waterfall. A small cave is next to the inlet of the river, but standing water isolates it from the sandy beach at the tunnel entrance.

This pool leads to the exits from this level, but it is difficult to navigate. The fast-moving river current keeps the pool flowing in a whirlpool motion; thus, crossing the room in the water requires a character to roll below his or her dexterity on 4d6. Creatures failing the check are swept into the reach of the **shambling mound** that dwells here (80%) chance or into the current that then pulls them over the falls.

A secret door to **Area 2-24** is located 20 feet above water level on the wall opposite the entrance tunnels. The wind generated in **Area 2-24** causes tendrils of slime concealing the door to move. Characters could climb along the walls (–25% Climb Walls due to the slick walls, or 20% chance for non-thief characters). Anyone falling into the pool is swept back toward the shambling mound near the entry (80% chance) or over the falls.

A narrow ledge begins at the far edge of the waterfall and leads to another exit, but the swift current at the very edge of the waterfall pulls characters over unless they roll below their dexterity on 5d6. Characters caught in the whirlpool's current can attempt to grab the walkway by making the check as they pass it. Otherwise, the go over the falls.

The shambling mound lurks between the entry tunnel and the mouth of **Area 2-23** and may be mistaken for another logjam of floating debris. Despite the name, the creature no longer shambles; it is rooted to the bottom of the pool lest it be swept over the falls. Still, its reach threatens the exits of both tunnels, and nearly everything coming downstream gets swept once around the whirlpool, so it has grown big and lazy. Any treasure the creature might have possessed has been washed away by the swift current (although a great amount of wealth awaits in **Area 2-23**).

Characters might come up with other ways to cross the water, using spells, rafts, or some ingenious tactic. You'll need to judge the success of the attempt.

Shambling Mound: HD 8; **HP** 55; **AC** 1[18]; **Atk** 2 fists (2d8 + enfold); **Move** 6; **Save** 8; **AL** N; **CL/XP** 11/1700; **Special:** enfold (if two fists hit, save or suffocate in 2d4 rounds), resists cold and weapons (50% damage). (***Monstrosities*** 419)

Tactics: The shambling mound has learned the value of patience in waiting for its meals to be delivered by the river current. It waits for the heroes to enter the room, either by the water or perhaps by picking their way across the rafts of driftwood that conceal the beast itself! It cannot move or flee, although clever heroes may decide to apply their energy to dislodging it and forcing it over the falls (which requires dealing 20 points of damage to its underwater extremities).

AREA 2-23:
RATS, RATS, AND MORE RATS

This area, a small cave on the edge of a great pool of water, is simply full of rats. It contains **10 rat swarms**. Area effect spells, oil, and acid are far more effective ways of dealing with their numbers than killing them one by one. Either way, their treasure, which is buried in the corner, can be accessed only if they are all neutralized. The treasure contains an ebony coffer (150 gp) wrapped in canvas containing 24 three-ounce platinum bars (90 gp each) stamped with the mark of a foreign merchant house. Revealing these in the city may have complex political results, but any development is up you. An underwater passage (see **Area 2-21**) leads to **Area 2-23**.

Rat Swarms (10): HD 5; **HP** 37, 33, 32, 28x2, 27, 26, 23, 22x2; **AC** 7[12]; **Atk** swarm (1d6); **Move** 12; **Save** 12; **AL** N; **CL/XP** 5/240; **Special:** 10% of contracting disease.

Tactics: As soon as they notice an infiltrator, the rats rush into a clawing, biting frenzy that does not subside until they are all killed. They do not pursue a character underwater or into the reach of the shambling mound (**Area 2-22**).

AREA 2-24: WATERFALL WELL

This cavern is shaped like a cylinder, nearly 150 feet from top to bottom. The roar of falling water makes conversation in this area impossible, and the air is full of spray. A huge waterfall rushes over a precipice halfway up, crashing 80 feet down to a churning pool. Opposite that, a smaller waterfall exits a small tunnel and trickles down the slimy wall. A narrow ledge looks like it connects the exit of the small tunnel to the edge of the large waterfall. The water below swirls and eddies before flowing out through a large tunnel opening.

This is the final area on this level. The waterfall flows into a deep well leading to Level 4, while a rough path leads to a tunnel to **Area 1-7**. A fall from (or being swept over) this waterfall results in 4d6 points of damage. A character in the pool at the base must roll below their dexterity on 4d6 to escape the incredible force of water or take 1d6 points of damage per round. After 2d4 rounds, objects in the pool are swept downstream toward **Area 4-1**.

CHAPTER SIX: LEVEL 3 – A RIVER RUNS THROUGH IT

This is the third level below the surface, although it may be reached by a direct tunnel from the Ironworks (**Area Q**). The level is made up of the lair of the Ebon Union in an abandoned halfling gatehouse and the tunnels by which it is approached. The tunnels are filled with dangerous creatures, some placed by thieves and others naturally occurring. Opponents on this level include gricks, monstrous spiders, mephits, and an enormous squid. Also present are Lilith's flame-spawned troll and the bulk of the Ebon Union, including their master, Devlin.

A mighty underground river dominates the level, cutting it in half. The approach to the lair of the Ebon Union crosses it several times, and some form of trap or creature protects the crossings. The halfling gatehouse once protected the entrance to the halflings' great underground city, but the entry tunnel has collapsed, leaving a handful of rooms and the halflings' deadly trap corridor to be inhabited by the thieves' guild.

AREA 3-1: ENTRY CHAMBER – THE IRONWORKS TUNNEL

Descent into this spray-dampened chamber lands the heroes on a stone ledge. A sluice channel has been carved into the floor to carry fast-moving icy water through the room to power the huge waterwheel. Past the thundering wheel is a matching ledge on the opposite side of the channel. The sluice is one of several powerful waterways that flow through the bedrock beneath the city. The builders of the forge cut this room out of the stone to access its forceful current to power their wheel, which drives the bellows and water pumps for the forges above. The party must slip through the narrow spaces around the thundering waterwheel and over the sluice itself to proceed; this route requires a character to roll below their dexterity on 4d6. Ropes, poles, ladders, or other items can be used to reduce the danger (and thus roll on 3d6).

<<Level 3: A River Runs Through It Map>>

Any character falling into the water is swept through a low tunnel to be expelled high over the river, where they fall into the river and take 2d6 points of damage. They are then swept downstream into **Area 4-1**, passing below **Area 3-11** on the way. A character falling into the sluice upstream from the wheel has the added pleasure of being crushed before falling into the river, taking 4d6 points of damage (or half that amount with a successful saving throw).

The far side of the room is the same 10-foot-wide ledge as the area at the base of the ladder. From here, five tunnels lead off in various directions. A poem Ulf Ironfist carved on the wall upstairs in **Area Q-8** reveals which one to take: the second from the right. The others lead to various dangerous traps and encounters that are not without reward, but do not take the heroes any closer to their goal.

AREA 3-2: A WILD RIDE

This tunnel seems to dead-end as the party moves around a corner. The end of the tunnel actually occupies the space directly over the sluice tunnel from **Area 3-1**. A **pit trap** here drops characters directly into the fast-moving flow and carries them swiftly to be expelled in a long freefall into the river gorge near **Area 3-13**. Falling into the river in this way inflicts 3d6 points of damage. Characters are then swept downstream into **Area 4-1**, passing below **Area 3-11** on the way.

AREA 3-3: SECRET DOOR

This small round chamber appears completely empty, but it hides a **secret door** to the location of the romantic union between Lilith and some of her victims. The ground is covered with loose stone rubble (from carving the doors).

AREA 3-4: STIRGE CAVE

A number of leathery-skinned **stirges** hang near the ceiling of this chamber. The blood-drained corpse of a guild prisoner lies bound at the back of the area, the result of a painful interrogation process involving the bloodsucking beasts. He is dressed in common clothing, but an astute character might notice his boots are unusually well made. In hidden compartments in the heels of his boots are the items the Ebon Union was after — the only treasure to be found here.

Stirges (7): HD 1+1; **HP** 6x2, 5x3, 4x2; **AC** 7[12]; **Atk** proboscis (1d3 + blood drain); **Move** 3 (fly 18); **Save** 17; **AL** N; **CL/XP** 2/30; **Special:** +2 to hit bonus, blood drain (automatic 1d4 after hit). (**Monstrosities** 461)

Tactics: The stirges attack as soon as they have reason to believe prey is below. They are deterred only by smoke; if it is introduced, they retreat to another area.

Treasure: Leather boots with secret compartments in the heels (sized to fit adult human male; worth 30 gp); three uncut sapphires (250 gp, 225 gp, and 200 gp, or quadruple that when cut and polished); a tiny map with landmarks but no names, except a drawing of a gem labeled "Temple of the Azure Eye." This map and the short adventure that goes with it are available as free downloads at *www.necromancergames.com*.

AREA 3-5: DIRE RATS

This small side-chamber is empty, but a deep hole in the back wall ends in shadows. It is full of **8 giant rats**, their non-combatant young, and a few bits of treasure.

Giant Rats (8): HD 1d4hp; **HP** 4x2, 3x3, 2x3; **AC** 7[12]; **Atk** bite (1d3); **Move** 12; **Save** 18; **AL** N; **CL/XP** A/5; **Special:** 5% are diseased. (**Monstrosities** 384)

Tactics: The giant rats attack as soon as someone begins exploring the entrance to their lair, most likely flying into the face of a single curious explorer. When six of them are killed, the remaining rats back into their lair and defend their offspring or flee into the dungeon.

Treasure: Human ear with pearl earring (120 gp), silvered dagger.

AREA 3-6: YELLOW MOLD

This room smells dry and musty and is bare of anything of interest except for a small, fungus-covered chest in the corner. The chest is contaminated with **yellow mold** just waiting to be disturbed. The chest was left as an emergency cache by a party of adventurers that did not

Level 3: A River Runs Through It

Entrances: The basement of the Ironworks (**Area Q-8**) has a secret passage to **Area 3-1**. Tunnels from **Area 1-6** and **Area 2-18** converge in **Area 3-9**.

Exits: The river flows over a waterfall to **Area 4-1**. The passage from **Area 3-29** leads to **Area 4-3**.

Wandering Monsters: Most of the creatures on this level have lairs and move around very little. As a result, most of the wandering monster encounters are with minor creatures or with thieves on their way in or out of the lair. Roll 1d20 every hour or after a loud event.

1d20	Encounter
1–2	**1d4 giant rats** (subtract from **Area 3-5**)
3–4	**Ebon Union thief** (shifter or cutpurse)
5–6	**Ebon Union gang** (1d4 knives, 1d3 bolts, and 1d2 thugs)
7	**Monstrous Spider** (subtract from **Area 3-11**)
8–20	No Encounter

Giant Rats: HD 1d4hp; AC 7[12]; **Atk** bite (1d3); **Move** 12; **Save** 18; **AL** N; **CL/XP** A/5; **Special:** 5% are diseased. (*Monstrosities* 384)

Bolt, Male or Female Human (Thf2): HP 2d4; AC 7[12]; **Atk** dagger (1d4) or light crossbow (1d4+1); **Move** 12; **Save** 14; **AL** C; **CL/XP** 2/30; **Special:** +2 save bonus vs. traps and magical devices, backstab (x2), thieving skills.
Thieving Skills: Climb 86%, Tasks/Traps 20%, Hear 3 in 6, Hide 15%, Silent 25%, Locks 15%.
Equipment: leather armor, 2 daggers, light crossbow, 20 bolts, pouch of caltrops (1d4 damage, halves movement in 10ft-diameter area), pouch with 1d8 gp and 2d10 sp.

Cutpurse, Male or Female Human (Thf2): HP 2d4; AC 7[12]; **Atk** dagger (1d4); **Move** 12; **Save** 14; **AL** C; **CL/XP** 2/30; **Special:** +2 save bonus vs. traps and magical devices, backstab (x2), thieving skills.
Thieving Skills: Climb 86%, Tasks/Traps 20%, Hear 3 in 6, Hide 15%, Silent 25%, Locks 15%.
Equipment: leather armor, 2 daggers, pouch of caltrops (1d4 damage, halves movement in 10ft-diameter area), pouch with 2d10 gp and 2d10 sp.

Giant Spider (6ft diameter): HD 4+2; AC 4[15]; **Atk** bite (1d6+2 + poison); **Move** 4; **Save** 13; **AL** C; **CL/XP** 7/600; **Special:** lethal poison (save or die), webs (save to avoid becoming stuck). (*Monstrosities* 451)

Knife, Male or Female Human (Thf1): HP 1d4; AC 7[12]; **Atk** dagger (1d4); **Move** 12; **Save** 15; **AL** C; **CL/XP** 1/15; **Special:** +2 save bonus vs. traps and magical devices, backstab (x2), thieving skills.
Thieving Skills: Climb 85%, Tasks/Traps 15%, Hear 3 in 6, Hide 10%, Silent 20%, Locks 10%.
Equipment: leather armor, 2 daggers, pouch of caltrops (1d4 damage, halves movement in 10ft-diameter area), pouch with 1d4 gp and 2d6 sp, 10 % chance of a small pouch of powdered silver skimmed from a previous heist (worth 1d4 gp).

Shifter, Male or Female Human (Thf2): HP 2d4; AC 7[12]; **Atk** dagger (1d4); **Move** 12; **Save** 14; **AL** C; **CL/XP** 2/30; **Special:** +2 save bonus vs. traps and magical devices, backstab (x2), thieving skills.
Thieving Skills: Climb 86%, Tasks/Traps 20%, Hear 3 in 6, Hide 15%, Silent 25%, Locks 15%.
Equipment: leather armor, net, 2 daggers, pouch of caltrops (1d4 damage, halves movement in 10ft-diameter area), scales, pouch with 2d10 gp and 2d10 sp, 10% chance of a small pouch of powdered silver skimmed from a previous heist (worth 2d4 gp).

Thug, Male or Female Human: HD 1; AC 6[13]; **Atk** short sword (1d6) or club (1d6), dagger (1d4); **Move** 12; **Save** 17; **AL** C; **CL/XP** 1/15; **Special:** none. (*Monstrosities* 254)
Equipment: leather armor, short sword or club, dagger, small wooden shield, pouch with 1d4 gp and 2d6 sp.

Shielding: The deep halfling stronghold is shielded with lead barriers. No magical detection or transportation is possible through the perimeter walls. The trap corridor is shielded as well, preventing detection and transportation magic within it.

Detections: The level radiates evil, although not to any overpowering degree.

Continuous Effects: The tunnels here are mostly dry, the water having drained off into the river. The reflected sunlight from the surface is far behind, as is the phosphorescent fungal growth; unless the party provides its own light, this area is in total darkness. The exception are the areas occupied by the Ebon Union, which are lit with torches or small fires.

Standard Features: In the tunnels, the walls, floors, and ceilings are all rough, unworked stone. These tunnels and chambers average 10 feet high, unless otherwise indicated. The river gorge is 100 feet from ceiling to water level on average, and the depth of the river averages 15 feet. The lair of the Ebon Union features the exquisite craftsmanship of the deep halflings: flawlessly fitted stone floors and walls with smooth stone ceilings. In these areas, overhead clearance is only seven feet, unless otherwise indicated. All interior doors are of worked stone and open inward.

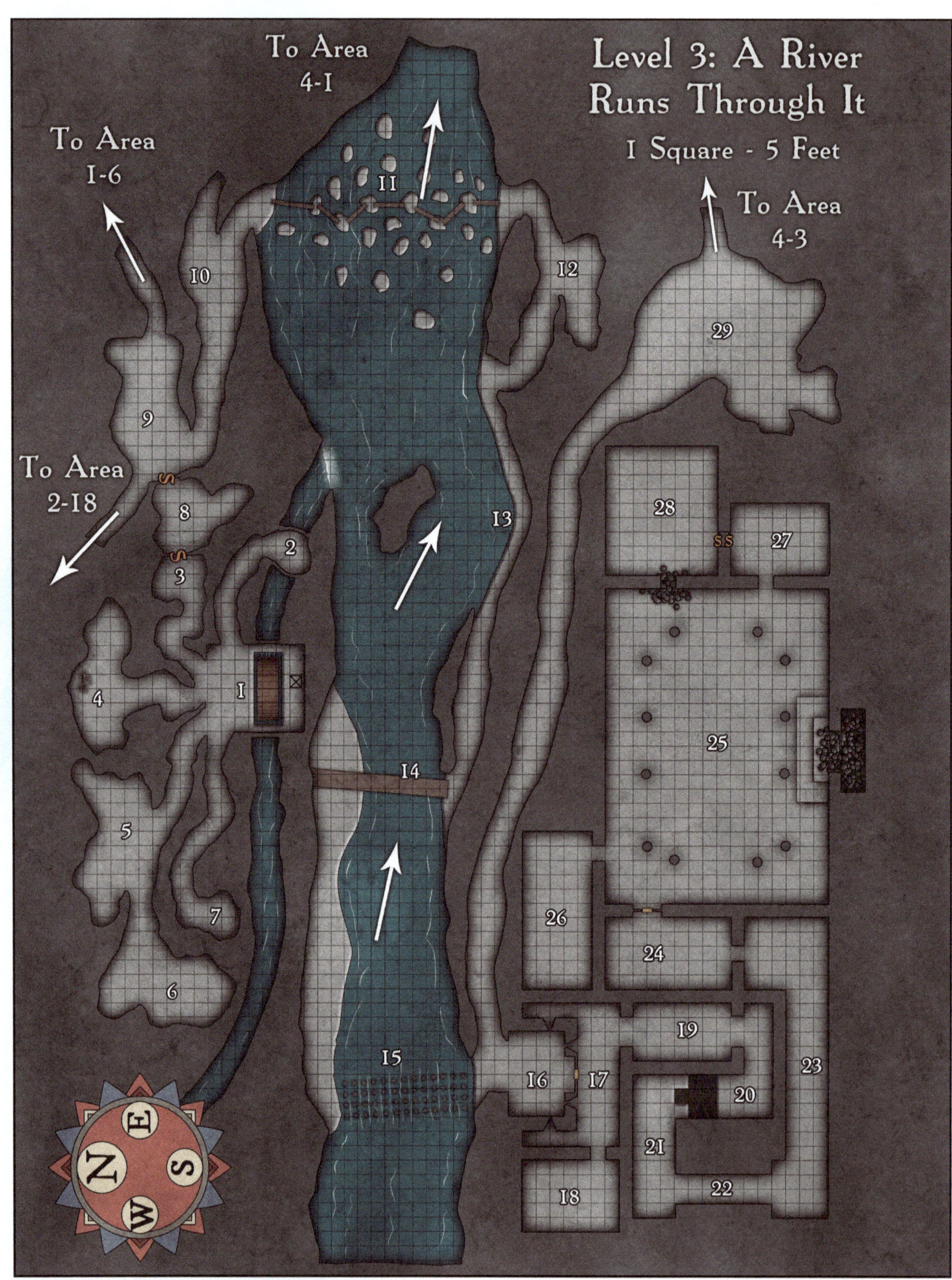

To Area 4-1
To Area 1-6
Level 3: A River Runs Through It
1 Square - 5 Feet
To Area 4-3
10
11
12
29
9
To Area 2-18
8
S
2
3
S
13
28
S S
27
4
1
14
25
5
26
7
24
19
6
23
15
16
17
20
21
22
18
N E S W

survive to retrieve it. It contains four flasks of oil, a hooded lantern, 10 torches, 50 feet of silk rope, 200 feet of cotton cord, a clay jug of water (stale), and four *potions of healing*.

Yellow Mold: HD n/a; AC n/a; Atk 1d6 damage + spore cloud; Move 0; Save n/a; AL N; CL/XP 3/60; Special: poisonous spore cloud (10ft diameter cloud, save or die), vulnerable to fire (destroys mold). (*Monstrosities* 336)

AREA 3-7: PIT TRAP

The tunnel appears to dead-end as the party turns a corner. In actuality, the last few feet of the corridor is a **concealed pit trap**. Anyone stepping on the trap has a 2-in-6 chance of springing it and falling into a 40-foot-deep pit and takes 4d6 points of damage.

AREA 3-8: THE LOVE SHACK

This area is at the end of the second tunnel from the right in **Area 3-1**: the only one of the five that leads somewhere productive. The tunnel opens into a small cavern that is musky with the smell of incense. Near the back, dozens of candles surround a pile of luxurious pillows and cushions and a small alabaster table. A complex mechanism of iron bars and latches is mounted to large slabs of rock that cover the tunnel entrances.

This chamber is one of the locations of the covert trysts between Lilith and Ulf Ironfist. Ulf manufactured the secret doors for Lilith to protect their cozy little hideaway. If the heroes come directly from the Ironworks, they are looking at the back of it; if they came from Levels 1 or 2, they probably detected it from outside.

Treasure: Alabaster table (90 lbs., 800 gp); jade incense burner and box of imported incense (550 gp); 10 silk pillows (7 gp each); jug of strong, high-quality dwarven mead (8 gp).

AREA 3-9: ENTRY CHAMBER — TUNNELS FROM LEVEL 1 AND 2

If the party descends to this level from Level 1 or 2, this is the chamber that it enters. The Ebon Union uses it as a storeroom and staging area, especially when they coordinate activities from more than one location. A rough map of Dun Eamon is sketched on one wall in chalk; the locations of the burglaries, the garrison, the tavern, and all the entrances to the underground are clearly marked. A well-made secret door conceals the exit to **Area 3-8** and the Ironworks access point.

AREA 3-10: GRICK LAIR

At this point, the narrow tunnel splits into two that seem to run parallel. Several sets of assorted tracks lead up the left-hand passage. A ranger has a 4-in-6 chance to notice flaws in the tracks: a dwarven stride is too long, a footprint is reversed, and so forth. All others have a 1-in-6 chance. An unusually intelligent pair of **gricks** that dwell here has intentionally laid these tracks. Fewer visible tracks go down the righthand tunnel due to a smaller quantity of dust.

The passage to the left narrows to little more than a crack but is long enough for the whole party to squeeze into before they realize it. In the back of the crack is a pile of grisly human remains, mostly lower legs and feet with boots and shoes held on by entrails and strips of flesh. The gricks use these to lure prey into their lair.

Once the party is inside, the gricks strike at the last party member in line. Their lair is on a hidden ledge above the chamber. On the ledge with the gricks is the body of a recent victim, a thief from the Ebon Union. The corpse possesses a *charm of silence* (see **Appendix C: New Magical Items**) that masks the sounds of the gricks. The remaining treasure is stored on the ledge behind the creatures.

Gricks: HD 4; HP 30, 23; AC 4[15]; Atk 4 tentacles (1d4), beak (1d6); Move 6; Save 13; AL N; CL/XP 6/400; Special: immune to blunt weapons. (*Monstrosities* 230)

Tactics: The gricks strike as soon as they judge the party has fully entered the chamber. The smaller grick lowers the corpse of the thief, using its area of *silence* to envelop the last character in line. The large one attempts to grab the character with its tentacles (a successful to-hit roll) and drag it up onto the ledge. Once the victim is on the ledge and silenced, both creatures turn to the attack. Unless that character finds a way to announce his plight to his comrades, he may not last long against both creatures.

Treasure: *charm of silence* (see **Appendix C: New Magical Items**), *+1 short sword*, large sack of powdered silver (45 gp).

AREA 3-11: CAVERN OF SPIRES

The smooth-walled tunnel opens abruptly into a huge cavern here that is roughly 100 feet across. The floor drops away over a steep cliff a few feet into the cavern, and whatever lies below is hidden by thick mist. Several dozen rough stone spires rise up from the mist, a series of stone islands in a sea of grey fog. On the opposite side of the cavern, a small ledge is visible, as well as a narrow tunnel entrance. Heavy wooden beams have been laid across the tops of the spires to form a makeshift walkway that leads to the mouth of the other tunnel. The sound of roaring water can be heard from far below.

The thieves' guild adapted this area to serve as the outer line of defense for their lair. The carefully-laid board walkway is a **trap** rigged to collapse under the weight of intruders and spill them into the web of the **monstrous spiders** imported from the forests outside the city. The spiders' treasure is found at the base of a large spire in the center of the chasm, along with the body of its previous owner, a guild thief who had stopped off for a few pints after a heist one night and took a bad step while returning to the lair.

Crossing the cavern by leaping from stone to stone is possible, as many of the thieves do. This method requires a character to roll below their dexterity on 3d6 to avoid falling. Characters must make one check for each jump, and seven attempts are required to cross the cavern. When the thieves must carry heavy objects across the chasm, they retrieve the boards stored in **Area 3-12**. The surface of the fog lies 10 feet below the tops of the spires, the spiders' webs are 10 feet below that, and another 60 feet farther down is the rushing underground river. Characters falling into the river take 2d6 points of damage. The river carries them through a low tunnel to **Area 4-1**.

Anyone trying to cross on the beams must deal with the trap set by the Ebon Union. The four-inch-square beams have been rigged to collapse. The first two beams are secure, but the third has been hollowed out; it appears the same as the others from above, but can hold only 150 pounds before snapping. A character can successfully leap toward the nearest spire by rolling below their dexterity on 4d6. Anyone falling lands in the spider web below. The rest of the beams are secure.

Giant Spider (1ft diameter) (8): HD 1+1; HP 9, 8x2, 7x3, 5x2; AC 8[11]; Atk bite (1hp + poison); Move 9; Save 17; AL N; CL/XP 3/60; Special: lethal poison (save or die, +2 saving throw). (*Monstrosities* 451)

Giant Spider (6ft diameter) (2): HD 4+2; HP 31, 27; AC 4[15]; Atk bite (1d6+2 + poison); Move 4; Save 13; AL C; CL/XP 7/600; Special: lethal poison (save or die), webs (save to avoid becoming stuck). (**Monstrosities** 451)

Treasure: Leather armor, short sword, dagger, satchel containing a pouch of silver dust worth 15 gp, a pouch of coins (8 gp, 19 sp, 12 cp), a tobacco pipe and a silver flask (12 gp) half full of cheap brandy. In the bottom of the flask are 3 jade beads (12 gp each).

AREA 3-12: STORAGE CAVE

This area is full of flea-infested grain sacks, empty casks, and other junk. The thieves store things here on the off chance they might come in handy. Several 10-foot beams kept here are used for carrying heavy items across the chasm in **Area 3-11**.

Also present in this area is the body of Tell, Elinda Bannon's pet owl. Tell was killed elsewhere in the dungeon, and Esme brought his body here (see **Area 3-13**).

AREA 3-13: MEPHIT GALLERY

The claustrophobic tunnel gives way to a narrow ledge that snakes along the cliff high above the fog-shrouded river. The ledge is two feet wide and can be traversed without incident, provided the heroes are not distracted by combat or other events. During combat on the ledge, characters must make a saving throw to avoid falling.

Characters who listen hear the sound of flapping wings, like some flying creature swooping through the darkness. The creature is **Esme**, a **smoke mephit**. Her history is intertwined with the other creatures in this encounter: a pair of **fire mephits** named **Iktor** and **Vlaus**, who have prepared a **trap** for the party. They have a small treasure stored on top of the isolated rock spire where they harass adventurers and thieves from out of reach. Esme has no desire to attack the characters, only to watch them or something else die. She likes to get to know the victims of an imminent accident or ambush, and she approaches the party if permitted.

> A small winged humanoid creature settles down onto the ledge in your path. Her slender figure is the color of smoke. She looks up at your party, a tragic little figure with an expression of morose curiosity.
>
> "Have you dealt in death today?" she asks morbidly. "I can sense it on you …"

Esme's obsession with death has kept her from leaving the other mephits, though she despises them for their mischievous attitudes. They manage to create enough carnage to fulfill her requirement for death, but she would just as happily watch them die as well. The party intrigues her, and she flies about pestering them about their acts of violence and asking how painful various deaths were until they reach the halfway point of the ledge. She stops suddenly and informs the party, "Oh, um, the others will try to kill you now," and flies away to watch the show.

The fire mephits attached four large rocks to chains on the cavern ceiling and release them to swing across the 30-foot gap and slam into the ledge. The rocks attack as a 5HD creature and do 2d6 points of damage. Characters who are struck must make a saving throw to avoid being knocked off the ledge. Characters falling from the ledge into the river take 3d6 points of damage and are swept over the waterfall into **Area 4-1**, passing below **Area 3-11** on the way.

Esme, Smoke Mephit: HD 2; HP 13; AC 4[15]; Atk 2 claws (1d2); **Move** 12 (fly 18); **Save** 16; **AL** N; **CL/XP** 2/30; **Special:** breath weapon (15ft cone, 1d4 damage, save or eyes burn for 3 rounds, −2 to hit), immune to fire, summon mephit (1/day, 25% chance to summon smoke mephit). (***The Tome of Horrors Complete*** 380)

Iktor and Vlaus, Fire Mephits: HD 3; HP 22, 20; AC 5[14]; Atk 2 fiery touches (1d3+1); **Move** 12 (fly 20); **Save** 14; **AL** C; **CL/XP** 5/240; **Special:** spit fire (3/day, 20ft range, 1d8+1, save for half), gaseous form. (***Monstrosities*** 327)

Tactics: Iktor and Vlaus attack from their prepared position on top of a tall spire in the middle of the river gorge. The spire is 30 feet away, and the fiery little figures can be seen dancing in excitement on the top. On the first round of combat, they release the chained rocks to swing into the ledge where the heroes stand, hoping to reduce their numbers and have a good laugh. The boulders continue to swing, coming close to the ledge every other round but losing momentum in each successive round. They could be used by heroes to cross to the mephits' spire. The mephits do not engage the heroes in melee unless they appear badly weakened. If they lose more than 75% of their hit points or if any mephit dies, the rest flee.

Esme, as indicated, bears no ill will toward the party, but she does hope that they either kill something in a spectacular fashion or die excitingly themselves. She can actually be a quite morbid little cheerleader throughout the conflict. She fights back if attacked, but does not flee if there is no immediate danger to her; she would rather watch the dying mephits/heroes expire.

Treasure: *potion of fire resistance*, half melted silver ingot worth 60 gp, pouch of 35 gold coins painted copper (35 gp).

Development: Esme, Iktor, and Vlaus were called using *Mamuthek's Aperture*. Lilith used a chip of obsidian as the material component, hoping for a fire elemental or something equivalent. Instead, she got Iktor and Vlaus, much to her disappointment. Esme was drawn into the bargain because of the layer of soot that Lilith failed to remove from the obsidian. Furious, Lilith expelled the mephits from the

lowest level of the dungeon, warning them to stay out of her way and not to attack or hinder the Ebon Union. The mephits have followed her orders out of fear, although they periodically "help" one of the thieves to his death. They know that Lilith's lair is on Level 4, but they are not aware of the greater plot or the events in the city. Esme, if she survives, can relate much of this information to the party; she thinks it unimportant, but she has no reason to withhold it. She may also accompany the heroes if they tolerate her company, as she sees them as a good source of death and suffering.

Area 3-14:
Bridge Over Foggy Waters

Nothing is unusual or dangerous about this sturdy hemp bridge, although it sways and creaks ominously with every step. On the far side, an iron ladder of individual rungs has been bolted to the wall. It descends to a narrow, gravelly beach at water level. This beach runs only one direction: along the chasm wall toward **Area 3-15**.

Area 3-15: Calamari, Anyone?

The beach narrows and disappears near the evidence of a bridge that once spanned the underground river. The waterway is wide, swift, and shallow, swirling around stone pylons that are arranged in rows of four all the way across. A large barrel of some stinking liquid stands on the beach with a bucket next to it, and a matching barrel is visible across the river.

This is the ruin of a halfling bridge. Identifying it as such may tell the heroes that they are close to the stronghold. A **large cave squid** defends this area. It lives in the swift-moving water downstream from the bridge, hanging on to the pylons with its tentacles to resist the force of the water. The barrels contain a strong tanning solution that the squid finds unpleasant. By flinging a bucket of it into the water upstream, the heroes can compel the squid to protect its sensory organs and thus make it safe to sneak by. This has no effect on the squid during combat, when hunger overcomes instinct.

Hopping from one pylon to the next is easy, although characters have a 10% chance of slipping (and then must make a saving throw to avoid falling into the river). The river is 50 feet wide at this point, so characters must make two checks to cross in this manner. During combat on the pylons, any failed attack requires the character to make a saving throw to keep from stumbling and falling into the water. Anyone hit by the squid must also make the saving throw to stay on a pylon.

Large Cave Squid: HD 6; HP 42; AC 7[12] head and tentacles; 3[16] body; **Atk** 10 tentacles (1d3); **Move** 0 (swim 9 or jet 27); **Save** 11; **AL** N; **CL/XP** 11/1700; **Special:** jet (move 27), ink cloud (as *darkness 15ft radius*), constrict (after tentacle hits, automatic 1d6 damage, 25% chance to pinion random limb). (*Monstrosities* 457)

Tactics: The squid attacks as soon as there are characters halfway across the pylons. Two of its arms are committed to holding itself in position against the current; of its remaining eight arms, it uses four for feeding and four for attacks. The four feeding arms wrap around characters and drag them to its mouth on the following round. The four attacking arms bludgeon characters for 1d3 points of damage.

If the arms holding onto the pylons are located and severed, the squid can make a saving throw to reallocate its arms to hold it in place. If both anchoring arms are severed and the squid fails the saving throw, it tumbles away downstream.

On the far side of the bridge, the tunnel turns back downstream toward **Area 3-29**, and **Area 3-16** is readily visible just ahead.

Area 3-16: Entry Alcove

This small area is carved from solid rock and adorned with images of halfling culture. If the party has not yet encountered any thieves on this level, the alcove is unthreatened. If a randomly encountered guild member or members survived, then four Bolts man **Area 3-17**. An iron door protects the entrance to the halflings' gatehouse.

Area 3-17: Gatehouse

If the party engaged thieves on this level but allowed survivors to escape, they returned to their lair with a report and the level of security has increased. If Devlin learns (presumably from survivors) that a party of adventurers is making its way down the tunnels, he posts **4 bolts** in this area (though they tend to post a single lookout and retire to **Area 3-18**). Subtract these thieves from the total in **Area 3-25**. Devlin keeps the heightened watch for 24 hours or until he has reason to believe the threat has passed. The thieves fire their crossbows at anyone not announcing themselves as loyal servants of the Ebon Union. If the sentries do not know the interlopers, they summon reinforcements and Devlin from within the lair.

Bolts, Male or Female Human (Thf2) (4): HP 8, 6x2, 5;
AC 7[12]; **Atk** dagger (1d4) or light crossbow (1d4+1); **Move** 12; **Save** 14; **AL** C; **CL/XP** 2/30; **Special:** +2 save bonus vs. traps and magical devices, backstab (x2), thieving skills. (see **Appendix A: NPCs**)
Thieving Skills: Climb 86%, Tasks/Traps 20%, Hear 3 in 6, Hide 15%, Silent 25%, Locks 15%.
Equipment: leather armor, 2 daggers, light crossbow, 20 bolts, pouch of caltrops (1d4 damage, halves movement in 10ft-diameter area), pouch with 1d8 gp and 2d10 sp.

Tactics: If the crossbowmen are here, then the party is expected. As soon as they become aware of the characters, the crossbowmen set up a lethal crossfire from the arrow slits, focusing on anyone trying to open the door. If the door opens, one of them tries to escape into **Area 3-19** to warn Devlin while the others cover his retreat. If half of them are killed, the others withdraw through the series of traps to make a report and prepare for the party as a group.

Area 3-18: Guardroom

This room used to house a small unit of halfling guards to man the gatehouse, but now it is set up to accommodate a few thieves who might be assigned to watch the entrance. An upturned crate serves as a card table, and numerous empty bottles are strewn around the room. The deck of cards has six aces.

Area 3-19: Spelling It Out

A soft, ambient glow lights this rectangular room. Stone tiles etched with letters and strange, unrecognizable icons cover most of the floor. A large slab of marble set into one wall bears an inscription, with something scrawled next to it in charcoal. In this chamber is the first of several traps and puzzles the heroes must overcome to gain access to the Ebon Union's lair. Since the lair is in the gatehouse of an ancient deep halfling stronghold, the engineers found it easier to recondition some of the halfling traps rather than create their own.

The floor here is divided into a series of stone tiles, each with a different letter or symbol on it. The letters come from every alphabet imaginable: Dwarven, Elven, Common, Infernal, Celestial, and so on. Only certain tiles can bear the weight of a person, and a riddle on the wall indicates which ones. On a marble slab recessed into the wall are four lines of text in halfling, but written using the Dwarven script. On the wall next to the marble slab, someone has written the Common translation in charcoal.

> *To find the way to city deep*
> *Follow the host into his keep*
> *But tread with caution lest you name*
> *An enemy and lose the game.*

This fairly straightforward riddle suggests that the tiles that spell out the name of the host are safe, which they are. The heroes, however, must puzzle out whose stronghold they are in. The party can do this by considering the text, analyzing the craftsmanship of the chamber, or by recalling rumors from the city. Halflings, dwarves, and elves have a 4-in-6 chance to know this information from the construction of the place. Furthermore, the answer ("halfling") must be spelled out using the Dwarven runes on the floor (just as the clue was written in Dwarven despite being the Halfling language).

If any tiles other than the Dwarven runes that spell out "halfling" in halfling are touched, the trap is triggered. When an incorrect tile is stepped on, all the tiles in a five-foot square area around the triggering tile collapse into a pit, including any otherwise correct tiles. The tiles are six inches square. Moving across the room requires three such checks. The bottom of the pit is hidden by magical *darkness* and *silence*. Anyone falling into the pit takes 4d6 points of damage from the fall.

Area 3-20: Illusionary Hallway Pincushion Trap

This rectangular chamber is lit like the first. A pit is in the floor whose bottom is lost in darkness. On the far side of the pit is the doorway in the wall, surrounded by age-tarnished spikes. There is no ledge at the threshold, only the hallways beyond. The doorway and corridor image is an **illusion trap**; that space on the wall is actually solid stone covered in sharp spikes. The visible spikes are illusions as well, for they cover the actual doorways to the corridors, one on either side of the spike field. The most likely initial response is a running jump into the concealed spikes. But actually, the only way in is to jump through the illusionary spikes and land in the hallway.

The jump itself is not very difficult, but the consequences are dangerous. The pit is 10 feet across and 15 feet wide (the width of the area). A jumping character needs to make a saving throw to clear the pit. If a character hits the real spikes, he or she is pierced by 1d4 spikes and takes 1d4+1 points of damage per spike. They must also make a saving throw to hold onto the spikes to avoid falling backward into the pit for 4d6 points of damage. Leaping into the illusionary spikes sends a characters skidding into the hallway beyond. The bottom of the pit is hidden by magical *darkness* and *silence*.

Area 3-21: Disassembled Trap

This area is cluttered with shattered chunks of stone, bent iron rods, gears, and vicious-looking blades. A doorway is on the far side of the rubble. The engineers of the Ebon Union were unable to determine the function and application of this trap and had to destroy it.

Area 3-22: Shocking Developments

This stretch of hallway is floored with simple grey and green marble tiles. There are 50 of them, in 10 rows of 5, set in no obvious pattern or order. Scrawled charcoal writing in Common is on the wall, but there is corresponding halfling script. A door is at the far end. This open expanse of hallway is **trapped**, and the charcoal writing on the wall again reminds the thieves (some of whom are not especially sharp) how to enter safely. The black scrawl near the door reads:

> *Foolish feet that walk astray*
> *Bring bolts of lightning from the floor*
> *Escape a frightening crisping — go*
> *Where every other went before*

Perhaps this is some halfling riddle used to grant safe passage, but when the Ebon Union restored it to operation for their purposes, such trivialities were done away with and they periodically reset the tiles in a completely random fashion. What is important is the arrangement of the pressure-plate triggers beneath the tiles, which are still arranged in the original halfling layout: a checkerboard grid. The clue in the rhyme is "where *every other* went before," meaning that *every other* tile is trapped, regardless of color. By starting directly opposite the entrance and skipping every other tile, a character can proceed unharmed with no checks at all. The first tile opposite the door is green and all the others in that row are grey; the party may have found a scrap of paper in **Area 1-3** that refers to this. There are an equal number of grey and green tiles because they used to be laid out in the checkerboard pattern, so counting tiles may help solve the puzzle (25 of each color). Stepping on a pressure plate deals 2d6 points of electrical damage (save for half damage).

Area 3-23: Halfling Barbecue

This corridor is longer and narrower than most, tiled rather simply compared to the last chamber. The air smells thickly of something aged and earthy, and the corridor turns a corner at the far end. The area beneath the floor is filled with a **natural gas trap**, and a character might recognize it as smelling like swamp gas. The simple stone tiles have wide cracks in between, which allows the gas to seep up. If an open flame is carried over the tiles, the gas ignites and flares up between the cracks in a spectacular wall of flame.

The halflings solved their problem with the sensitivity of the gas by causing the doorway from **Area 3-22** to extinguish all non-magical fires brought through it (torches, lanterns, candles, and so forth). Conveniently, this allows parties to proceed safely into the darkness without igniting the gas.

Yet the magic extinguishes only open flames, not sparks. If a character attempts to relight his torch with flint and steel or otherwise creates a source of ignition, the gas explodes, causing 6d6 points of fire damage to all characters within 30 feet of the blast (or half that amount with a successful saving throw).

Area 3-24: Antechamber

The chamber at the end of the series of trapped hallways is wider by several feet and is unlit. A large iron door is on one side. Stacked against the walls are several long poles, a few polearms, ladders, coils of rope, and some small casks and crates. This is the anteroom to the halflings' gate chamber (**Area 3-25**). The only treasure is the collection of items that the Ebon Union needs only during their forays to the surface or items they have not yet brought into their lair.

Treasure: Canvas bundle with 4 polearms, two 100-foot coils of hemp rope, 20 torches, cord of firewood, miner's pick, shovel, two buckets, and a cask of ale (10 gp).

Area 3-25: Gates to the Deep

This chamber was the focal point of the old halfling stronghold, as it held the massive stone gates to their underground community. In events that may or may not have been connected to the halflings' departure, the tunnel beyond the gates collapsed, sealing off access to their city and isolating the gatehouse complex. The gatehouse stood empty for untold years before the Ebon Union discovered it. The room is easily three times the height of the corridor that approached it, and massive, ornately carved columns support its vaulted ceiling. A stone ledge runs all the way around the room at a height of 10 feet. On one wall, a pair of enormous doors stands wide open, revealing piles of rock and rubble beyond. The chamber is obviously in use as a makeshift dormitory and mess hall; pallet beds, hammocks, trestle tables, and cooking fires contrast sharply with the stately stone edifices.

This room is a significant encounter, most likely a showdown with the core of the Ebon Union thieves' guild. If the Ebon Union is expecting trouble (probably because a thief escaped a previous encounter and made it back), they have used the time to prepare a nice welcome for the party. If the party manages a stealthy approach to the lair (that is, without encountering any thieves or triggering any of the traps in **Areas 3-19, 3-20, 3-22, 3-23**), then they may catch the thieves at rest and off their guard. The encounter is structured based on the high probability of the former; if the party achieves complete surprise, a few modifications may be necessary.

If the thieves are aware of the heroes' approach, they have taken up positions in hiding around the room and in adjacent chambers. The **bolts** and **nets** occupy the high ledge, hidden by shadows, pillars, or piles of trash and bedding. The **knives** are hidden around the lower portion of the room, under tables, in beds, behind crates, and so on.

Bolt, Male or Female Human (Thf2) (6): HP 8, 7, 6x3, 4; AC 7[12]; **Atk** dagger (1d4) or light crossbow (1d4+1); **Move** 12; **Save** 14; **AL** C; **CL/XP** 2/30; **Special:** +2 save bonus vs. traps and magical devices, backstab (x2), thieving skills. (see **Appendix A: NPCs**)
Thieving Skills: Climb 86%, Tasks/Traps 20%, Hear 3 in 6, Hide 15%, Silent 25%, Locks 15%.
Equipment: leather armor, 2 daggers, light crossbow, 20 bolts, pouch of caltrops (1d4 damage, halves movement in 10ft-diameter area), pouch with 1d8 gp and 2d10 sp.

Cutpurse, Male or Female Human (Thf2) (2): HP 6, 4; AC 7[12]; **Atk** dagger (1d4); **Move** 12; **Save** 14; **AL** C; **CL/XP** 2/30; **Special:** +2 save bonus vs. traps and magical devices, backstab (x2), thieving skills. (see **Appendix A: NPCs**)
Thieving Skills: Climb 86%, Tasks/Traps 20%, Hear 3 in 6, Hide 15%, Silent 25%, Locks 15%.
Equipment: leather armor, 2 daggers, pouch of caltrops (1d4 damage, halves movement in 10ft-diameter area), pouch with 2d10 gp and 2d10 sp.

Knives, Male or Female Human (Thf1) (5): HP 4, 3x2, 2, 1;
AC 7[12]; **Atk** dagger (1d4); **Move** 12; **Save** 15;
AL C; **CL/XP** 1/15; **Special:** +2 save bonus vs. traps
and magical devices, backstab (x2), thieving skills. (see
Appendix A: NPCs)
Thieving Skills: Climb 85%, Tasks/Traps 15%, Hear 3 in 6,
Hide 10%, Silent 20%, Locks 10%.
Equipment: leather armor, 2 daggers, pouch of caltrops (1d4
damage, halves movement in 10ft-diameter area), pouch with
1d4 gp and 2d6 sp, 10 % chance of a small pouch of powdered
silver skimmed from a previous heist (worth 1d4 gp).

Net, Male or Female Human (Thf2) (2): HP 7, 4; AC 7[12];
Atk net (save or entangled) or dagger (1d4); **Move** 12; **Save**
14; AL C; **CL/XP** 2/30; **Special:** +2 save bonus vs. traps
and magical devices, backstab (x2), thieving skills. (see
Appendix A: NPCs)
Thieving Skills: Climb 86%, Tasks/Traps 20%, Hear 3 in 6,
Hide 15%, Silent 25%, Locks 15%.
Equipment: leather armor, net, dagger, pouch of caltrops
(1d4 damage, halves movement in 10ft-diameter area), 50ft
silk rope, grappling hook, pouch with 1d8 gp and 2d10 sp,
10% chance of a small pouch of powdered silver skimmed
from a previous heist (worth 2d4 gp).

Shifter, Male or Female Human (Thf2): HP 5; AC 7[12];
Atk dagger (1d4); **Move** 12; **Save** 14; AL C; **CL/XP** 2/30;
Special: +2 save bonus vs. traps and magical devices,
backstab (x2), thieving skills. (see **Appendix A: NPCs**)

Thieving Skills: Climb 86%, Tasks/Traps 20%, Hear 3 in 6,
Hide 15%, Silent 25%, Locks 15%.
Equipment: leather armor, net, 2 daggers, pouch of caltrops
(1d4 damage, halves movement in 10ft-diameter area),
scales, pouch with 2d10 gp and 2d10 sp, 10% chance of a
small pouch of powdered silver skimmed from a previous
heist (worth 2d4 gp).

Thugs, Male or Female Human (5): HP 6, 5x2, 4, 2; AC 6[13];
Atk short sword (1d6) or club (1d6), dagger (1d4); **Move** 12; **Save**
17; AL C; **CL/XP** 1/15; **Special:** none. (see **Appendix A: NPCs**)
Equipment: leather armor, short sword or club, dagger,
small wooden shield, pouch with 1d4 gp and 2d6 sp.

Note: If any bolts were killed in **Area 2-17**, subtract them from
those found here. Do not subtract any thieves killed elsewhere in the
dungeon, as it is assumed that they were coming or going on business
in the city. This group represents the number that can be found here
at any given time.

Devlin, Male Human, Master of the Ebon Union (Thf8):
HP 27; AC 6[13]; **Atk** +1 rapier (1d6); **Move** 12; **Save**
8; AL C; **CL/XP** 8/800; **Special:** +2 save bonus vs. traps
and magical devices, backstab (x4), darkvision (60ft), read
languages, thieving skills.
Thieving Skills: Climb 92%, Tasks/Traps 50%, Hear 5 in 6,
Hide 55%, Silent 60%, Locks 55%.
Equipment: +1 rapier, +1 leather armor, *potion of
invisibility*, thieves' tools, key to door in **Area Q-2**.

Description: Devlin inherited leadership of the Ebon Union after the organization was devastated by the inquisition of a group of paladins, Lawful priests, and ambitious adventurers. The previous guildmaster and his lieutenants were killed, and many of the thieves were incarcerated for their crimes or returned to petty thievery and extortion. Of the small group that remained together and fled the city, Devlin was the most charismatic and held the highest rank. The group subsisted on highway robbery for a time before settling under Dun Eamon (a portion of the gang remains in the Eamonvale wilderness; see **Appendix D: Wilderness Encounters**). Despite the fact that he had few men and almost no resources, Devlin's tactical instinct and clever plans have helped turn the Ebon Union into an efficient and wealthy organization. He has impressed upon his men the value of preparation and teamwork and taught them that abandoning a heist before it turns sour is sometimes best. In return, he demands ultimate loyalty from his men and punishes turncoats and skimmers ruthlessly. The men respect and obey him and would die before betraying him or their brothers.

Devlin is a slender, dark-haired man with a smooth voice and an aura of cool confidence. He always attempts to talk instead of fight during a transaction, but when the deal is too far gone to salvage, his rapier is as quick as his tongue and as sharp as his mind.

Tactics: The thieves of the Ebon Union are very likely aware of the party's approach, either from encountering them elsewhere in the dungeon, engaging them in **Area 3-16**, or by listening to the various sounds resulting from the triggering of traps along the corridor. If this is the case, the bolts and nets take up positions hiding around the gallery in the chamber. The knives hide around the bases of the columns and amid the pallet beds and other furnishings on the floor. If the party achieves surprise, the thieves are scattered about sleeping, playing cards, drinking, or training. In either case, they respond to the party's entrance immediately, attempting to gain a surprise round of missile fire and net dropping before entering melee. The thugs and the other specialists enter from **Area 3-26** to join the fray. **Devlin** enters from **Area 3-27**, along with any unique NPCs who may have survived previous encounters, such as Kubris, Thurf, or Gulik. This development increases the difficulty of this encounter; consider having these NPCs advance and become recurring villains instead. If Tabitha survived, she is not present, but rather stayed in the city.

Devlin is a skilled swordsman, but he prefers to escape alive if possible. He joins the fight in such a way as to minimize his apparent ability if he has a clear shot at the exit corridor (he does not want to be targeted as the leader if the battle is going poorly). If death is imminent and his escape is blocked, only a heroic death will do. The other thieves flee or surrender if two-thirds of them are killed. If the heroes use the doorway to protect their flanks and cast area effect spells to deal damage, the thieves should not present an undefeatable challenge. The only treasure in this area is the equipment of the thieves; the rest is hidden away in **Area 3-28**.

Development: The further exploration of the halfling tunnels beyond the rubble-choked gates is a possibility, but the results of such a venture are left to you to devise (see **Resolution**).

Area 3-26: Chapel

This room was clearly a religious fixture of some type, but it now serves as more of a kitchen. Crates and barrels are stacked near an altar, several strings of vegetables are hung in place of ruined tapestries, and a large barrier now serves as a scummy stewpot. This room was originally a shrine to a halfling god, either a recognizable deity or one long forgotten, at your discretion. It has now been modified to serve as the Ebon Union's primary cooking and food storage area. The dry goods that are stored here are of poor quality and are aged well past freshness, but several cases of salted meats make the stews worth eating. The brazier is the only treasure in the room.

Treasure: Bronze brazier (worth 200 gp).

Area 3-27: Private Quarters

Devlin has taken for himself the quarters that were once given to the commander of the halfling garrison. A few of the items here are valuable bits of treasure that serve enough of a purpose to be kept out of the hoard. The room features running water piped in by some unknown method, although the receiving basin is shattered and replaced with a wooden tub. Devlin's sleeping arrangements consist of a massive pile of silken pillows draped with several bolts of valuable fabric stolen during the days of highway banditry. A large table dominates the room's center and holds several maps of the city and the surrounding wilderness, a magnifying lens, scales, and a pair of oil lamps.

Treasure: two oil lamps, magnifying glass, 10 silk pillows (7 gp each), two slightly-soiled bolts of woolen cloth (30 gp each), map with location of Hobark's camp marked in red (see **Appendix D: Wilderness Encounters**). A secret door leads to **Area 3-28**.

Area 3-28: The Hoard

This room is dirty and filled with rubble except for a raised platform in the back corner. Piled upon this platform are the ill-gotten gains of dozens of heists: stacks of shining silver coins, gem-encrusted serving pieces, and gold-embroidered tapestries. Stacked around the bottom of the platform are two wooden chests, canvas wrapped bundles, a large mirror, a small casket trimmed in silver, and several other items of exquisite beauty, exemplary craftsmanship, and, presumably, great value. The treasure is dominated by silver coin (of which there is simply a lot) and unique or hard-to-market items; the simple serving pieces and jewelry have already been fenced. The chests are **trapped** to protect their contents from the prying fingers of greedy thieves as well as from outsiders.

Treasure: *+1 bastard sword*, *+1 plate mail with winged helm*, canvas bundle containing silvered short sword with amethysts in cross guard (580 gp), canvas bundle containing curtain of glass beads and freshwater pearls (1,000 gp), canvas bundle containing four bolts of trade-grade silk (100 gp each), canvas bundle containing two bolts of exquisite silk (200 gp each), full-length mirror in ivory frame (60 lbs., 750 gp), silver pitcher (35 gp), silver serving platter (20 gp), six lead-crystal goblets in wooden case (15 gp each, or 100 gp for entire set), two gold marriage goblets (50 gp each), gold-rimmed bowl (28 gp), set of six jeweled masquerade masks (wolf, 90 gp; lion, 95 gp; hawk, 100 gp; bull, 100 gp; unicorn, 105 gp; dragon, 110 gp), and 6,780 sp.

The large chest is trapped to fire a cloud of tiny darts from inside the lid when it is opened to strike the person opening it. The character must make a saving throw or be struck by 1d4 darts that do 1 point of damage each. The darts are also coated in scorpion venom that does 2d4 points of damage (no save). The chest contains 978 gp, a leather belt (15 gp) that hides eight gold bars (20 gp each) in concealed pockets, wooden case holding 30 small silver bars (5 gp each), iron box with 25 pp, and two small platinum bars (50 gp each).

The small chest is trapped with a poison needle that jabs the person opening it (save or die). The chest contains a variety of trade gems: 50 assorted agates, azurite, turquoise, and other gems (10 gp each, or 4d4 gp each); and 10 bloodstone and quartz gems (50 gp each, or 2d4 x 10 gp each)

The silver-trimmed casket is cursed. Anyone opening it contracts horrible boils across their body (−2 to hit, damage, and saves) until they receive a cure disease spell. The casket contains the mummified remains of an infant prince of an ancient desert kingdom (not an undead creature) wearing a hammered-gold death mask with garnet eyes (1,500 gp). The casket is worth 900 gp.

AREA 3-29:
TOUGHER THAN THE AVERAGE TROLL

This cavern is one of the largest on this level, with several smaller caves and a tunnel exiting the far side. A huge, black-skinned humanoid beast is digging in the sandy floor at the base of a crack in the wall, as if it were looking for something. This **flame-spawned troll** was called from the Abyss after Lilith obtained the items from the Seer's Parlor and the Root-Cutter's Shop. She placed it at the edge of Level 3 to protect her domain and to keep thieves from wandering down into her lair. The **Band of the Crimson Mantle** is hiding here, injured and cornered by the troll. They take advantage of the party's arrival to escape, taking some cheap shots at them on the way.

Flame-Spawned Troll: HD 6; HP 42; AC 4[15]; Atk 2 claws (1d4 + 1d6 fire), bite (1d6 + 1d6 fire); **Move** 12; **Save** 11; **AL** C; **CL/XP** 10/1400; **Special:** fiery (additional 1d6 damage), immune to fire, regenerate (3hp/round), vulnerable to acid and cold (200%). (***The Tome of Horrors Complete*** 569)

Band of the Crimson Mantle: The Band's stats are listed in **Appendix A: NPCs**. For the purpose of this encounter, they are all at 50% of their maximum hit points. Unless you chose otherwise, Dresden the Mad has already been killed (his body may have been found on Level 2).

Pratchett, Male Half-Elf Thief (Thf5): HP 14 (currently 6); AC 6[13]; Atk short sword (1d6) or *+2 light crossbow* (1d4+1) or leather sap (1d4 nonlethal); **Move** 12; **Save** 11; **AL** C; **CL/XP** 5/240; **Special:** +2 save bonus vs. traps and magical devices, backstab (x2), darkvision (60ft), detect secret doors (4-in-6 chance), read languages, thieving skills. (see **Appendix A: NPCs**)
Thieving Skills: Climb 89%, Tasks/Traps 35%, Hear 4 in 6, Hide 30%, Silent 40%, Locks 30%.
Equipment: *+1 leather armor*, short sword, leather sap, *+2 light crossbow*, 20 bolts (8 pre-poisoned); large vial of purple worm poison (8 applications; save or additional 1d6 damage); 50ft silk rope, grappling iron, thieves' tools, flint and steel, hooded lantern, 2 flasks of oil, 2 days' trail rations, waterskin, pouch (contains 65 gp, 18 sp, and 4 garnets [worth 120 gp, two worth 100 gp each, and 90 gp]), map to his secret cache of supplies and treasure.

Isidra, Female Human Priest of the God of Death (Clr5): HP 23 (currently 12); AC 3[16]; Atk heavy mace (1d6); **Move** 12; **Save** 10 (+1, ring); **AL** C; **CL/XP** 5/240; **Special:** +2 save vs. paralysis and poison, banish undead, spells (2/2). (see **Appendix A: NPCs**)
Spells: 1st—*cause light wounds* (x2); 2nd—*hold person, silence 15ft radius*.
Equipment: *+1 ring mail* (see special note below), small steel shield with unholy symbol of the God of Death, heavy mace, *ring of protection +1, potion of healing* (x3), scroll (*detect magic* and *speak with dead*), mummified hand of a small child, 2 days' trail rations, waterskin, 2 torches, pouch (containing 32 gp and 18 sp), silver necklace with 3 tiny black pearls worth 500 gp total.

Yelm, Male Human Barbarian (Ftr5): HP 31 (currently 15); AC 5[14]; Atk *+1 bastard sword* (1d8+3) or throwing axe (1d6+2) or strike (1d4+2); **Move** 12; **Save** 10; **AL** N; **CL/XP** 5/240; **Special:** +2 to hit and damage strength bonus, multiple attacks (5) vs. creatures with 1 or fewer HD. (see **Appendix A: NPCs**)
Equipment: chainmail, stained kilt, *+1 bastard sword*, 4 throwing axes, 2 flasks of oil, wineskin, flask of whiskey, 5 days' trail rations, 6 torches, 50ft hemp rope, silver beck torc worth 20 gp, silver-trimmed drinking horn worth 12 gp, hacksilver armband worth 8 gp, pouch containing 25 gp and 16 sp.

Tactics: The troll is easily distracted from his project and attacks as soon as he becomes aware of the party. He ignores the fleeing Band and continues to attack the heroes until killed.

The Band of the Crimson Mantle has been pinned in the small cave for several hours as they recovered and monitored the troll's activities. As soon as the troll leaves the opening of the cave (most likely to fight the party), the Band grabs its possession and races for the tunnel exit to Level 4. On the way, it targets the party with a few minor attacks, such as a crossbow bolt from Pratchett and a spell from Isidra, mostly adding insult to whatever injuries the troll is inflicting. Unless the party goes to great lengths to stop the Band, its members successfully exit the area.

Development: The Band of the Crimson Mantle has proven to be cruel, cowardly, and evil, but Yelm still has an opportunity to redeem himself. If the party lost members or is in need of support, you may consider having Yelm desert the Band and join the party. If this is the case, Yelm turns from his flight and attacks the troll from behind (he is not inclined to run from a good fight and has been less than enthusiastic about Pratchett's leadership of the Band). This premise can be used to introduce Yelm as a new character or NPC; simply hand over his sheet to a player. The extra muscle will be of use on Level 4, and this is an easy way to replace casualties or add hirelings without the party needing to revisit the surface. Consider the party's past dealings with the Band when determining the outcome of this development. If the party is faring well, Yelm flees with the rest of the Band.

Chapter Seven: Level 4 – Mamuthek's Managerie

This is the lowest known level of the underground network of caverns and rivers. It is smaller than the others, but populated with more powerful creatures. The terrible products of Lilith's experimentation with *Mamuthek's Aperture* are here: a demonic minotaur, a cursed treant, dretches, mongrels of Yith, and the usual dungeon vermin. Lilith awaits the party with roleplaying and combat challenges.

Area 4-1: Twin Falls

Two powerful waterfalls crash from considerable height to churn the pool below into brown foam. Bits of driftwood and debris float at the edges of the pool. A small, sandy beach on one side of the chamber features a water-carved corridor leading into the rock wall. The water flows out through a low, dark tunnel. The sandy beach leads into Lilith's lair, passing several of her powerful minions on the way. Following the river leads past two additional beaches, one of which has an entrance to the lair. Being swept over either of these waterfalls results in 4d6 points of damage. A character in the pool at the base must roll below their dexterity on 4d6 to escape the incredible force of water or take 1d6 points of damage per round.

Area 4-2: Giant Rats

A chorus of hissing squeaks can be heard from within a small side-cavern. Above those sounds, the crunching of bone and the popping of ligaments is audible. In a grisly display of scavenger appetite, the 6 **giant rats** here are dismembering the bloated corpse of an adventurer that washed down from somewhere upriver (at your discretion, this corpse and its items could be replaced with the body and items of a party member lost in one of the rivers on a previous level). The adventurer's body is torn, waterlogged, and distended with the gaseous byproducts of advanced decay. In its smelly pouches is the treasure found in this chamber.

Giant Rats (6): HD 1d4hp; HP 4x2, 3x3, 2; AC 7[12]; **Atk** bite (1d3); **Move** 12; **Save** 18; **AL** N; **CL/XP** A/5; **Special:** 5% are diseased. (*Monstrosities* 384)

Treasure: *potion of extra healing*, *dust of disappearance*, a chain shirt, a battle axe, a shortbow and quiver of 10 arrows, and a pouch of 35 gp.

Area 4-3: Entry Chamber – Tunnel From Level 3

The floor of this chamber is flat and sandy, with a great confusion of tracks pointing in every direction. A tunnel exits into darkness on one side and another gives way to a corridor on the opposite side that branches in two directions. This room is empty of anything of interest except for two clues. A ranger, druid or elf has a 3-in-6 chance to detect tracks from mongrels of Yith, dretches, and humanoids (the members

---

Level 3: A River Runs Through It

Entrances: The river from **Area 2-24** flows through a low tunnel to **Area 4-1**. A river from Level 3 flows over a falls into **Area 4-1** as well. A tunnel from **Area 3-29** leads to **Area 4-3**.

Exits: The only exit from this level leads out of the underground caverns and into the gorge below the city. The river that flows through this level joins the flow of the waterfalls that spill from around the island city and falls several hundred feet into a deep pool.

Wandering Monsters: With the exception of a few minor creatures, the denizens of this level stick to their respective areas. Check on 1d20 for wandering monsters only every two hours; loud events do not produce any special interest, but they do warn the occupants of the trespassers' presence.

1d20	Encounter
1–2	Screaming, demonic bellowing or mad gibbering noises
3–4	1d4 **giant rats** (subtract from **Area 4-2**)
5–6	1d2 **dretches** (subtract from **Area 4-8**)
7–20	No Encounter

Dretch Demons (1d2): HD 4; AC 2[17]; **Atk** 2 claws (1d4), bite (1d6); **Move** 9; **Save** 13; **AL** C; **CL/XP** 6/400; **Special:** spell-like abilities. (*Monstrosities* 92)
Spell-like abilities: 1/day—*darkness 15ft radius*, *stinking cloud* (20ft radius, save or nauseated for 1d4+1 rounds), summon 1d4 giant rats.

Giant Rats (1d4): HD 1d4hp; AC 7[12]; **Atk** bite (1d3); **Move** 12; **Save** 18; **AL** N; **CL/XP** A/5; **Special:** 5% are diseased. (*Monstrosities* 384)

Shielding: No areas are shielded on this level, but Lilith wears an *amulet against scrying*.
Detections: The entire level radiates evil and chaos. The demonic auras of the various creatures and the foul acts that have taken place here saturate the place with a palpable aura of darkness. The cursed treant in **Area 4-6** radiates an aura of desperation and anguish.
Continuous Effects: These lowest caverns are mostly dry. Unless the party provides its own light source, the area is in total darkness.
Standard Features: The walls and ceilings are rough with stalactites and mineral formations. The floor is covered with sand from the river and is generally dry. Overhead clearance is 10 feet unless otherwise indicated.

Level 4: Mamutheks Menagerie
1 Square - 5 Feet
To Outside Waterfall
N
W
E
S
15
14
13
12
10
11
9
7
8
5
6
4
1
2
3
To Area 2-24
To Area 3-11
To Area 3-29

of the Band of the Crimson Mantle), but not which direction they went or how long ago. Carved on the wall near the corridor entrance is another "EB" sigil from Elinda Bannon.

AREA 4-4: KNOCK, KNOCK, OOZE THERE

This room is vaguely wedge-shaped, and puddles of water cover the floor in places. Water also drips from every stalactite, making a chorus of dripping tones. The drips seem to fall especially heavily from a crack in the ceiling toward the rear. The crack in the ceiling is far too small to fit through without magic. It goes nowhere of importance, unless you wish to insert a connecting passage for future development. It probably engages the interest of the heroes long enough to allow the **grey ooze** in the corner to attack. Its treasure of 20 glass marbles and *lenses of charming* (without frames) are scattered on the ground.

Grey Ooze: HD 3; HP 19; AC 8[11]; **Atk** strike (2d6); **Move** 1; **Save** 14; **AL** N; **CL/XP** 5/240; **Special:** acid (dissolve metal [save resists]), immunities (blunt weapons, heat, cold, spells). (*Monstrosities* 229)

AREA 4-5: WHO LET THE DOGS OUT?

A heavy stone block rests against what appears to be an opening in the tunnel wall. Marks in the sand would indicate that the block was dragged there and wedged into the crack. A faint scratching can be heard from somewhere behind the stone. With the help of the demonic minotaur, Lilith keeps **2 mongrels of Yith** penned up in this small cave. The heroes may be tempted to move the boulder and explore the cave. Moving the huge stone requires a combined strength of 35, and multiple characters may need to collaborate on this effort. Using levers, digging pits, and so on can help as well, and reduces the combined strength to 30. While the party is so engaged, the mongrels of Yith within hide themselves among their "toys" — a collection of driftwood and grisly body parts. They prepare to charge as soon as the stone moves away — unless they immediately see their beloved mistress Lilith or the minotaur, who has thumped them badly in the past.

Mongrels of Yith (2): HD 4; HP 30, 24; AC 4[15]; **Atk** bite (1d6+1); **Move** 15; **Save** 13; **AL** C; **CL/XP** 4/120; **Special:** terrifying howl (save or flee in fear for 1d6 rounds). (see **Appendix B: New Monsters**)

Tactics: Unless the mongrels of Yith see one of the two figures mentioned above, they attack immediately and fight until killed. They burst forth immediately to surprise the characters, if possible.

AREA 4-6: ONLY YOU CAN PREVENT FOREST FIRES

This cavern is lit from within by a flickering yellow light. An odd groaning can be heard, punctuated periodically by a mighty bellow and the sound of heavy logs crashing onto stone. The chamber is home to what may be the most bizarre creature called by *Mamuthek's Aperture*. Lilith very much wanted a fire elemental to guard her lair (and keep it warm). She tried accessing the Elemental Plane of Fire the first time with a chunk of obsidian, but this material instead produced the mephits in **Area 3-13**, much to her disappointment. In her next attempt, she endeavored to put a live flame on the tray of the summoning device and

included a tiny sliver of wood to fuel it. Because of the wood included on the tray, her results were far from desirable.

Shurr'arrin, Insane Flaming Treant (8HD): HD 8; HP 55; AC 2[17]; **Atk** 2 strikes (2d6 + 1d6 fire); **Move** 6; **Save** 8; **AL** L; **CL/XP** 10/1400; **Special:** control trees (60ft range, 2 trees animated, move 3, strike 1d6), fire (additional 1d6 damage), immune to fire. (*Monstrosities* 485)

Description: Shurr'arrin is an ancient treant that once ruled as the lord of a great forest. He raised an army to defend against a cult of fire worshippers, but he was defeated and his forest burned. As punishment for his insolence, the elemental priest that led the cult cursed him and banished him to the Elemental Plane of Fire, where he remained until Lilith's summons drew him through the *Aperture*. His curse is a heinous one: he is immune to fire and the damage caused by it, but not immune to the resultant pain. A second curse makes extinguishing his burning limbs once they are alight impossible — something that happened immediately following his arrival on the Elemental Plane of Fire. He has been imprisoned there for unknown eons, always burning but never consumed. Shurr'arrin is now thoroughly insane from lifetimes of agonizing pain and now acts without reason. He looks like an enormous tree engulfed in raging flames.

Tactics: Shurr'arrin is completely insane and attacks as soon as he is aware of something upon which he can vent his anguish. As he charges, he shouts out a garbled moaning in a mix of Treant, Ignan, and Common: "*Let me die ... Why won't I burn? ... Just let me die ...*"

The party may try to amend his condition. A *remove curse* spell lifts the curse that keeps him burning but does not actually extinguish the flames — that must be done by some other means, such as immersing him in a great deal of water. The greater curse that renders him immune to flame but not to pain requires more extensive efforts to break — the exact nature of this curse is up to you.

Extinguishing the flames does nothing to restore Shurr'arrin's sanity, although once extinguished he may break off the attack and act randomly instead. Restoring his mind requires a *restoration* or *wish*. If no efforts are taken to help him, he fights ferociously until killed (by means other than fire).

AREA 4-7: STIRGES

This small cavern is reachable only by following the river (more likely by drifting down it) to the small beach on one shore. The cave is filled with **stirges**, one of which has a bracelet stuck on its neck; this treasure can be removed only after death.

Stirges (8): HD 1+1; HP 8, 7, 6x2, 5x2, 4, 3, ; AC 7[12]; **Atk** proboscis (1d3 + blood drain); **Move** 3 (fly 18); **Save** 17; **AL** N; **CL/XP** 2/30; **Special:** +2 to hit bonus, blood drain (automatic 1d4 after hit). (*Monstrosities* 461)

Tactics: The stirges attack as soon as they realize they are not alone. They fight until five of them are killed or until smoke is introduced. Randomize the ones that flee the area to see if one of them wears the bracelet.

Treasure: Gold bracelet with single emerald charm (1,200 gp).

Development: At your discretion, this chamber could contain an access tunnel to some point inside the Angus keep.

AREA 4-8: DRETCH PIT

Fires dot this large, circular cavern, surrounding an uneven platform made of lashed driftwood and planks that occupies the center of the room. The shadowed mouths of several smaller caverns and recesses are visible. A low murmuring comes from below the wooden panels. This is the chamber that turned Elinda Bannon around to look for another way in. It is the home of Lilith's **dretches** and their "caretaker," a **demonic minotaur**. The side caverns house the minotaur's lair and the captured members of the **Band of the Crimson Mantle**. The dretches are in the pit, where they are kept out of the way and out of trouble until Lilith lets them loose on the city. If the minotaur has his way (see below), the strength of the boards figures in the combat here. Any character walking on the wooden covering has a 2-in-6 chance of causing a structural collapse that sends the character and anyone within 10 feet crashing 20 feet into the pit of dretches. Characters who fall take 2d6 points of damage (or half that if they make a saving throw).

Demonic Minotaur: HD 8; **HP** 60; **AC** 6[13]; **Atk** head butt (2d4), bite (1d6) and battle axe (1d8); **Move** 12; **Save** 8; **AL** C; **CL/XP** 10/1400; **Special:** never get lost in labyrinths, magic resistance (10%), resist fire (50%), spell-like abilities.
Spell-like abilities: 3/day—*darkness 15ft radius, pyrotechnics*.

Description: Describe the minotaur in such a way that its fiendish nature is obvious — flaming hooves, glowing eyes, and so on. If the players jump to the conclusion that this is the "demon" their characters have sought, then humor them; such assumptions may come back to haunt them!

Dretch Demons (8): HD 4; **HP** 27, 24, 22x2, 20, 17, 14, 12; **AC** 2[17]; **Atk** 2 claws (1d4), bite (1d6); **Move** 9; **Save** 13; **AL** C; **CL/XP** 6/400; **Special:** spell-like abilities. (*Monstrosities* 92)
Spell-like abilities: 1/day—*darkness 15ft radius*, stinking cloud (20ft radius, save or nauseated for 1d4+1 rounds), summon 1d4 giant rats.

Tactics: The minotaur waits to attack until the pit distracts the party's attention, if possible. When it does attack, it charges and attempts to head butt a character standing close to the edge of the pit.

If successful, the character must make a saving throw or be forced onto the flimsy wooden covering in the hopes the structure collapses with them. If given a choice, the minotaur strikes a heavily-armored warrior instead of a thief or spellcaster. It attempts to head butt other characters if they are foolish enough to get between it and the edge of the pit.

The dretches in the pit attack zealously as soon as an opponent is present, although they cannot get out of the pit alone.

Treasure: Possessions of the Band of the Crimson Mantle; see **Appendix A: NPCs**.

Development: Whenever the characters explore the side caverns, they find any survivors of the Band of the Crimson Mantle being held prisoner there. This may include Pratchett, Isidra, and possible Yelm, or none of them, depending on what occurred with the encounter in **Area 3-29**. They are unconscious and buried up to their necks in the sand. They have only 20% of their hit points left, and Isidra has no spells. Their weapons are buried at their feet and all their other items are still on their persons. Without healing and rest, they will do the party little good, but dispatching them or leaving them to die on their own should be considered an evil act, as they currently pose no threat. Their interactions with the party over the course of the adventure and the party's general alignment should factor into an interesting quandary. This turn of events presents a good roleplaying challenge, especially if the party is divided on what to do.

If allowed to survive and recover, Pratchett resents any implied obligation to the heroes, but does not attempt to challenge them unless the odds favor him. Isidra has seen death up close and is more intrigued by it than ever; she has no gratitude or animosity and does not challenge the party. Yelm nobly regards himself indebted to the heroes if they save him, although he is shamed by his defeat and wishes to redeem himself. This moment allows another opportunity for him to join the party as a replacement character or NPC. Generally, the Band presents no threat if they are allowed to leave — consider it a temporary truce in what might become an ongoing rivalry.

Area 4-9: Beach

This small beach is the only way to bypass **Area 4-8** and its dangerous tenants. While there is no inherent danger on the beach or in the tunnel leading away from it, overshooting the landing can be quite deadly. This is the last stop on the underground river before it exits the caverns and joins the massive waterfalls thundering down from overhead. Beyond the beach, there is no dry ground and no tunnels — only rock-walled tunnel and rushing water. Being washed over the falls in this manner results in 10d6 points of damage, with no save.

Area 4-10: Alarms

In this area, Lilith has placed magic mouths here to secure her inner sanctum. They are located at the exit of the tunnel from **Areas 4-8** and **4-9** and at the tunnel opening leading to Area **4-12**. The magic mouths repeatedly scream out "Intruders!" when triggered.

Area 4-11: The Garbage Disposal

This small chamber is splattered with shattered bodies and reeks like a charnel house. Creatures of unrecognizable nature have been torn limb from limb, their entrails strewn about among splinters of bone and bits of fur. Not all of Lilith's summonings produced creatures that were willing or able to serve her dark purposes. The minotaur from **Area 4-8** provides the service of eliminating them from her affairs. The room causes nausea in characters who fail a saving throw, resulting in a −1 penalty to hit and saves for 1d4 hours.

Area 4-12: Lilith

This is the inner sanctum of Lilith, the succubus demon. The encounter needs to be modified if the party managed to avoid all creature encounters, alarms, and traps on this level, which is unlikely. The unworked stone walls of this chamber are nearly invisible beneath its opulent furnishings. A silken canopy is slung overhead between stalactites, and the mysterious light source above it is tinted pale yellow. Piles of cushions are strewn carelessly about, and a luxurious round bed is centered against the far wall. An iron cage hangs from the ceiling with a wilted female form inside.

The figure locked in the cage is really **Lilith** using her shapechange ability. Unless the party has prior history in Dun Eamon, they have never met the real Elinda Bannon and have no reason to doubt that she should be here. She wears Elinda's *amulet against scrying*. Some of Elinda's other items are still in her pack, opposite the cage, and might be useful if a battle ensues. These stolen items are listed as the treasure for this area, but are not included in the treasure balance for this level (Elinda would like to see them again). The fact that the heroes came here hoping to find the missing wizard and the cinematically heroic nature of the rescue may aid in Lilith's deception as well.

If the heroes did good detective work in the city above, however, they may suspect that some form of shape-shifting seductress is at work. They may also have the knowledge needed to trap Lilith in a lie, but to do so will require roleplaying cleverness. The following encounter is critical to the outcome of the adventure, so play out the scene carefully.

The party may or may not realize that the real Elinda Bannon is still in danger. Her prison is a deep hidden pit (**Area 4-13**) beneath the plush bedding in this chamber.

Playing Lilith: Lilith feigns unconsciousness until disturbed, when she "awakes" and is overjoyed to find that her saviors have arrived. She demands to know if they have destroyed "the demon," which the party may or may not believe has been accomplished. She also insists that the party escort her from the dungeon quickly so that she may deliver a warning to Lord Angus. Use the following text, or adlib your own.

"I had given up hope of ever seeing sunlight again! Who are you? Please, tell me you have defeated that foul, otherworldly creature! Regardless, we must make haste to the surface. I fear a most sinister plot is brewing between the outsiders and those they possess in the city. Lord Angus and all of Dun Eamon are in grave peril: I must speak with him immediately!"

Already, Lilith has made one small slip — she has not spent enough time on the surface to know that the sun never really shines in the Grey Citadel. She makes several more as time goes on, but only attentive heroes can catch them. Even the persona she adopts is that of a waifish damsel-in-distress, an image copied from an illusion Elinda has intentionally projected about herself since her capture; yet the players may have learned enough about Elinda to doubt this image. The party might also be able to trap Lilith with a few careful questions regarding people in her life, such as Stump or the Angus brothers. Their ability to do so depends on how they phrase their questions and how much Lilith may have learned in the city. Elinda Bannon has been deliberately vague during her imprisonment, hoping that such an opportunity would arise. This encounter can be as roleplaying oriented as the group wishes, within the limits of your creativity and flexibility.

Some parties may be satisfied at this point and head immediately for home, but most will have a few more questions, giving Lilith a few more chances to give herself away. Her responses on certain issues are detailed below:

HER CAPTURE

The troll in **Area 3-29** subdued Elinda, but she was backtracking to bypass the minotaur in **Area 4-8**. The party may have found her "EB" sigil in **Area 4-3**.

HER ROUTE

When pressed, Lilith recites the route she used most often, but the party may have found Elinda's sigil in **Area 2-14**. Again, clever questioning can trap Lilith in her masquerade.

HER LEVEL OF RESPONSIBILITY

If the heroes pursue this conversation, they may realize that Lilith does not know that Elinda was only trying to communicate, not summon.

HER TRAIL OF CLUES

Lilith does not know what the actual clues were. Depending on how the heroes word their questions, they may be able to catch her in a lie.

THE NATURE OF THE "DEMON"

Lilith would like the party to believe that they killed the demon, so she describes the demonic minotaur from **Area 4-8**. This tactic may arouse suspicion if the heroes (a) followed up the theft of minotaur body parts from Caledon's shop or (b) established a strong case in favor of a demonic seductress.

THE EBON UNION

This is essentially the truth as Elinda would know it.

Lilith, Succubus Demon: HD 6; HP 43; AC 9[10] or 2[17] (missile) and 4[15] (melee) from *shield* spell; **Atk** 2 scratches (1d3); **Move** 12 (fly 18); **Save** 11; **AL** C; **CL/XP** 10/1400; **Special:** +1 or better magic weapons to hit, level drain (drain 1 level with kiss), magic resistance (70%), shapechange (at will), spell-like abilities, spells (4/2/2), summon demons (40% chance, baalroch or nalfeshnee). (*Swords & Wizardry Complete Rulebook*)
Spell-like abilities: at will—*charm person, clairaudience, darkness 15ft radius, ESP, suggestion.*
Spells: 1st—*magic missile* (x2), *shield, sleep;* 2nd—*magic mouth, web;* 3rd—*hold person, lightning bolt.*

Description: Lilith is a power-hungry schemer, not terribly surprising for one of the more duplicitous demons of the Abyss. She is unique in the number of enemies she has amassed among the demon princes, however, and in the number of factions that want her dead for reasons best left to future development. As a result, she is determined never to return to the underworld, especially when life on the Material Plane is so enjoyable. To those ends, she is very deliberate about how she uses the artifact, and she is very hesitant to summon other demons lest those that arrive be inclined to collect on one of her various bounties. She is cunning, deceitful, and manipulative to the utmost and should be played as a shrewd, calculating villain. When not masquerading as another female humanoid, she prefers a form that features straight dark hair and green eyes, with alabaster skin and ideal human proportions.

Tactics: If the heroes confront Lilith with her deception, she attempts to excuse her errors with the intensity of her experiences. If that fails, she uses *charm person* on the most powerful male party member, saying to him, "How can you doubt me? I am in as much danger as any of you!" If she can get one or more party members to support her, she attempts to flee toward the surface and escape. Also, if the party runs across a powerful foe, she takes advantage of the distraction and flees. She tries to lead the chase through areas where she knows her minions dwell and fights if escape is not an option.

If combat ensues or if it benefits her escape, Lilith casts *lightning bolt* then turns to using Elinda's *wand of magic missiles* (14 charges remaining).

Lilith knows that she is effectively cornered here and imagines that many if not all of her summoned creatures have been defeated. Her intention is to convince the party to escort her to the surface, where she hopes to escape into a crowd. If they do not contest her identity, she insists that they pack up the artifact (found in **Area 4-14**) "lest it fall into evil hands" and depart immediately. Once released from her cage, she also retrieves a satchel with Elinda's spellbooks (from **Area 4-14**) and a backpack with her other items (see below). In the bottom of the satchel are several material components meant for use with the artifact. If given the opportunity, Lilith combines the giant constrictor snakeskin with the last of the Abyssal ore to call (she hopes) a **monstrous giant constrictor** snake (see **Area 4-14**).

Monstrous Fire Snake: HD 10; **AC** 2[17]; **Atk** bite (1d8 + 1d6 fire + paralysis); **Move** 12 (climb 9); **Save** 5; **AL** C; **CL/XP** 12/2000; **Special:** fiery bite (additional 1d6 fire damage), immune to fire, paralysis (1d6 rounds, save avoids, 75% chance to be set on fire by bite), surprise (1–4 on 1d6), vulnerable to cold (200%). (***The Tome of Horrors Complete*** 244)

If the party is thoroughly convinced that Lilith is Elinda, she could follow through on her request to be escorted all the way to Arb Angus, whom she then tries to seduce and *charm*. If she accomplishes this feat, her conquest of the Grey Citadel will be nearly complete, and the characters will have failed in their quest, at least for now. These events and their repercussions are beyond the scope of this adventure, although the material is present to adapt to such an eventuality. Such elaborate twists are left to your discretion.

Treasure: Elinda's *+1 staff*, *wand of magic missile* (14 charges remaining), dagger, a spellbook, and a backpack with three days' rations, a waterskin, and a blanket.

AREA 4-13: PRISON PIT

The real **Elinda Bannon** still needs to be rescued. She is bound in a deep pit beneath the bedding in **Area 4-12**. The pit has a narrow mouth, but widens as it descends into a conical chamber that is 30 feet high at the entrance and 60 feet in diameter. A magical *darkness* effect is centered in the chamber, leaving a 10-foot perimeter of normal (but also dark) conditions. Elinda is badly injured and without spells, and she is guarded by another of Lilith's summoned creatures, a **demonic monstrous scorpion**.

Elinda Bannon, is unconscious, regardless of when the party finds her. She has 6 hit points remaining and no spells prepared. Her familiar was killed elsewhere in the dungeon (see **Area 3-12**). She has her armor and one of her rings, but her staff, wand, and amulet are in Lilith's possession.

Elinda Bannon, Female Human (As Lilith's Prisoner) (MU6): HP 17 (currently 6); **AC** 4[15]; **Atk** none; **Move** 12; **Save** 10; **AL** L; **CL/XP** 6/400; **Special:** +2 saves vs. spells, wands and staffs, spells (4/2/2). (see **Appendix A: NPCs**) **Equipment:** *bracers of defense AC 6[13]*, *ring of protection +2*. **Note:** When found in Lilith's trap, Elinda has no spells remaining, very little of her equipment, and her pet owl was killed.

Demonic Monstrous Scorpion: HD 8; **HP** 58; **AC** 3[16]; **Atk** 2 pincers (1d10 + 1d6 fire), sting (1d4 + lethal poison); **Move** 12; **Save** 8; **AL** C; **CL/XP** 9/1100; **Special:** fiery claws (additional 1d6 fire damage when claw hits), immune to fire, lethal poison (save or die). (***Monstrosities*** 411)

Tactics: The scorpion lurks on the far edge of the magical *darkness*, out of sight of the party. It waits to attack until the pit or the prisoner distracts the heroes in some way. After that, it knows no restraint. Its claws dance with flames when it snaps them open and closed.

AREA 4-14: SUMMONING CHAMBER

A thinly wrought sphere of golden metal sits on a four-legged stand in the center of the room. Lines of soot trace the stone walls and floor of this chamber. A table against one wall is cluttered with odd bits of junk, chipped rocks, and vials of liquid. This area is the resting place of *Mamuthek's Aperture*, the ancient artifact that called Lilith and began the saga that is presumably about to come to an end, one way or another. For a description of the device, see **Appendix C: New Magical Items**.

A secret door on the far wall leads to an escape tunnel for Lilith and a final trap for the party. Among the treasure on the table is a satchel with Elinda's spellbooks and some potential material triggers — the remains of what was stolen from the civilians on the surface. Among the items are a mummified feline paw (of a tiger), a carefully rolled snakeskin (from a giant constrictor), and a bleached skull (of an ape). These are all normal animals; Lilith has already used the more exotic components to call her troll, minotaur, and so on. Also in the satchel are the leftover mineral samples — a few chunks of Abyssal ore, the Astral moonstone, and the vial of Elysian soil. These components, plus any other items the heroes may have with them, can be used to activate the artifact. Lilith is temporarily out of powdered silver, and she knows better than to summon demons who might attempt to collect on her bounty if they were free to do so. The heroes might have silver of their own, or they may be willing to call an unbound creature … the possibilities are numerous, depending on how much the heroes know (or think they know) about the artifact.

The use of the *Aperture* in or after whatever conflict develops between Lilith and the party can shift the balance of power considerably. If Lilith is permitted to use the artifact, she calls **monstrous fire snake** with the last chips of ore and the snakeskin. If the heroes choose to use the device, they might end up with an Elysian tiger, or something far more bizarre, or nothing at all: the products of *Mamuthek's Aperture* are entirely left to your discretion.

Treasure: *Mamuthek's Aperture* (see **Appendix C: New Magical Items**) and Elinda Bannon's spellbooks.

AREA 4-15: PIT TRAP

The door opens to reveal a tunnel that is visible in dim light for a few feet and then disappears into inky blackness. The secret door in **Area 4-14** has another secret door just beyond it that hides the true exit tunnel. This tunnel leads to the river channel, but there is no beach or dry ground. Lilith uses this tunnel to exit her lair and then fly up to **Area 4-1**. The more obvious tunnel continues past the second secret door to a concealed pit trap that is hidden in magical darkness. Characters running after Lilith may be taken in by the false corridor and could fall to their deaths without a bit of restraint. The pit is 100 feet deep, and characters who fall in take 10d6 points of damage (save for half).

Chapter Eight: Resolution, Rewards, and Development

When the heroes emerge from the tunnels having eliminated the demonic threat and rescued the wizard, throngs of cheering crowds await them. Experience rewards should be finalized and booty sorted out (remember that some items of treasure may cause reactions if used in the city). A job well done — but not necessarily the end of the adventure …

Lord Angus pays out the agreed upon reward of 2,000 gp in full. If the party can prove that the demons were much more powerful than the dretches and mongrels of Yith that terrorized the surface, he readily doubles the reward; if the party can prove that the underground caverns are free of thieves, demons, undead, and all other threats, he triples the reward.

If Elinda was rescued, she may be willing to reward the party with one or two custom minor magic items, but such work is not easily undertaken. First, her lab and library must be restored, and the process of gathering materials and making preparations may lead the heroes on yet another quest. Her gratitude is unconditional, but her services may depend on how thoroughly the heroes looted her tower and their willingness to return her items stolen by Lilith. Ulf Ironfist is similarly willing to craft weapons or armor for the party or collaborate with Elinda on one magical weapon or suit of armor. They are willing to absorb up to 6,000 gp worth of costs to create an item or items. The party must handle any further costs.

If *Mamuthek's Aperture* was retrieved, the party now has the responsibility of deciding what to do with it. If Elinda was successfully rescued, she certainly factors into that discussion, as will Arb Angus, who feels it is his responsibility to keep it from doing harm again. A quest to destroy it could result, or a trip to deliver it to some inaccessible place or noble order for safekeeping.

After the party deals with the threat of Lilith and her demons, other threats may possibly be left underground. Gethrax, the Ebon Union, the *box o' darkness traps*, and even the naturally occurring predators of the underground should be dealt with to ensure the city's safety. Even after the dungeon is cleared, thieves certainly remain in the city — and quite likely a few demons as well. Continued service to Lord Angus as he begins to restore order is a definite possibility. If Lilith, Gethrax, Devlin, or the Band of the Crimson Mantle survive, they could easily become recurring antagonists, especially if the party stays in the area.

After encountering Gethrax and his *box o' darkness traps*, the party most likely has the clues needed to pursue the destruction of his order, following a trail of *boxes* to seek out their fortress-temple in the Stoneheart Mountains. Cael Angus and the Temple of Fortitude might sponsor such a venture.

Even after the Ebon Union is ousted from the caverns, they may yet present a threat. If Devlin escapes, he returns to lead the highwaymen in the forest, if they still exist. If Tabitha or any of the other guild agents escaped, they may continue to haunt the party as well.

The ancient halfling stronghold beneath the city still beckons. An extensive (and expensive) excavation project would require the services of engineers and laborers, but the potential wealth of the halfling ruins is tempting. Alternatively, the halflings might still occupy their underground city and might request (or require) the party's assistance in dealing with an external subterranean threat.

Several citizens still suffer from the damage inflicted by Lilith and might need advanced healing that comes only at the end of the specific holy quest. The citizens hope that the party might stay nearby, and they continue to treat them as heroes. Indeed, it should be difficult for a character to pay for a meal with his own coin or empty his glass without it being refilled within moments. The party should have time to rest, recover, and reap the benefits of being the heroes of the Grey Citadel.

Appendix A: NPCs

Many of the important power figures and influential people of Dun Eamon may be found in several different locations or may be encountered frequently enough that their profiles need regular reference. Listed below are the profiles for the primary NPCs of the adventure. Their backgrounds are detailed so they can be paraphrased in part when the heroes inquire about them during their investigation. The primary villains (**Gethrax**, **Devlin**, and **Lilith**) are encountered in more predictable locations; their profiles are found in their encounter areas.

The Angus Clan

The three Angus brothers share the responsibilities of leadership in Dun Eamon and are regarded by most to be just and capable.

Arb Angus

Arb Angus, Male Human, Lord of Eamonvale (Rgr9):
HP 71; AC 2[17]; Atk *+2 bastard sword* (1d8+2) or longbow x2 (1d6); Move 12; Save 4 (+2, ring); AL L; CL/XP 9/1100; Special: +9 damage vs. giants and goblin-types, alertness, spells (1), tracking.
Spells: 1st—*detect evil*.
Equipment: *bracers of defense AC 4[15]*, *+2 bastard sword*, short sword, longbow, 20 arrows, *ring of protection +2*, gold band of lordship, amulet of the Angus crest, emerald signet ring (500 gp).

Description: Arb Angus is a tall, robust man with thick brown hair and a well-trimmed beard. Despite his social rank, he disdains ceremonial dress and usually wears simple clothing of high quality leather and wool. The only indicator of his lordship is the unadorned gold circlet on his brow and the ancestral Angus blade on his hip.

The eldest of the three Angus brothers, Arb rules Eamonvale, a remote river gorge in a temperate rainforest. He inherited title and land from his father, and the region has developed well under his reign. He is young, having just entered his 30th year, and he rules with the confidence and vigor of youth tempered by the strict discipline and wisdom of his father. His policies on trade and tax ensure a place for the local farmers and craftsmen in the economy, and his strict prohibition on foreign guild influence has drawn much controversy. While many abroad would see him overthrown, he is well-loved by his citizens.

His youth was spent in close contact with his brothers, engaged with the activities of aristocratic life. He is a skilled hunter and falconer and a competent horseman, but he never adjusted well to courtly life and is always quick to dispense with etiquette if such can be done without offense. He trusts his brothers implicitly, and they are involved in every important decision he makes. It is known that he does not intend to take a wife until later in life, but that has not stopped Elinda Bannon from being drawn to him.

While in the city, he spends as little time in the keep as possible. He often speaks with craftsmen and merchants around the market or stops to listen to a traveling minstrel and share a pint in a tavern. He can be encountered nearly anywhere in the citadel.

Bron Angus

Bron Angus, Male Human, Captain of the Mist Watch (Ftr8): HP 56; AC 1[18]; Atk *+2 longsword* (1d8+4); Move 12; Save 7; AL L; CL/XP 8/800; Special: +2 to hit and damage strength bonus, multiple attacks (8) vs. creatures with 1 or fewer HD.
Equipment: *+2 chainmail*, *+1 large shield*, blue tabard, grey cape, *+2 longsword*, chain of office, signal horn.

Description: Bron Angus is tall and slim, tightly strung with wiry muscle from training with the watch. His brown hair is cropped shirt, and he wears a handlebar moustache to age his appearance. He is almost never seen out of his uniform of mail, blue tabard, and grey cape.

Three years younger than his brother Arb, Bron is the captain of the Mist Watch. As a young man, Bron's father apprenticed him to his uncle, who was a mercenary captain. He traveled extensively until his father's death and became wise in the ways of war and the nuances of command. He operates with his father's strictness, but lacks the compassion that ensured his brother's success. Despite his grim personality and apparent lack of emotion, Bron is passionate about his duty to the city, and this commitment has won him the extreme loyalty of his men.

Bron is being actively sought as a husband by many of the wealthy maidens of the citadel and surrounding region, especially those whose merchant fathers have financial interests at stake. He avoids their advances on the pretense that a commander's duty is to his men and his city, but in reality, he is badly smitten with Elinda Bannon. Only his knowledge of her affection for his older brother Arb and his deep respect for him keeps Bron from acting.

Bron is fanatical about his work and spends nearly every waking hour at it. He meets regularly with the officers of the watch in their mess, trains recruits personally in the garrison yard, and can often be seen striding purposefully along the ramparts of the citadel, inspecting his men. He also lingers at the gates, measuring those who come and go under jurisdiction.

Cael Angus, Master of the Temple of Fortitude

Cael Angus, Male Human Priest, Master of the Temple of Fortitude (Clr7): HP 34; AC 4[15]; Atk *+1 flail* (1d8); Move 12; Save 9; AL L; CL/XP 7/600; Special: +2 save vs. paralysis and poison, banish undead, spells (2/2/2/1/1).
Spells: 1st—*cure light wounds*, protection from evil; 2nd—*bless, hold person*; 3rd—*cure disease, prayer*; 4th—*cure serious wounds*; 5th—*raise dead*.
Equipment: *bracers of defense AC 4[15]*, vestments of the temple, wide leather belt with removable holy symbol, *+1 flail*.

Description: Cael Angus is a short, barrel-chested youth. His head is shorn in the tonsure of his order, and he is rarely seen in other than his coarse brown robes. His arms bulge with powerful muscles, and he wears thick leather armbands gilded with the icons of his faith.

Cael is the master of the Temple of Fortitude, the favored place of worship in the Grey Citadel. While many other religions are practiced openly, most of the citizens are devoted to the God of Strength. Cael and his priesthood minister to the needs of the locals and also venture out to the mines, lumber camps, and farms that surround the city. He has discovered a means by which the temple can sustain itself on minimum tithes: while not at prayer or training, the burly acolytes hire themselves out as laborers and stevedores to visiting merchant caravans.

The youngest brother of the Angus clan entered the priesthood at the temple at an early age and proved to be an excellent study and devoted acolyte. Cael rose quickly in the clergy, and before his 20th year, he took over the duties of the aging head priest. Now 25, Cael is responsible for the spiritual well-being of hundreds of citizens. His devotion to his god is the only force that exceeds his devotion to his older brothers, whom he admires greatly.

Cael leaves the citadel only on the direst business. He can usually be found at the Temple of Fortitude, where his time is divided between meditation, mentoring his acolytes, and meeting with his congregation.

He also moves freely about the city, overseeing the activities of the laborers, making house calls, and considering the rants of the prophets in the marketplace.

KEY INDEPENDENTS

These characters are some of the more powerful or notorious citizens, for one reason or another. Elinda, currently missing, is not encountered until the end of the adventure. Fitch, Brother Melph, Rasputin, and Stump all have their roles to play in the development of the mystery, but once those encounters are completed (or deleted), these NPCs are available to replace a deceased character or act as henchmen; with minor modifications to the adventure, any or all of them could serve as pre-generated characters. The Band of the Crimson Mantle is an adventuring party whose efforts will rival those of the heroes.

ELINDA BANNON

Elinda Bannon, Female Human (MU6): HP 17; **AC** 4[15] or 2[17] (missile) and 4[15] (melee) from *shield* spell; **Atk** *+1 staff* (1d6+1) or dagger (1d4); **Move** 12; **Save** 10; **AL** L; **CL/XP** 6/400; **Special:** +2 saves vs. spells, wands and staffs, spells (4/2/2).
Spells: 1st—*light, magic missile, shield, sleep*; 2nd—*invisibility, mirror image*; 3rd—*dispel magic, lightning bolt.*
Equipment: *bracers of defense AC 6[13], +1 staff,* dagger, *ring of protection +2, amulet against scrying, wand of magic missiles* (14 charges), backpack with three days' rations, waterskin and blank, pet owl (Tell).

Note: Elinda's magic items are extensive and scattered throughout this adventure. The heroes are likely to encounter some of these items in the hands of the villain. While Elinda does not mind her items being used to facilitate her rescue, she expects them to be returned and offers to craft something especially for the party. These items are NOT part of the demon's "treasure."

Tell, Owl (Pet): HD 1; **HP** 4; **AC** 6[13]; **Atk** 2 claws (1d3), bite (1d2); **Move** 2 (fly 12); **Save** 17; **AL** N; **CL/XP** 1/15; **Special:** −2 to all die rolls in bright light, flies silently. (*Monstrosities* 369)
Note: Tell does not survive the events of *The Grey Citadel*.

Description: Elinda is a tall, slender beauty with thick brown hair, usually braided to keep it from interfering with her tinkering. Her clothing is always simple and of the highest quality. When she travels, she favors sensible outfits of blouses and trousers, while at home and about town she wears the clothes of a craftsman, including a leather apron laden with tools and smudged with soot and grease.

Elinda is a wizard who focuses her studies on the use of ancient magical devices and artifacts. She travels widely in search of relics and spends a great deal of time sifting through rotting times for obscure clues and references to the resting places of powerful magical items. She has great skill in the creation of magical items as well, although she considers that to be merely a means by which to fund her continual research, the expansion of her library, and her acquisition of rare treasures. She often collaborates with the craftsmen of the city, especially weaponsmiths, as the city's forges are the best for miles around and can produce enchantment-quality blades with ease.

Elinda grew up in the Grey Citadel, for her father was the chief steward of the previous lord. She spent her childhood with the three brothers and all are very close, although their adult lives have led them down different paths. She longs to wed herself to Arb, the eldest of the brothers, but she thinks she lacks the femininity to attract him (in reality, he feels his duties to his citizens prevent him from taking a wife). Bron, the middle brother, is badly smitten with Elinda, but

keeps his distance out of respect for his older brother. Her relationship with Cael is the strongest, and they play a weekly game of checkers at the temple.

When she is not traveling, Elinda can usually be found in her apartments in a tower on the curtain wall of the citadel, where she has a large library in addition to a modest living space. She visits the brothers regularly and also spends a fair bit of time at the forges, conferring with the masters on metallurgy and technique.

RASPUTIN

Rasputin, Half-Elf Male Thief Performer (Thf6): HP 20; **AC** 5[14]; **Atk** *+1 dagger that returns to the hand* (1d4+1) or short sword (1d6) or throwing dagger (1d4); **Move** 12; **Save** 10; **AL** N; **CL/XP** 6/400; **Special:** +2 save bonus vs. traps and magical devices, backstab (x3), darkvision (60ft), read languages, thieving skills.
Thieving Skills: Climb 90%, Tasks/Traps 40%, Hear 4 in 6, Hide 35%, Silent 45%, Locks 35%.
Equipment: *bracers of defense AC 6[13]*, gaudy clothing and jewelry, *+1 dagger that returns to the hand* (in boot), short sword, 4 throwing daggers, *ring of protection +1*, balalaika, props (dice, cards, juggling balls, and so forth), pouch containing 54 gp, 22 sp, 18 cp, and hacksilver ingot worth 90 gp, pet monkey (Vlado).

Vlado, Monkey (Pet): HD 1d4 hp; **HP** 3; **AC** 7[12]; **Atk** 2 claws (1d3); **Move** 15; **Save** 18; **AL** N; **CL/XP** A/5; **Special:** none.
Equipment: vest, fez, hurdy-gurdy, tin cup.

Description: Rasputin is a half-elf performer of dark complexion and slender build. His foreign heritage is evident in his dress and grooming; he favors loose, colorful silk clothing and has thick side-whiskers and long hair.

He is popular around the city, known for performing sleight-of-hand tricks for the local children and pulling bouquets from his sleeve for blushing ladies. His balalaika is always at hand and his repertoire ranges from tear-jerking romantic ballads to bawdy folk songs, but some carry special messages, for Rasputin is an information merchant. He conceals his information in his lyrics so that only their intended listener may recognize them, and he divulges the requested information only after payment has been made to his tip jar, which is managed by his monkey Vlado. In addition to gathering and selling information, Rasputin often serves as a coordinator and go-between for illicit business deals and is willing to violate the city's trade policies, so long as it doesn't involve murder, dark magic, or slavery.

His youth was spent on the road with a troupe of entertainers, and in addition to his music, he possesses considerable skill as a blade thrower — a skill he prefers to keep secret until it is needed. Concealed beneath his cheerful personality is the driving force in his life: an unfulfilled promise he made to an older brother who lay dying after a bandit raid. His brother's child Elisabeta, a rare beauty with a talent for dance, had been abducted during the fighting, surely destined for the slave markets of the arid south. Rasputin pursued and dispatched the band of highwaymen with a vengeance, but not before his niece was sold to a gang of slavers. Since then, Rasputin has drifted from city to city, investigating every brothel and pleasure den and infiltrating the highest royal houses to examine their harems.

He has stayed in the Grey Citadel for several months now, waiting out the winter, saving traveling funds, and talking with merchants and caravan laborers coming in from the trade roads. He can usually be found by day in the caravan camp and performs most evenings at the Market Tavern.

Brother Melph

Brother Melph, Male Human Priest (Clr5): HP 21; AC
7[12]; Atk *+1 staff* (1d6+1); **Move** 12; **Save** 11; **AL** L; **CL/XP**
5/240; **Special:** +2 save versus paralysis and poison, banish
undead, spells (2/2).
Spells: 1st—*cure light wounds* (x2); 2nd—*bless, hold person*.
Equipment: cleric's vestments, leather armor, heavy cloak,
+1 staff (a gift from the nymph Bernya, in return for his
service along the roads of her wilderness), bedroll, holy
symbol, 3 days' trail rations.

Description: Brother Melph is a lighthearted man in his late youth. He
is tall and slim, even frail-looking — but this is far from the truth. His
brown hair is swept back from the temple, and his skin is deeply tanned
from long journeys under the sun. His manner is reserved and quiet.

For many of the crofters and trappers of Eamonvale, he is the only
man of the cloth to visit with any regularity, and he has been present
at a great many births, deaths, weddings, harvest festivals, and barn
raisings in the valley. Those who know him are always glad to see
him, for he invariably brings news from afar and a new story or joke.
His traveling companions are often surprised by his wry wit, just as
his enemies are surprised by his agility and whirling attacks with his
unassuming walking staff.

A compulsive wanderer, he rarely settles in one location for long
unless his services are needed. Nobody knows where he comes from
originally, and when asked about his homeland, he responds, "Origins
and destinations are unimportant … it is the journey that matters."

Melph can be encountered outside of Dun Eamon (see the
Wilderness Encounters Appendix), as well as in the caravan camp.

Fitch the Barman

Fitch the Barman, Male Dwarf (Ftr5): HP 32; AC 4[15];
Atk *+1 battle axe* (1d8+1) or leather sap (1d4 nonlethal);
Move 12; **Save** 9 (+1, ring); **AL** L; **CL/XP** 5/240; **Special:**
+4 save vs. magic, darkvision (60ft), multiple attacks (5) vs.
creatures with 1 or fewer HD.
Equipment: +1 battle axe, dwarven chainmail, ring of
protection +1, potion of heroism, leather sap, 85 gp.

Description: Fitch is the barkeep, a grizzled, broad-shouldered,
dwarf who says nothing but heard everything. He usually wears
a coarse woolen shirt and trousers, but his armor is kept oiled and
locked away should it be needed.

His services at the bar are varied, but mostly relate to pulling pints
and keeping inventory for the extensive cellars. Customers regard him
as trustworthy, mostly because he is rarely heard to speak a word to
anyone. The safety of the Market Tavern, its staff, and its customers
is of utmost importance to him. He is especially fond of Molly and
Horace, the two young folks that work at the Tavern, as they are
without family, and he has none of his own. He maintains a friendship
with Stump, a compatriot and former business partner who frequents
the bar.

Fitch is a retired adventurer. He traveled the land as a young dwarf,
fighting wars, crusading against goblinkind, and delving deep into
perilous dungeons. The patrons at the Market Tavern have learned,
however, that those are not days he likes to revisit, and he is very hesitant
to discuss adventuring with anyone. He does not even discuss them with
Stump, who was the leader of their adventuring band. He is content with
his current life and prefers to keep his previous one a secret.

Fitch is almost always encountered at the Market Tavern, although
he can be found during the slow hours in the market looking out for
exotic spirits with which to stock the shelves.

Stump the Halfling

Stump, Male Halfling Thief (Thf6): HP 17; AC 6[13]; Atk
+1 short sword (1d6+1), dagger (1d4), or light crossbow
(1d4+1); **Move** 12; **Save** 10; **AL** N; **CL/XP** 6/400; **Special:**
+1 to-hit missile weapon bonus, +2 save bonus vs. traps
and magical devices, +4 save vs. magic, backstab (x3), read
languages, thieving skills.
Thieving Skills: Climb 70%, Tasks/Traps 30%, Hear 4 in 6,
Hide 45%, Silent 55%, Locks 25%.
Equipment: *+1 leather armor*, *+1 short sword*, light
crossbow, 20 bolts, maps of several dungeon complexes, extra
prosthetics, thieves' tools, *potion of invisibility*, *potion of
frozen concoction*.
Note: Stump (which is a nickname) lost his left hand while
defusing a trap and has since had it replaced with an
eight-inch-long steel spike. This spike deals damage as a
dagger. The sharp spike is interchangeable with a hook and
blunt-tipped spike as well. The loss of his hand has hurt his
thieving skills, however.

Description: Stump is an aging, unpleasant halfling with short grey
hair and thick eyebrows and beard. His left hand is missing at the wrist
and has been replaced with a steel spike. He bathes infrequently and
usually smells like alcohol.

Stump's cheer has gone out of him and been replaced with bitterness
and resignation; he takes joy only in monitoring the success of his
adopted daughter, Elinda Bannon. Most of the citizens regard him as
a sad old drunk, not knowing the truth of his past. He also maintains
contact with Fitch, the barman at the Market Tavern. Fitch is an old
adventuring partner of his and one of the only survivors of the expedition
that cost him his hand. He periodically gives advice to Lord Angus, who
respects his wisdom and experience in foreign lands.

Stump has explored some of the most notorious dungeons in the
land. His academic dedication and mastery of ancient tongues served
him well in such endeavors, and he achieved renown to such a degree
that he was able to pick and choose from lucrative financial offers
from some very powerful figures. His last expedition as a dungeon
guide met with great tragedy, and Stump was one of three survivors of
a party of 20. The failure of that outing compromised his reputation,
but the booty allowed him to retire comfortably in the valley.

Stump can be encountered at the Market Tavern or at the Hole, but
spends most of his time drinking and sulking in his run-down hovel.

The Band of the Crimson Mantle

This group of adventurers has been in Dun Eamon only a few
days longer than the party. They are greedy and unscrupulous, but
not all of them are necessarily evil. The heroes may clash with
them above and beneath the ground as they investigate the mystery
surrounding the underground caverns. Because Dun Eamon is a city
of adventure on a busy trade route, some of the locals may know of
the Band; the background information is provided as rumor material
as well as a roleplaying aid. The Band has adopted a red cloak as
its symbol, although the members wear theirs in different fashions.
Since joining forces, the Band has established a system of common
phrases for communication.

Pratchett

Pratchett, Male Half-Elf Thief (Thf5): HP 14; AC 6[13];
Atk short sword (1d6) or *+2 light crossbow* (1d4+1) or leather
sap (1d4 nonlethal); **Move** 12; **Save** 11; **AL** C; **CL/XP** 5/240;
Special: +2 save bonus vs. traps and magical devices,
backstab (x2), darkvision (60ft), detect secret doors (4-in-6
chance), read languages, thieving skills.

Thieving Skills: Climb 89%, Tasks/Traps 35%, Hear 4 in 6, Hide 30%, Silent 40%, Locks 30%.

Equipment: *+1 leather armor*, short sword, leather sap, *+2 light crossbow*, 20 bolts (8 pre-poisoned); large vial of purple worm poison (8 applications; save or additional 1d6 damage); 50ft silk rope, grappling iron, thieves' tools, flint and steel, hooded lantern, 2 flasks of oil, 2 days' trail rations, waterskin, pouch (contains 65 gp, 18 sp, and 4 garnets [worth 120 gp, two worth 100 gp each, and 90 gp), map to his secret cache of supplies and treasure.

Description: Pratchett is a handsome half-elf with wavy black hair and bright eyes. He wears his sword and crimson cape in the most dashing manner he can imagine, but his bravado is sometimes transparent, allowing his greed and lust for power to show through.

Pratchett was an orphan raised by a band of thieves in a distant city. He spent his youth lifting merchant purses and holding up caravans, but he was always dissatisfied with his share of the booty. After he was caught skimming a few coins from a stolen pouch, he fled before an assassin's blade could end his career. He decided that adventuring rather than thievery was the way to make money, and he formed his own company. His years at the bottom of the pecking order led him to crave authority; he does not tolerate any threat to his leadership. It is rumored that the Band's last fighter lost sight of who was really in charge and fell victim to a poisoned crossbow bolt. Money matters most to Pratchett; he cares nothing for his companions or his clients. Other adventuring parties drive down profits and take away jobs; therefore, they are competition and must be harassed and handicapped by any means possible.

Pratchett knows that Dresden is completely unstable and would gladly replace him, but he needs a spellcaster and does not mind paying him in shiny knickknacks. He sees Isidra as a harmless eccentric who is good in a fight and can heal the party, and her obsession with death distracts her from the treasure and its distribution. He knows Yelm is a great fighter, and the only pay he requires is enough cash for drinks and another fight.

Isidra

Isidra, Female Human Priest of the God of Death (Clr5): HP 23; AC 3[16]; **Atk** heavy mace (1d6); **Move** 12; **Save** 10 (+1, ring); **AL** C; **CL/XP** 5/240; **Special:** +2 save vs. paralysis and poison, banish undead, spells (2/2).

Spells: 1st—*cause light wounds* (x2); 2nd—*hold person, silence 15ft radius*.

Equipment: *+1 ring mail* (see special note below), small steel shield with unholy symbol of the God of Death, heavy mace, *ring of protection +1*, *potion of healing* (x3), scroll (*detect magic* and *speak with dead*), mummified hand of a small child, 2 days' trail rations, waterskin, 2 torches, pouch (containing 32 gp and 18 sp), silver necklace with 3 tiny black pearls worth 500 gp total.

Note: Isidra's armor was a gift from her mentor. Unlike most magical armor, this suit of ring mail adapts to a new owner's race/build/gender only if the armor and the new wearer are immersed in unholy water. It is currently in the form of a revealing bustier and corset, a scale skirt, bracers, and leggings.

Description: Isidra is a pale, slender woman who might have been beautiful if it was not for her dark, sunken eyes and sardonic smile. She wears black robes over her armor, and her crimson mantle is the only color on her person.

Isidra's upbringing was happy at first, but later led her down the dark path she now treads. Her parents, caretakers at a small cemetery, were slain when they stumbled into a priest of death robbing bodies for his rituals. The evil cleric took over the position of caretaker and became Isidra's only family. He raised her and schooled her, and she grew morbid and detached through lack of contact with living beings. When the villagers mobbed up and razed the cleric's dwelling, she escaped, returning later to the smoldering ruins. She heard her mentor's cries for her, but could only sit and watch with fascination as death took him. She fled one crime scene after another until she found the band; they needed a healer, and they usually managed to leave a pleasant trail of corpses wherever they went.

Isidra is starting to realize that Pratchett is just using her, but she does not care enough about money to be concerned. She ignores Yelm; his carefree approach to life is why she prefers the company of the dead. She leaves Dresden in his own little world, but is concerned that her chosen path may drive her to the same fate.

Dresden the Mad

Dresden the Mad, Male Halfling Mage (MU5): HP 14; AC 6[13] or 2[17] (missile) and 4[15] (melee) from *shield* spell; **Atk** dagger (1d4) or sling (1d4); **Move** 12; **Save** 11; **AL** C; **CL/XP** 5/240; **Special:** +1 to-hit missile weapons bonus, +2 saves vs. spells, +4 save vs. magic, wands and staffs, spells (4/2/1).

Spells: 1st—*charm person, magic missile, shield, sleep*; 2nd—*invisibility, web*; 3rd—*fireball*.

Equipment: *bracers of defense AC 6[13]*, dirty red robes, dagger, sling with 30 stones, *ring of fire resistance*, *potion of flying*, *potion of gaseous form*, 2 scrolls (*haste* and *knock*), assorted rocks (his "friends"), 2 days' trail rations, clay flask, pet toad named Pebble.

Description: Dresden is thin and scrawny, and he usually stands by himself, mumbling and casting about wild glances. His pet toad nestled in his mangy hair, his rotten teeth, and his bizarre personality make him a thoroughly unpleasant individual. His red cloak has been fashioned into a loose toga and is torn and ridden with lice, much to Pratchett's disgust.

Dresden is dangerously unbalanced and unpredictable. He was born in a quiet little halfling village that was completely unprepared to have a spellcaster in its midst. Dresden spent many childhood hours alone, talking to rocks and experimenting with his powers. The explosive destruction of his parents' house was the result of one such experiment. He miraculously escaped unharmed and was seen skipping into the woods holding a conversation with only himself. Since then, he has found employment on and off as an adventuring spellcaster, but as his grip with reality slips, work becomes harder to find. Dresden speaks almost exclusively in Terran, although it is unknown how or why he learned that language. He is mischievous and sadistic and uses his spells to heckle and annoy people.

Only Pratchett seems able to communicate effectively with him, which Dresden tolerates because it keeps him from having to deal with other people. He finds Yelm and Isidra to be very dull because they do not seem to be a part of the world in which he currently lives.

Note: Dresden does not survive the events of *The Grey Citadel*.

Yelm the Barbarian

Yelm, Male Human Barbarian (Ftr5): HP 31; AC 5[14]; **Atk** *+1 bastard sword* (1d8+3) or throwing axe (1d6+2) or strike (1d4+2); **Move** 12; **Save** 10; **AL** N; **CL/XP** 5/240; **Special:** +2 to hit and damage strength bonus, multiple attacks (5) vs. creatures with 1 or fewer HD.

Equipment: chainmail, stained kilt, *+1 bastard sword*, 4 throwing axes, 2 flasks of oil, wineskin, flask of whiskey, 5 days' trail rations, 6 torches, 50ft hemp rope, silver beck torc worth 20 gp, silver-trimmed drinking horn worth 12 gp, hacksilver armband worth 8 gp, pouch containing 25 gp and 16 sp.

Description: Yelm is a tall, powerful man with a booming voice and a fierce look in his green eyes. His long red hair is braided into his thick beard, and intricate blue tattoos cover half of his face and most of his body. His red swath of cloth is worn in a primitive but functional fashion, loosely pleated around him and held with a thick leather belt.

Yelm has been many things in his life — wandering barbarian, slave, pit fighter, caravan guard, beggar, soldier, wilderness guide, prisoner, outlaw, gambler, and more. Yet he has come to realize there are only two activities he truly enjoys: drinking and fighting. Those two activities can keep him in plenty of trouble, and he needs the Band to stay out of it. He is not evil, but he is immoral and unruly. He has no tolerance for weakness or cowardice and always prefers a stand-up fight to sneaking about in the dark.

Yelm likely follows Pratchett as long as he finds things to fight and gives him money to drink, although he does not approve of some of the leader's methods. He looks on Isidra as a challenge and is always trying to get her to find a bit more enjoyment in life. He leaves Dresden in his own world, but is tempted to put the little madman out of everyone's misery.

THE MIST WATCH

The maintenance of law and order in and around the Grey Citadel is the responsibility of the Mist Watch. The force is made up of career soldiers, citizen militia, and wilderness outriders. There is no law of mandatory service for the citizens, but any man living within the city walls is subject to conscription in times of war.

Bron Angus is the Captain of the Watch and has been highly successful despite his young age. His experiences as a young man in a mercenary company taught him to be intolerant of sloth, insolence, and drunkenness, and his strict orders have resulted in an elite fighting force. The members of the Mist Watch are trained to a basic level with all weapons and tactics, but many of them have additional areas of expertise. All the watchmen are rotated through various duty stations to avoid boredom and complacency.

MIST WATCH SOLDIER

Mist Watch Soldier, Male or Female Human Warrior: HD 1; AC 5[14]; Atk longsword (1d8), spear (1d6) or longbow x2 (1d6); **Move** 12; **Save** 17; **AL** L or N; **CL/XP** 1/15; **Special:** none. (*Monstrosities* 257)
Equipment: ring mail, steel shield, longsword, spear, longbow, quiver of 20 arrows.

MIST WATCH SERGEANT

Mist Watch Sergeant, Male or Female Human Warrior:
HD 3; AC 4[15]; Atk longsword (1d8), spear (1d6) or longbow x2 (1d6); **Move** 12; **Save** 14; **AL** L or N; **CL/XP** 3/60; **Special:** none. (*Monstrosities* 256)
Equipment: chainmail, steel shield, longsword, spear, longbow, quiver of 20 arrows, potion of healing, signal horn, rank chain.

MIST WATCH CONSTABLE

Mist Watch Constable, Male or Female Human Warrior (Ftr3): HD 3; AC 4[15]; Atk *+1 longsword* (1d8+1) or longbow x2 (1d6); **Move** 12; **Save** 12; **AL** C; **CL/XP** 3/60; **Special:** multiple attacks (3) vs. creatures with 1 or fewer HD.
Equipment: chainmail, large steel shield, *+1 longsword*, longbow and quiver of 20 arrows, signal horn, rank chain.

MIST WATCH SPECIALISTS

Some specialists do exist within the ranks of the watch: cavalry units known as **Outriders**, **Lookouts** manning the city walls, **Woodsmen** patrolling the wilderness areas of the valley, and the **Mist Mages** supporting the watch with magic.

Outriders patrol the wilderness surrounding the citadel, on the lookout for brigands and threatening monsters. They are always accompanied by a **Warden** when outside the city. See the **Wilderness Encounters Appendix** for outrider profiles.

Lookouts man the walls to watch for trouble.

Mist Watch Lookout, Male or Female Human Warrior:
HD 1; AC 5[14]; Atk longsword (1d8), spear (1d6) or longbow x2 (1d6); **Move** 12; **Save** 17; **AL** L or N; **CL/XP** 1/15; **Special:** none. (*Monstrosities* 257)
Equipment: ring mail, steel shield, longsword, spear, longbow, quiver of 20 arrows, signal horn, spyglass.

Woodsmen are skilled hunters and trackers who patrol the thick woods beyond the reach of mounted patrols and act as scouts in time of war. See the **Wilderness Encounters Appendix** for their profiles.

The Mist Mages are spellcasters who back up the traditional troops with their displays of magic.

Mist Mage, Male or Female Human Wizard (MU4): HD 4d4; AC 9[10] or 2[17] (missile) and 4[15] (melee) from *shield* spell; **Atk** dagger (1d4) or *wand of magic missiles* (1d4); **Move** 12; **Save** 12; **AL** L or N; **CL/XP** 4/240; **Special:** +2 saves vs. spells, wands and staffs, spells (3/2).
Spells: 1st—*charm person, light, shield*; 2nd—*detect evil, phantasmal force.*
Equipment: robes, dagger, *wand of magic missiles* (2d4 charges), *potion of healing*, spellbook.

Common patrols are as follows:
Mist Watch City Patrol: 9 soldiers, a **sergeant**, 25% chance of a constable, 10% chance of a mist mage.
Mist Watch Night Patrol: 9 soldiers, a **sergeant**, 50% chance of a constable, 25% chance of a mist mage.
Mist Watch Mounted Patrol: 7 outriders, a **warden**, 10% chance of a **woodsman**.

THE EBON UNION

The Ebon Union is a displaced guild of criminals and cutthroats. They were ousted one year previous to this adventure from their lair in the city of Reme (or any convenient urban location in your campaign world) by a coalition of adventurers and city guardsmen. Devlin, the highest ranking survivor, took the remnants of the gang and fled into the wilderness, where they survived as highwaymen for several months (the party may have even encountered their bandit gangs in the past). The approach of autumn and a taste for the luxuries of city life finally drove them to seek out a new home. The aspiring assassin Tabitha was one of several outriders sent to seek out a potential home for the guild. When she investigated the rumors of a halfling fortress below Dun Eamon, she knew the Ebon Union had found a place to make its new home. Some of the Union did not fancy a life underground; they remained in the wilderness under command of the ranger Hobark and are described in **Appendix D: Wilderness Encounters**.

The Ebon Union has developed a unique character through its trials of the past year, and some of its members that made the transition are very specialized. A few of them (called **Nets**) became adept with the net during their escapades as bandits, hiding in trees and using weighted nets to drag horsemen to the ground. These thieves found their nets to be useful in the city as well, especially for taking uncooperative merchants or rogues into custody for a "discussion" with Devlin. Their crossbowmen (known as **Bolts**) developed remarkable accuracy while providing cover fire for raids on merchant caravan camps, and these thieves now provide cover from the rooftops while the burglars are at work. The booty of their caravan raids needed to be marketed, so a number of fences (**shifters**) exist within the organization. Thanks to the heavily restricted trade sanctions in Dun Eamon, these scoundrels have also found continued demand for their skills. Thieves with more traditional skills (**cutpurses**) supply the guild with its most consistent income.

The union's lair is in the fortified gatehouse of a long-abandoned halfling stronghold on **Level 3** of the underground cavern complex. The thieves dwell in the darkness much of the time, and they have adapted to their surroundings. Treat all members of the Ebon Union as having darkvision (30ft); this ability is lost if they spend a day or more aboveground in the daylight. The thieves have specific orders regarding the secrecy of their location and a number of locations in the city that they can use as staging points for their entries and exits from the sewers.

The Ebon Union is very conscious of any investigation the party conducts, and their eyes and ears all over the city keep them informed of the heroes' progress. As the adventure progresses, **Timed Encounter 3.1** (see **Chapter Two**) and a possible assassination attempt at the Bathhouse (**Area P**; see **Chapter Three**) represent the union's efforts to protect its identity and activities. Allow the Ebon Union to react to the heroes' actions, especially if they encounter thieves and allow them to escape — the Ebon Union is quick to exploit any information the survivors can provide about party composition and abilities. Similarly, if any thieves survive encounters with the party in the dungeon, the thieves in the lair in **Area 3-25** (see **Chapter Six**) are prepared for the group's arrival.

Note: The party might possibly try to infiltrate one or more of its members into the Ebon Union. This strategy is not unreasonable — after all, the Ebon Union would rather have the local thieves contributing to its coffers than working against it. The process is not easy, however. First, they must make contact with a representative, which can be done by detaining a randomly encountered member or approaching one of the guild agents (such as Rorin, Kinnan the Dark, or Edgar). They require a heist of the character's choosing that must yield a profit of at least 200 gp, with all of the profits going to the guild. The applicant is then rewarded with a cloth token and a vague set of directions to the lair (enter the market drain and follow the flow of the water, cross and recross the river, and so on). If the applicant survives the trip, he must surrender his personal treasure to the guild hoard for "safekeeping."

Devlin is very untrusting of new recruits — the character can expect several dangerous assignments before he is fully accepted. This is a complicated plot development that is not fully accommodated by the adventure text, so you may choose not to allow it to occur. Infiltration is unlikely after the group begins an investigation into the robberies or tangles with any of the thieves.

The profiles of Devlin and his lieutenants are detailed in the locations or events in which they are encountered:

NPC	Role	Location
Edgar	informant	Public Stables (**Area B**)
Molly	informant	Market Tavern (**Area D**)
Rorin	shifter	The Hole (**Area O**)
Tabitha	assassin	Bathhouse (**Area P**)
Kubris and **Thurf**	agents	**Timed Encounter 3.1** (see **Chapter Two**)
Gulik	agent	**Timed Encounter 3.3** (see **Chapter Two**)
Devlin	guildmaster	**Dungeon Area 3-25**.

The bulk of the Ebon Union membership is as follows:

BOLTS

Bolt, Male or Female Human (Thf2): HP 2d4; AC 7[12]; Atk dagger (1d4) or light crossbow (1d4+1); **Move** 12; **Save** 14; **AL** C; **CL/XP** 2/30; **Special:** +2 save bonus vs. traps and magical devices, backstab (x2), thieving skills.

Thieving Skills: Climb 86%, Tasks/Traps 20%, Hear 3 in 6, Hide 15%, Silent 25%, Locks 15%.

Equipment: leather armor, 2 daggers, light crossbow, 20 bolts, pouch of caltrops (1d4 damage, halves movement in 10ft-diameter area), pouch with 1d8 gp and 2d10 sp.

CUTPURSES

Cutpurse, Male or Female Human (Thf2): HP 2d4; AC 7[12]; **Atk** dagger (1d4); **Move** 12; **Save** 14; **AL** C; **CL/XP** 2/30; **Special:** +2 save bonus vs. traps and magical devices, backstab (x2), thieving skills.

Thieving Skills: Climb 86%, Tasks/Traps 20%, Hear 3 in 6, Hide 15%, Silent 25%, Locks 15%.

Equipment: leather armor, 2 daggers, pouch of caltrops (1d4 damage, halves movement in 10ft-diameter area), pouch with 2d10 gp and 2d10 sp.

KNIVES

Knife, Male or Female Human (Thf1): HP 1d4; AC 7[12]; **Atk** dagger (1d4); **Move** 12; **Save** 15; **AL** C; **CL/XP** 1/15; **Special:** +2 save bonus vs. traps and magical devices, backstab (x2), thieving skills.

Thieving Skills: Climb 85%, Tasks/Traps 15%, Hear 3 in 6, Hide 10%, Silent 20%, Locks 10%.

Equipment: leather armor, 2 daggers, pouch of caltrops (1d4 damage, halves movement in 10ft-diameter area), pouch with 1d4 gp and 2d6 sp, 10 % chance of a small pouch of powdered silver skimmed from a previous heist (worth 1d4 gp).

NETS

Net, Male or Female Human (Thf2): HP 2d4; AC 7[12]; **Atk** net (save or entangled) or dagger (1d4); **Move** 12; **Save** 14; **AL** C; **CL/XP** 2/30; **Special:** +2 save bonus vs. traps and magical devices, backstab (x2), thieving skills.

Thieving Skills: Climb 86%, Tasks/Traps 20%, Hear 3 in 6, Hide 15%, Silent 25%, Locks 15%.

Equipment: leather armor, net, dagger, pouch of caltrops (1d4 damage, halves movement in 10ft-diameter area), 50ft silk rope, grappling hook, pouch with 1d8 gp and 2d10 sp, 10% chance of a small pouch of powdered silver skimmed from a previous heist (worth 2d4 gp).

SHIFTERS

Shifter, Male or Female Human (Thf2): HP 2d4; AC 7[12]; **Atk** dagger (1d4); **Move** 12; **Save** 14; **AL** C; **CL/XP** 2/30; **Special:** +2 save bonus vs. traps and magical devices, backstab (x2), thieving skills.

Thieving Skills: Climb 86%, Tasks/Traps 20%, Hear 3 in 6, Hide 15%, Silent 25%, Locks 15%.

Equipment: leather armor, net, 2 daggers, pouch of caltrops (1d4 damage, halves movement in 10ft-diameter area), scales, pouch with 2d10 gp and 2d10 sp, 10% chance of a small pouch of powdered silver skimmed from a previous heist (worth 2d4 gp).

THUGS

Bandit, Male or Female Human: HD 1; AC 6[13]; **Atk** short sword (1d6) or club (1d6), dagger (1d4); **Move** 12; **Save** 17; **AL** C; **CL/XP** 1/15; **Special:** none. (*Monstrosities* 254)

Equipment: leather armor, short sword or club, dagger, small wooden shield, pouch with 1d4 gp and 2d6 sp.

Appendix B: New Monsters

Mongrel of Yith

Hit Dice: 4
Armor Class: 4[15]
Attacks: bite (1d6+1)
Saving Throw: 13
Special: Terrifying howl
Move: 15
Alignment: Chaos
Number Encountered: 1, 1d6+4
Challenge Level: 4/120

Mongrels of Yith are the offspring of hounds of Yith breeding with normal dogs, wolves, and coyotes. The large mongrels' terrifying howl is a result of their supernatural parent, and causes anyone who fails a saving throw to flee in fear for 1d6 rounds. The mongrels are usually bigger than their hound of Yith parent thanks to their normal parent. They are more intelligent than a normal animal and often work together to surround foes.

Mongrel of Yith: HD 4; AC 4[15]; **Atk** bite (1d6+1); **Move** 15; **Save** 13; **AL** C; **CL/XP** 4/120; **Special:** terrifying howl (save or flee in fear for 1d6 rounds).

Appendix C: New Magical Items

Unique Item

Mamuthek's Aperture

A power-hungry magic-user named Mamuthek created this ancient device (see **Adventure Background** in the **Introduction**). It is formed of thin gold bands that pivot on tiny rivets and can be collapsed into a small wooden box or expanded to create a globe of interwoven strips. When unfolded, it sits on a four-legged stand and looks deceivingly flimsy. A small gold plate hangs from the top of the globe from four fine chains. When activated (by giving it a gentle spin), the globe accelerates to blinding speed, opening an aperture to another plane of existence and summoning a creature (or creatures). The device can call up to 12 HD worth of creatures or a single creature of no more than 12 HD.

The plate is used for determining the source plane and target creature to be called. A mineral placed on the tray determines the plane on which the gate opens; this includes minerals from alternate Material Planes and Inner or Outer planes. A piece of organic matter placed on the tray determines the nature of the creature called; there is no limit on how long the organic material has been lifeless or how large it must be. If both organic and mineral materials are provided, the artifact attempts to locate a creature of that type on that plane. For example, a chunk of ore from the Abyss and the top of a minotaur's horn produce a demonic minotaur, if one exists. If no material is provided when the device is activated, it attempts to locate the last being it contacted and retrieve it again, regardless of how much time has passed since the previous activation.

Mamuthek's Aperture does not force any action or obligation on the creature beyond a compulsion to step through. Called creatures with 6 or fewer HD cannot resist; creature with more than 6 HD can resist the compulsion with a saving throw. Around the equator of the golden globe is a shallow tray that can be used to establish a ward against the creature. If filled with powdered silver (25 gp worth per use), a *protection from evil* circle is created to ward against the called creature. A creature that fails its saving throw is contained within the ward.

If the creature is contained, a service agreement may be negotiated as normal. If it has the opportunity or if no task is assigned, the creature may return by activating the artifact while inside the globe, but this is possible only before the device is used to call another creature. Also, creatures called using *Mamuthek's Aperture* are never forced to return, even after completing the service; there is no maximum duration, and a creature can stay and act independently if it so desires.

Several liabilities exist in this faulted artifact. The lack of obligation on the part of the creature puts the user at risk. Also, the inability to send a called creature back has resulted in the introduction of some very powerful beings to the Material Plane over the years.

Note: Called creatures do not disappear when slain; their bodies figure into the events of *The Grey Citadel*.

Medium Miscellaneous

Magical Item

Belt of Reduction

Elinda Bannon crafted this magical belt to facilitate her comings and goings through her ring gates to her secret laboratory. The belt is elegantly crafted of brown leather and gold chain and reduces the wearer by 10% to 50% of their original height. The degree of reduction is established based on the link of chain that is fastened, and the effects are reversed when the belt is removed.

Lesser Miscellaneous

Magical Item

Charm of Silence

This small charm is worn on a non-magical chain around the neck. It consists of an onyx stone within a tiny silver globe that can be opened to expose the charm. When the onyx is exposed, it projects an area effect identical to the *silence* spell with a radius of 10 feet. The area of silence prevails until the globe is closed and the onyx is concealed or the charm is removed (**Note:** The death of the wearer does not end the effect). The charm of silence can be activated only once per day; once it is deactivated, it cannot be used again for 24 hours, regardless of how much time has passed since the original activation.

Ring

Ring of Animate Dead

This ring carved from bleached bone allows the wearer to raise 2d6 zombies or skeletons once per day. The corpses remain animated until slain or until the wearer uses the ring again, at which point they crumble into mounds of gore. Usable by magic-users and clerics.

Unique Trap

Box o' Darkness Trap

The *box o' darkness trap* is used by Gethrax to protect his lair in **Dungeon Level 1**. While it is a magical item (created by Gethrax's unholy order), it is also considered a trap and its effects are fully described in **Area 1-9** (see **Chapter Four**). The heroes should continue to encounter these items if they pursue the cult that manufactures them.

The traps are armed when wound up and from then on are triggered by the approach of any Lawful humanoid within 50 feet. When triggered, they begin to play a pleasant tune as would a child's music box, and the sound of laughing children can be heard. After five rounds, the music slows and thick black fog seeps out of the box, expanding to cover a 50-foot radius. This sickly fog animates 2d6 dead creatures (as the *animate dead* spell) in that area (if available). Each newly raised undead creature receives +1 hit point and a +1 bonus to attacks, damage, and saving throws. Checks to turn undead in this area suffer a –3 penalty for 10 hours. On the bottom of the box is an engraved sigil that may be able to lead the party to the powerful creator of the devices in a later quest.

APPENDIX D: WILDERNESS ENCOUNTERS

<CH>Appendix D: Wilderness Encounters

This appendix details the wilderness areas around the city of Dun Eamon. It is presented separately because it is not crucial to the main adventure. You are encouraged to set the Grey Citadel in your own world and use the wilderness encounters as appropriate in your own campaign. The following information is provided either as a more fleshed-out campaign setting or as source material for you to cut and paste and use as you will in your own setting to expand upon the main adventure contained in this book.

The Grey Citadel is located in a remote area many miles from anywhere of note. This most likely means — if you are using this material to detail the trip to Dun Eamon — that the heroes will spend a few days (and nights) en route to the city on whatever business has drawn them there. These encounters should help impart the flavor of the various creatures, conditions, and organizations that make the frontier such a dangerous place to adventure.

A few of these encounters have ties to the plot as detailed in the city, but none of them is critical to the success of the adventure, so feel free to run as few or as many of these as desired or to save them for future adventures in Eamonvale. They have been geared toward the party levels indicated for the adventure — with a few exceptions — but their treasure generally reflects the poor economy of the frontier wilderness. Some of them (notably the lizardfolk and highwaymen lairs) may need additional development and/or mapping.

The wilderness surrounding Dun Eamon is mostly forested mountain slopes, although some areas feature steep rocky bluffs, trackless moors, or boggy hollows. For extended wilderness adventuring in Eamonvale, three encounter tables are provided below: one for trade road traffic, one for wilderness encounters, and one for use at night in either location.

In addition to the road and wilderness encounters, two other regions of note are found in Eamonvale. One is the Trackless Mire, a vast blanket bog that is utterly inhospitable. It is covered with hidden sinkholes, quickmud, limestone fissures, caverns, and easily confused landmarks, making it a lethal place for adventuring. The wizard Elinda Bannon keeps a secret workshop here (see **Area L-9** in **Chapter Two**). No encounters of importance occur in this desolate area.

The other type of encounter region is the village, of which there are several scattered every 10 or 12 miles along the road. These small communities are almost exclusively made up of farmers, trappers, and shepherds. A village of 100 citizens or more has a magistrate and a small militia; the most influential citizens usually administrate the smaller ones. Encounters in these small communities might also include caravans, mounted patrols, and woodsmen.

THE SURROUNDING WILDERNESS

The River Eamon flows down out of the Stoneheart Mountains, first through snow-fed mountain streams before crashing down through rocky gorges and finally calming and widening as it flows across the lowland plains toward the sea. The region surrounding the river valley (known as Eamonvale) is governed from the city of Dun Eamon. The authority of the lord of Eamonvale extends from the river's headwaters in the rugged mountains to the edge of the grasslands that stretch endlessly away from the foothills of the Stonehearts. Encounters in the region immediately surrounding the city are described in this chapter.

The trade road runs from the more-civilized lowlands over the forbidding peaks of the Stoneheart Mountains into exotic distant lands. Merchant traffic is consistent on the road for as long as the mountain passes are open, but it peaks during the summer and fall seasons when rivers are down and the first snow has not yet fallen. Even after the merchant trade across the mountains has fallen off for the season, local hunters, trappers, farmers, craftsmen, and adventurers still travel to the Grey Citadel with regularity, so the trade road is never without encounters.

Some of the regions that frame the trade road are desolate and uninhabited, but most of the Eamonvale region is alive with animal life and dotted with small settlements. Wandering off the road is not advised by anyone who knows the area — bandits, highwaymen, and humanoid tribes are always nearby. Outrider patrols from Dun Eamon travel the tradeways and police the villages and hamlets, but even they do not wander far from the road.

WILDERNESS WEATHER

Weather in Eamonvale is commonly chilly, damp, and grey. Assume that at any given time there is some combination of light fog and mist in the air, which has the same effect as the weather described in the city. Heavier fog and rain are included on the encounter tables and described below.

Heavy Fog: Visibility is obscured beyond five feet. Heavy fog lasts 1d4 hours.

Rain: A steady rain reduces visibility range by half. These rainstorms last for 2d4 hours.

Downpour: A strong but short-lived cloudburst combines the effects of rain and fog as described above. These storms last for only 1d4 hours.

ENCOUNTERS ON THE TRADE ROAD

The trade road is a wide boulevard of crushed gravel spotted with periodic potholes and washouts. It is 20 feet wide in most places, with a five-foot-wide grassy verge on either side. Beyond the verge, the landscape varies from rocky gorge to thick forest to steep precipice, and often the terrain beyond the road is invisible in the drifting mist. For encounters on the road, roll 1d20 every hour.

1d20	Encounter
1 (unique)	**Logan the Furrier**
2 (unique)	**Fallen Messenger**
3 (unique)	**Brother Melph**
4–5	**Merchant Caravan**
6 (unique)	**Kamvase**, wandering minstrel
7–8	**Lizardfolk Hunters** or **Hobark's Highwaymen**
9–10	**Outrider Patrol**
11	Heavy fog
12	Rain
13	Downpour
14–20	No Encounter

LOGAN THE FURRIER

Logan is a typical trapper who lays his trap lines along the wooded mountain creeks around the city. When encountered, he appears with an enormous bundle of furs slung across his back, a canvas bag at his side, and a spear in his hand. He uses the trade road for travel to and from the city's market, where he sells his tanned skins in Raiment Row. He has a small shack up in the hills where he does his own

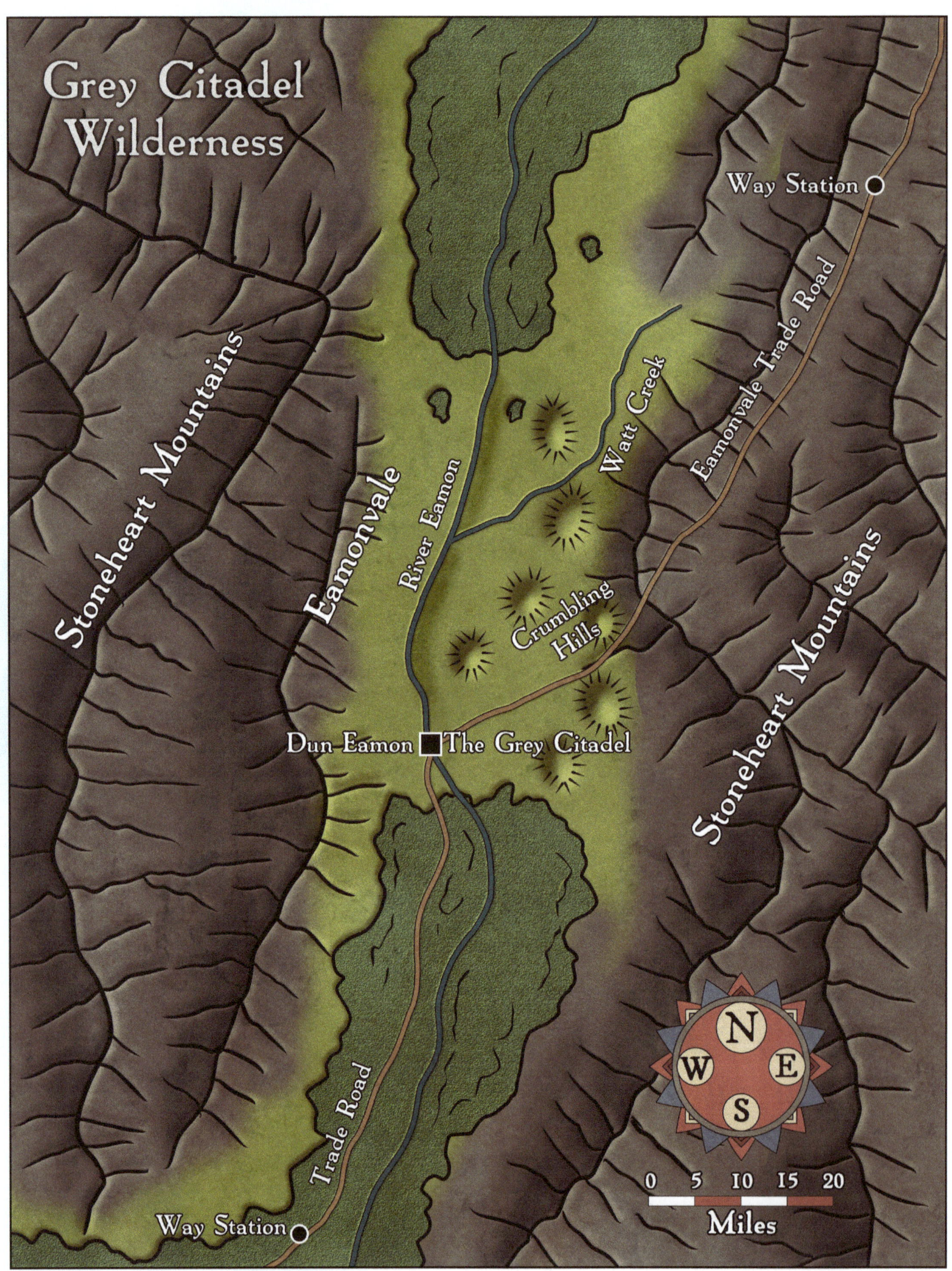

Grey Citadel Wilderness
Stoneheart Mountains
Stoneheart Mountains
Way Station
Eamonvale Trade Road
Watt Creek
Eamonvale
River Eamon
Crumbling Hills
Dun Eamon
The Grey Citadel
Trade Road
Way Station
N
W
E
S
0 5 10 15 20
Miles

tanning and curing. He visits the Grey Citadel once or twice each week and can give the party a rumor or two from the **City Rumors Table** (see **Chapter Two**), most likely dealing with the demons or some other current event, but it may be slightly inaccurate due to the word-of-mouth process his rumors usually come by.

If Logan is encountered at night, the party comes upon his small roadside camp. Day or night, he is always ready to share a few words of gossip, directions, or idle conversation. He is especially eager to trade a pipe of his cheap, coarse tobacco for a pinch of some exotic imported variety, he touts the quality of the local product in hopes of an exchange.

Logan the Furrier, Male Human Trapper: HP 6; AC 9[10]; Atk spear (1d6); **Move** 12; **Save** 18; **AL** L; **CL/XP** B/10; **Special:** none. (*Monstrosities* 254)
Equipment: leather armor, spear, well-cured furs (10 gp), pouch with 8 gp.

FALLEN MESSENGER

At the beginning of the encounter, a large furry creature can be seen on the slope below the trade road tearing at something clothed in fabric. The creature in this encounter is a brown bear, a powerful omnivore common in these mountains. This one is scavenging from the corpse of a murdered messenger, although the party initially has no way of knowing this. The bear fights if threatened, but other options include distracting the bear with another food source or luring it away.

The body, which is already cold, is that of a messenger from a large temple of a Laful deity in a lowland city. The message was intended for Cael Angus, master of the Temple of Fortitude in Dun Eamon. Gethrax and a few bandits from the highwayman gang murdered the messenger to keep his message from reaching the city. An examination of the body reveals that not all of the acolyte's injuries are from the bear's meal; he has several sword wounds as well. The message is detailed below:

> Master Cael,
> I hope this message finds you in good health, for we are in need of your support. A servant of darkness by the name of Gethrax escaped our agents of justice, though we purged the cult that he had founded. He is known to be fleeing to his home somewhere in the Stoneheart Mountains, and we believe his path will lead him through Eamonvale. He must be detained or destroyed at all costs, for he is an ambassador of purest evil. He is associated with this sigil, though we know not what it means. Be warned, and shelter your flock well against his malign touch.
> Yours in Faith,
> *Father Grom Billig*

An odd icon follows the message (the heroes may encounter this sigil in **Dungeon Areas 1-9** and **2-17**). It is the mark of a powerful cadre of necromancers whose temple is hidden deep in the mountains, although only a learned sage would recognize it.

Brown Bear (Grizzly): HD 6; HP 41; AC 6[13]; Atk 2 claws (1d6), bite (1d10); **Move** 9; **Save** 11; **AL** N; **CL/XP** 6/400; **Special:** hug (additional 2d6 if both claws hit). (*Monstrosities* 37)

Treasure: On the messenger's body are a *potion of healing* and a ruby ring (250 gp).

BROTHER MELPH

The party encounters this young man on the trade road, mostly likely as he strides purposefully toward Dun Eamon with a light pack and sturdy staff. Brother Melph is an itinerant wanderer and a priest of the God of Roads. He is returning to the city from his usual journey through the valley, stopping in at taverns and roadside inns to offer healing, counseling, and news. For many of the more remote villages, he is the only man of the cloth that visits with any regularity. The party may meet him eventually (or again) in the caravan camp at Dun Eamon. He is available as a replacement or surrogate party member. He can usually be heard whistling before he can be seen. He was in Dun Eamon fairly recently and so might be able to share a slightly out-of-date rumor from the **City Rumors Table** (see **Chapter Two**). Brother Melph can be encountered any time of day, but only along the road. If encountered at night, he is not camped, but he may come striding along in the darkness on the road he knows so well.

Brother Melph, Male Human Priest (Clr5): HP 21; AC 7[12]; Atk *+1 staff* (1d6+1); **Move** 12; **Save** 11; **AL** L; **CL/XP** 5/240; **Special:** +2 save versus paralysis and poison, banish undead, spells (2/2). (see **Appendix A: NPCs**)
Spells: 1st—*cure light wounds* (x2); 2nd—*bless, hold person.* (see **Appendix A: NPCs**)
Equipment: cleric's vestments, leather armor, heavy cloak, *+1 staff* (a gift from the nymph Bernya, in return for his service along the roads of her wilderness), bedroll, holy symbol, 3 days' trail rations.
Note: Brother Melph is a cheerful priest of the God of Roads who offers his clerical skills and traveling stories at the caravan camp. Brother Melph is one of several NPCs who can serve as a pre-generated or replacement characters or as a temporary addition to or permanent part of the party.

MERCHANT CARAVAN

Up ahead, a number of wagons have convened at a broad turnout in the road. Horsemen are present, clad in fine clothing in the colors of the wagons. These horsemen are young aristocrats and courtiers, the arrogant sons of noble merchant houses learning the ways of caravans. The caravan master is an elderly man who spent his life in service to the house; he is skilled and competent, but allows himself to be bullied by the young nobles. In addition to the cargo of textiles and spices, they carry a few passengers — wealthy women and their servant girls on their way to join their husbands at a distant trading emporium. The encounter with the merchant caravan can be handled in several different ways (or in each of these ways at different times, or with different caravans).

• The young aristocrats insist that the party wait in the road until their caravan has gotten underway and moved on. Any objection is seen as a challenge to their authority and any insult is read as an affront to the dignity of the merchant house and a personal assault. They may issue a challenge to a fencing match, a test of skill, or some other duel, while the caravan master and guards roll their eyes and look the other way.

• The party comes upon the caravan just after highwaymen have attacked it. Several people are injured; two wranglers are dead. The master and the passengers are eager to pay for additional escorts, but without their purses they can pay only in promises. The young noblemen are adamant about needing no assistance and may even go so far as to accuse the party of being in league with the bandits.

• The party comes upon the caravan *while* highwaymen are attacking it. If the party makes the young nobles look bad, the accusations of being allied with the bandits may still come out, as does the request for an escort.

• The heroes find the caravan as they make camp for the night and are invited to join for a meal and a drink. In the morning, the arrogant nobles accuse the characters of stealing goods from the wagons, which one of them has actually left for his allies in the highwayman gang. The heroes must defuse the situation and possibly reveal the traitor.

Caravan Guards (6): HD 1; HP 7, 6, 5x3, 4; AC 7[12]; **Atk** longsword (1d8), dagger (1d4) or light crossbow (1d4+1); **Move** 12; **Save** 17; **AL** Any; **CL/XP** 1/15; **Special:** none. (*Monstrosities* 257)
  Equipment: leather armor, cloak, longsword, dagger, light crossbow, 20 bolts, pouch with 3d6 sp.

Caravan Laborers, Male or Female Humans (6): HD 6, 5, 4x2, 3x2; AC 9[10]; **Atk** dagger (1d4); **Move** 12; **Save** 18; **AL** Any; **CL/XP** B/10; **Special:** none. (*Monstrosities* 254)
  Equipment: cloak, dagger, shoulder yoke or wheelbarrow, pouch with 2d6 sp.
  Note: The caravan laborers in the camp are usually hard at work during the day and hard at play during the night.

Caravan Master, Male Human: HP 14; AC 9[10]; **Atk** dagger (1d4); **Move** 12; **Save** 16; **AL** N; **CL/XP** 2/30; **Special:** none. (*Monstrosities* 254)
  Equipment: dagger, written trade agreements representing terms with several merchant houses, strongbox with 200 gp
  Note: The caravan master is an aging man with little tolerance for trouble, from his young lords or from travelers.

Young Nobles, Male Humans (4): HP 4, 3x2, 2; AC 6[13]; **Atk** rapier (1d6); **Move** 12; **Save** 18; **AL** Any; **CL/XP** B/10; **Special:** none. (*Monstrosities* 254)
  Equipment: ring mail, rapier, foppish shirt, signet ring (20 gp), pouch with 25 gp and 20 sp, light warhorse.
  Note: These young men are cocky and have imperious attitudes.

Young Noblewomen, Female Humans (3): HD 4, 3x2; AC 6[13]; **Atk** none; **Move** 12; **Save** 18; **AL** Any; **CL/XP** B/10; **Special:** none. (*Monstrosities* 254)
  Equipment: dress, jewelry (80 gp).
  Note: These young women are sheltered and pampered, and may find adventurers to be uncouth and boorish or may be intrigued and attracted to the wild life.

Treasure: In addition to the NPCs' items, the caravan holds a cargo of textiles, spires, and other trade goods worth hundreds of gold pieces on the open market, but is fairly worthless to adventurers without good mercantile contracts, trade agreements, and bartering ability.

KAMVASE, WANDERING MINSTREL

From a distance, the party hears the idle strumming of a lute and a lilting, melodic voice. Upon sighting the party, a chubby halfling seated on a boulder shifts his ballad to one that features the heroes as the subject:

"… when mighty adventurers come around, the beasties tremble 'pon the ground, and soft swoons many a winsome lass, and men are quick to raise their glass … Well met, travelers!"

This is Kamvase, a halfling with a larcenous streak. Many welcome his company on the road, only to find their purses lightened and the minstrel nowhere in sight when they turn around. He is eager to share the road with a powerful party, mostly for his protection, but also to relieve them of a few choice items.

Kamvase readily shares his plentiful music and his limited wine and cheese if it looks as if the heroes will accept his company. If they do, he waits until they are camped to make his move. When watches are distributed, he accepts one on his own, if the party is agreeable. If a character shares a watch with him, he uses his lute and soft singing to lull the hero to sleep (saving throw to avoid). If given a moment with the entire party asleep, he quickly pinches a few small items and makes off into the woods (he avoids large or obvious things such as swords, preferring something that will not be missed immediately). The party's reactions may be diverse, depending on what was stolen from whom. The item may be lost forever, you may choose to allow a manhunt, or Kamvase could surface again in Dun Eamon. When in the city, Kamvase usually makes contact with Kinnan the Dark at the caravan camp to liquidate his ill-gotten gains (see **Area C** in **Chapter Three**).

Kamvase, Male Halfling Minstrel (Thf4): HP 13; AC 6[13]; **Atk** short sword (1d6) or sling (1d4); **Move** 9; **Save** 11 (+1, ring); **AL** N; **CL/XP** 4/120; **Special:** +1 missile weapon bonus, +2 save bonus vs. traps and magical devices, +4 save vs. magic, backstab (x2), thieving skills.
  Thieving Skills: Climb 88%, Tasks/Traps 35%, Hear 4 in 6, Hide 35%, Silent 45%, Locks 35%.
  Equipment: leather armor, short sword, sling with 30 stones, *ring of protection +1*, lute, gold ring (45 gp), pouch with 35 gp and 22 sp.

LIZARDFOLK HUNTERS

Through the mists that drift across the road ahead of the heroes, a ghostly shape appears momentarily and then disappears just as quickly. A low, hissing cry rises and falls somewhere amid the fog-shrouded trees. Characters have a 2-in-6 chance to notice that the creature walked upright like a human, but was much taller and balanced itself with a thick, serpentine tail.

The figure crossing the road was a lone lizardfolk hunter, but his hunting party is just ahead of him in the forest. The hunting party does not respond immediately to an attack on the straggler, preferring to sacrifice him to enhance their own attack on the characters. If they are successfully shadowed or tracked, they lead the characters back to their lair, described in the **Lizardfolk Valley** section, below. If the party is accompanied by the lizardfolk youth described in **Area U** (see **Chapter Two**), the hunters are more receptive to negotiations and may escort the party to their village, but they do not lower their guard. The lizardfolk are most active upriver of the city, where their lair is located; downriver of the city, this encounter should be replaced with **Hobark's Highwaymen**.

Lizardfolk (6): HD 2+1; AC 5[14]; **Atk** javelin (1d4 + sleep poison), 2 claws (1d3), bite (1d6); **Move** 6 (swim 12); **Save** 16; **AL** C; **CL/XP** 2/30; **Special:** breathe underwater. (*Monstrosities* 302)
  Equipment: javelins (x3), shield, sleep poison (save or sleep for 1d4 hours).

HOBARK'S HIGHWAYMEN

A band of highwaymen prepared an ambush on a lonely stretch of the trade road. Their leader Hobark is with them. Some are mounted, and some are armed with nets or crossbows. They attack any party that does not obviously outnumber or overpower them. This encounter might be used effectively with the **Merchant Caravan** encounter, providing the additional consideration of noncombatants to defend and work around. It may turn into a dangerous running battle in the form of a high-speed chase on foot or horseback through the damp, foggy woodland. The highwaymen are most active south of the city where their lair is located; north of the city, this encounter should be replaced with the **Lizardfolk Hunters**. The stats below describe the standard complement of bandits for an ambush.

Hobark, Male Human Highwayman (Rgr6): HP 49; AC 6[13]; **Atk** throwing axe (1d6); **Move** 12; **Save** 8 (+1, ring); AL N; **CL/XP** 6/400; **Special:** +4 damage vs. giants and goblin-types, alertness, tracking.
Equipment: leather armor, throwing axes (x6), *ring of protection +1*, 6 gp attached to his armpit hair with wax, light warhorse.

Bolts, Male or Female Human (Thf2) (4): HP 2d4; AC 7[12]; **Atk** dagger (1d4) or light crossbow (1d4+1); **Move** 12; **Save** 14; AL C; **CL/XP** 2/30; **Special:** +2 save bonus vs. traps and magical devices, backstab (x2), thieving skills. (see **Appendix A: NPCs**)
Thieving Skills: Climb 86%, Tasks/Traps 20%, Hear 3 in 6, Hide 15%, Silent 25%, Locks 15%.
Equipment: leather armor, 2 daggers, light crossbow, 20 bolts, pouch of caltrops (1d4 damage, halves movement in 10ft-diameter area), pouch with 1d8 gp and 2d10 sp.

Nets, Male or Female Human (Thf2) (2): HP 2d4; AC 7[12]; **Atk** net (save or entangled) or dagger (1d4); **Move** 12; **Save** 14; AL C; **CL/XP** 2/30; **Special:** +2 save bonus vs. traps and magical devices, backstab (x2), thieving skills. (see **Appendix A: NPCs**)
Thieving Skills: Climb 86%, Tasks/Traps 20%, Hear 3 in 6, Hide 15%, Silent 25%, Locks 15%.
Equipment: leather armor, net, dagger, pouch of caltrops (1d4 damage, halves movement in 10ft-diameter area), 50ft silk rope, grappling hook, pouch with 1d8 gp and 2d10 sp, 10% chance of a small pouch of powdered silver skimmed from a previous heist (worth 2d4 gp).

Riders, Male or Female Human Horsemen (6): HD 1; AC 6[13]; **Atk** short sword (1d6) or club (1d6), dagger (1d4); **Move** 12; **Save** 17; AL C; **CL/XP** 1/15; **Special:** none. (*Monstrosities* 254)
Equipment: leather armor, short sword or club, dagger, small wooden shield, pouch with 1d4 gp and 2d6 sp.

Tactics: The bolts take up positions on either side of the road to bait the party into approaching the ambush site. The nets hide in the trees above and just in front of the crossbow positions until characters pass below them, at which time they attack with their nets. The riders wait on either side of the road behind the crossbowmen to sweep into the road in a countercharge or to surround fallen heroes.
Hobark accompanies the horsemen, but he is quick to leave his horse and attack on foot unless an entire party is mounted.
Treasure: The bandits have several pouches of coin from this day's raids, worth 120 gp and 200 sp.

OUTRIDER PATROL

The mounted outrider patrols originate in Dun Eamon and are charged with protecting the trade road and the travelers on it as they approach the city. They have a range of roughly 50 miles in any direction — rarely more than a day's ride from the city. There are exceptions to this limit, such as when the outriders are on specific business: i.e., responding to a crisis or escorting a diplomat, priest, or magistrate. When out of the city, they prefer to billet themselves in a village tavern, a home, or a barn, but they are equipped to camp outdoors if no other option is available. A writ from Lord Angus gives them authority over most citizens of the valley, although they cannot overrule an appointed agent of Lord Angus (such as a magistrate) unless circumstances are extreme.

Outrider patrols travel in groups of eight, one of whom is a warden. They wear the livery of the Angus clan (blue and grey tabards over mail) and carry blue banners at their lance tips. They are obliged to stop every group of travelers when they enter the valley and inquire about their destination, business intentions, and length of stay. They also assess a party's composition and include it in their report when they return to the city. Their high rate of travel ensures that most visitors to the region are expected by the time they arrive in Dun Eamon. In extreme circumstances, the warden may dispatch two riders to return at full speed to request further support or deliver important information.

The outriders are not at leisure to discuss current events in the city, although they have been instructed to be on the lookout for capable adventurers that might be of use to the community.

Mist Watch Outrider, Male or Female Human Warrior: HD 1; AC 5[14]; **Atk** longsword (1d8), lance (1d6 or 2d6 with charge) or shortbow x2 (1d6); **Move** 12; **Save** 17; AL L or N; **CL/XP** 1/15; **Special:** none. (*Monstrosities* 257)
Equipment: ring mail, steel shield, heavy lance, longsword, shortbow, quiver of 20 arrows, warhorse, tack and harness, rations, waterskin, bedroll.

Mist Watch Warden, Male or Female Human Warrior (Ftr3): HD 3; AC 4[15]; **Atk** *+1 longsword* (1d8+1) or shortbow x2 (1d6); **Move** 12; **Save** 12; AL C; **CL/XP** 3/60; **Special:** multiple attacks (3) vs. creatures with 1 or fewer HD.
Equipment: chainmail, large steel shield, *+1 longsword*, shorbow and quiver of 20 arrows, signal horn, rank chain, writ of authority from Lord Angus, *potion of healing*, warhorse, tack and harness, rations, waterskin, bedroll.

Warhorse: HD 3; AC 7[12]; **Atk** bite (1d2), 2 hooves (1d3); **Move** 18; **Save** 14; AL N; **CL/XP** 3/60; **Special:** none. (*Monstrosities* 252)

Valley Woodsman: There is a 15% chance that a valley woodsman on horseback accompanies any outrider patrol.
Valley Woodsman, Male Human (Rgr4): HP 5d8; AC 7[12]; **Atk** longsword (1d8) or short sword (1d6) or longbow x2 (1d6); **Move** 12; **Save** 10; AL L; **CL/XP** 4/120; **Special:** +4 damage vs. giants and goblin-types, alertness, tracking.
Equipment: studded leather, longsword, short sword, longbow, quiver of 20 arrows, *2 potions of healing*, signal horn, bedroll, waterskin, 3 days' worth of rations.

ENCOUNTERS

OFF THE TRADE ROAD

If the heroes choose to leave the relative safety of the road, they may already be tracking one of the preceding factions. If they are wandering aimlessly or looking for a place to camp, use the following table to determine their encounter, rolling 1d20.

1d20	Encounter
1	**Bernya** the nymph
2–4	**Wolf pack**
5–6	**Dire boar**
7–8	**Shaw**, Valley Woodsman
9–10	**Lizardfolk Valley** or **Highwaymen's Camp**
11	Heavy fog
12	Rain
13	Downpour
14–20	No Encounter

BERNYA THE NYMPH

The party most likely encounters Bernya standing on a tree limb over the road, challenging their passage with an arrow set to her bowstring. Bernya is one of several fey creatures that dwells in the misty forests of Eamonvale, but she is unique among her kind. She is troubled by her past and by the unrest in the valley, and her attitude is unlike that of any other nymph. She usually contents herself with monitoring the passage of adventuring bands and merchant caravans, but periodically her rage boils over and she confronts a party openly, demanding to know its business in the valley. This reaction is more likely if the party shows evidence of evil tendencies or travels with servants or thralls, and she attacks without notice if any party obviously keeps slaves. She reacts the same when encountered at night.

Several human generations ago, a band of slavers came to the valley. They raided the outlying villages and readily dispatched or evaded the militias that opposed them. Internal affairs kept the Angus clan from mounting an efficient defense, and many of the citizens retreated to within the city walls. Bernya and a few farmers and woodsmen fought against the slavers, but their efforts were ineffective, and the band prepared to leave the valley with its human cargo. During a final, desperate attack on the slavers' camp, Bernya was badly injured and taken as a prize slave herself, bound and masked to contain her beauty. A small group of woodsmen and adventurers attacked the caravan repeatedly as it wound its way out of the mountains, eventually managing to free the nymph. She joined their guerilla band, vowing that she would not rest until all the slaves had been freed and the slavers dispatched. They eventually completed the task and eliminated the slavers, but by the time Bernya returned from the pursuit across distant lands, she was unable to return to the life she had known. She has sworn to keep that kind of evil from rising in her domain again.

Bernya, Nymph: HD 6; HP 40; AC 7[12]; Atk +1 *scimitar* (1d6+1) or dagger (1d4) or longbow x2 (1d6); **Move** 12; **Save** 11; **AL** N; **CL/XP** 8/800; **Special:** spells (3/1/1). (***Monstrosities*** 351)
Equipment: leather armor, *+1 scimitar*, dagger, longbow, quiver of 20 arrows.
Note: Bernya's downtrodden attitude and disfiguring scars mean anyone who looks on her is not subject to death or blindness. She is still extremely striking, but her deep-seated

rage, cold determination, and intuition rise to the forefront.

Description: Bernya is a stunningly beautiful creature, but the scars of her battles against the slavers mar both her appearance and her personality. Her hair is dirty and tangled, her face is smudged with dirt, and a long scar cross from below her right eye to the corner of her jaw. She wears bloodstained armor and carries an ash bow, a scimitar, and a dagger — souvenirs of the defeated southern slave raiders.

Two wolves of Lassilim's pack almost always accompany Bernya while she patrols the wilderness.

Wolves (2): HD 2+2; HP 15, 13; AC 7[12]; **Atk** bite (1d4+1); **Move** 18; **Save** 16; **AL** N; **CL/XP** 2/30; **Special:** none. (***Monstrosities*** 513)

WOLF PACK

Many packs of wolves roam the forests around Dun Eamon, but two are uniquely large and powerful. A worg named **Gorian** leads one pack; a winter wolf named **Lassilim** leads the other. Lassilim's pack has allied itself with Bernya and assists her in seeking balance in the woodlands. Gorian and his wolf pack want to force the human hunters and farmers out of the area so that the beasts might once again dominate the mountain slopes, with Gorian himself as lord of the realm.

The heroes have an equal chance of encountering either wolf pack, as well as the chance of encountering a non-aligned pack of normal wolves. Lassilim's pack does not attack the party unless provoked or if asked to do so by Bernya. Gorian's pack attacks immediately, trying to kill or drive off any trespassers in "their" realm. The other wolf packs size up the party before attacking, and usually try to separate a weaker member from the group and chase him or her into the mist.

1d20	Wolf Pack Encounter
1–5	4d4+4 wolves plus **Gorian**
6–10	3d4+4 wolves plus **Lassilim**
11–19	3d4+4 wolves
20	Gorian's pack *and* Lassilim's pack

Wolf: HD 2+2; AC 7[12]; **Atk** bite (1d4+1); **Move** 18; **Save** 16; AL N; **CL/XP** 2/30; **Special:** none. (*Monstrosities* 513)

Gorian, Worg: HD 4; HP 28; AC 6[13]; **Atk** bite (1d6+1); **Move** 18; **Save** 13; AL C; **CL/XP** 4/120; **Special:** none. (*Monstrosities* 515)

Winter Wolf: HD 5; AC 5[14]; **Atk** bite (1d6+1); **Move** 18; **Save** 12; AL N; **CL/XP** 6/400; **Special:** breathe frost (1/turn, 10ft range, 4d6 damage, save for half). (*Monstrosities* 514)

LIZARDFOLK VALLEY

Exploring beyond the trade road, rescuing the lost lizardfolk child from the city, or tracking the lizardfolk hunting party may lead the heroes to the lair of the lizardfolk tribe. This area is a deep gorge with a geothermal hot spring at the rear. The warm water flows under a bridge at the road, where the party might feel a warm breeze blowing out of the valley. The reptilian humanoids occupy a small village at the back of the valley, but have extensively trapped the entire area.

They arrived only a few years before the events of this adventure. The Angus clan has always kept a zero tolerance policy on slavery and allows no person in bondage across the ford. A slave caravan managed to pass off its human cargo as servants, but they had also been carrying a number of lizardfolk captives from the distant south. The reptilian humanoids were not doing well in the cold mountain environment, nor had they adjusted well to captivity, so they were clubbed and left to die outside the city. They made their way into the forest, where they managed to scavenge and hunt enough to survive.

When they discovered the hot springs in the small valley, their chances for survival and their quality of living increased. The temperature was reminiscent of their tropical home, and the mineral-rich plant life supported numerous small creatures for them to hunt and trap. The small tribe has flourished here, built a village, and begun to explore the mountain slopes and venture in disguise into the city nearby. Still, they dream of returning to their tropical home in the south, but they cannot begin to plan such a journey and are content to stay where they are for now. They have no connection to the events of the adventure.

The lizardfolk have found plenty of time to establish their presence in the area, and the village is well defended by cunning traps and ambushes, most of which use fungal poisons. There is a 20% chance that a trap is watched by a group of lizardfolk hunters.

LIZARDFOLK VILLAGE TRAPS

Characters have a 2-in-6 chance to set off any trap.

Type	Description
Punji Stakes	1d4+1 spikes coated with fungal sleep poison (save or sleep for 1d6 hours), 1d4 damage; save avoids trap
Spore Pit	40-foot-deep pit, 4d6 damage; bottom covered with tiny mushrooms with fungal sleep spores, save or sleep for 1d6 hours
Poisoned Darts	1d6 darts attack as 3HD creature, 1d2 damage, darts coated in fungal sleep poison, save or sleep for 1d6 hours

Ank'M'Tak, Lizardman Chieftain: HD 6; HP 41; AC 5[14]; **Atk** javelin (1d4), heavy stone pick (1d8), or 2 claws (1d3), bite (1d6); **Move** 6 (swim 12); **Save** 11; AL C; **CL/XP** 7/600; **Special:** breathe underwater, spells (Drd 3/2/2). (*Monstrosities* 302)
Spells: 1st—*detect magic, faerie fire, locate animals*; 2nd—*cure light wounds, obscuring mist*; 3rd—*cure disease, plant growth*.
Equipment: javelins (x3), shield, heavy stone pick, totem staff with several dangling humanoid skulls, loincloth decorated with bits of jewelry stolen from the Highwaymen (900 gp).

Description: Chief Ank'M'Tak wears a loincloth of snakeskin pierced with pins, brooches, and other jewelry. His totem staff is rumored to give him the power of his defeated enemies. He is powerfully built and carries himself with pride. His only concerns are for the survival and growth of his tribe.

Shar'M'No, Lizardman Shaman: HD 5; HP 34; AC 5[14]; **Atk** javelin (1d4), heavy stone pick (1d8), or 2 claws (1d3), bite (1d6); **Move** 6 (swim 12); **Save** 12; AL C; **CL/XP** 6/400; **Special:** breathe underwater, spells (Clr 2/2). (*Monstrosities* 302)
Spells: 1st—*cure light wounds, detect magic*; 2nd—*hold person, snake charm*.
Equipment: ragged robe, javelins (x3), shield, heavy stone pick, medicine bag (holy symbol), staff with gems pressed into the cracks (4d4 x 10 gp in gems).

Description: Shar'M'No wears a ragged robe stolen from a traveler. His is the only one in the tribe to wear humanoid clothing and stands out as such. He is smaller that Ank'M'Tak and often looks around with paranoia, hissing under his breath. He covets the chief's position and wishes to overthrow him.

Lizardfolk Hunters (20): HD 2+1; AC 5[14]; **Atk** javelin (1d4 + sleep poison), 2 claws (1d3), bite (1d6); **Move** 6 (swim 12); **Save** 16; AL C; **CL/XP** 2/30; **Special:** breathe underwater. (*Monstrosities* 302)
Equipment: loincloth with ornamental shells and bones, javelins (x3), shield, sleep poison (save or sleep for 1d4 hours).

Description: These lizardfolk are prepared for battle; they carry only their weapons and wear only loincloths decorated with shells and bones.

Lizardfolk Noncombatants (10): HD 2+1; AC 5[14]; **Atk** none; **Move** 6 (swim 12); **Save** 16; AL C; **CL/XP** 2/30; **Special:** breathe underwater. (*Monstrosities* 302)

Description: The village is home to a number of elderly or infant lizardfolk who do not take part in any conflict. The elders have the respect of the tribe, and the young cannot survive without the hunters to provide them with food.

Tactics: The shaman Shar'M'No has advised Chief Ank'M'Tak that the extraction of information from (and eventual roasting of) captives is critical to survival, so they do not attack sentient beings on sight. When the lizardfolk do encounter humanoids, they attempt to take them prisoners and deliver them to their village for a meeting with their leaders.

There is a 20% chance that a party of lizardfolk hunters is watching any of the traps in the valley, as the traps do not kill or permanently detain most creatures. These hunters assess the danger of the trapped creature and either move to surround it or send for reinforcements from the village. The lizardfolk attempt to time their attack so that it takes advantage of whichever trap the party has triggered. Most of their traps involve fungal sleep poison, so they focus on heroes who remain awake. They attack those characters with their javelins at range and then close to melee. When in close combat, they fight defensively against anyone who appears to be succumbing to the poison's effects, as they are under orders to bring survivors in if possible.

When the lizardfolk fight as a tribe, the hunters throw their javelins as they close in and then rush into melee with their heavy picks. The chief and the shaman stand back and support the tribe with their spells, using their javelins if a threat comes near. If Chief Ank'M'Tak is wounded, weakened, or otherwise vulnerable, Shar'M'No tries to kill him with *cause light wounds* or another method to ensure his place as leader. If the heroes notice this act, they may intervene and win the chief's favor.

If the party gains access to the village, as prisoners or otherwise, the chief and shaman take an audience with them. Should the party stumble onto the camp, the hunters immediately move to surround it,

but do not attack without orders from Ank'M'Tak. The chief questions the heroes as to their motives and attempts to ascertain the threat level. The shaman covets the leadership of the tribe and tries desperately (and often successfully) to influence the chief's decisions. A gift to the tribe improves relations considerably, while insults and threats are not taken well. Depending on the heroes' actions, the chief may offer to trade with them, challenge them to a trial, or simply order the tribe to kill them. A test of strength and hunting prowess might be called on to settle any issue that might arise — the party must enter the valley and defeat an equal number of lizardfolk hunters, including the chief … without the use of their equipment!

If the party arrives at the village as a result of making contact with the lost lizardfolk youngster from **Area U** in Dun Eamon (see **Chapter Two**), reactions may be very different. The tribe is grateful to have the child returned, but they immediately subject the youngster to harsh reprimands and interrogation to ensure that he acted without fear and battled well while in the city. If the party supports this image, the young creature receives only the rebuke. If the party reports that it was hiding in fear, a harsh punishment is in order. Alternatively, the heroes could be asked or required by the tribe to determine the fate of the youngster when they visit the city.

Regardless of how the youngster fares, the chief and shaman both thank the heroes and offer them sanctuary. If the lizardfolk village remains in the valley, the heroes have a place where they can rest and store supplies. At your discretion, the leaders may approach the party with their desire to leave the valley and return to their ancestral homeland, which could become an involved process. The shaman continues to covet the chief's position and conspire against him, and the heroes might become pawns in his clever schemes as their relations with the tribe progress.

Highwaymen's Camp

The highwaymen are camped on a high bluff above the road. The camp consists of a few dozen tents, dugouts, and temporary shacks, plus two wagons stolen from merchant caravans. Several fire pits are scattered about, as well as cords of wood, game-smoking lean-tos, latrines, and food caches.

Their camp's natural defensive position is ideal; many **traps**, **deadfalls**, and **pits** have been prepared on the approaches to it, and it is always under careful guard. Characters may stumble upon this area if they leave the road, but it is more likely that they will track the ambushers back here or force its location from a captive under duress. Planning an invasion of the camp is a difficult affair, and the party is almost certainly outnumbered. Infiltrating the camp by stealth or deception is just as difficult, but all are potentially viable tactics. Defeating the bandits also brings the party into good favor with the government of Dun Eamon.

Wilderness Traps

Characters have a 2-in-6 chance to set off any trap.

Trap	Description
Hidden Pit	20-foot deep, 2d6 damage
Log Deadfall	4d6 damage, all in path must save for half damage
Rolling Boulder	4d6 damage, save for half damage
Spear Trap	Attacks as 4HD creature, 1d8 damage

This particular band of highwaymen is a splinter group of the Ebon Union. Some of them came with the thieves' guild after they were ousted from their previous home city, but most of them joined the group later, during the months that the entire band relied on robbery on the trade road. Most of the men who joined during this time were outdoorsmen and had no desire to dwell in a city, much less below one. Devlin wisely allowed them to stay in the wilderness under the command of **Hobark**, his old lieutenant. By doing so, he has maintained his influence on the trade caravans while having a ready market for the goods he steals. He provides supplies to the bandits in exchange for marketing their stolen caravan goods — goods that he can sell for a higher price than Hobark could find for them and still turn a profit for the Ebon Union. In some cases, he might conspire with Hobark and his men to steal the same item a second time as it leaves the region in the hands of its new owner.

Hobark was one of the first to join the Ebon Union during their wilderness era. He had previously made good money and a bad name for himself as a bounty hunter and freelance killer. Highway robbery suits him well and favors his skills, for he is cruel and sadistic and yet fancies himself noble, and no man in the gang can match him in combat or on horseback.

Hobark, Male Human Highwayman (Rgr6): HP 49; AC 6[13]; Atk throwing axe (1d6); Move 12; Save 8 (+1, ring); AL N; CL/XP 6/400; Special: +4 damage vs. giants and goblin-types, alertness, tracking.
Equipment: leather armor, throwing axes (x6), *ring of protection +1*, 6 gp attached to his armpit hair with wax, light warhorse.

Description: Hobark is a bounty hunter and mercenary for hire. He was one of Devlin's lieutenants before the Ebon Union divided, and he fell naturally into leadership. His position is based on the most elementary "law of the jungle": He was the strongest, fastest, and most skilled of the highwaymen that remained behind. Devlin's tactics using the crossbows and nets have continued to serve the gang well, and none of Hobark's men finds fault with his leadership. Hobark is a tall, black-haired man with a look of intensity on his face and a brace of axes crossed over his chain shirt.

The highwaymen are a diverse bunch of ruffians. In addition to the ruffians normally found in the Ebon Union below the city, two other NPC types are in the wilderness gang: riders and hunters.

Bolts, Male or Female Human (Thf2) (10): HP 2d4; AC 7[12]; Atk dagger (1d4) or light crossbow (1d4+1); Move 12; Save 14; AL C; CL/XP 2/30; Special: +2 save bonus vs. traps and magical devices, backstab (x2), thieving skills. (see **Appendix A: NPCs**)
Thieving Skills: Climb 86%, Tasks/Traps 20%, Hear 3 in 6, Hide 15%, Silent 25%, Locks 15%.
Equipment: woodland camouflage cloak (1-in-6 chance to spot in wilderness), leather armor, 2 daggers, light crossbow, 20 bolts, pouch of caltrops (1d4 damage, halves movement in 10ft-diameter area), pouch with 1d8 gp and 2d10 sp.

Knives, Male or Female Human (Thf1) (14): HP 1d4; AC 7[12]; Atk dagger (1d4); Move 12; Save 15; AL C; CL/XP 1/15; Special: +2 save bonus vs. traps and magical devices, backstab (x2), thieving skills. (see **Appendix A: NPCs**)
Thieving Skills: Climb 85%, Tasks/Traps 15%, Hear 3 in 6, Hide 10%, Silent 20%, Locks 10%.
Equipment: leather armor, 2 daggers, pouch of caltrops (1d4 damage, halves movement in 10ft-diameter area), pouch with 1d4 gp and 2d6 sp, 10 % chance of a small pouch of powdered silver skimmed from a previous heist (worth 1d4 gp).

Nets, Male or Female Human (Thf2) (6): HP 2d4; AC 7[12]; Atk net (save or entangled) or dagger (1d4); Move 12; Save 14; AL C; CL/XP 2/30; Special: +2 save bonus vs. traps and magical devices, backstab (x2), thieving skills. (see **Appendix A: NPCs**)
Thieving Skills: Climb 86%, Tasks/Traps 20%, Hear 3 in 6, Hide 15%, Silent 25%, Locks 15%.
Equipment: leather armor, net, dagger, pouch of caltrops (1d4 damage, halves movement in 10ft-diameter area), 50ft silk rope, grappling hook, pouch with 1d8 gp and 2d10 sp, 10% chance of a small pouch of powdered silver skimmed from a previous heist (worth 2d4 gp).

Shifters, Male or Female Human (Thf2) (2): HP 2d4; AC 7[12]; Atk dagger (1d4); Move 12; Save 14; AL C; CL/XP 2/30; Special: +2 save bonus vs. traps and magical devices, backstab (x2), thieving skills. (see **Appendix A: NPCs**)
Thieving Skills: Climb 86%, Tasks/Traps 20%, Hear 3 in 6, Hide 15%, Silent 25%, Locks 15%.
Equipment: leather armor, net, 2 daggers, pouch of caltrops (1d4 damage, halves movement in 10ft-diameter area), scales, pouch with 2d10 gp and 2d10 sp, 10% chance of a small pouch of powdered silver skimmed from a previous heist (worth 2d4 gp).

Thugs, Male or Female Human (18): HD 1; AC 7[12]; Atk battle axe (1d8) or longsword (1d8); Move 12; Save 17; AL C; CL/XP 1/15; Special: none. (see **Appendix A: NPCs**)
Equipment: leather armor, longsword or battle axe, pouch with 1d4 gp and 2d6 sp.

Riders, Male or Female Human Horsemen (16): HD 2; AC 6[13]; Atk flail (1d6) or shortbow x2 (1d6); Move 12; Save 16; AL C; CL/XP 2/30; Special: none. (*Monstrosities* 254)
Equipment: leather armor, small wooden shield, light flail, shortbow and quiver of 20 arrows, warhorse, tack and harness, rations, waterskin, and bedroll.

Warhorses (16): HD 3; AC 7[12]; Atk bite (1d2), 2 hooves (1d3); Move 18; Save 14; AL N; CL/XP 3/60; Special: none. (*Monstrosities* 252)

Hunters, Male or Female Humans (Rgr2) (8): HP 3d8; AC 7[12]; **Atk** longsword (1d8) or short sword (1d6) or longbow x2 (1d6); **Move** 12; **Save** 13; **AL** N; **CL/XP** 2/30; **Special:** +2 damage vs. giants and goblin-types, alertness, tracking.
Equipment: leather armor, longsword, short sword, longbow and quiver of 20 arrows, rations, waterskin, and bedroll.

Tactics: The Highwaymen fight very aggressively to defend their camp. Hunters or bolts guard the perimeter, looking out over the approach to the camp and the network of traps. The guards have a 2-in-6 chance to hear the characters' approach each time a trap is triggered or some other noisy event occurs; success means the camp is alerted to the party's presence. If the perimeter is lost, the Highwaymen gather around their leader (if he still lives) and fight ferociously, but they fall back into the forest and flee if they sustain 50% casualties.

Treasure: The Highwaymen have their personal items, the provisions of their camp, and a stash of gold and silver coins worth 1,200 gp.

WILD BOARS

Wild boars are one of the most dangerous creatures on the forest slopes. While not as organized as the wolves or as powerful as a bear, their sheer ferocity makes them the bane of locals and travelers alike. A campfire or the sounds of a group often draw boars, for they require nothing more than the promise of food to ransack a camp. Normal boars usually attack singly or in pairs, while dire boars are almost always alone. At your discretion, a wereboar could be introduced for further plot development.

1d20	Wild Boar Encounter
1–7	1 wild boar
8–13	2 wild boars
14–16	1 giant wild boar
17–20	Reroll twice, or **wereboar** if desired

Giant Wild Boar: HD 6; AC 5[14]; **Atk** gore (4d4); **Move** 15; **Save** 11; **AL** N; **CL/XP** 7/600; **Special:** continue attacks 2 rounds after death. (*Monstrosities* 48)

Wild Boar: HD 3+3; AC 7[12]; **Atk** gore (3d4); **Move** 15; **Save** 14; **AL** N; **CL/XP** 4/120; **Special:** continue attacks 2 rounds after death. (*Monstrosities* 48)

Wereboar: HD 5+2; AC 4[15]; **Atk** bite (2d6); **Move** 12; **Save** 12; **AL** N or C; **CL/XP** 6/400; **Special:** +1 or better magic or silver weapons to hit, lycanthropy. (*Monstrosities* 306)

SHAW, VALLEY WOODSMAN

The valley woodsmen are wilderness experts in the employ of Lord Angus, although many hunt and trap on the side. They patrol the areas of mountainous forest that are beyond the reach of the outriders — and these areas are vast. The valley woodsmen cover many miles each day, traveling cross-country with only a mentally ingrained map of their beloved wilderness to guide them. They report weekly (give or take a few days) to Bron Angus or to one of his officers at the Mist Watch Garrison (see **Area J** in **Chapter Two**) before refreshing their supplies and heading back out into the wilds.

Most woodsmen are rangers, but some barbarians serve as well. Nearly all are human males, although elves and half-elves have entered into such contracts with Angus, and at least one woman is listed among their ranks. If this encounter is rolled, the party most likely does not notice anything until the woodsman announces himself; the woodsman may track the heroes for miles and may emerge only if they are attacked. Woodsmen assume an aloof, detached demeanor toward adventurers, although they warm to a druid or accomplished ranger in the party. Unless the party is engaged in some forbidden act or misdemeanor, the woodsmen usually inquire about the party's experiences in the wilds, sightings of game, or news from beyond the valley. They recommend that travelers make their way back to the road as soon as possible and are willing to provide an escort if needed. If encountered at night, the woodsman listens at the edge of camp to assess the party's nature before entering or moving on.

Shaw, Valley Woodsman, Male Human (Rgr4): HP 33; AC 7[12]; **Atk** longsword (1d8) or short sword (1d6) or longbow x2 (1d6); **Move** 12; **Save** 10; **AL** L; **CL/XP** 4/120; **Special:** +4 damage vs. giants and goblin-types, alertness, tracking.
Equipment: studded leather, longsword, short sword, longbow, quiver of 20 arrows, 2 *potions of healing*, signal horn, bedroll, waterskin, 3 days' worth of rations.

NIGHT ENCOUNTERS

Most of the night encounters are simply encounters with the common traffic of the trade road that take place after dark; the others are with nocturnal hunters and foragers. The NPCs have guidelines for night encounters in their descriptive text, above.

1d20	Encounter
1	**Bernya** the nymph
2–5	**Wolf pack**
6–7	**Boar**
8	**Brown bear**
9	**1d3 ronus**
10	**Brother Melph** (see **Appendix A: NPCs**)
11	**Shaw**, valley woodsman
12	Heavy fog
13	Rain
14	Downpour
15–20	No Encounter

BERNYA THE NYMPH

Bernya is one of several fey creatures that dwells in the misty forests of Eamonvale, but she is unique among her kind. More details about Bernya can be found in the list of daytime encounters on the Trade Road.

Bernya, Nymph: HD 6; HP 40; AC 7[12]; **Atk** *+1 scimitar* (1d6+1) or dagger (1d4) or longbow x2 (1d6); **Move** 12; **Save** 11; **AL** N; **CL/XP** 8/800; **Special:** spells (3/1/1). (*Monstrosities* 351)
Equipment: leather armor, *+1 scimitar*, dagger, longbow, quiver of 20 arrows.
Note: Bernya's downtrodden attitude and disfiguring scars mean anyone who looks on her is not subject to death or blindness. She is still extremely striking, but her deep-seated rage, cold determination, and intuition rise to the forefront.

WOLF PACK

If a wolf pack attacks the party at night, a few members break away to create a distracting howl from a distance. The howling still seems far-off when the pack strikes. A worg named **Gorian** leads one pack; a winter wolf named **Lassilim** leads the other. Lassilim's pack has allied itself with Bernya and assists her in seeking balance in the woodlands. Gorian and his wolf pack want to force the human hunters and farmers out of the area so that the beasts might once again dominate the mountain slopes, with Gorian himself as lord of the realm.

The heroes have an equal chance of encountering either wolf pack, as well as the chance of encountering a non-aligned pack of normal wolves. Lassilim's pack does not attack the party unless provoked or if asked to do so by Bernya. Gorian's pack attacks immediately, trying to kill or drive off any trespassers in "their" realm. The other wolf packs size up the party before attacking, and usually try to separate a weaker member from the group and chase him or her into the mist.

1d20	Wolf Pack Encounter
1–5	**4d4+4 wolves** plus **Gorian**
6–10	**3d4+4 wolves** plus **Lassilim**
11–19	**3d4+4 wolves**
20	Gorian's pack *and* Lassilim's pack

Wolf: HD 2+2; AC 7[12]; **Atk** bite (1d4+1); **Move** 18; **Save** 16; AL N; **CL/XP** 2/30; **Special:** none. (*Monstrosities* 513)

Gorian, Worg: HD 4; HP 28; AC 6[13]; **Atk** bite (1d6+1); **Move** 18; **Save** 13; AL C; **CL/XP** 4/120; **Special:** none. (*Monstrosities* 515)

Winter Wolf: HD 5; AC 5[14]; **Atk** bite (1d6+1); **Move** 18; **Save** 12; AL N; **CL/XP** 6/400; **Special:** breathe frost (1/turn, 10ft range, 4d6 damage, save for half). (*Monstrosities* 514)

WILD BOAR

When the boars attack at night, no notice is given. They rush into the camp and tear into sleeping characters, though food scraps may distract them.

1d20	Wild Boar Encounter
1–7	1 wild boar
8–13	2 wild boars
14–16	1 giant wild boar
17–20	Reroll twice, or **wereboar** if desired

Giant Wild Boar: HD 6; AC 5[14]; **Atk** gore (4d4); **Move** 15; **Save** 11; AL N; **CL/XP** 7/600; **Special:** continue attacks 2 rounds after death. (*Monstrosities* 48)

Wild Boar: HD 3+3; AC 7[12]; **Atk** gore (3d4); **Move** 15; **Save** 14; AL N; **CL/XP** 4/120; **Special:** continue attacks 2 rounds after death. (*Monstrosities* 48)

Wereboar: HD 5+2; AC 4[15]; **Atk** bite (2d6); **Move** 12; **Save** 12; AL N or C; **CL/XP** 6/400; **Special:** +1 or better magic or silver weapons to hit, lycanthropy. (*Monstrosities* 306)

BROWN BEAR

This large creature is often drawn to a camp by the smell of food being prepared. Sometimes, it waits at the edge of the camp until the party retires before foraging, but whenever it decides to take its meal, it expects the food to be surrendered without contest. It attacks only if the party resists or threatens it.

Brown Bear (Grizzly): HD 6; HP 41; AC 6[13]; **Atk** 2 claws (1d6), bite (1d10); **Move** 9; **Save** 11; AL N; **CL/XP** 6/400; **Special:** hug (additional 2d6 if both claws hit). (*Monstrosities* 37)

RONUS

These fearsome predators drift down from the higher slopes to hunt along the road at night. They prefer an individual or a small group of travelers to a large caravan, but they are not terribly picky, especially if the seasonal traffic has died off. Between the mist, the dark, and the creatures' natural coloring, they can be very difficult to defeat (1-in-6 chance; 2-in-6 for elves and rangers). The creatures have the brownish-gray body of a wolf and the head of a falcon.

Ronus (1d3): HD 3; AC 4[15]; **Atk** bite (1d6+2); **Move** 24; **Save** 14; AL N; **CL/XP** 3/60; **Special:** none. (*The Tome of Horrors Complete* 465)

SHAW, VALLEY WOODSMAN

The valley woodsmen often patrol silently through the wilderness after sundown. If encountered at night, the woodsman listens at the edge of camp to assess the party's nature before entering or moving on.

Shaw, Valley Woodsman, Male Human (Rgr4): HP 33; AC 7[12]; **Atk** longsword (1d8) or short sword (1d6) or longbow x2 (1d6); **Move** 12; **Save** 10; AL L; **CL/XP** 4/120; **Special:** +4 damage vs. giants and goblin-types, alertness, tracking. **Equipment:** studded leather, longsword, short sword, longbow, quiver of 20 arrows, 2 *potions of healing*, signal horn, bedroll, waterskin, 3 days' worth of rations.

IDEAS FOR FURTHER DEVELOPMENT

These encounters are simply meant to provide some colorful roleplaying and a bit of conflict en route to the Grey Citadel. With some attention, however, they could easily be enhanced into several sessions' worth of gaming. Consider the following hooks:

• Bernya contacts the party with concerns that Hobark and his men have turned to kidnapping. She does not have the resources to go against them herself, but the party may be able to bring in some woodsmen and perhaps an outrider unit to assist. Plotting and coordinating the attack on the camp requires good intelligence, timing, and execution.

• Lord Angus wants the lizardfolk threat neutralized. On reaching their valley, the party realizes that the lizardfolk just want to return to their jungle home. The heroes must avoid the conspiracies of the greedy shaman and escort the lizardfolk out of the region, hopefully finding some way to claim their reward as well.

• Lassilim and his pack find the party one night to report that Gorian's pack and some unknown humanoid agents have captured Bernya and a few woodsmen. Finding Gorian's hidden burrow is just the beginning, because Hobark and his men have negotiated with the would-be wolf king for the enslavement of the nymph and the murder of the woodsmen.